Betrayed...

Service for sanctuary—that was the deal for 250 years. Now the government is breaking the treaties, but the shifters won't surrender without a fight.

Werewolf Ethan Calhoun's mission to secure his pack's future sends him to Minnesota to solicit support from a powerful congressman who has used their services in the past but now wants to renege on the covenants protecting the packs. Ethan never expected this assignment would lead to the truth behind his family's mysterious heritage—or reveal his fated mate.

Despite knowing she and Ethan are destined to be together, Selena Wolfe believes she is too damaged to be anyone's mate. Besides, she's busy plotting retribution against the politician who betrayed her pack, leaving her no time for the sexy new lobo in town.

But when her blackmail plan backfires, Ethan is not only there to console her, but he helps her regroup, heal...and implement the revenge she so sorely deserves.

TROPES/THEMES/CHARACTERS: Werewolves, fated-mates (but not insta-love), shifters, vampires, witches, supernatural, crooked politicians, betrayal and revenge, attempted genocide, patriotism.

TRIGGER WARNING: non-graphic rape scene.

Each book in the series is a stand-alone romance, but because of the overarching story, books are best read in order.

Betrayed by the Moon

Service For Sanctuary Book 1
MJ Compton

Comptonplations Publishing

Betrayed by the Moon (Service for Sanctuary Book 1)

Cover designed by Getcovers

Published in the United States ofAmerica by Comptonplations Publishing

EBOOK ISBN: 978-1-959923-13-8

PRINT ISBN: 978-1-959923-14-5

www.comptonplations.com

For survivors everywhere.

Acknowledgements

My wonderful husband Steve; Central New York Romance Writers; and the Purples: Gayle Callen, Kris Fletcher, Carol Lombardo, and Christine Wenger.

Also: Renee Kloecker for use of her country cottage, and Andrea and Walt Kaczor for opening their home to the Thistle Dew Writers.

Contents

Prologue

"They're breaking the treaty."

Ethan Calhoun stopped twirling his tone bar between his fingers and clutched the cold steel in his palm. So, a governmental dilemma prompted Tokarz, pack alpha, to summon the pack to the Full Moon Lodge. Ethan had hoped Tokarz was going to announce a new tour for Toke Lobo and the Pack. The band hadn't been on the road in months.

"What?" someone asked.

"The United States government wants to break the treaty with us."

Ethan tightened his grip on the tone bar. Mitchell Jasper, the pack's government liaison, slunk into the room with Tokarz. Ethan figured something bad was coming. The man looked...terrified.

"Washington no longer wants to offer sanctuary in return for our services," Tokarz clarified, in case any werewolf in the room didn't understand the implications of a broken treaty. As if the threat to their existence was a concept too complicated to be stated only once.

Or maybe shock made everyone slower than usual.

Ethan didn't have the words to describe the sensation of melting from the inside out. Granted, he wasn't a descendent of one of the original French families comprising most of the Loup Garou pack. The treaty cut with Thomas Jefferson wasn't sacred to him as it was to the others. He was ignorant of his own family's history.

His grandfather remained mute about the pack he'd abandoned. Although Loup Garou had accepted the Calhoun family, Ethan was always aware he was an outsider.

"We need your help." Jasper cleared his throat before he spoke. The words still emerged weak and diluted. It was a miracle the man didn't piss himself.

"Why should we help you?" Tokarz asked.

"Most people don't want the treaties abandoned."

"Most people aren't aware there are treaties." Tokarz spoke in a voice so cold, Ethan expected the windows to frost over.

Why didn't Tokarz ask Jasper to define *we*? *Who* wanted the pack's help?

"Look." Jasper channeled some testosterone from somewhere. "*I* know it's a bad idea to break the treaties. *I* know how valuable having a...secret weapon of...your nature...is to the security of our country. I'm a patriot, and I am not going to let ignorance and short-sightedness destroy something costing the government nothing and still works."

Tokarz smirked. "So. You want us to be a *secret* secret weapon?"

The phrase sounded ridiculous. Tokarz watched too many old movies.

Jasper cleared his throat again. "My department isn't the only one trying to work around the new administration's dictates. While I am in Loup Garou to officially tell you the treaties will be rescinded, I am also here, personally, to tell you *our* country has never needed you more."

The man deserved points. He played the room perfectly. Every werewolf present, including Ethan, was deeply patriotic.

"Not to say there isn't an element who would like to see you...your species eliminated."

"Say what you mean," Tokarz said. "Don't use fifty-dollar words when nickel ones will do. Dead. Some folks want us dead."

Only if a lobo observed Jasper closely, as Ethan did, would he see the slight inclination of his head.

"We need to remind some members of congress who are privy to the agreements precisely what they know and why the treaties matter."

"You mean threaten them." Tokarz glowered.

"The treaties have served our nation for two centuries. Some influential people need to be reminded."

"And on whose behalf would we be reminding them?" Tokarz asked the first question Ethan would have asked in his place.

"Your own." Jasper lifted his chin, as if daring Tokarz to contradict him.

"Go on," Tokarz said after several moments of a staring match. Jasper did not blink.

"I have a list of names. Men who have availed themselves of the special services guaranteed by the treaties, and who are currently in positions of power to help—maybe force—the preservation of the treaties."

Maybe Ethan's imagination spoke, but Jasper sounded stronger. Surer of himself.

"And how do you suggest we *remind* these people they owe us sanctuary?"

As Jasper laid out his plan—and his idea didn't sound like much of a plan—Ethan's gut churned. He was surprised he hadn't snapped the tone bar he always carried in his front pocket. His fingers worked the steel hard enough.

Jasper's so-called plan involved sending emissaries to meet with the politicians who had availed themselves of lycan services in the past. Ethan wasn't clear on what the emissaries were supposed to do;

every instinct he possessed shrieked Tokarz planned to send him. He'd worked on a couple missions the band had been involved in and was one of the few band members not yet mated. Mated males needed to stay put and protect their females.

After the meeting broke up, Tokarz asked Ethan to stay. The request prompted Ethan's father and grandfather to also remain.

"My grandson is the sole survivor of my line," Pa told their alpha.

"When my grandfather accepted you into the Loup Garou pack, you—"

"My agreement with the Loup Garou hasn't changed."

Ethan exchanged a glance with his father, who didn't seem any more in the know than Ethan was. Pa nursed his secrets; his family respected Pa's reticence.

"My agreement hasn't changed," Pa repeated. "The treaty your ancestors signed with the government has nothing to do with me or mine."

"My grandfather's conditions for accepting you included honoring our ways. The treaty is a part of this pack's heritage."

"Has Ethan not participated in missions as required? The time you met your mate? The time a crazy man in Idaho threatened to overthrow the government? Ethan has fulfilled his generation's obligation to your family."

"I don't have a choice."

"You do. You're alpha. You could send anyone."

"You're right. I'm alpha, and I've made my decision."

A LOPSIDED SILVER MOON transformed the random snowflakes drifting around Ethan from white to glitter as he made his way home. His breath, puffing into the frigid winter night, sparkled where moonbeams brushed the warmer air.

The streets were empty despite lycans preferring the night. Everyone must have been celebrating the fact they weren't being sent on a fool's errand.

The moon appeared lonely, as if she needed a song or two. Ethan considered obliging her.

Except he didn't feel much like singing at the moon or into a microphone or even in the shower. He was unmated; naturally Tokarz volunteered him for a mission. The mated guys got to stay home with their females, while the single males were obligated to treaty fulfillment.

Even without a treaty.

Even if a lobo's family wasn't included in the treaty.

Even if the lobo wasn't part of the pack.

Chapter 1

Ethan sat in his bright red truck—not the most unobtrusive vehicle for surveillance—and tried to stay awake. Not only had he been forced to volunteer for the mission, he'd been exiled to northern Minnesota to do so. Pro-lycan factions considered Congressman Bryant Peters a crucial swing vote on the treaties between the werewolves and the United States. His vote, rumor claimed, was on the fence. Ethan's job was to convince him favoring the treaties was in his best interest.

Ethan wasn't sure how to approach the mission. He'd researched the congressman's itinerary, ending with him outside a regional office in Warwick, Minnesota, trying to decide what to do next. Worry about bungling the mission played havoc with his body and his senses. He couldn't blame being in a strange city. Too many years on the road with Toke Lobo and the Pack taught him every night was a new adventure.

A lot of people entered and emerged from the professional building. The congressman wasn't the only person who rented offices at the address.

Something smelled...unusual. Out of place.

One woman stomped out the door. Ethan straightened in his seat, gaze riveted on her. She was clothed in the same black every other woman wore. Her neat pantsuit gave her a professional appearance.

Long brown hair was caught at her nape with a barrette, exposing her mating spot.

Her mating spot. The place Ethan would use his teeth to mark her when he claimed her. His penis swelled.

Ancient Ones. He was in Warwick to meet his mate. No wonder his heart raced. He wasn't suffering from anxiety. Mating fever caused his agitation.

He gripped the steering wheel to keep from bolting from the truck, sprinting across the street, and tossing the female over his shoulder. He didn't want sapien witnesses who wouldn't comprehend the urgency quickening in his blood.

He had a mate. No longer single. No longer stuck on a senseless mission. He could mark her, take her back to Colorado, and let some other lobo deal with Congressman Peters.

A tall, thin man followed her out of the building. The female kept walking. The man grabbed her arm to stop her.

The shock of the woman's reaction pierced Ethan like a spike. Her face flushed, and her nostrils flared. She planted her feet as if preparing for battle.

Her response was all Ethan needed. He leapt from his truck and crossed the street before his heart could beat twice.

"Let go of her," he snarled at the tall man.

"Mind your own business," the man snapped.

"She is my business."

"Selena, who is this guy?"

Selena. My mate's name means moon.

Her eyes, a brindle color not unlike a doe's pelt, widened. Her nostrils flared. "He's my...intended."

Ethan hoped the other guy didn't catch the bewilderment in Selena's tone. Then her words registered. She'd recognized him the

same way he'd known her. She was lycan. Not sapien. "Her fiancé."
He used a word the sapien mates in the pack used before they'd been
marked.

The man dropped Selena's arm. "Well, he puts a different spin on
your—"

"He changes nothing."

The man's blue eyes narrowed. Ethan had the impression he was
peering through the man's skull into the sky on the other side of his
head.

Ethan cupped Selena's elbow, and a shock of genetic recognition
latched on to his bones. "Are you finished?"

She tensed beneath his touch. "Yeah."

"Come on." Ethan steered her toward his truck.

"Tell your father I'll be paying attention," she called to the man on
the sidewalk.

Ethan helped her climb into the cab of his truck before he took his
place behind the wheel.

"Your arrival is inconvenient." She fastened her seat belt once he'd
closed his door.

"Ethan Calhoun is the name. Welcome to my life."

"Please tell me you aren't here for me." Desperation edged her
words. Not the good kind of desperation, as in she couldn't wait for
him to claim her. "What are you doing in Varulv territory? Where are
you from?"

"One thing at a time. I'm from Loup Garou, Colorado."

"You're not in Warwick to find me. Right?"

"I did not come to Warwick to find you, but seeing how we've
met—"

"No." She stared straight ahead, her gaze as rigid as the rest of her
body. "You've found no one."

Ethan sniffed. He hadn't mistaken the earthy, spicy scent of werewolf. "My mating instinct says different."

"And mating instinct is never wrong." She recited as if by rote. "Except I have no intention of mating. Nothing personal." She glanced at him. "I'm sure you're a nice lobo."

"There's only one way to find out." He twisted the key in the ignition. A peek across the street revealed the tall man still in front of the building, staring at Ethan's truck. "Where did you park?"

"Park?" She sounded confused or distracted. Probably by pretty boy.

"Your car."

"Oh. I don't drive. I took the bus."

Ethan wasn't sure he'd ever met another adult who didn't drive. Well, except for Luke's mate. "Okay. Where are we going?"

"We?"

He didn't dare look at her. Heavy city traffic required all his attention. If the skepticism behind an arched eyebrow had a sound, it escaped from Selena's throat.

"There is no *we*. There's Evan and there is Selena."

"Ethan," he muttered. He swallowed his annoyance. "Where do you want to go?"

"I told you I don't drive, and vehicles tend to warp my sense of direction."

"Do you have an address?" He spotted familiar giant yellow arcs ahead. Perfect.

She rattled off numbers and a street name as he pulled into the fast-food parking lot. "What are you doing?"

"I'm going to program your address into the map app on my phone. Then I'm going to get something to eat." He parked the truck. "Repeat the address, please."

"Here." She reached for the phone. "I'll program the address. You get your food."

He handed her his phone. Her smaller fingers would be more agile on the tiny keys than his. He backed out of the parking spot and got in line at the drive thru. "You want anything?"

Well-deserved contempt filled her glare. No werewolf in his right mind would eat a fast-food burger. "No. Thank you."

She zipped her way around the cell phone better than he did. His was new. He'd never seen a reason for needing one until Tokarz exiled him to Minnesota.

"One yogurt berry thing," he told the speaker. Static confirmed his order.

"The parfait better not be for me," Selena warned as she activated his phone's voice option.

"Sorry. It's for you." Ethan contorted in his seat to pull out his wallet.

"What part of *we're never going to mate* don't you get?" She slid his phone on top of the CD jewel cases in the space beneath the truck's radio.

"What part of *we don't have a choice* don't *you* get?" he countered. "The Ancient Ones make mating decisions. Not me. Not you."

"I'm not accepting berries from you."

For some reason, her refusal hurt more than her words and attitude. The time-honored mating ritual included the male offering berries to the female. One band member improvised with blueberry muffins. Luke, his former on-the-road roommate, inadvertently gave his mate-to-be strawberry lemonade. Since Ethan's mate was another werewolf, unlike the mates of any other band member, he wanted tradition. The fast-food yogurt cup contained fresh blueberries and strawberries.

She still rejected him. He wasn't aware such a thing could happen. Maybe she didn't care for people from Colorado. Or men with black hair and eyes. Or men.

He dropped the brown bag containing the yogurt into the beverage holder and pulled into the street. Except for the annoying female voice of his cell phone telling him where to drive, the interior of the truck was silent.

Inhaling his future mate's fragrance did things to his body he'd seen on the pornographic websites Luke surfed on the Internet. Ethan's penis was as hard as the steel tone bar in his pocket. The erection didn't sit well in his tight jeans. He wanted nothing more than to flip Selena onto her stomach and let instinct take over.

He parked in front of a shabby house. "Here?" he asked again, horrified she lived in a place the wrecking ball should have claimed a decade earlier.

"Yes, here." She still sounded testy.

Ethan put the transmission in park and shut off the ignition. Selena climbed out of the truck before he could race around the hood to open the door for her.

"Thanks for the ride, Ian. Good luck."

He met her on the front porch. He didn't touch her. Physical contact would be his undoing. Instead, he braced his hands against the exterior wall, trapping Selena between his outstretched arms. "My name is Ethan."

Her brindle eyes were wide, as if she couldn't believe he would threaten her. He might not be alpha, but he was male. She couldn't continue to insult him.

"Maybe you can deny me my right to mate, to sire children, and the privilege of honoring and protecting you, but you will not deny me my name. Say it."

"E-Ethan," she stammered.

He'd terrified her. The rank scent of her fear smothered him. Sickened him. He didn't want her afraid of him. He wanted her to want him. Honor him.

He dropped his arms and headed toward his truck. He didn't deserve her contempt or her fear.

"Wait."

The fright in her voice was as discordant as a drummer dropping a cymbal on an out-of-tune guitar.

"E-Ethan. Please."

He stopped; leaned against the porch rail to face her. The wood creaked beneath his weight. The cool spring wind played havoc with his hair, so he tucked the longer strands behind his ears. He crossed his arms over his chest and tried to erase emotion from his face.

She exhaled as if she were deflating. "Look. Why don't you come in for a cup of tea or something?"

"You're scared of me."

"I don't know you. If the gods of our elders have designated you as my mate, I shouldn't have reason to fear you. Except I don't want to mate. With anyone."

"Then what's the point of me coming inside?"

"How did you find me?"

He wasn't going to share the nature of his secret-secret mission. "How did you know where I'd be when I arrived?"

She forgot her fear long enough to roll her eyes.

He raised his eyebrows. His question was as pertinent as hers.

Her gaze flickered toward the house next door. "Can we move our discussion inside?"

Ethan dropped his arms. She showed him her back as she unlocked her door, a gesture he took as a victory.

"The last thing in the world I will ever do is hurt you, and if anyone else hurts you—"

"Please." She opened the door. "Stop with the male lobo posturing." She stood aside and let him pass.

He entered a small, dingy room. The stale smell suggested fresh air hadn't bothered with the space in the current millennium. Rodents scrabbled in the walls. What little furniture populating the room appeared worn.

"Who did you bring home?" Another male spoke from the shadowed corner.

"Ethan," Selena replied, while he bristled, ready to defend his mate from the intruder.

"Nathan? Nathan who?" The voice cracked.

"My name is Ethan Calhoun. Who are you?"

"Channing Wolfe, Varulv pack alpha. You look familiar. Where are you from?"

Ethan grabbed his temper before irreparable damage resulted. "Loup Garou, Colorado."

The man emerged from the shadows. He was old. Too old, in Ethan's opinion, to be a pack alpha. The sparse hair on his head was as gray as his eyes and the circles beneath them. Ethan thought he heard joints creaking.

"Ethan, meet my grandfather."

His intended mate was an alpha's granddaughter? *Whoa.* Intense, especially considering his own alpha mated a sapien.

"You're a long way from home. Were you planning on checking in?"

"Of course," Ethan lied. Tokarz hadn't mentioned another pack might claim northern Minnesota. Courtesy demanded he check in with the ruling pack. "I ran into your granddaughter as soon as I arrived."

A quick check of Selena showed one brow arched. She didn't contradict him.

"Mating fever brought you to Minnesota?" Channing was old, not stupid.

Ethan said nothing.

"New one on me." Channing continued fishing.

"Strangest thing," Ethan agreed.

"Is this any way to treat your intended?" Channing asked Selena. "Get him something to drink. To eat. You were raised better than a sapien girl."

Selena opened her mouth, as if to argue, glared at Ethan as if he were to blame for the situation, and then stalked from the room.

"You have to forgive the girl. She hasn't had a lot of female influence. Her mamma died when Selena was real young, and my mate died before Selena was born."

"My appearance shocked her." Ethan sought to placate the old man. Although Channing wasn't *his* pack elder, Ethan was determined to be polite, while at the same time protecting Selena.

"Are you going to court her in the traditional way?"

Ethan tried not to be offended by the question. He failed.

Channing must have read Ethan's mind. "Your pack brews beer, right? Moonsinger? If making beer isn't flouting the ways and nature of our kind, I don't know what is. How can I be sure you'll do right by my girl?"

Okay, yeah, brewing beer was weird. Lycan allergy to alcohol versus the pack decision to brew craft beer as a method of supporting the pack was a hotly debated subject. Ethan's grandparents still argued about whether to stay with the Loup Garou pack or find a more traditional place to spend their waning years. Channing's concern was valid. Still, Ethan had to force his teeth to unclench before he spoke.

"On the way here, I stopped and bought a blueberry and strawberry yogurt parfait. I made the offering. It's still in my truck. I would never dishonor my mate by violating our rituals. If you're concerned traditions won't be honored, you should explain why your granddaughter refused the berries I offered."

"Humph."

"I don't need my grandfather's permission," Selena said as she returned to the front room. Somewhere along the way, she'd discarded her shoes. She carried a tray with a carafe of water garnished with floating lemon slices and a platter of what smelled like fish. She placed the tray on the table in front of a sagging sofa. "Sorry the walleye is partially cooked. I thawed it in the microwave."

Ethan's stomach rumbled. He hadn't eaten in hours. "Smells great." He helped himself to a chunk. "Thanks."

"Have a seat." Channing waved a hand toward the room. "You remind me of someone. Can't think who, though."

Ethan studied the limited seating options as he chewed on his fish. Channing reclaimed a worn recliner in the corner. Ethan's only choice was a battle-scarred sofa. If he sat, he'd have to share with the female who had rejected him.

"I've been driving all night. I need to stretch my legs." The perfect excuse to avoid proximity with her. He had his pride.

"Where are you staying?" Channing asked.

Selena—who leaned against the door jamb, as if she, too, were avoiding physical closeness to Ethan—winced.

Or flinched. Neither reaction flattered him. He dreaded what was coming next. "I haven't had a chance to find a motel."

"Nonsense." Channing sounded as if he were trying to be hearty and jovial. He failed. Miserably. "You'll stay with Selena."

"Gramps—"

"Staying here isn't a good idea, sir." Dread weighted Ethan's stomach.

"Nonsense," Channing repeated. "The sofa pulls out if you're being...modest."

"Practical." Ethan stole a glance at Selena, who appeared upset. "I have other business in town and don't want to inconvenience anyone."

"What other business? You're in Varulv territory."

Right.

The lie came easily. "I'm with a band, and we're between booking agents, so I'm scouting possible venues for us to play."

"Doesn't the Loup Garou alpha have a side gig besides the brewery? What's the band's name?"

"Toke Lobo and the Pack."

"Aren't they on the radio?" Channing asked, while Selena exclaimed, "Get out. You are not."

Ethan now had an excuse to look directly at her. "Sure I am. I play steel guitar."

"You do not."

Ethan scowled.

Selena narrowed her eyes. "Prove it."

"Okay. I'll be right back."

He grabbed the *Full Moon Lady* CD and the bag with the yogurt stuff from his truck. He tried to hand both to her.

Selena ignored the brown paper bag in favor of the jewel case. She studied the photo on the cover. "Which one are you?"

Ethan gripped the tone bar he always kept in his jeans pocket. "Steel guitar."

"No hat?" She eyed his head as if she suspected he had high-maintenance hair.

"No hat. The band is half and half on head gear." Something she could see for herself. He set the yogurt on the table next to the tray of fish before jamming his hand into his pocket.

Selena continued to ignore the bag and focused on the jewel case in her hand. "The photo is tiny. How do I know it's you?"

"Quit trying to redirect our attention," Channing snarled. "He shouldn't have to pay for a hotel when you're his mate, and he can sleep here."

"I don't want to impose," Ethan repeated. "And I'm not going to force myself where I'm not wanted. You two don't know me. I don't belong sleeping on her sofa."

He studied her as he spoke. Her eyes widened and her complexion paled. Her mouth opened as if she were going to speak.

The stench of her fear wasn't his imagination. Ethan watched Channing to gauge his reaction. Nothing. Maybe his sense of smell was waning in his old age. Pa complained his senses weren't as keen as they'd once been.

"You can stay. On the sofa." Her lips parted, baring her teeth in what Ethan assumed was supposed to be a smile. She sounded as if she might cry. "With Gramps."

Channing barked. Maybe laughed. "Good try. I told you before. I'm heading home tonight. The city is no place for an old wolf at night."

"Gramps—"

"No arguing. I need to get going. I don't care for driving after dark." Channing slowly rose from his chair. "I only stuck around to make sure you followed through with your task."

Ethan wasn't sure if the recliner or Channing creaked.

"You don't like driving," Selena muttered.

"I do not." Channing stooped and kissed Selena's cheek.

"Text me when you get home."

Channing made a face. "I don't like gizmos and gadgets."

"Text me anyway."

The old man made a sound in the back of his throat, not unlike one Pa made. He cocked his head at Ethan, before striding across the room and out the door.

Ethan squared his shoulders and braced his courage to deal with Selena. Who was in the process of straightening her back and lifting her chin.

Apparently, her grandfather's presence had dampened Ethan's mating urges. They were currently making themselves known in some embarrassing ways. "I, uh, am going to, uh...I need to..." He gestured toward the door. If he didn't remove himself from her presence, things could happen he might later regret.

"Good idea."

Her lips quivered. If Ethan hadn't been obsessed with her mouth, he might have missed the miniscule betrayal of her nervousness.

She lifted the tray from the table. "I'm serious. You have to stay with me. Gramps is right. We don't want you going back to Colorado and telling other packs the Varulv are inhospitable."

No one had mentioned hospitality, as if being welcoming mattered. What mattered was knowing Selena's fear wasn't his doing. "If sleeping on your sofa makes you happy, I guess I'd better not insult your grandfather by finding a motel."

She exhaled as if she'd been holding her breath. "Thank you. Hospitality is important to him." She carried the tray of fish from the room.

Ethan stared a long moment at the still-unopened bag containing the berries and yogurt. His lips tightened. He shook his head and left.

SELENA WAITED UNTIL THE front door snicked shut behind Ethan before she leaned against the closed kitchen door and slid to the floor. She couldn't have been limper if her bones decided to abandon her body. Her respiration consisted of nothing more than gasps and wheezes. She was amazed she'd managed to hold herself together for as long as she had.

She never should have let her grandfather bully her into going to Congressman Peters' office. She should have disobeyed. Run off to some remote mountain top and stayed until...

But no. Her pack alpha issued an order, leaving her no choice. She'd gone to the Congressman's office. Although she did not have an appointment, she'd been shown inside at once. Stating her piece had been more difficult than she'd imagined. She managed to speak without emotion.

When the congressman's son, Liam Peters, on whom she'd once had a crush, followed her out the building and grabbed her arm, she believed she would lose control. Until her second worst nightmare materialized...

Her mate arrived on the scene to rescue her.

She believed the gods of her elders had decided she wasn't mating material. As her grandfather's only heir, she was prepared to assume leadership of the Varulv pack on his death and was already planning a future beyond her rule. For ten years, she believed she understood her fate. Until this morning. Until Ethan.

A mate. Something she didn't want or need. He'd opened his mouth, and his deep baritone nested in her soul. Her good-girl inner wolf wanted to throw herself into Ethan's arms. The howling guilty-girl who dictated her every action was smarter.

She pulled the Toke Lobo and the Pack jewel case from her blazer pocket. Every werewolf in America knew the band. Ethan was hard to miss now she'd met him. His smile. The slight indentation in his chin. The way his black hair curved around his entire head. An earring adorned his left ear in the photo. She or her grandfather would have noticed if he wore a hoop or anything shiny. She hadn't seen a hole in his earlobe; she'd purposely studied him, searching for flaws.

Using the tip of her index finger, she traced the outline of his face. He was the handsomest band member. Hers, whether she wanted him or not.

Maybe you can deny me my right to mate, to sire children, and the privilege of honoring and protecting you.

He couldn't have chosen a more accurate way to humiliate her. To remind her life didn't always follow destiny.

A minute later, she dropped the brown paper bag containing the fresh berry parfait into the trash.

Chapter 2

"I wasn't aware Channing Wolfe was still alive," Tokarz told Ethan. "He's my grandfather's contemporary."

"He's old," Ethan admitted. He'd driven to a nearby decrepit park to make his phone call. All metal had been stripped from the playground equipment. Graffiti decorated what pieces remained. The basketball hoop drooped as if weary of hanging around such a dreary space.

"The Varulv didn't die out after the old man's son was killed?" Tokarz continued. "He was doing treaty work for some politician—maybe the one you're in Minnesota to persuade—and got caught in the Pentagon on September eleventh."

Although Ethan barely remembered the terrorist attacks himself, he knew the stories. All Americans did. Tokarz's words clicked. "Erik Wolfe?" The man was a hero among the werewolf packs. A legend.

"Yeah. Why?"

Holy scat. Ethan's mate was Erik Wolfe's daughter?

"Did he have offspring?" Regardless of whose child Selena was, Ethan didn't want to blurt out he'd found his mate to his alpha.

"Offspring? I don't remember."

"Selena." Finally. Ethan spoke the name aloud. The word was a symphony in his mouth. The sibilant start; the languorous long vowel after tongue play against the backs of his teeth.

"And why should either of us care?" Tokarz's sharp tone cut through the nonsense. "The Varulv isn't a particularly powerful pack. They're not particularly reputable, either. I didn't know they were still around."

"The Varulv pack is alive and active. I'm working in their territory without their permission." Ethan carefully worded the statement as not to blame Tokarz for disregarding diplomacy. And, for the time being, he decided to ignore the insult to his mate's lineage. Tokarz remained his alpha. "Me approaching the congressman could present a problem."

"How did they find out so quickly you're in town?"

"Selena Wolfe was at the congressman's office when I arrived." Ethan spied a dilapidated gazebo in the distance. The neighborhood clearly abandoned a nicer past.

"Sounds as if Jasper confused the matter, asking two packs to negotiate with Peters."

"I don't know why she was at the congressman's office."

Or the identity of the tall man who'd accosted her.

"You've confirmed she's Erik Wolfe's daughter?"

"She's Channing Wolfe's granddaughter. I might be jumping to conclusions." He wasn't. His marrow told the truth.

"Channing, if I remember right, had only the one son." Another Toke Lobo silence, as if he were waiting for Ethan to argue. "Anything else?"

Ethan clenched and unclenched his teeth several times before answering. "Not sure yet."

Yes, Selena was his mate, as decreed by the Ancient Ones, cooperating or not. Sharing his failure to claim her with the world, even with his alpha, would embarrass him.

"What aren't you telling me?"

He couldn't refuse to answer a direct request. "Selena Wolfe is my mate."

Ethan thought he heard a muttered *scat*.

"I suppose you want to come home." Tokarz sounded irritated.

So, his resentment at being shipped off to Minnesota due to his unmated state hadn't gone unnoticed. "Still working on the logistics." Not a lie as much as an intentional misdirection of the truth. Tradition dictated Selena would leave her pack and join his.

He would no longer be a single male, meaning he would no longer have to be active in treaty work, if any treaties existed after the upcoming vote. Tokarz wouldn't be able to ship him off to Minnesota or Siberia or any other damned place on a whim.

"So, your convince-the-congressman job turned out to be a two-fer for you. You get to serve your pack, and you found your mate."

Naturally Tokarz would twist reality to make the situation sound better than the truth. Ethan wasn't going to confess he had no idea how to approach the congressman or deal with Selena's refusal of the berries he'd offered.

"You need to touch base with Channing Wolfe. Otherwise, he could stop me from doing my job."

Tokarz wasn't the only one who could spin.

"Yeah, he's my future mate's grandfather," Ethan continued, "but mating still doesn't give me the right to barge into Varulv territory to do Loup Garou business."

"Do you plan to claim her soon?"

"Our relationship is between Selena and me." Maybe he shouldn't have been so blunt, but some things weren't anyone's business, including his alpha. Ethan finding his mate had nothing to do with the mission. He called Tokarz to make sure his presence in Warwick wasn't going to create political issues, not for mating advice.

Tokarz must have decided Ethan needed instruction. "There are two important rules to remember about mating. First, don't hurt her. Second, make sure she's happy."

Happy. Ethan didn't believe anything would make Selena happy. Beneath her fear, sadness clung to her in a swampy funk.

"If you claim her, I don't need to make amends with Channing."

"If I claim her, I'm no longer qualified for the mission," Ethan reminded him. Spending his efforts on Selena instead of Congressman Peters appealed to every cell in his body.

"The policy is not etched in stone. I finished my mission after I met Delilah."

As if Ethan would ever forget being on the road with a sapien who refused to adjust to the reality of werewolves. She'd been Ethan's first prolonged exposure to a *homo sapien* female; Delilah went out of her way to be unpleasant. He still wasn't fond of her.

Tokarz continued defending his mate. "Delilah didn't have an easy time, learning our ways while looking for a serial killer."

"I was there."

Thank the Ancient Ones Selena's lycan blood was as ancient as his own. Maybe he wasn't a legacy descendent of the Loup Garou pack, but his mate-to-be could match her lineage to the Garniers any time.

At least he spoke to Tokarz on the phone instead of face to face. The distance allowed him to grin. His mate was worthier of the Garniers than the sapien chosen for Tokarz.

"I need to get going." Ethan hoped Tokarz had run out of advice to impart. For some reason, he'd expected his alpha to be...wiser. Better at giving him direction. Ethan was floundering, and Tokarz's lackadaisical attitude didn't help.

"Keep me posted." Tokarz disconnected the call.

Ethan stared at his phone for a full minute before reacting.

The world—his world—was falling apart. First, the treaties keeping him safe were going away, followed by Pa's statement Ethan should not be doing Loup Garou business. His mate, the female meant to be with him forever, refused him. Now his alpha was...fading. Yeah, Tokarz put up a good front until Mitchell Jasper left. Once the liaison was gone, Tokarz lost his focus.

A VEHICLE PULLED UP to the curb outside Selena's house. She peered out the window. Hard to miss—or mistake—Ethan's blood red truck. He extracted a dark brown duffel from behind the driver's seat. He'd accepted her invitation to crash at her place.

After her conversation with Congressman Peters, she didn't want to be alone.

She hated herself for being cowardly. An alpha female, more than capable of defending herself, should be brave. She'd taken steps years ago to ensure the new moon, her most vulnerable time, would never betray her again.

Still...

She opened the door before he could knock, stepping aside to let him enter. "How long will you be in town?"

"Hello to you, too." He grinned, letting her know her abruptness hadn't offended him. "I have no idea how long my official business is going to take. My personal business is going to take a lifetime."

Her cheeks heated and her insides shivered. His voice, deep and dark, burrowed further into her psyche. "You have no personal business."

The smile slid from his face as if it were a pie she'd tossed at him. "Don't I?" He dropped his duffel to the floor before lifting his hand as if to touch her cheek.

She jerked from the caress and spun away from him. Although she'd just met him, he was the only male in the world, other than her grandfather, she trusted enough to show her back. She couldn't figure out what her instinct meant. "What part of no don't you get?"

"I understand your words." His hand fell to his side. "I don't believe them."

"No means no." Her voice quavered. *"No means no."*

"Look at me." From the sound of his voice, he maintained the gap between them. He honored the distance she needed.

She verified what she'd heard. "What?"

"I don't know what's going on with you, but I'm patient. We can't change our destinies." His eyes were bright, mimicking lasers trying to pierce her defenses.

Maybe letting him stay with her was a mistake.

"There are circumstances, situations I can't explain."

He waited, as if she were going to spill her sorrows.

"I'm sorry I can't be what you need me to be. I know it's unfair to you. I'm depriving you of offspring and mated bliss. We live in a complicated world. The old ways—"

"Are still relevant as far as mating. If another female interested me, I wouldn't be able to do anything. I wouldn't be attracted to her."

Her head drooped. "I'm sorry," she whispered. The words were inadequate.

"Maybe I should find another place to stay."

She shook her head. "I...I trust you."

"You trust a male in the grip of mating fever?"

She raised her head again and met his stare. She lifted her chin. "Yeah. I do. The minute I don't, you'll be the first I'll tell. Or maybe you've never met an alpha female with her temper up."

"I'm not high enough in rank where I have a lot of interaction with my so-called betters. Except with the band. No females in the band."

His admission surprised her. "How low are you?"

"My status is moot if we're not going to mate."

He was right, although a lesser-status male insulted her own alpha rank and reinforced the low regard by the gods of her elders.

"Anyway, I got sidetracked. Sorry. I'm going out in a bit. I don't have a spare key for you. Are you okay to stay alone while I'm gone?"

"I can drive you," he offered.

"While I appreciate the offer, I want to run. I need to run. Clear the fog from my brain."

"Two legged or four legged?"

"Two." She forced her lips into an upward curve.

"Will you be safe? You don't live in the best neighborhood."

Her inner wolf-bitch bared her teeth and considered growling. "I can take care of myself."

"I would rather you didn't have to."

She hated him. He shouldn't be able to annihilate her defenses with a few simple words.

"I hope you're at least going to put on some shoes."

"Why? It's easier to shift if I need to without shoes."

He narrowed his eyes. "Funny."

"Look, I don't want you to get too invested in me. On any level. I can't be your mate. I can't even be your friend."

"Only my hostess."

"On behalf of the Varulv pack."

"For your grandfather's sake."

Her stare, willing him to concede, was her only answer.

SELENA WAS MORE BEAUTIFUL in her pinkish-red sweater and blue jeans than she'd been in her black suit. And her toes...he'd forced himself not to stare at them in her grandfather's presence.

He'd seen plenty of women's toes in the bars and dance clubs where the band played. Most of those toes were coated in nail polish. At least the ones he'd noticed.

Selena's were not. They were well-trimmed and naturally pink. Incredibly sexy. Did his reaction mean he had a foot fetish? Luke, his on-the-road roommate, loved Internet porn sites. Ethan would never be able to un-see some stuff Luke had forced on him, including some of the odder sexual fixations, like foot fetishes. True lycans had sex only with their mates. Luke was part sapien, an excuse used to minimize a plethora of foibles.

Remembering such scat insulted his mate, who stood in front of him, lovelier than any female had a right to be. A sign for sure his trek to Minnesota was going to be a disaster. Tokarz could congratulate himself all he wanted for ordering Ethan to Warwick, so he could meet his mate. Meeting and marking were two different things. Ethan could force the matter but having Selena's consent seemed like a better way to embark on their life together.

She walked toward the door, and he glimpsed her ass in jeans for the first time. *Ancient Ones.* A more perfect female behind had never been created. Her backside distracted him from the whole rank and status dilemma.

Focus.

Ethan accepted his place as theta in the Loup Garou pack. He wasn't as short-tempered as most others in the pack. He preferred to sit back and observe before making decisions.

His reaction when he first laid eyes on Selena was an anomaly. Which reminded him — "Who grabbed your arm this morning outside the congressman's office?"

She twitched, as if changing the subject unnerved her. "Liam Peters."

"How do you know him?" He sounded jealous, which was ridiculous.

"He's Congressman Peters' oldest son." Her cautious tone scraped at him like a dull blade. "Congressman Peters and my grandfather go way back."

She couldn't hide the strain in her voice. Her attention shifted away from him for a couple of quick blinks. She wasn't telling him everything relating to Liam Peters.

"How far back?"

"Before I was born. Doesn't your grandfather have old friends or colleagues?"

She'd guessed his problem. Ethan's grandfather never spoke of his origins. The Calhouns weren't a Loup Garou legacy family. Ethan's true status remained a mystery. Until now, rank hadn't mattered. As far as he knew, he had no pedigree, unlike the congressman's blue-eyed son.

"So, you've known the son for a long time?" He struggled and failed to sound neutral.

Selena didn't seem to notice. "Since I can remember."

"Are the two of you close?"

Her head jerked. "No."

Ethan didn't believe her. He glimpsed the ghosts in her eyes before she averted her face again.

What if she loved, or believed she loved, the congressman's son? A lump the size and texture of a peach pit lodged in his throat.

Pursuing his suspicions could wait. Selena needed to get used to the idea the Ancient Ones were not going to tolerate her disregard for their plans. Female werewolves didn't have the restriction on them the males had. Only their morals, upbringing, and a pack's isolation from the rest of the world prevented the women from taking lovers as their sapien counterparts did.

The peach pit wedged tighter.

What if she'd been in a relationship with Peters?

Ethan was the better male. Now he had to prove it.

"So. Where are you going tonight?"

"I don't answer to you."

Wow. That was hostile.

"I'm only trying to be friendly. If we're going to be roommates, we ought to try to not be at each other's throats."

"I teach a class on Tuesday nights."

"What type of class?" He wanted to learn everything about her.

"My life is boring. Let's discuss you. I noticed you're wearing an earring on the CD cover, yet you don't have a hole in your ear."

"What?"

She pulled the jewel case from her pocket. "Here. You have an earring. I don't see a hole in your earlobe."

Heat flooded his cheeks. "It's magnetic. Why?"

"Curiosity. Trying to be a good roomie. It's funny. New country versus cowboys and stuff."

"Yeah. Some guys wear the traditional hats. I wear an earring." He resented having to defend his stage appearance. Unless she preferred the stud. "Do you want me to wear one?"

Her mouth gaped before she answered. "No."

"Afraid you might swallow something sharp while we're necking?"

She narrowed her eyes. "Hardly. Anyway, I put fresh bedding on the sofa. I need to get going, or I'm going to be late."

"Don't forget your shoes."

SELENA STOPPED NEXT TO a neon cowboy hat advertising roast beef sandwiches and lifted her face to the night sky. Light pollution from the city cloaked most of the stars, although a few planets pierced the haze. The moon, waxing her way to the Milk Moon of May, begged for a song.

Selena sniffed the air as a precaution. No danger mingled in the hint of rancid grease from fast-food franchises, a rotting dumpster, or the dog droppings someone hadn't scooped. A smoldering cigarette added to the potpourri. Faintly, indiscernible to most sapiens, lilies of the valley leant their fragrance to the night.

Selena resumed her jog. College town, the area around Warwick College, was safe enough. Still, she remained alert, her nose, her ears, and her eyes at the ready. She'd been careless once. Never again.

ETHAN WAITED FIVE MINUTES before following Selena. He left his truck at her house. Tracking her was easier on foot. Besides, he feared

she might see and recognize the Colorado plates and be furious with him. He merely needed to follow the direction his penis pointed, as the old lycan adolescent joke went. Didn't seem so funny now that mating fever afflicted him.

A couple of times she stopped and lingered for no reason he could discern. He took care she wouldn't sense him behind her.

Several women called greetings to her, joining her as she approached a low building. She laughed, tilting her face to the sky, and offering her joy to the moon.

Desire shot through him.

He stood in the shadows of a clump of shrubbery at the edge of a parking lot and focused. His mate's voice carried out an open window. He couldn't make out the words, but he knew her voice. Not as well as he wanted or intended to, but he knew it.

"Hey, Selena!" someone called. "What kind of bombs are we making tonight?"

"You're late," Brittany chided, as Selena hurried into the chemistry classroom.

"I had some—" Selena broke off. Britt might be a friend, but she was sapien and wouldn't understand the concept of mates.

"No matter. I started without you. It's not as if I've never made a bomb before."

Selena laughed. She and Britt had gone into the candle and bomb-making business last year. Their products were popular with the New Age community on the fringes of college town.

Britt wanted to expand their line with other related items. Selena agreed. The Varulv needed an industry to sustain them the way the Loup Garou pack used their brewery. She could apply her knowledge of healing plants to create therapeutic lotions, soaps, and lip balms in addition to the candles and bath bombs they were currently producing. Their merchandise would be organic. Healthy. A counterpoint to the poison of Moonsinger Beer.

Ethan stayed in the shadows outside the low building and jiggled his head. Something must be wrong with his ears. Or his brain. He could have sworn someone asked his mate how to make bombs.

Maybe she'd said bonbons. Weren't bonbons a fancy candy or cookie? Maybe Selena liked to bake.

She might have said barn. Barn could be misconstrued for bomb. Except Selena didn't strike him as a builder, making a barn-raising wishful thinking on his part.

He crept closer to the open window and sniffed. He wouldn't know how a bomb or the components smelled. If he could describe the scent, maybe Luke could research it on his computer.

Bombs. His heart boomed in his chest.

He tried to banish his outrage. His mate, the one for whom he'd waited all his life, engaged in terrorist activities. Maybe she'd planted an explosive device in the congressman's regional office during her visit.

She'd left Ethan, her newly found mate, to teach others how to build bombs.

Ethan thought Selena replied, "basal." He hoped basal was a better type than nuclear. Nor could he be sure what he'd heard. Maybe she'd said *missile*. Didn't matter. She built bombs and trained other terrorists to do the same.

What if Tokarz ordered him to kill her? She could be executed for treason. Ethan would have to choose between country and mate. How did one determine the most honorable of two hideous options?

He wanted nothing more than to shift. Running might clear his head and settle his gut. Stretching his muscles until they ached might alleviate some of the hurt in his heart. Howling his frustration might soothe his soul. Neither action was an option. Instead, he stalked to his adopted shrubbery clump at the edge of the parking lot. Lightning bugs signaled his approach.

Maybe Selena's treachery was the Ancient Ones' karma for gloating his mate was a better female than his alpha's woman.

At least he hadn't marked Selena right away. Living with the shame of a mate gone bad was more than he had the strength to endure. He needed to learn gratitude for the small gifts from the Ancient Ones.

No. He'd come to Minnesota to persuade Congressman Peters to uphold the treaties. If Selena had to be trussed and locked in a closet until he could get her to Loup Garou, he'd buy the rope.

He got it. He did. If anyone had a valid reason to go after the congressman, Selena topped the list. Her father had been killed in service to the congressman; now the politicians were going to disavow their debt to the lycan population. Selena had to be furious, if not devastated. Her father's death meant nothing to Peters.

Selena's class lasted two hours. Ethan stayed, lurking in the shadows. Although he couldn't prevent her from making bombs tonight, he could stop her from doing anything with them. He'd wait until she went to bed, then return and confiscate them. Or he could stay to grab the evidence after everyone left for the night.

Except transporting explosives worried him. He was not hero material, not the type of lobo who could swoop in and save the day. Low-totem guys like him followed orders well. Someone needed to issue those orders and make life-and-death decisions. Half the time, Ethan had trouble deciding what to eat for supper. How was he supposed to deal with bombs?

He'd better wait until Tokarz could send reinforcements.

People—females—emerged from the building.

"Be careful, Cassandra! If you drop the bomb, you'll make a real mess." Laughter followed.

The women were leaving the premises with their handiwork. Were they suicide bombers? A moment after the light snapped out, Selena and another woman emerged.

"Good class tonight." The other woman raised her hand and pointed at something. "Do you want a ride home?"

The sole car remaining in the parking lot chirped and the locks plinked.

"No thanks. I like to walk."

"And I like to dance, but I wouldn't dance my way into your crappy neighborhood."

"I'll be fine. See you next week, Britt."

Selena hitched her backpack onto her shoulder and headed for the street.

Foolish female. She should have accepted the offer of a ride.

He waited another fifteen minutes by his calculations before he broke into the low, one-story building. Manufacturing flimsy locks ought to be illegal. He closed his eyes to visualize the location of Selena's room. Closing his eyes also helped focus his nose. He found her unique aroma. The thread of scent led him directly to the door he would have selected anyway.

Another insubstantial lock delayed him less than ten seconds.

Chapter 3

Selena arrived home to an empty house. She tried to recall if Ethan mentioned going out. His truck, the big shiny red monster, still lurked at the curb. His duffel slouched in the living room corner, evidence he hadn't relocated to a motel.

He must have gone out for a run. She didn't blame him. The gorgeous night called for running and moon singing.

His absence gave her time to regroup. She usually loved teaching her class; tonight, the emotional tsunami she'd been on all day exhausted her. She decided to grab a shower before going to bed. Ethan would be back at any moment. Dealing with him required full use of her brain.

Something outside the closed bathroom door thumped after she shut off the water. Ethan must have broken in. Typical arrogant lobo. She had a few choice words for him.

Instead of waiting to dry off, Selena opted to shift. The heat generated by the energy involved would evaporate the water clinging to her skin. First, though, she unlatched the door as quietly as she could, so she could nose it open once she'd changed.

She'd dropped to all four feet when the door burst inward.

The stink hit her first. *Gods of the elders, what is that creature?* She growled as she leapt for its throat.

The…thing must not have expected a wolf. The beast's awkward and clumsy reaction granted Selena a moment to recoup. It stumbled and fell backward, rolling out of Selena's way.

She whirled to attack again. The human-looking creature flashed fangs and hissed at her. Her wolf vision, usually so sharp and clear, translated the putrid being's movements as blurs.

Scat. The fangs were the giveaway.

Selena wasn't prepared for a battle with the undead. Females weren't taught Vampire 101. She was so screwed. Her thoughts were a tangle as undefined as the vampire in motion. Smeared. Smudged. Distorted.

She was going to die or become the world's first ever werewolf vampire. She would never hear Ethan play guitar with her new favorite band. Never make love with Ethan. Never bear his children. She would be forever remembered as the werewolf who wimped out to a victorious vampire. A lesson to be taught to other lycan children as to what not to do.

My beautiful tail-end.

She bared her teeth at the prancing monster. She wanted Ethan's babies, and if survival meant fighting a piece of reconstituted offal, she would battle. She'd trained to use her innate skills to her advantage. She possessed expertise this creature couldn't imagine.

The vamp feinted left, left, right, its image trailing. Maybe the creature was trying to glamour her, trick her into believing a lie.

Ethan deserved better than to be unmated. He deserved her. She deserved him. Somehow. *Gods of our Elders*, she vowed, *I'll try.*

The vamp rushed her. She leapt out of the way.

Only to be hit in the hindquarters by the door crashing inward.

A black wolf, snapping and snarling, surged into the room.

The vamp careened off the far wall. A mirror shattered on the floor, the tinkle of splintering glass merging with the cracking of the windowpane as the monster smashed its way out of the house.

Coward didn't want to handle two lycans.

The black wolf gave chase. Selena resisted the temptation to follow. Instead, she returned to the bathroom to shift. She donned her robe, belting the brown chenille tightly at her waist.

Every nerve in her body jittered and the vamp wasn't the only reason.

She wanted Ethan's babies. Damn the mating instinct. Damn it all to a vampire's lair.

Ethan was shrugging into his shirt as she exited the bathroom. She paused in the doorway, absorbing the sight of his naked torso, the play of muscles stretching his skin, sleek and defined; the ebony pelt of the wolf now a wedge of wiry curls in the center of his chest. His jeans hung low on his hips, revealing the taut skin below his navel. Selena forced herself to look away.

"I lost the vampire," he admitted. Although Ethan had resumed his human form, he growled as if he were still lycan. "Why was a vampire in your house? Did you invite it?"

Every hint of tenderness she might have harbored fled. "Invite? What is 'invite' supposed to mean? I was in the shower. It attacked when I got out. And where were you? You were going to wait for me."

"If you didn't order the vamp out, you invited it!"

"You aren't making any sense. I didn't know it was a vamp until it broke the bathroom door."

"You didn't smell it?"

"Hey! Female here. Protected. Cherished. Sheltered." *Not quite.* Not helpless, either. "Intro to Vamps and Other Abominations wasn't part of my education."

She did her best to match his glare. "Where was your big, strong masculine backside when I needed protection?"

Not that he had a big backside.

Ethan resumed buttoning his shirt. "The creatures know where you live."

Waves of rage surrounded him like an aura. He still hadn't answered her question. "Yeah. No kidding. I wish I knew what to do."

Ethan sat, socks in hand. "You have to declare your house a vampire-free zone."

"That is one of the stupidest things I've ever heard." Vamps were sly creatures. Sneaky. How could merely declaring one's space vampire-free make it so?

"Don't roll your eyes at me." Ethan yanked on his boots. "I don't make the rules. I only know what they are."

"Don't blame me if no one ever taught me the rules."

Ethan stood. Strode across the room to stand in front of her. He loomed, as if trying to intimidate her. Although she was female and expected to be cowed by her mate, she was also descended from a long line of alpha werewolves.

If only she weren't clad in her robe. Asserting authority without testicles to reinforce her position was difficult enough; with him fully dressed in jeans, a brown and navy checked flannel shirt, and his boots, she was at a distinct disadvantage.

Wait a minute.

Ethan had gone outside to get dressed. *His clothes were outside and intact.*

She stood on tiptoe and leaned into him. "I see you didn't rush to my rescue when you smelled vampire."

He took a step back. His scowl rearranged itself, adding a touch of wariness.

"I mean," she continued, poking her forefinger into his chest for emphasis. The shock of contact gobsmacked her equilibrium. "You were able to shift without destroying your clothes. Or am I interpreting what happened all wrong?"

Tell me I'm wrong.

He captured her hand in his and trapped it against his body. "I smelled the vampire and figured I could better fight him four-legged. His stink masked your presence. Otherwise I wouldn't have taken the time to undress before shifting."

Oh, his excuse sounded logical enough, except mating fever allegedly suppressed logic.

Selena stared at him for several heartbeats before rolling her eyes and heading for her bedroom.

He still hadn't told her where he'd been.

She emerged a few minutes later to find Ethan sweeping the glass from the broken window and mirror into a pile.

"It didn't have a reflection." Right before the mirror crashed to the floor, the vampire passed by the silvery glass. The memory hit her like an ice bath.

"No," Ethan dug the broom bristles into a corner. "They don't. I don't suppose you have any plywood lying around."

"No." Her voice quavered. She hated the sign of weakness. "I only rent. Let me call the landlord and tell him about the break-in."

Ethan propped the broom against the wall, then crossed the room in three strides and enveloped her in a near-suffocating embrace. He couldn't have hugged her after the vampire abandoned the house? He couldn't have comforted her when she needed solace instead of waiting until she recovered on her own?

"Too late, wolf." She pulled away from him. Then fought the urge to rest her head against his chest and be soothed.

"You don't have to be alpha strong all the time."

She stopped, her back toward him. "You met me this morning. You don't know me well enough to make any judgements."

"You had a scare tonight. *I* had a scare tonight. Vampires aren't part of our normal world. Maybe we should comfort each other."

She considered laughing in his face. "Except we aren't mated and never will be."

Warmth increased at her back, betraying his nearness. If he touched her again, she might shatter like the mirror.

"We'll see," he replied. "Will you do one thing for me?"

Wishing she could decipher the nuances of his voice, she faced him. "Depends."

"Declare your house off limits to vamps."

"Are we back to inane solutions?" She started to walk away from him.

"Can speaking the words hurt?"

His question stopped her. He had a point. Saying the words wouldn't make a difference. Neither could they do harm. "What should I say?"

"I've never dealt with vampires before either. How about 'I declare my house to be a vampire-free zone?'"

"I, Selena Wolfe, do declare this house to be a vampire free zone. Vampires are not welcome." She put all her alpha strength into the statements, hoping to increase the power of the words. "All vampires will be staked on sight." She lifted her chin in a silent dare to contradict her.

He raised an eyebrow. "I guess we'd better stock up on stakes."

ETHAN STARED AT THE cracks in Selena's living room ceiling. He shifted on the lumpy mattress of the pullout bed.

His mate-to-be had a vampire after her. The horror of the indisputable fact still stabbed him, piercing his usually inner calm. Not much disturbed him. Of all the members of Toke Lobo and the Pack, he considered himself the most levelheaded. The emotions involving Selena were as unsettling to his normal as she was.

Vampires and making bombs. If marking his mate-to-be could force her to leave Minnesota, he would. Marking her wouldn't be a hardship. Imagining Selena naked and beneath him had him erect.

Her alpha heritage did not give her the right to fight the Ancient Ones' desires.

He twisted in the sheets again. A metal bar supported the middle of the bedframe, and the flimsy mattress did nothing to pad the steel from pressing into Ethan's back. The springs creaked as he squirmed.

The fresh night air, courtesy of the broken window, cooled his heated body and helped rid the room of vampire stink.

Bombs. His mate-to-be made bombs.

Yeah, he'd whisk her off to Loup Garou where Tokarz would assign someone to keep an eye on her while Ethan returned to Minnesota to fulfill his mission.

Except keeping an eye on her was his responsibility. His duty included making sure she did nothing to embarrass him or the werewolf community. He finally grasped Stoker's dilemma when his sapien mate wanted to...think.

Selena's alpha heritage had trained her to think and offer wisdom to her pack, unlike some sapien twit with no clue about lycan culture. She'd been raised to lead.

He climbed out of bed. He wore only his boxers, tight and uncomfortable. The front resembled a tent. The lousy mattress and worse bed frame weren't keeping him from sleep. His own body betrayed him by mimicking the steel bar.

He padded across the room, hoping they'd managed to find all the broken glass. His lycan blood meant he'd heal quickly; not exempt from pain.

He stopped at Selena's closed bedroom door.

"I wouldn't if I were you." Her voice rang clear.

Naturally she'd heard him get up and cross the room. She would recognize the staccato rhythm of his heart. Which meant she couldn't sleep either.

"I only want to talk."

"I had a full and disturbing day today, and tomorrow doesn't promise to be much better. I need to sleep." She sounded sullen.

"You're awake now."

"Are you threatening to bore me to sleep?"

He grinned. He couldn't help himself. "You're lycan. Nocturnal. The night is your friend."

"Vampires are creatures of the night, too. I'm safer in daylight."

The forlorn, barely audible confession encouraged him.

"I will never intentionally hurt you." He rested his forehead against the flimsy panel. "I'm supposed to protect you. Keep you safe."

Whisk her out of Minnesota, away from the vampires, away from her bomb making. Away from the temptation of another male, Congressman Peters' son.

"I know."

"You're killing me."

"Me? I didn't have run-ins with vampires before you showed up. Did you bring them with you from Colorado?"

"No."

"I never smelled one until after I met you."

Curious. "Conversely, I never smelled one until I came to Warwick."

Silence for several heartbeats before he heard, "Oh."

"Maybe we should mate."

"You believe vampires attacked us because I won't mate with you?" The statement might have been punctuated with a snort. "You do have creative arguments."

"I'm dealing with a new situation. How many females do you suppose have refused their mates?"

"Ethan?"

"Yes?"

"I told you. My refusal is nothing personal. It has to do with me."

"Maybe I need a better answer. You're asking me to defy the will of the Ancient Ones. You're asking me to forgo offspring. You want me to sacrifice everything our species holds sacred. I deserve a better explanation than what you've given me thus far."

"You do." Another whispered reply. A long silence. "It's . . . complicated."

"You think you're in love with someone else." He didn't ask, and he didn't name names.

More quiet, while Ethan's guts knotted tighter.

"How did you guess?"

He pressed his forehead against the door and dug his fingers into the frame, as if he could read vibrations using the wood as a conduit. The frame splintered beneath his grip. Slivers of painted wood embedded beneath his nails.

"Your grandfather claims he raised you right." He could barely force the words past the tightness in his throat. "He worried I would dishonor you by ignoring our traditions."

She made a sound he didn't recognize and couldn't identify.

His instincts screamed for him to crash through the door and claim her. He could easily overpower her. His inner wolf baited him.

The cool calmness he'd inherited from Pa urged him to wait. To consider.

His penis agreed with his inner wolf; still, he would not force her. She'd feared him when they'd first met, and the memory of her terror's stench still clung to his olfactory.

He really wanted to force the man's name from her, so he could kill whoever had stolen his mate's heart. Her heart belonged to *him*, not some sapien facsimile of what a male should be. He flexed his fingers against the ruined door frame, ignoring the pricks of his slivers, and imagined using them on his competitor's throat before shifting and tearing his still-beating heart from his chest.

Neither scenario would endear him to Selena. She needed to come to him on her own. And she would. No sapien male would fight vampires for her. No sapien male would treasure her ability to defend herself the way she had against the vampire. No sapien male could fathom the nuances of lycan life. A sapien male probably couldn't impregnate a female—she would be too strong for his measly seed. Ethan knew of no *homo lupus* woman joined with a *homo sapien* man. Mixed matings were always—*always*—sapien female, lycan male.

He tried to take comfort in the concept and failed. "He will never cherish you the way I will."

The foreign noise continued, the only sound from behind the door.

What if the vampire had returned and — Ethan didn't finish the imaginary scenario as he smashed his way into her room.

Selena lay alone in her bed.

She jerked upright, clutching her pillow to her breasts. Gaps in her window blinds allowed moonlight to seep into the room, painting silvery white stripes across the walls and floor. One band revealed pink flowers on the shoulders of her nightwear. Her breasts rose and fell in harsh rhythms.

"I'm sorry." His voice clawed its way out of his throat. "I thought the vampire returned. Are you okay?"

"Get out."

He jerked his head once, recoiling from the venom in her tone. Yeah. She was okay. He backed out of the room, hesitating by the broken door. He swallowed hard. He wanted to say something soothing, something reassuring. He couldn't find the words.

He'd glimpsed a desolation in her eyes, a wretchedness deeper than anything he'd ever experienced. He fed her misery, and he didn't know how to stop.

"Go."

He needed to fix her mood. Fix her pain. Fix their ill-fated future. Life would be much easier if he could stay in the room with her. Hold her. Savor her unique aroma. Listen more closely to the nuances of her breathing, her heartbeat, and sighs.

"I'm worried," he confessed. "I'd be more comfortable nearer to you."

"Not a good idea."

"It's a great idea. I belong in bed with you."

"What part of go away do you not get?" A tremor vibrated beneath the anger.

"I'm never going away." He wadded his fingers into a fist. "I'll leave you alone in your room tonight, but I am staying."

Chapter 4

ETHAN FELL ASLEEP AT moonset. The aroma of cooking food woke him. He needed a shower. He called out a greeting to Selena before heading for the bathroom.

Like the rest of the house, the bathroom contained only necessities. No frou-frou, no fuss, reflecting (he hoped) the taste of its tenant. He appreciated her style. She was a *what-you-see-is-what-you-get* werewolf. The soap and shampoo in her shower weren't heavily perfumed—he could wash without worrying how he smelled to the outside world.

He showered quickly, his stomach rumbling. The aroma of bacon triggered his hunger.

He sauntered to the table wearing clean jeans and nothing else.

Selena started to say something to him and stopped, her mouth open, sparking ideas he shouldn't be having. She held a spatula in her hand as if she wielded a charm to ward off his shameless thoughts. Her brindle eyes widened.

"What?" Ethan asked. He glanced down, expecting to see blood or a blob of toothpaste in his chest hair—except he hadn't brushed his teeth yet.

"N-Nothing," Selena replied. She faced the stove and thrust the spatula into the frying pan of bacon. The sizzling, hot...

Bacon. Focus on the bacon, not on the way her ass fills out her jeans. Except part of his body responded only to Selena.

"Um, maybe you want to put on a shirt." Her voice sounded funny, as if she were choking. "The bacon is hot and greasy. You don't want to get burned."

"I usually eat breakfast without my shirt." *And jeans.* Except on the road. The band always ate in coffee shops or diners. "Did you sleep okay?"

Her shoulders hunched, hiding the back of her neck. "Fine. I, uh, hope you like bacon."

"Love bacon." For something supposedly a cure for anything, the scent of bacon sure didn't have an effect on what ailed Ethan. "Soft, crispy. I don't care. I'll eat bacon any way it's cooked."

"How do you want your eggs?"

Ripe and ready. Okay. Never mind. Think about the bacon, not how her fine ass will feel in my hands as I — "Over easy." Except nothing was easy about Selena. Here she stood, behaving normal, as if a vampire hadn't been in her living room. As if their tear-filled confrontation in the middle of the night never happened.

She didn't look at him again until she slid his plate in front of him. A couple of minutes later, she sat across from him with her own breakfast.

"What are your plans for today?" he asked.

She continued to stare at his chest. He checked again. Still nothing amiss.

"Tell me how the brewery works." Selena used her fork to spear a strip of bacon.

"What brewery? Moonsinger?" Ethan cut into his eggs.

"Are you familiar with any other brewery?" She addressed his pecs. Maybe his nipples.

"The pack hires brewers and...buys hops... and now you know everything I do."

Selena rolled her eyes. "The brewing is not what I meant. I meant how the financial aspects work."

"I'm out of the loop."

"Don't you get a share of the profits?"

"Indirectly. The profits mostly maintain the infrastructure of Loup Garou. The utilities. Roads."

"You mean you have to work?" Selena propped her elbows on the table and leaned across her plate to stare at Ethan. Her breasts hovered dangerously near her food. Egg yolk wouldn't go well with the blue and purple striped shirt she wore over a pink turtleneck.

Her stare made him...uncomfortable, as if she judged him and found him somehow lacking.

"Yes." He swallowed hard and forced himself to look her in the eye. "I mean, the band is my main job. Although we don't tour much anymore, recording and rehearsing all takes time."

She stopped slouching, as if preparing for battle. "Seriously? You told my grandfather you were scouting venues for a series of concerts."

Right. "We perform. We tour, but we're not on the road the way we were."

"Hard to build a fan base if you aren't visible."

"Not my call." Ethan happened to agree with her. Tokarz wanted to stay home. Maybe once Ethan claimed Selena he'd appreciate why hanging out with a mate and child appealed more than the road. Nowadays, only Ethan and Restin missed touring. Except the rooming-with-Luke part.

"We're working on another CD," he told her.

"So, you have a recording studio in Loup Garou, too. Right?"

"Yes."

"And the profits—"

"Go back into the community." He bit into a slice of bacon. "Why are you asking me these questions?"

"The Loup Garou pack is a...prototype for financial freedom. Beer is a weird product for werewolves to produce. I guess it's a decoy."

"The people who drink Moonsinger don't necessarily believe in werewolves."

"True."

"So why all the questions?"

"Gramps wants to do something similar for the Varulv. I'm curious how the financial aspects work."

"Similar? To Moonsinger?"

"Well, the product wouldn't be *beer*. Or fish. We need to diversify. Other things can be an industry to support the pack."

"What did you have in mind?" He didn't expect her to confess to making bombs.

She fidgeted. Squinted at him. "I have a degree in botany," she muttered. "I'm a trained herbal healer—Old Olivia from my pack has been working with me for years."

"I'm not following you," Ethan confessed. "Teas?"

"No, toiletries."

"Toiletries? You mean toothpaste? Deodorant? That stuff?"

"Not quite. More along the line of products females prefer. My college roommate used nice-smelling creams, lotions, and bath products. Not overpowering. She told me she made them herself. So we made some candles and sold them. We're working on formulas we can patent and mass produce. We can't make our stuff fast enough." Her cheeks were pink by the time she'd finished her recitation. "We're going into business together."

"Sounds...interesting." Too many scents mucked up a guy's head. Playing in the honkytonks favored by fans of Toke Lobo and the

Pack could clog a lobo's olfactory for a month. At least sweat smelled honest. The masks people wore were far more offensive.

"It's girly," Selena explained. "Females spend a fortune on products that make them feel girly."

"Nothing wrong with girly if you're female. You don't need to justify anything to me."

"You're right. I don't." Selena straightened in her chair, lifting her chin and squaring her shoulders. She met his gaze, for only a moment.

"I wish I knew how the financials with the brewery work."

"Maybe I could talk to your alpha," she suggested.

No. Bad idea. He didn't want Selena anywhere near Tokarz. Well, not Tokarz. Lately, Tokarz doled out too many tasks to his beta, and Ethan loathed Restin. He didn't want Restin's nose in his business. And Selena's business was Ethan's business, no matter how much she insisted she would not mate with him.

"I'll ask."

"You don't need to snarl at me." She continued to gaze elsewhere.

"My face is up here." He pointed to his eyes.

Her cheeks flamed from pink to red. She lifted her gaze until her eyes locked with his. "If you don't want to be treated like a sex object, cover yourself," she snapped.

Wait a minute. She couldn't stop staring because she thought he had a sexy chest?

He peered down again. Still only a chest. "What do you know about sex objects?"

"Oh, for the love of the gods of our elders." Her fork clattered to her plate. "Can you stay on topic?"

"Me? You're the one who can't look me in the eye and is babbling about sex objects."

"You're distracting me. If I sat here without my shirt, how would you react?"

Ethan's throat closed. The saliva in his mouth dried. He'd seen more than his share of naked breasts. Loup Garou mothers openly nursed their babies. Besides, rooming with Luke Omega, the only werewolf in the world with a pornography addiction, exposed Ethan to sights he wished he could forget. "The female breast is meant to nurture her young. I wouldn't—"

"Oh, vampire scat." She propped her chin on a fist and raised an eyebrow.

"You're supposed to be my mate. How am I supposed to react?"

"The same way I am." Selena sounded smug. "You're not the only one with mating fever."

"You admit we're mates?"

"I never claimed we weren't. I'm fighting the compulsion, too."

News to him. "What's stopping us?"

The color leeched from her face. "I can't..." She hung her head. Her unbound hair brushed her uneaten breakfast.

He fisted his hand to keep from swiping the strands out of the way. Clenched teeth kept him from howling his heartbreak. His female loved another, and the other male had her building bombs. His conclusion kept him awake the other half of the night.

Congressman Peters' son had Selena Wolfe making bombs.

"Did you call your landlord regarding the window?" he asked. Safe change of subject. As much as he'd liked the fresh air last night, security mattered more.

"Don't forget you trashed my bedroom door, too." Only a hint of a warble in her voice betrayed any emotion.

"Yeah. Right." He didn't want to talk about his middle-of-the-night mini meltdown. "So, what's your plan for the day?"

"Besides wait around for the landlord? I can skip my afternoon class. Since you're here, and I can pick your brain, I want to work on a business plan."

Another damned class. What subject? Advanced bomb-making? "I've told you what I know. I'm a musician, not a brewer or a businessman. Why don't you share your information regarding Congressman Peters?"

She recoiled as if he'd struck her. "Congressman Peters? Why would you ask me—"

"I found you with his son yesterday."

A muscle in her jaw pulsed.

"I believe you told the son to tell his father you'd be paying attention. Paying attention to what?"

She tugged the collar of the turtleneck she wore beneath her flannel shirt closer to her chin, then tucked her hair behind her ears, egg yolk and all.

Her ears were nice. Tiny. Flat to her head. She was a neat, compact female.

"Selena?"

"His vote." Her brindle eyes were bright. "What else would I be watching? In case you're not aware, the government plans to break the treaties with the individual packs. Congressman Peters' vote is crucial. His party is leading the betrayal."

Ah. So, she knew the new administration wanted to break the werewolf treaties. At least they had the same goal.

"I've heard rumblings. The congressman is part of the movement?"

"He's the one who sent my father to his death," she reminded him.

"How?"

"I was a kid on September eleventh." Frustration gave her words an edge. "All I know is he died doing something for Congressman Peters."

"Your father is a legend, at least to the Loup Garou."

Her lips parted. The anger in her eyes softened to something he didn't recognize and didn't dare try to define. "I'm glad. He didn't deserve—"

"The only people who deserved to die were the hijackers." Ethan's fork clattered on his plate as he dropped it. "Your father died a patriot, fulfilling his pack's obligation. Not one single lycan would do differently. You are the daughter of a martyr. The granddaughter of an alpha. For you to diminish either heritage by doing anything to jeopardize your legacy, to bring shame to the Varulv would be criminal."

She continued trying to justify her terrorist activities. "There's a lot of criminal stuff going on in the world, in case you haven't noticed."

"Doesn't mean we have to be part of the problem." Ethan pushed aside his plate. Elbows on the table, he leaned closer to her. "We're the good guys. We're the true patriots. We recognize persecution and prejudice, despite people who don't believe we exist. We don't need to do anything except be upstanding citizens."

And not make bombs.

"Member of the choir here." She waggled her fingers as she spoke. "Why don't you tell me why you're really in Warwick. Researching concert venues? Please."

"We're not talking about me."

"We are now."

"Fine. Why do you believe I'm here?"

"Your alpha knows Gramps is old, and he's making a power play to commandeer the Varulv."

Ethan couldn't help himself. He laughed, even though laughing might hurt Selena's feelings. "I am not the one who had a vampire after her last night. Why do you suppose you were attacked?"

Her eyes widened. "Me? How do you know the creature wasn't after you?"

"You can't be serious. This is your house. Your town. You were alone when it broke in." He ticked off each point on his fingers. "Other than you and your grandfather, no one knows I'm in Warwick."

"Your alpha?"

"Okay, and maybe my alpha, who would not sic a vampire on anyone even if he did know I was in Warwick. I doubt your grandfather has much to do with those assholes either."

"No one else in your pack—"

"Until I arrived, even I didn't know my destination. I first met you yesterday afternoon. If anyone was after me, blame the congressman's son."

Her mouth gaped. Her eyes were nearly as wide. "You believe Liam or his father sent vampires after me?" Her voice squeaked.

Ethan stared at her. She'd have to make the connection sooner or later.

"How would the congressman know how to contact vampires?"

"He works with werewolves." He struggled to remain patient. "Why not vampires?"

Selena stared at the wall as she spoke. "If vampires have a deal with the government, wouldn't the government want out, the same as they do with us? If lycans have treaties, who's to say the vamps don't?"

Terrifying concept.

She swallowed hard. "All we know is—"

"They smell bad," he interjected. "And they're assholes."

"They smell disgusting," Selena agreed.

He'd always heard vampires stank. The stench had something to do with the blood they consumed. Although werewolves loved fresh blood, they didn't subsist solely on the stuff. Nor did blood stay in lycan systems, whereas vampires required blood to function. Undead was creepy enough. They didn't need to be assholes when it involved their survival. As if being undead required survival instead of being a contradiction.

"Why would a congressman want to work with vampires?" Selena asked.

"Why would he want to work with werewolves? Same reasons, I reckon." Ethan expanded on his theory. "We operate under the radar. Our skills don't require technology and can't be detected. We make great secret weapons. Vampires—or any undead creature—could be the same. Except for their stink."

"Creepy." Selena shuddered.

"Creepy?" Ethan snorted. "Spotting that thing coming after you scared me scatless. I'd never encountered one before."

"So you mentioned."

"I think our agenda for the day—"

"*Our* agenda?"

"—should include getting the window fixed and finding out what type of stakes we need for protection, then getting some."

"Gods of our elders, I wish I could argue with you."

Nothing like adversity to form a team.

Chapter 5

ETHAN SAT IN HIS truck to make his phone calls. He didn't trust Selena. Although he hadn't shared the true reason for his Minnesota trip with her, he could smell her secrets on her. Mostly her tender feelings for the congressman's son.

"We were attacked by a vampire last night," he greeted Tokarz.

"Well, scat," his alpha replied.

Ethan couldn't argue with a reaction mirroring his own. "I need intel on what kind of stakes we need for protection."

Tokarz made a rude noise. "Call Luke. He's the research guy. Did you claim your mate?"

"We were busy last night, fighting off vampires and all."

"Mating is a nice way to relax after being in danger. The danger gets the blood flowing. Mating reduces the pressure."

Ethan ignored the advice. His agenda for the call didn't include mating talk. "What do you know about building bombs?"

The prolonged quiet on the other end made Ethan wonder if he'd lost the connection. "Hello?"

"I'm listening." Tokarz sounded cranky. "Vampires and bombs? What's going on?"

"I'm trying to figure out why you sent me," Ethan snapped.

"To talk to Congressman Peters and get him to vote for continued support for the treaties between the werewolf packs and the federal government. I sent you to Minnesota for one simple task, and now you're spinning tales involving mating, vampires, and bombs. What in the name of the Ancient Ones are you doing?" Not cranky. Furious.

"You dropped me into the middle of a mess. Chasing Congressman Peters was not my idea," Ethan reminded him.

"What's this bomb-building scat?"

"Someone might be building bombs, and I'm ignorant of the process."

"Have Luke research it!"

Ethan exhaled through his mouth to keep from growling. Growling at one's alpha when one's alpha was already cranky could be hazardous. He muttered a few conciliatory words before disconnecting the call.

Ethan didn't want to call Luke Omega for anything. So what if Luke legitimatized his obsession by becoming a full-fledged federal agent working to arrest Internet child pornographers? He'd mated. Sired twin offspring. And continued to surf the web searching for naked females and people having sex.

Still, Ethan needed info on making bombs, the best wood to stake a vampire, and additional background on Congressman Peters.

Luke answered the phone after two rings.

"Tokarz told me to call you," Ethan explained.

"Good morning to you, too," Luke replied. "Abby and the twins are fine. Thanks for asking."

"Sorry," Ethan muttered. Being civil to a lobo one didn't like was difficult.

"Rumor says you met your mate. Is she happy yet?"

If Ethan could have lunged across the cell signals to wrap his hands around Luke's throat, he'd have leapt without blinking.

"Nope. The vampire attack put a damper on our evening," Ethan answered in a low, growly voice. A gaggle of children ran toward the park. They looked too young to be unaccompanied.

"Vampire? Scat." Luke, who always had something to say, said nothing more.

"So, what's the best wood to shove in a bloodsucker's heart?"

The faint tapping of Luke's fingers on his computer keyboard brought back memories of nights when Luke's activities kept Ethan awake. "Oak. Hawthorn. Ash. I'd suggest dipping the pointed end in garlic. Can't be too careful with undead assholes."

"And it's not a myth, like silver bullets are for us?"

"How am I supposed to know?"

"Your computer isn't telling you?"

"Doesn't matter. Just make sure to pierce the heart."

"Have you ever personally encountered a vampire?" Ethan asked.

"Nope."

"Then how accurate is the stuff on the Internet?"

"Anybody can post anything they want," Luke explained. "I try to find at least three unrelated sources. The hawthorn, oak, and ash triad is pervasive. It's a fairy thing."

"A fairy thing?" Ethan drummed his thumbs on the steering wheel as he scanned the now empty streets, his attention on finding movement before movement found him.

"Yeah. The three together form a magical shield or portal."

"Do we believe in magic?" Ethan regretted the question as soon as the words left his mouth.

"People don't believe in us, so I'm keeping an open mind. Including about the nature of vampires."

"They do stink. Bad," he warned Luke. In case vampire covens or whatever planned to invade Loup Garou.

Nope, they're right here in Warwick, Minnesota.

Where the sun beamed like a lover's smile. Like safety, assuming vampires and sunlight didn't mingle. He didn't want to embarrass himself by asking Luke to research something so trivial.

The street sign on the corner caught his eye. Pine and Oak. Selena's house was on Pine. Maybe she should move around the corner onto Oak, one of Luke's mystical triad of trees.

"Okay, thanks." Ethan hated owing Luke, but Tokarz had given him no choice. "Now let's discuss bombs. Basal bombs."

More tapping. A baby fussed in the background.

"I get basal," Luke said a moment later. "B-a-s-a-l. I get bombs. Nothing together. Now, if you were asking about basil—b-a-s-*I*-l bombs, I'd be more help."

"Isn't basil with an 'i' an herb?"

"Lucy makes pesto out of the leaves," Luke replied.

Ethan thought he'd smelled pesto outside Selena's bomb-making facility. "How does an herb figure into making bombs?"

"According to all the do-it-yourself websites, herb bombs are something you toss into water to make taking a bath smell good or food wrapped in dough balls. Take your pick."

"Bucks, not does, have balls. And what does 'make your bathwater smell good' mean? Why would you want your bath water to smell like food?"

Toiletries. Selena had mentioned toiletries. Herbal toiletries.

"How would I know? I have more important stuff to do than surf the net for stupid scat."

"Tokarz sent me to you." Ethan made his tone as cold as he could. "Would you have me disobey my alpha's order?"

Ethan easily pictured Luke's physical reaction, a cross between a glower and a pout accompanied by twitchy fingers.

"One last question, then I'll let you get back to your naked females."

"They're not naked females. They're little girls being sexually exploited." Luke's irritation grew more apparent the longer Ethan spoke to him.

They're still females without clothes. Ethan didn't call to bait Luke. He suspected he was going to need a lot of Internet help on this mission. "What can you find on Liam Peters, Congressman Bryant Peters' son?"

"Son of a politician? I imagine only squeaky-clean stuff on the Internet."

"Can you search the other places you go? The deep, dark net places."

"If he's on the dark web, he won't be using his own name, especially being a congressman's son. You have a smart phone. Why don't you do some digging? I have my own treaty fulfillment work to do."

"Ogling naked females on the Internet from the safety of your own home isn't as challenging as vampire-slaying," Ethan snarled.

"I had my own dragons to slay for my mate," Luke reminded Ethan.

"I remember." Except Luke's adversaries had been sapien. *Homo lupus* could take *homo sapien* any time. Vampires? Werewolves didn't know scat about the undead bloodsuckers.

A black pickup chugged up the street. Ragged clouds of dark smoke burst out of a rusted tailpipe, staining the air. The rough-sounding engine coughed as the truck pulled next to the curb in front of Ethan's newer model. A couple sheets of plywood wobbled against bright blue nylon rope in the truck bed.

The man behind the wheel stared at Ethan before he climbed out of the cab. A cigarette clung to his lower lip. Blue smoke curled in ribbons around his head. The bottom part of his face hadn't seen a razor in a day or two.

"Are you there?" Luke's aggravation broadcast loud and clear.

"Hold on a second," Ethan snapped.

The newcomer hitched his greasy jeans and sauntered up the sidewalk to Selena's porch. His unbuttoned flannel shirt flapped like a spastic bird attempting flight.

Selena opened the door wide enough to peer out. She stared at Ethan as if trying to tell him something.

Ethan did not trust the looks of the landlord. "See what you can find on Liam Peters," he told Luke. "I'll call you back."

He disconnected before Luke could sputter another word.

Moving nearly as fast as last night's nocturnal visitor, Ethan reached the door as the landlord spoke.

"So what happened?" The newcomer's whiny voice grated on Ethan's nerves. Ethan longed to wipe the lechery from the man's gaunt face. No one had the right to leer at Selena.

"Someone broke in." Selena relaxed her stance. "I want the window replaced."

The man hefted the wood. "Uncle Tony wants plywood for now. He'll put in a new window in a couple weeks."

"Is Tony your landlord?" Ethan asked Selena.

The man jumped as if Ethan had bitten his backside instead of merely speaking. "Where did you come from?"

"Who are you if you're not the landlord?"

"Tony's nephew. Curtis. He hired me to board up the broken window."

"Good." Ethan jerked his head toward the door. "Come on. Let's let Curtis work in peace and quiet."

He expected Selena to argue. Instead, she grabbed her shoes and followed him on to the porch. "Thanks. He gave me the creeps. Where are we going?"

"Do you have anything of value in there?" he asked in a low tone.

"This house is only a place to eat, shower, and sleep. My home is in Ulvskog."

Ethan held open the truck door. "We should find you a new town-side den. A safer place with no vampire breaches."

"Okay." She clambered into the truck cab.

He'd expected an argument. Her agreement without debate surprised him.

"Are all the streets in this neighborhood named after trees?" he asked once he sat behind the wheel.

"What? How should I know?" She drew her shoulder strap across her breasts.

"You live here."

"I guess. I never paid much attention."

He jammed the key into the ignition and twisted. A quick check of his side-view mirror confirmed no traffic. "Oak Street is up ahead."

"So?"

"So I learned something today, and I want to test a theory." He rounded the corner and drove on Oak until he got to Ash Street. "Bingo."

Elm, not Hawthorn, was the next cross street. He turned onto Elm, and bingo again. There was Hawthorn, one block away. Taking a right onto Hawthorn led him to Ash. One block of Ash ran between Hawthorn and Oak. The sacred triad. An anti-vampire zone.

"What are you doing?" Selena asked.

"Searching for a new place to live."

"Shouldn't a new place be further away from the breached house?"

At least she wasn't arguing with him.

"The traditional stakes to kill vampires are oak, ash, and hawthorn. The three trees growing together create a portal to the fairy world."

"You're scattin' me," followed a snort of laughter.

"According to the research expert I consulted." *Ha*. Wouldn't Luke *love* being called a research expert.

"So you believe if I move to this particular block, I'll be protected from another vampire attack."

"Moving can't hurt." He wasn't going to commit to anything. "I mean, you aren't emotionally attached to the place on Pine, are you?"

"No."

Only two houses lined this side of Ash Street on the block between Oak and Hawthorn. One wore a shade of purple deep enough to avoid being garish, although it did sparkle.

"There's a place for sale." Selena pressed her finger against the window, leaving a smudge. "It's a dump."

"Most houses in this neighborhood are dumps."

Ethan drove around the block again, slowing as he neared the orange-painted bungalow. The bright blue trim didn't subdue the color. "I can't believe I missed seeing this house the first time around."

How much could the ugly house possibly cost? He possessed some assets. He'd need more but getting his hands on what he needed shouldn't be a problem. A smart lobo would have a home base in Warwick if his mate refused to relocate. Why not on a hopefully charmed block?

He'd rather be in the woods. Away from sapien so-called-civilization. But if Selena lived in Warwick, he needed to be in Warwick. The Ancient Ones wanted him with her.

"Got the realtor's phone number?" he asked.

"You aren't serious."

"Never mind." He pulled out his cell phone and tapped in the number on the 'for sale' sign. He studied the façade as he waited for someone to answer. The rest of the short block on that side of the street consisted of an empty lot.

A chirpy woman answered the phone.

"Hi. My name is Ethan Calhoun, and I'm sitting outside forty-two Ash Street in Warwick. I'd like to see the inside as soon as possible."

ETHAN CALHOUN HAD LOST his mind. Selena studied him, searching for more signs of the madness in him. "You want to buy this house?"

"Maybe."

"Are you insane?"

"Crazy about you."

He had a good line. And yeah, she'd been grateful he'd been present for the vampire attack and relieved he'd butted in when the landlord's creepy nephew had shown up. Buying a house based on the names of the streets surpassed weird.

"Look at the house, not me," he said in a gentle voice. None of the anger, tainting his tone with her all morning, remained.

She twisted in her seat, trying to see what he viewed. If the property included the empty lot next door, she could plant a garden, giving her ready access to ingredients. Except the house would be Ethan's, not hers.

"Are you cold?" he asked. "I can turn on the heat."

"What?" The question caught her off guard.

"You're wearing a turtleneck, a shirt, and a sweater, and you're still shivering. If you're cold, I can run the heater."

Werewolves didn't chill as easily as sapiens did, and Ethan ought to know that. Every lycan knew their body heat attributed to their higher metabolism. He was messing with her again. What would he imagine if he discovered she wore both a bra and tank top beneath the turtleneck? "I'm fine. Well, confused. Why are you looking at property?"

"You're here."

Such a simple answer to a complex situation. "You can't—"

"I can do anything I please. I'm not saying I'm going to buy the place. I only want to see the inside. I want to determine if it's a safe place. Unless your landlord's nephew is using hawthorn plywood, I'm not going to be happy staying in your house."

"So disinviting vampires isn't going to work." She never believed the incantation would. Life and sorrows were never simple.

"I'd rather be safe. Wouldn't you?"

"Of course. Maybe I should go back to Ulvskog."

"Why aren't you there now?"

"College. I have a degree in botany. I'm working with my former roommate on the botanical toiletries. It's easier to work in town where the non-plant ingredients are more available. Brittany lives here. She and Ulvskog wouldn't mix."

"And Liam Peters is here."

She sank against the back of the seat and stared at Ethan. "What does Liam Peters have to do with anything?"

"You were with him yesterday. *His hands were on you.*"

"Are you jealous of Liam?" How absurd.

"Should I be?"

"No." She kept it short and to the point.

"Then why were you with him?"

"I had an appointment with his father." She strained to keep her fear and disgust hidden. "Liam wanted to continue our discussion. I didn't. You rescued me. My hero."

She spoke in such a fake tone of voice, Ethan should have laughed. He did not.

"I interrupted something."

"Yes. Exactly what I told you."

"And why did you meet with his father?"

"He's my congressman. He has used the sanctuary-for-service treaties."

Ethan thumped the steering wheel with his thumbs.

"I want to peer in the windows." She released her shoulder harness. "I can't sit here with your angst poisoning the air I'm breathing."

Flouncing out of the truck would have been tacky, flirtatious, and far too girly. She tried to exit gracefully. And failed.

Why had she ever let her grandfather con her with tales of Varulv hospitality? Nothing outweighed her need to keep distance between her person and her designated mate. *Stupid, stupid, stupid,* she cursed as she stomped up the three surprisingly solid steps to the porch. *You were afraid of what Bryant Peters might do once you were on his radar again,* her conscience reminded her.

And how did Ethan get next to her so quickly? "Are you part vampire?" she asked.

"What?"

"How did you get to the porch so fast?"

"Oh. I'm quick. I've always been quick." He stomped on the floor. "Solid."

Selena brushed past him to peer through cobweb-strewn glass. What she could see of the interior surprised her. She blamed the distortion on the condition of the windows.

"Hey there!"

She spun at the sound of a perky female voice. A beige minivan had pulled to the curb behind Ethan's truck. The name of the realty company on the door matched the sign jammed into the lawn.

"Hi," Ethan replied.

The woman, dressed in a light brown business suit, scurried to the porch. "I'm Rita Anderson," she said, as she thrust her hand toward Ethan.

Ethan shook the hand. "Ethan Calhoun and my fiancée, Selena Wolfe."

Fiancée? Oh, he had a lot of nerve.

A lobo shouldn't be any other way.

"We were driving around the neighborhood and were intrigued by the house," Ethan explained.

"Yes. Such an unusual paint job," Selena replied. She bared her teeth and hoped Rita the Realtor would mistake the grimace for something else. "Like a carnival ride."

"We're looking for a starter home," Ethan continued as if Selena hadn't interrupted.

"Of course," Rita agreed with too much enthusiasm. "Let's go inside and poke around."

Selena glared at Ethan across Rita's back as she struggled with the lockbox on the door. He had the audacity to wink at her.

"How many bedrooms?" Ethan asked.

Selena got into the game. "I'd like an in-law apartment for my mother."

Rita straightened, her face a mask of noncommittal. "I'm afraid Ash Street isn't the neighborhood for amenities such as in-law apartments."

"She's kidding. Her mother's dead." Ethan draped his arm across Selena's shoulder and steered her into the house after Rita.

The smell hit Selena first. No mustiness lingered like in her place on Pine. She scented no mice or other rodents living in the building.

Surprisingly, the walls weren't papered in gloomy, overblown flowers or painted in garish colors. The orange and blue exterior paint job, she decided, camouflaged a miracle. The neighborhood required something.

"Is this woodwork oak?" Ethan asked. He removed his arm from her person and rapped on a windowsill.

Rita consulted a manila folder. "Yes. The house is built in the Craftsman style, which utilized primarily oak."

Whatever Craftsman meant. Architecture didn't interest Selena.

"All of the exposed wood is either oak or ash stained to resemble oak. The kitchen cabinets were handcrafted especially for the house."

"Excellent."

Selena rolled her eyes. She couldn't help herself. She didn't believe in fairies or *magick-with-or-without-a-k*. Or any other woo-woo stuff. Of course, she hadn't believed in vampires until one attacked her.

"And Rita doesn't believe in us," Ethan murmured against Selena's ear.

She hated the way he read her mind, or at least her facial expressions. She wanted to be mysterious. Aloof.

The house consisted of a good-sized front room, a compact kitchen with wooden cupboards, a dining room, three bedrooms, combination laundry room-mudroom, and two bathrooms. The back porch, as deep and wide as the front, overlooked a generous yard fully enclosed by a tall hedge. A huge tree, branches shivering beneath the weight of a flock of birds, dominated a far corner.

"Is there a basement?" he asked.

Again, Rita consulted her folder. "Full basement with a kitchenette and three-quarter bath."

"An in-law apartment, sweetheart. Do you think your grandfather can manage the stairs okay?"

Ethan Calhoun was positively hateful.

"Are the appliances included?" he asked.

"The house is being sold as is. The lot next door is part of the property."

"And the asking price?"

"Honey, I'm not ready to buy," Selena interjected. As if she had a say in how he spent his money. Toke Lobo and the Pack's success, along with the Moonsinger Brewery, secured the future of Loup Garou. "We can't buy the first house we see."

"I like the address. I like the wood. It's a good size for a family."

Compared to her home in Ulvskog, the place was enormous.

Oh, what did she care what he did with his money? His buying a house didn't mean she would be living with him. Assuming he included her in his plans was arrogant.

Except they were supposed to be mates. Ethan kept behaving as if she hadn't refused him. Repeatedly.

"I suppose I could organize my business in the basement," she said, trying to get a rise out of Ethan.

Rita flipped open the manila folder again. "The property is zoned—"

"I do crafts," Selena lied.

"Tell the truth." Ethan grinned at Rita. "She makes bombs."

Chapter 6

"B—Bombs?" Realtor Rita stammered.

Ethan shouldn't have baited her or Selena. "You know, stinky stuff women toss in their bathtubs to make the water smell."

"Bath bombs," Selena clarified. She glared at him. "I'm developing a line of natural, herbal-based toiletries."

The shock on Rita's face faded. Her lips parted, showing many white teeth.

Selena's teeth were prettier.

"Oh. The parcel next door would come in handy for growing ingredients."

"I had the same idea." Selena showed only the tips of her teeth. "I'm making a mental list of what I should plant."

"You impress me. You're always thinking ahead, even though you contradict yourself." He opened a door and peered down a staircase. "Let's check the basement."

The dry basement pleased him. Lurking dampness couldn't hide from Ethan's nose. The furnace and hot water heater were partitioned off from the main space and appeared new. A tiny kitchenette and a bathroom with a shower stall, toilet, and sink completed the lower level.

"What do you think, sweetheart?" he asked. "We could get you some tables, put in shelving. You could make a great factory for your stinky stuff."

Selena narrowed her eyes and clamped her lips.

Ethan wandered upstairs and out the back door to scope out the lawn. A lush green hedge, formidable from a distance, became impenetrable when closely scrutinized. Long, sharp spikes would draw blood if a living creature tried to crash through the branches. He took out his phone and fumbled around trying to figure out how to snap a photo. He sent the results to Luke.

Ten minutes later, he had his reply. Hawthorn. The hedge shielded the house from vampires.

Why would anyone create a vampire-proof residence in the middle of a derelict neighborhood? Maybe an infestation, unrelated to Selena, plagued the area.

What were the chances of this specific property being available right when he needed a safe house? How many times had he been told, *there's no such thing as coincidence.*

He could stash Selena inside the house and protect her from bloodsucking assholes. Maybe. The trick would be getting her to stay.

Rita stood at the back door—not sliding glass patio doors, thank the Ancient Ones—doing something on her phone. Behind her, Selena dug into her pocket and pulled out her own phone.

Yeah. He needed to swap phone numbers with her. Technology created whole new sets of problems.

"What's the asking price?" he asked Rita, as she stepped onto the porch.

She quoted a ridiculously low number to him.

He countered with three quarters of the asking price.

Rita hemmed and hawed.

"Cash."

He had her attention.

"How did you get my number?" Selena snapped into her phone.

Her words got *his* attention. He tried to focus on what the other party said. *Did you enjoy your company last night?*

"Who is this? Why are you calling me?" Nothing in her voice gave away any emotion except anger.

For two seconds, he considered snatching the phone from her and dealing with the caller himself. He squelched the urge. Let her caller believe her alone. Ethan could be a secret weapon, along with Selena's own lycanthropy. He continued to eavesdrop.

Selena noticed him, gave him her back, and stomped from the room.

"Let me reach out to the owner and see if he'll accept your offer." Rita interrupted his brooding.

"I want to settle in as quickly as possible. I'll throw in another thousand if I can move in today. Call it rent until we can close." He wanted to follow Selena.

"The owner isn't averse to a rent-to-own agreement."

Renting might not be a bad idea. He and Selena were going to need a place in town. Even if the manufacturing took place in local werewolf territory, they would need a more urban setting for business reasons, if only to keep homo sapiens away from the werewolf village.

He could no longer see Selena, and despite the vampire proofing, he feared for her safety.

He left Rita on the back deck, making her phone call to the owner, while he searched for his female. Selena emerged from a white on white bathroom. Her complexion matched the color of the tile wall behind her.

"Are you okay?" he asked.

"Yeah." She kept her face averted.

"Who called you?"

The question earned him more of a scowl than a glare. "None of your business."

"How do you figure? I was present last night, too."

"What are you talking about?"

"I didn't enjoy your guest," Ethan answered.

Her expression betrayed nothing. "Do you always eavesdrop on personal conversations?"

"If it involves your safety? You bet your tail, I do."

The muscles in her jaw tightened; he guessed she clenched her teeth.

"Selena." He wanted to caress her face, cup her cheek in his palm. Instead, he jammed his hands into his jeans pocket, found his tone bar, and gripped it hard enough to bend the steel.

"How do you like the place?" he asked. *There.* He could show her he respected her reticence.

"It's okay. Why?"

"I'm buying it and stashing you in it. It's vampire-proof," he added before she could argue with him. "If such a thing exists. Besides, the bloodsucker won't know where to find you. We're moving in today."

She stared at him for a moment. "You don't have any furniture."

"We can move yours."

"It's not mine. I rented the house furnished."

"Okay." He wouldn't miss the ugly, uncomfortable sofa. "We'll go shopping as soon as we're finished dotting the T's and crossing the I's."

"Life doesn't work that way," she said.

"Unless you pay cash. I'm willing to pay anything to keep you safe."

"You must be making a fortune from the brewery."

Right. He had what she wanted for her pack.

"You're what matters. I want you behind all this ash, oak, and hawthorn. Damn the cost."

"Sounds like a whiny English folk song," she said, as she tried to step past him. "Do you want me to morph into a swan or something?"

Selena excelled at deflecting him off-topic. "Let's hope vampires hate swan blood."

Her lips parted. Her eyes widened. "What if vampires don't like lycan blood?"

"The asshole last night didn't have a problem going after yours," Ethan replied.

"The asshole didn't know we were werewolves until it encountered us. It didn't see either of us change. We could have been household pets."

Ethan hated dog comparisons. "I suspect flawed recon info. The question is why. And I believe you know the answer."

A muscle in Selena's cheek twitched.

"My gut is telling me," he continued, "whoever called you also sicced the vampire on you."

She blinked.

They stared at each other.

"Another question would be who would know how to contact vampires? The congressman. Who would want to do business with such disgusting creatures besides a politician?"

"Excuse me?" Rita rapped on the doorframe. "The owner is perfectly amenable to your moving in today. Shall we go back to my office and deal with the paperwork?"

ETHAN PURCHASED THE HOUSE. He and Selena left the realtor's office and climbed into his truck.

Selena's many reasons to argue the transaction vanished when she recalled the attack. Fear? Terrified. Yeah, her caller instigated the vampire attack—or at least was aware of it—and she had a good idea to whom the anonymous voice belonged.

They'd left her alone for ten years. Ignored her existence...until she threatened to expose them.

Vampires. The last thing in the universe she'd ever expected from them. The naïve girl of ten years ago no longer existed. Stronger, more secure in her heritage, Selena could handle anything. Except bloodsuckers.

"Ready to shop for furniture?" Ethan asked.

Selena studied the sky. The morning and a good chunk of the afternoon were gone. Only a few hours of daylight remained. Come nightfall, she planned to be behind the hawthorn hedge, in the house with the ash and oak woodwork. With Ethan.

"Where are you getting the money to pay for a house and furnishings?" she asked.

"Money is my concern. We'll manage."

"What's this *we* stuff?" She hoped he didn't expect her to kick in toward his living arrangements. She had no money.

Ethan leveled his dark eyes on her. The deep baritone of his voice drugged her. "We'll manage."

One of her few memories of her father was hearing him tell Gramps, "I need to pick my battles." Weird, why she remembered his words now, but the sentiment fit. What Ethan did with his money was his business.

Turned out Ethan didn't dawdle at anything. He didn't fuss. After signing the rent-to-own agreement and writing the realtor a check, they drove to the largest furniture warehouse store in the area, where he bought the barest minimum of what they'd need for the night. He didn't bother with price tags, and he didn't angst over style. He wanted simple and plain, so that's what he purchased.

Although her opinion didn't matter—he owned the house—but yeah, everything he chose matched her own preference. When he did ask her opinion, she concurred with his choices. She would have picked the same items.

He used a credit card, then drove his pickup to the loading dock. Beds, mattresses, a sleeper sofa, and a flimsy table with four matching chairs filled the back of the truck. He stopped at the Pine Street house, where Selena gathered her belongings, including food.

The sun blazed low in the western sky by the time they returned to Ash Street. Ethan didn't want her help to unload the truck. She assisted anyway because he couldn't manage himself. The mattresses were too awkward for one individual to handle.

Selena put a package of walleye to thaw in the kitchen sink, then stood in the master bedroom doorway while Ethan assembled the queen-sized bed. "You don't mess around."

"Nope." He barely glanced at her as he tinkered with nuts, bolts, screws, and wrenches. "And I don't trust vampires."

They were on the same page.

"Can I help you?"

"I've got it."

"Thank you for finding a safe house."

"We need a place to live in town—our own home, and don't argue with me—and this place is vampire proof." He finally looked at her. "You can build your business here, where you'll be safe. I'm not trying to be the boss of you or control you or force you into letting me mark you. I simply don't want you undead."

"Thank you." She hesitated. "Are you sure I can't help?"

His brows rushed together like clouds roiling in a stormy sky. "You can make a list of whatever else we're going to need. Tables, chairs, bureaus, additional appliances."

Annoyance sparked. Female stuff. Her role in a traditional lycan household.

"If you need an industrial strength dishwasher for your vials and test tubes, write the kind on the list," he continued. "A restaurant quality stove with twelve Bunsen burners to cook your concoctions? Go for it."

Her heart pinged. "I can't let you—"

"Nobody *lets* me do anything. I do what I want and what I need."

She sensed kitchen appliances weren't on his mind.

She wandered from room to room, examining everything with fresh eyes. He'd immediately seen the potential for the basement as a workspace for her.

The gods of her elders sent her a mate to meet her needs. To recognize what she needed before she grasped her neediness. Falling in love with Ethan would be too easy. He would break her heart. After he learned the truth about her, he would flee from her in disgust. Her heart would shatter.

The basement kitchen would suffice for the time being. Eventually she hoped to do business on a sizeable scale. Until then, the space would work. More than appliances, she needed shelving units and work tables. Maybe she could build a makeshift greenhouse at one end of the space. She could install grow-lights to germinate seedlings in a secure place. Growing and harvesting the ingredients for her products appealed to her. Ethan had foreseen her use of the empty lot next door.

She meandered to the first floor again to check out the laundry facilities—conveniences the house on Pine did not have. An unusual sound stopped her at the top of the stairs. Deep, rich, slightly rough. The croon echoed from the room where Ethan banged around putting together the bed.

She slipped across the bare wooden floors until she lingered outside the door. Ethan was...humming. No, not quite humming. More like muttering a song under his breath, yet perfectly in tune. She closed her eyes, enabling her to better focus on his music. His voice sounded rough and gritty as if tainted by whiskey and tobacco although he neither smoked nor imbibed.

The lyrics were vaguely familiar. Poignant. The low baritone dipped into the deepest recesses of her fears and memories, stirring emotions she didn't want to experience.

She opened her eyes and peered around the corner. Oblivious to anything except assembling the bed, he tinkered with his tools, all the while seducing her with no awareness of what he did.

Chapter 7

Did she know how the moon enhanced her beauty?

Ethan stood in the living room doorway, fixated on Selena. She leaned against a window overlooking the back yard. No interior lights spoiled the ambiance. Stripes of silver moonlight slanted across the bare wood floor. White outlined her cheek, casting the rest of her face in deep shadow. Sorrow molded her stance.

The half-moon preened in the midnight sky, as if jealous of Selena's beauty.

"Too bad we can't run with the moon tonight," he spoke in a low voice. "She looks lonely, as if she could use a friend."

"It's too dangerous." Selena's wistful tone panged in his heart. "I don't care if you believe this house is vampire proof. The night is dangerous. Besides, the stars are keeping the moon company."

"Sounds like the title of a country song." He joined her at the window, his sock feet making no sound on the bare wood floor.

"There's something intrinsically wrong if we can't be outside playing. We're prisoners because of the night."

"Because vampires attacked us, not the night."

"What if the attack was random?" The wistful note in her voice hinted she didn't believe the theory.

"The creature kept attacking, even after it recognized you—us—as shifters," he reminded her. "And while the truth might have surprised it, your form didn't deter it."

Her sigh misted the window pane. "Yeah. I figured."

He didn't want to have this conversation. Not at this moment. He wanted to savor the way the moon's glow caressed Selena's features. He wanted to study each millimeter of her face so he would be able to read her mood with only a glance.

"The moon used to mean safety to me," she said.

"She's our friend."

"Where were you last night when I got home from my class?" Selena still stared into the yard, as if searching for signs of another attack.

While her words weren't precisely an accusation, her tone carried hints of blame. If he wanted her to trust him, he needed to be honest with her.

"I followed you. To your class. Stayed outside while you made your bombs." He smiled and hoped the humor would reflect in his tone. "I admit your bomb-making upset me—until I smelled the pesto."

"Basil," she corrected.

"Stoker Smith's mate is a caterer, and she makes stuff called pesto."

"I'm impressed you know bath bombs are a thing. I don't expect you to understand herbs."

Maybe she wouldn't be pissed at him. "I confess, I called Luke. Luke Omega, the band drummer. He's good on computers. He did the research for me."

"You thought I was a terrorist?"

"I was afraid you were training terrorists." He needed a quick change of subject. "Doesn't the flowery, herby plant stuff clog your nose?"

"Some. I've been trained in healing for the pack, so I've developed a tolerance, and I let my college roommate formulate when my alleged allergies act up. I've never heard of lycan terrorists."

"She knows?" Ethan gestured out the window, refusing to give the terrorist thread a chance to develop into something out of his control.

"No. No one—almost no one knows."

The faintest catch marred the ease of her words. Without his musical knowledge, he might not have caught the break.

"It's not difficult, living in the sapien world," Selena continued. "If you don't draw attention to the moon cycles, no one notices you always have other plans on the night of the full moon."

"Yeah. We learned the same thing on the road. The full moon is better with your own kind. With those who identify with you. Who can sing with you. After Tokarz mated with Delilah—"

"Why did you follow me last night?" Selena no longer leaned against the window frame. She'd balanced her weight evenly on both feet.

Ethan recognized the position. Sapien self-defense. She'd used the stance before. He jammed his hand into his pocket, where his fingers wrapped around the tone bar. "You were being secretive. Furtive. Acting guilty."

"Guilty? I don't think so."

"You're my mate. I need—I want to learn everything I can about you."

"By stalking me like a creep?" The accusation echoed in the empty room.

"Why couldn't you simply tell me you taught a toiletry-making class?"

"I don't answer to you."

The past twenty-four hours changed everything. "You have no idea how rough being a male werewolf is nowadays. Females are less sheltered but we males are still trapped by our biology, unlike you females."

He observed her muscles tighten as she took offense to his words.

"Are you accusing me of something?"

The hitch in her voice betrayed her. A wave of pain threatened to drown him. Pain and frustration.

"Not at all." He tried to keep his tone light, belying the heaviness in his gut. "You have to remember my biology insists I protect you. Keep you safe. You're going to be the mother of my offspring. Nothing is more important."

She might have rolled her eyes at the same time the rigidity left her posture. "Mating fever. You're blaming your behavior on mating fever."

"I'm a victim of my biology. Unlike you."

"Maybe we're biological victims in different ways."

She had no reason to be bitter or angry. Females weren't dependent on blood flow and other physiological occurrences in order to mate. She could snuggle with the congressman's son and have at it. Or let Peters have at her.

The image of Peters touching what belonged to him enraged Ethan. He gripped the tone bar tighter.

"I apologize for being creepy." His stiff, formal tone matched his rigid posture. "Making you uneasy has never been my intention. I want you to feel safe. Secure. Cherished."

"Apology accepted."

SELENA WADDED HER FINGERS into her palm. Ethan stood close. Too close. She could have counted the black hairs in the stubble of his beard. He smelled of the outdoors, of the detergent used to wash his clothes, and of the experimental nettle shampoo she'd left in the shower.

Her heart hurt trying to keep pace with her lungs, which were straining to suck in enough oxygen.

His face hovered closer to hers. He wanted to kiss her. She just knew it. She *told* him she wasn't going to submit to the mating instinct. She *told* him they could never be a couple. She *told* him no meant no.

How would he taste? His mouth would have a different flavor than his cheek. His throat. Would his flesh have a salty tang? Would his mouth taste of the fish tacos they'd eaten for lunch or something better, something addictive? Or would his unique aroma overpower her other senses?

His nostrils flared, as if he were imprinting her scent on his memory.

Don't kiss me.

"Your pulse is racing," he murmured. He lifted his hand; she thought he would caress her cheek. Instead, his finger skimmed the knit cotton of the turtleneck hiding her collarbone.

She shivered. Her nipples tightened and tingled. Other body parts pulsed and grew heavy.

Why didn't he kiss her?

"You're not afraid of me." His dark eyes searched hers, as if searching for a spark of fear.

"Nope." She hadn't been since the moment on the porch at the Pine Street house.

His finger continued tracing the route along the fabric covering her collarbone until the tip sank into the hollow in the center of the bone.

She tilted her head to meet his gaze, exposing her throat.

He accepted her gesture of submission by adding a finger to the first, drawing the duo past her larynx to her chin. Chills blossomed on her skin like dandelions in spring.

"You smell nice." The deep rumble of his voice sparked vibrations that spanned the space between their bodies and added to her confusion. His fingers drifted back to her throat. "Do you taste as good as you smell?"

The light pressure of his touch on her throat created a lump as she swallowed. He was reading her mind, a disaster in the making. She tried to step back. His touch temporarily paralyzed her.

No. Not his touch. Mating fever, complete with chills, aches, hot flashes, and mental distress. If she could sleep off the symptoms and stay away from Ethan, she'd survive. His disease transferred his pathogens to her flesh with his fingers, the microbes penetrating the fabric of her turtleneck.

Still, she could not move. His stare mesmerized her as any hunter with prey. He added a third finger and traced them along the bottom of her chin to her jaw. Her cheek.

Her muscles quivered involuntarily.

Yet she'd yearned to bear his children while she fought off a vampire. Wanting his children had given her the strength she needed in a moment of weakness. She couldn't let the wanting happen again.

"Aren't you curious?" he asked. "Two beings, meant for each other—how sex would be between us?"

"I don't dare," she confessed.

"Ah. So you admit—"

"I never denied we're mates. I only said I can't mate with you."

"What if I say you can?"

"Your male prerogative?" She deliberately added snark to her tone.

He cupped her cheek. "No. My flexibility. My open mind. Whatever is keeping you from my arms, my bed, we can—"

She jerked away from him, stumbling several paces to ensure physical distance. Her feet slid on the bare wood floor. "There is no *we*."

He closed the gap in a vampiric blur. "Are you so certain?" he asked, as he grasped her shoulders. Not tightly.

She wouldn't need to expend any energy to free herself. Nor did she.

"You want to kiss me as much as I want to kiss you. It's only a kiss, Selena."

"A kiss this time." Had he read her mind? "What next?"

"Why don't we try and see?"

"You ruined the mood." She made no effort to repel him. She should have thrown off his touch. The heat from his body reignited the fever she'd hoped to banish.

"Did I?"

Walk away. Just take one step backward. "Yeah."

"Maybe I can recapture it. Should I try?"

What if Ethan truly courted her? Wooed her instead of handing her a bag of berries with yogurt from a fast food franchise because some ancient deity commanded a male give berries to his intended. To have him pay attention to *her*, Selena Wolfe, not to what she was.

"You can try," she said. "No promises."

"Our destinies were promised to each other."

"By the stars? The moon herself?" Selena shook her head. "No mysticism, Ethan. You and me. No gods of our elders, no celestial mysteries. Ethan and Selena."

"You've lived in the sapien world too long. Their attitudes have tainted you."

The mood vanished. He'd killed it. Snuffed the spark of attraction she'd been willing to admit having.

Easy to step back, to put distance between their bodies. "Do you need help assembling the second bed?" she asked, in as polite a tone as she could manage. "This place could use some furniture."

Confusion and maybe something else rearranged the shadows on his face. "What just happened? Something I said or did upset you."

"You reminded me we can never be. A kiss is pointless. Why bother?" She believed she suppressed her shudder well.

Ethan noticed. "Are you cold?"

"No. I'm afraid of you." This interlude taught her fear lurked in many guises.

"I wish you were. I could understand fear."

"You don't believe me?"

"I've smelled your fear of me on you. You're not afraid of me right now."

"Maybe not physically," she conceded. "But you're wrong. You terrify me. You make me believe I can be a good female werewolf, settle in with my mate, and live happily ever after."

"You can."

She ignored his interruption as she wrapped her arms around her torso. Her toes curled against the cool wood floor. Any moment, her teeth would start chattering and her breath would be visible. "A happy mating can never happen for me. You'd only end up hating me—and breaking my heart."

She mistakenly believed he wouldn't use his speed against her. He, a low-ranking lobo, would respect her alpha female status. She forgot to calculate mating fever into the equation. She'd barely confessed to future heartbreak when she found herself surrounded by his warmth. His searing body heat penetrated her layers of clothing. Her skin. Her body mass. Her bones. He touched her, melting her defenses.

The heat diffused more of his unique aroma. Lilacs, fresh venison, a frigid January night—every scent that had ever made her happy emanated from the perfection of Ethan Calhoun. Her muscles lost their ability to function. His hands, with their clever, marvelous fingers, pressed into her back. They generated so much heat she feared her body might fuse to his, forever connected.

She might have moaned. Maybe whimpered.

His lips, slightly chapped, brushed hers. Her pulse leapt. White blood cells did cartwheels while the red somersaulted along her veins, and plasma eddied around the corpuscles' antics. Balance deserted her. If he hadn't been holding her so closely, so tightly, she would have collapsed at his feet. The brush became pressure, became an answer instead of a question. No matter how much she didn't want to respond, biology—maybe physiology—joined forces with ancient and cruel gods. She wanted more.

Ethan's tongue thrust past her lips, sending sparks like swarms of lightning bugs into her inner darkness. His tongue touched hers, and flavors exploded; berries, sweet and cool against the heat threatening to consume her. Lilacs again—she hadn't known one could taste a flower. Her entire body morphed into a tight, throbbing bundle of need.

She couldn't remember the last time someone held her with affection...held her at all.

Only a kiss, he'd said. There was nothing *only* about his kiss. Nothing simple. Nothing innocent. This moment was everything she'd feared his kiss would be.

She couldn't breathe. He stole her air. Crammed his tongue into her mouth, disabling her protest. She couldn't scream. Couldn't summon — Instinctive strength burst in her arms. She wrenched free, shoving him away. She gulped in oxygen, the heaving of her chest mirroring Ethan's attempt to breathe.

They stared at each other.

"Yeah." Her voice quavered. "You're going to break my heart."

Chapter 8

"WHAT ARE YOUR PLANS for the day?" Ethan asked as he sauntered into the kitchen the next morning.

Selena flipped the bacon sizzling in her favorite cast iron frying pan. "I have a class this afternoon. I skipped yesterday, so I do need to go." He must have forgotten she'd told him her plans the previous evening...before the brain cramp of his kissing her.

"More bombs?"

Her paranoia provided the emotion to his neutral tone.

She faced him. At least he wore a shirt. After last night, she was surprised neither of them had run off to avoid facing the other.

"No." She didn't offer anything else. "You?"

"I have some errands." He scraped a chair across the kitchen floor and sat. He propped his elbows on the table. "I'll run them this morning."

"I don't need a bodyguard during the day." She hoped.

"Depends on where you're going." He never missed a beat. "I don't want you going near Congressman Peters' office until we can rule out the vampire connection."

Fair enough. She didn't want anything more to do with Congressman Peters. "I thought I'd invite my business partner to stop by, so I can show her around."

"The sapien woman?"

"Yep."

He glowered.

"We can take care of ourselves. No vampire is going to show its face in broad daylight," Selena reminded him. She bared her teeth. "And my better half adores this moon phase."

His scowl melted. The corners of his lips twitched, as if he wanted to smile.

"Ethan, I've lived without you my whole life. I can take care of myself." Better than he could ever imagine. "I get you're wallowing in instinct. Give me some credit, though. Okay?"

His lips stopped twitching, and while his frown didn't return, his somber expression betrayed his mindset.

"And no, you can't follow me to my class today."

"How are you getting there?"

Selena checked on the bacon. "I'm going to walk. The weather's nice enough. I'm not made from sugar. I won't melt in the rain."

"You took a bus to the congressman's office."

"I was dressed up and didn't want to arrive appearing less than sapien-professional." She shut off the burner and transferred the bacon to a paper towel-lined platter.

"You couldn't give me the directions to get home from there."

"Right. You should know better. The world is different using wolf senses."

"Good answer."

"True answer. You don't have to worry I'll return to the congressman's office. I was only obeying Gramp's order."

Ethan waited with the patience worthy of an alpha.

"Oh, stop," she snapped. "I was at the congressman's office for the same reason you were—Peters needs to vote to continue supporting the pack treaties."

"I never told you I wanted to see Peters."

"Please." Selena slammed the platter of bacon on the table. "Why else would you have been parked outside the congressman's the other day? Planning a Toke Lobo performance in the lobby?" *Honestly.*

"Maybe your presence drew me."

She snorted. Being angry and impatient with him was easier than remembering how he'd kissed her. How she'd reacted to his kiss. "My grandfather might have bought your line of scat. Not me. What are your errands? Checking out more implausible concert venues?"

"Maybe."

Now who was being evasive? "Maybe you should stay in to see if this place is zombie proof."

"I will if you will," Ethan taunted her.

"I've got a life, lobo. I'm carrying on."

"Nice house." Brittany brushed past Selena through the open door. "Love the outside color scheme. Owned by a rabid sports fan?"

"Musician," Selena said, as Britt entered the main room. "He bought the place as is. Maybe from a sports fan."

"I hope he got a break on the price. And how did you meet a musician?" Britt looked around the echoingly empty space. "Okay, I can see the interior appeal."

"Consider the exterior camouflage."

Britt sniggered. "Love all the wood. It's been well maintained."

"It's a great house. Lots bigger than it looks. The property includes the empty lot next door."

"Really?" Britt raised her pale eyebrows. "As in—"

"We have a place to headquarter the business and grow our own ingredients." Selena couldn't keep the smug tone from her voice. Britt had supplied all the expertise. Now Selena could contribute something besides knowledge of healing plants.

"How did you manage to convince your musician to set you up in such splendor?"

Selena opened her mouth. Not a sound emerged. Explaining her relationship—or lack thereof—with Ethan wasn't something she could do. Britt's ignorance of Selena's true nature made sharing impossible.

"A friend of the family wanted to invest." Ethan leaned against the door jamb.

What was he doing? He'd given her the impression he'd be gone for a long time. "You're back early."

"I forgot something. Aren't you going to introduce me to your friend?"

As if he didn't recognize Britt from his spying.

"Yes," Britt said, her voice husky. "Please do."

"Brittany Hauge, Ethan Calhoun, an alleged friend of the family. Ethan, this is Brittany, my business partner and former college roommate."

"Ethan Calhoun? As in the steel guitarist for Toke Lobo and the Pack?"

Selena had forgotten Britt loved country music.

Ethan's slow, lazy smile was sexier than it needed to be. "Why, yes I am. Selena has good taste in friends."

"Who else is your family friends with?" Britt asked Selena, her regard never leaving Ethan.

Okay, the lobo looked good. What he did to blue jeans ought to be illegal. His evergreen-colored Henley enhanced his complexion. He should button the top two buttons, though. Showing off his chest hair was playing dirty. She didn't want to have to bitch-slap her friend.

"Let me give you the fifty-cent tour." Selena needed to get Britt away from Ethan. She needed to get away from Ethan herself. Britt's reaction proved the Ethan distraction quotient created havoc.

She hustled Britt to the basement and didn't consider pushing her until they were two steps from the bottom. "Work tables and shelving units here. Maybe grow lights at one end to germinate seedlings." She sounded as if putting the business in Ethan's house was a done deal.

"It's a great workspace," Britt agreed. "What's it going to cost you?"

Selena stilled. "What?"

"Hey, I have eyes in my head. Your Ethan Calhoun is incredibly easy on those eyes. What does famous hot guy want in return?"

Selena couldn't decide whether to laugh or rage. "He's not sniffing around for sex."

"Honey, he's a guy. They're all sniffing around for sex. Trust me. While you were being the virtuous girl, I was—"

"I remember what you were doing."

"What you don't know concerning men . . ." Britt's voice echoed a thousand times in the cavernous space.

"Ethan isn't a horn dog." He never could be, even if he wanted to. She was the only female in the world with whom he'd be able to be sexual, something she couldn't contemplate right now.

"I won't say I tried to tell you when you come crying to me because he—"

"Deal," Selena said. "Now. Can we talk business? And leave Ethan out of the mix. What equipment will we need? The kitchenette is this way."

"Ethan is very much in the mix. Men like him don't do favors without expecting something in return."

"You have no basis for lumping him with all the losers in your life."

Britt crossed her arms. "How long have you known him?"

Probably *forever, in my soul* wasn't going to be a good answer.

"I told you. He's a family friend. My grandfather approves."

"Gramps approves? Well, all right then." Britt couldn't have been more sarcastic. "So. Tables. We'll need more tables than we need shelves."

"Where will we keep the finished product until it's ready to go out?"

"You're awfully optimistic. Let's hope we can sell what we make." Selena squared her shoulders. "Better optimistic than miserable."

Britt rolled her eyes but didn't mention Ethan again.

"Do you have an appointment?" The young woman with the blond hair and sky-blue eyes outlined in too much black gunk emitted boredom the way a septic emitted effluvium. File folders, papers, and "Vote for Peters" pens covered the desk. An old computer monitor sat like a boulder on one corner.

"No," Ethan admitted.

"The congressman is an important, busy man," the receptionist told him.

"If he wasn't important, I wouldn't need to see him. If you can't squeeze me in today, can I make an appointment?" Ethan fought his natural impatience. Sapien protocols could be so aggravating. As much as he wanted to leap across the desk and show the waif his fangs, the strategy not only wouldn't get him in to see the congressman, aggression might get him tossed out, if not arrested.

She tapped a few keys on her keyboard. The computer tower wheezed like the death pangs of a dinosaur. "The congressman is only in Warwick a short time, and his time is booked solid. Would you care to speak to one of his aides?"

If he wanted to speak to an aide, he'd have asked for an aide. "If the congressman isn't available, I want to schedule an appointment with him."

"Can I help you?"

Ethan recognized the voice. The congressman's blue-eyed son.

They stared at each other for a long time before Junior broke the stalemate. "You're Selena Wolfe's so-called fiancé."

"You're the congressman's son."

"One of them. May I help you?"

"Can you get me in to see your father?"

Junior's eyes narrowed. "Depends on why you want to see him."

Ethan rocked on his feet for a moment, before firmly planting them on the carpeted floor. His arms dangled at his sides. He had, by his estimation, at least twenty pounds on the scrawny politician-in-training. This homo sapien was not going to best him at anything. "My business is between Congressman Peters and me."

Junior was smooth. Too smooth. "If you give him a heads up, he can familiarize himself with the topic."

"Then I lose the element of surprise."

"My father doesn't care for surprises."

"Your father doesn't have to care for them. He has to serve his constituents."

"Judging by your accent, I doubt you're a constituent."

Busted. Ethan turned his back on Junior and continued his conversation with the receptionist. "The name is Ethan Calhoun. See if you can fit me in."

SELENA WIPED HER BROW. The studio where she attended her weekly self-defense class reeked of sapien perspiration and other unidentifiable stinks.

Krav maga didn't share the niceties of other self-defense philosophies. The maneuvers she learned and practiced lacked class. Lacked philosophical manners. No polite bows, no show of respect. If kicking someone in the balls did the trick, then kick someone in the balls.

Her wolf could handle any situation, except on the night of the new moon. She vowed never to be victimized by her physiology again. She'd discovered krav maga in her sophomore year of college. Someone in one of her classes mentioned the technique as the best method for self-defense. She researched it and found her style. She learned how to finish a fight as quickly and aggressively as possible.

Whether or not the opponent suffered temporary or permanent injuries didn't matter. If the attacker died, well, death was what he deserved for attacking in the first place.

Krav maga combined boxing, wrestling, Akido, judo, karate and intuitive street smarts. Learning the basics hadn't taken long. Krav maga wasn't meant to be a lifestyle. The method focused exclusively on fighting. Nothing more.

Selena left each session confident she could control her environment. Thanks to her lycan genes, she was the best student in the class, strong, fast, and determined to hurt the other guy. Maim the other guy. The practice soothed her soul.

Today was no different. Another crank phone call interrupted her meeting with Britt. *When the fat lady howls.* She fobbed off Britt's curiosity by claiming the call was a wrong number.

When Selena emerged from the studio, she discovered Ethan waiting for her. "How did you find me?" She didn't bother trying to hide her annoyance.

"I picked up your scent a couple of blocks away and figured I'd surprise you. Surprise?" He hooked his arm through hers.

Scat. She hated the thrill of his touch and her pleasure at his assertiveness. She should knock him on his tail.

"Self-defense class, Selena?" he asked, as he escorted her toward his truck.

"Comes in handy. Sometimes taking the stance is enough for some sapien males."

His arm tensed. "Aggressive sapien males are why past generations kept females close."

"So I've been taught." A vague but safe reply. "Thank goodness for modern times."

He stopped. Un-looped their arms. Grasped both of her shoulders and spun her to face him. His dark eyes were more serious than she'd ever seen. "Modern times or not, you're still vulnerable."

She gestured toward the krav maga studio. "Want to try to take me?"

"Okay." He released her. "Okay. I respect your need to protect yourself. You any good?"

"Better. I have advantages others in the studio can only dream of having."

One corner of his mouth tightened. "I hope you use them."

"Using your skills is why krav maga succeeds."

"Okay. Good. I couldn't stand it if anything happened to you."

She tried not to react. Hoped he didn't sense the cringe of guilt as he linked arms with her again. "You underestimate me. Where are we going?"

"I parked my truck on a side street," he said, as he tried to resume walking.

The too-familiar neighborhood clued her to the nature of Ethan's errand. She yanked her arm free. "You went to Congressman Peters' office."

"I did."

"I told you I'm taking care of him!"

"Shh." Ethan peered around to make sure no one watched. He grabbed Selena's arm and pulled her along with him.

"You have no right to come into Varulv territory and throw your male pheromones around." She lowered her voice as he dragged her in his wake. "You are in *my* territory. Peters is *my* congressman. Erik Wolfe was *my* father."

A knot throbbed in Ethan's jaw. "Don't get your panties in a wad. I didn't get to see him."

Don't get your panties in a wad? He was going to be one hurting lobo by the time she finished with him. "Hang out with a lot of sapiens, do you?"

"I play in bars and roadhouses. Comes with the territory."

"Well, don't bring their disgusting habits home to me, including wadding anyone's panties."

"Home to you sounds wonderful." He yanked open his truck's passenger door. "I would *love* to come home to you every night for the rest of my life. Especially now. You've shown me how great the physical part of our mating is going to be." He grabbed her waist and tossed her into the truck.

"I knew I shouldn't have kissed you," she blurted.

He slammed the door in her face. The wind's invisible fingers rippled through his long hair as he stalked around the hood.

Melting her panties was more of an issue than wadding them. *Stay angry*, she reminded herself.

"The mistake is mine," he said, once he'd slammed his own door. He jammed the key into the ignition and twisted. "I should have ignored your modern ways, tossed you on the ground, and mounted you the moment I saw you. Right in front of your congressman's son. Who, by the way, is a vampire."

The blood rushed from her head, leaving her dizzy. "He's not a vampire." She struggled to remain upright.

"I meant the slur as an insult, not literally."

Selena closed her eyes and tried to enjoy the patches of sun glancing off her face as Ethan drove. "Why don't you go back to Colorado?"

He calmed a notch or two. "I can't. First, my alpha sent me. You ought to appreciate duty."

Unfortunately, she did.

"And more importantly, you're here."

Not important enough to be first. Never mind she didn't want to be important or first. *Yes, you do.*

"I'm here. In your house."

"You aren't here for me to come home to."

"I'm not a meek female."

"Nor should you be. I accept your alpha female status. I don't expect subservience. I expect you. The real you. Not some imposter you're hiding behind."

"I'm not an imposter." She wished she could put more assurance into the statement. He was right. She was a complete fraud.

Ethan drove to the Pine Street house. "Let's finish moving you out."

"Fine." Forty-two Ash was a nicer house. Ethan was providing headquarters for her business. The hawthorn hedge surrounding the property added to its appeal. The vampire attack scared her more than she wanted to admit, at least to Ethan.

She happily left behind the rodent-infested walls and the lumpy, always damp furniture. The creepy, empty house next door would not be missed. She'd always sensed someone was spying on her. Plywood hiding the broken window didn't lessen the impression of being exposed and vulnerable.

She didn't have much. Werewolves weren't attached to possessions. With Ethan's help, she emptied the house of every trace of her and left her key on the kitchen counter. She'd call the landlord to tell him. Rent on her month-to-month lease was paid through May.

"We can go shopping for more stuff later," Ethan said once they'd loaded his truck and headed for Ash Street.

"For what?" She still felt out of sorts with him.

"Stuff. House stuff. Curtains. Stuff."

She'd never paid attention to house stuff. Gramps had everything she'd ever needed in Ulvskog. The Warwick house was merely shelter. "Curtains? Pictures for the walls?"

"More furniture."

"We have beds. A table and chairs. I need work tables and shelves for the basement."

They were still bickering when Ethan pulled to the curb. The neighborhood lacked driveways. Anyone could see what they dragged into the neon orange house.

They'd unloaded the last bag of clanking housewares, when someone knocked on the door. Selena and Ethan glared at each other. *You answer. No, you.* The knock repeated. Ethan stomped to the door. Selena lifted two plates from the bag.

"Welcome to the neighborhood." The woman's voice with a distinctive lilt carried from the front door to the kitchen. Selena decided to rescue Ethan, who probably wasn't as well versed in sapien etiquette as she.

"I brought you a hot dish," the woman continued.

"Thank you." Selena cut off Ethan and took the casserole from the woman. "You're too kind. I'm Selena. This is my fiancé, Ethan."

"I'm Helga." Her vivid blue eyes were Viking bright. "Are you renting or buying?"

"Rent to own," Ethan replied, his voice deeper than usual.

"And where are you from?" Helga tried to peer past Ethan to the empty living room.

"Up north," Selena said before Ethan could answer. Thank the gods of her elders she'd been living among sapiens in Warwick for five years. Her familiarity with the protocol rescued her. "I'd invite you in for coffee, but we haven't had a chance to lay in supplies."

"Oh, I understand," Helga chirped. "We were curious if you planned to keep your hedge."

"Isn't the hedge great?" Selena asked. "Big selling point for us."

"Oh." Helga sounded disappointed. "So many long thorns. The neighborhood cats and dogs get scratched on them all the time."

"As Selena said, it's what drew us to the house in the first place." Ethan's face was as immobile as granite.

"Not the color?" If Selena had to live across the street from a Day-Glo orange house, she might complain.

"No, the hedge," Helga repeated. "It's full of long thorns."

"Well, I do plan to plant a garden, so I wouldn't want the neighborhood pets wandering in." Selena kept her smile stretched tight.

"Oh. We were hoping we could convince the new owner the hedge is an eyesore and a danger."

"The paint job," Ethan explained, "is an eyesore. The hedge is a security system."

The brightness in Helga's eyes flared. "It's not particularly welcoming."

"Security systems seldom are."

"Oh. Well. I live across the street, in forty-one, if you ever need anything."

The dark purple house.

"Thanks," Selena said. "And thanks for the hot dish. I'll bring your pan back after we're done."

"No hurry." Helga's smile was as wide as the door frame. "Nice meeting you."

Ethan quickly closed the door behind her. "What the scat?" he whispered.

"It's a sapien tradition. She was only being nice."

"She wants us to get rid of the anti-vampire hedge."

"If you say so." Selena hefted the glass casserole pan. "Shall we see if we want to eat the hot dish?"

Chapter 9

Ethan visited Congressman Peter's office the next morning while Selena met with Brittany to price business supplies for the basement.

Junior waited for him.

"I forgot to leave my phone number with the receptionist, so she could call me with the time of my appointment with the congressman," Ethan said.

"I did some research on you, Ethan Calhoun. You're not from my father's congressional district. He doesn't waste time with people who aren't constituents."

"Yet."

"I beg your pardon?"

"I'm not one of his constituents yet. He can still waste his time with me."

Junior seemed confused by Ethan's statement, as if he didn't comprehend his father had been insulted.

"Would he speak to an entrepreneur who's investing in a start-up company?" Ethan shoved his hands in his pockets. He found his tone bar and took comfort in gripping the familiar steel.

"You're a country music guitar player for a band based in Colorado."

"Among other things."

"No other things." Junior sounded smug. "Merely a mediocre country band."

The tone bar snapped into two pieces.

"Not a mediocre band. We've had a number one hit. And now I'm investing in a local start-up company. I assume your dad would want to encourage new business. If I'm lending my name to an enterprise, why, anything could happen." He skirted the truth.

"Excuse me," the receptionist interrupted. "Liam, you have an important phone call on line three."

Junior didn't bother with manners. He stalked away as if Ethan angered him with his persistence.

"The congressman doesn't have any free time today." The receptionist stared at her telephone. She hadn't checked the schedule. Ethan had been aware of her every twitch since he'd arrived. "Why don't you leave your number with me? I can call you if something becomes available."

"Sure," Ethan said, sensing her lie. He'd have to find some other way to get an audience with the man.

"WE NEED A COMPUTER." Britt paced Ethan's kitchen as if she needed to generate power to her brain. "Before we do anything else, we need a computer. Without one, we can't set up a program to keep track of expenditures, we can't research how to structure a DBA, what type of business we want to be, register our name—Selena, we have to have a computer."

"We don't have money for a computer." Selena leaned against the kitchen counter, a glass of tap water in her hand. "We don't have money for anything."

Britt paused and raised her glass to her mouth and drank; swallowed. "What about your phone?"

"It's a stupid phone. You have a smart phone. Don't you have your laptop from college?" Selena asked.

"Don't you?"

"Nope. I sold it. I'm not techno-girl."

Britt sighed. "All right. I'll bring my clunker tomorrow. Does this house have Internet access?"

Why did homo sapiens have to complicate everything? If not for Selena's hope this venture with Britt would have a positive impact on her pack, she would have dashed out of Ethan's house right then and run all the way back to Ulvskog. "I'll ask Ethan."

Among many other topics she intended to quiz Ethan on. Such as the nature of his errand. He wouldn't admit it, but Selena's gut told her he had returned to Congressman Peters' office after she'd told him to stay away. What other errand could he possibly have?

"Have we settled on a name yet?"

"I vote we toss the ideas into a hat and draw the winner," Selena suggested.

"We can't be random. We need something we can market."

"Fine." Selena sat at the table and pulled a pad of paper closer. "Let's make a list. What have we brainstormed thus far?"

"You suggested Wolf Wood Naturals. Sounds creepy to me."

"Moon Maiden Magic?" Selena offered.

Britt rolled her eyes. "No."

They bantered possibilities for several moments.

"Wolf Wood Naturals is the best," Britt conceded. "Why Wolf Wood?"

"Ulvskog means wolf wood."

Britt snorted.

Ethan arrived while they were eating leftover Helga-Hot-Dish. Selena offered to fix him a plate.

"No, thanks." He barely suppressed his shudder. He handed a big plastic bag to Selena.

"This is a good hot dish." Britt fluttered her eyelashes. "Trust me."

"I don't know you well enough to trust you with my dietary preferences." He punctuated his words with a laugh, as if to lessen their sting.

Selena unwrapped the package he'd given her. She stared. "I can't accept anything else from you." He had no business buying a laptop computer, not after he'd purchased the property.

"You need a computer. I consulted an expert who does computer stuff for the government. He recommended this model."

"A computer? Great! Thanks," Britt gushed.

Selena glared at her partner, who appeared oblivious to anything except Ethan. "No. We can't accept anything more from him."

"I'm investing in your company. Do you have a name yet?"

Selena sensed he wanted to say more. Britt's presence hindered confidences.

"Wolf Wood Naturals."

Ethan made a face. "It has a certain appeal."

"No, it doesn't." Britt wrinkled her nose. "It's not feminine enough."

"Moonsinger?" Ethan suggested.

Selena stopped her jaw from dropping.

"Like the beer?" Britt asked. "Wouldn't the makers sue us?"

"Maybe we could negotiate," he suggested.

Ethan was right. Moonsinger portrayed romance, femininity, mystery. All three hooks made for great promotional opportunities. What were the chances the Loup Garou pack would be willing to share the trademark?

Or would use of the name come with a price she could not pay?

ETHAN DRAGGED A CHAIR across the kitchen floor and straddled it backward. "Have you written a business plan yet?"

"No. We need a name," Selena pointed out.

"If you want investors, government start-up funding, et cetera, you need a business plan. You need a mission statement."

"We plan to make bath products from all-natural ingredients with a focus on healing properties of plants."

"And? Anything else?"

She narrowed her eyes at him. "Why are you giving us a hard time?"

"I did some research." After a long phone conversation with Luke, who told him to find a library, get on a computer, and type in, *What You Need to Know to Start a Small Business.*

"The first item was buying a computer. Next, I need to arrange for Internet access for the house."

"We were just saying we needed a computer and Internet access," Britt said.

Ethan spent the rest of the afternoon listening to Selena and her sapien friend debate the technicalities they'd never considered. Their entire focus had been on product development. If someone had asked him a week ago if he'd be content listening to two females talk soap and herbs, he'd have snarled in the person's face. He wouldn't have known one of those females was his. Although they hadn't formalized their bond, Selena was his. She was his future. He needed to get used to his new reality.

"WHAT DID YOU REALLY do this morning?" Selena asked. She once again stood at a window overlooking the yard, where the hawthorn hedge and the tree reshaped the moonlight into shadows.

"I talked to someone in Loup Garou, who suggested I go to the library."

"Did they also suggest the Moonsinger name?"

"No. Moonsinger was my idea." He was proud of his suggestion.

"Even if Loup Garou lets us use the name, I'm not sure I want to be associated with beer." Her breath formed clouds on the cool glass pane.

"Hey. Moonsinger is all natural. Aren't hops supposed to be healing?"

"Hops are good for several things," she conceded. "I don't know how effective they are, distilled."

"Beer is fermented."

"Whatever. I'm trying to say that while I love the idea of Moonsinger as a brand name, I'm afraid my products would be associated with Loup Garou instead of Varulv. Your pack changes nature's goodness to poison. I want something better for my pack."

A lobo couldn't argue with her. "Moon plucked. You could gather all your plants at night and—"

"Please. I can hear the comedians now."

"We wanted to call the beer Howler. Someone beat us to the name," Ethan admitted. "Which is another reason to get Internet installed as quickly as I can. You need access to research and register names and trademarks and other stuff."

"Are you done dissembling?" Selena asked.

"We're not having a deep, meaningful conversation?"

"What else did you do this morning?"

Busted. "I tried to make an appointment to see the local congressman. After all, I'm investing in a start-up, which makes me a local businessman. A congressman ought to curry the support of local businesses. Encourage and foster them."

Her reaction scared him. "You *what*? How could you? You're *not* investing in my plan to help my pack."

"I'm not?" He struggled to stay cool. The heat of her rage required a chill factor.

"You've gone ahead and insinuated yourself into my life. You're trying to commandeer my life."

"Not your life. Your trust. Your love."

"By going behind my back?"

"I haven't gone behind your back. I've told you everything I've done. I'm trying to help you. And me. Using your business start-up is a good reason to want to see Congressman Peters."

"Using *me*. I told you. Peters is *my* responsibility. I don't want or need you interfering." She pushed herself away from the window and vanished into one of the shadows in the room; shadows so dense, Ethan's werewolf vision couldn't penetrate their depth. The blackness was her anger. Her rage.

Her fear.

"We are mates. Your life and my life are the same." He tuned his senses on her, using his instincts to find where she hid. "Of course, I am going to do everything I can to assist you with your business. You want to secure your pack. How can I not love and admire you? I'm proud of you and want to help you in every way I can."

"Save the blather for the next song you help Toke Lobo compose."

"The emotions belong to you. Why would I give them away?"

"I don't want them."

She protested too much.

"Yeah, you do. For some reason, though, you believe you don't deserve them. Maybe you think you're in love with the son of the man responsible for your father being in the Pentagon on September eleventh."

"I'm not in love with Liam Peters. I had a crush on him years ago, but believe me, I outgrew it real quick."

Something in her tone bothered Ethan. Every note in her voice rang false.

His gut twisted. His first reaction insisted he leave her in the black hole. Higher instinct clamored against his anger. Higher instinct insisted devotion meant more than pride. Higher instinct urged him to take a step toward her.

She stood completely still, cloaking herself in the darkness.

"I'm waiting for my goodnight kiss." He wished he didn't feel predatory.

"I agreed to one kiss," she muttered.

"A day," he amended for her.

"You never specified a time frame."

"I implied one. Especially after the first kiss."

"Don't beg. It's unattractive."

"Don't you find my desire ego gratifying?" he teased.

"Your lust is involuntary."

Her words were a bucket of cold water on his libido. Still, he tried. "If desire was involuntary, would I be waiting for consent or doing what the instincts the Ancient Ones blessed me with demand I do?" His voice roughened. Sometimes, as the full moon drew closer, one didn't have all the patience one needed.

"You won't." She sounded as if she believed he could control his baser nature.

A low buzz shattered the mood. Her jeans pocket glowed, betraying her position.

Ethan tamped a spurt of annoyance. "Answer your phone," he said before stalking away. He headed toward the smaller bedroom, where he'd slept the previous evening. He didn't close the door. He'd give her a semblance of privacy. Eavesdropping in his own house, however, wasn't a crime.

Except he heard nothing. Selena didn't say a word.

SELENA DISCONNECTED THE CALL immediately. The number on the screen differed from all the other calls. Not one duplicate number. The message hadn't varied. She must have received ten anonymous calls since visiting Congressman Peter's office. If not for Gramps, she would have shut off the phone.

She couldn't stop shaking. Or maybe the room reeling around her affected her balance. Her preoccupation with hiding her shame from Ethan prevented her from thinking clearly. Except vampires and heavy-breathing cranks had ways of forcing a she-wolf's decisions. All Selena could do was thank the gods of her elders for sending Ethan to her.

"An important call?" Ethan asked as she stumbled past the door to the bedroom he'd claimed.

"No." She struggled to regulate her respiration.

"Another prank call isn't important?" He left his room, hand outstretched. "May I?"

She tucked the phone into her jeans pocket. "Don't make assumptions."

"You're trembling."

"You're overwhelming." She grinned, as if she were making a joke. She needed a quick change of subject. "Do you want to come home with me for the full moon?"

"What? That came out of nowhere."

"The full moon is the day after tomorrow," she reminded him. "Unless you have other plans."

"You know I don't."

"Good. You can drive. I hate taking the bus to Ulvskog." She tried to slink past him.

He was quick. "Thank you."

"I'm not going to kiss you."

"Then I'll kiss you." He held out his arms.

She could have easily sidestepped, knowing he wouldn't pursue. Instead, she sidled closer, telling herself she dared him to take liberties with her. Admitting she wanted him to kiss her, to touch her would open them both to irreparable heartache.

His lips claimed hers, his tongue invaded her mouth. She didn't fight.

Did that construe consent?

The voice in her head assured her she was resisting. Ethan was taking advantage. Her inner voice lied. A lot.

After he released her from the spell he'd cast on her, she felt lonelier than she ever had in her life. Emptier.

A shared life has been stolen from me.

"Good night, Ethan."

"Stay awake with me. You've been living in the sun too long. You need more moon. You need her magic."

"We all need her magic." Easy to sidestep words.

"So, stay with me. Let's go to the backyard. Bring some walleye. We'll have a picnic."

"I suppose a picnic table is next on your shopping list. Midnight picnics and songfests."

"Why not? Our souls are nocturnal, and we naturally prefer the outdoors. Of course, the neighbors might object to a songfest."

"I prefer a nice snug house with central heating to the outside, come winter," Selena said.

"You don't like running in the snow?" He sounded surprised.

"Don't all wolves love running in the snow? Stop stereotyping me." All her willpower focused on not snapping at him. She loved snow running.

"I'll bet snuggling is more fun in the cold. We'll have to experiment."

"Good night, Ethan."

Chapter 10

Selena donned her favorite green and brown checked flannel shirt over her off-white cotton turtleneck before she left the privacy of her bedroom. The room overlooked the backyard. The lack of curtains or blinds wasn't a privacy issue. The sun made its own rules. Morning light slanted across the bed with an insistence she couldn't ignore.

Ethan was right. She'd lived in the sapien world too long. She belonged to the night, a creature of the moon.

Her pack would prefer working on her line of personal products at night. "Night shift," she muttered. "Handcrafted by the light of the moon."

She'd have to remember to share the potential branding statement with Britt.

"Are you cold?" Ethan asked as she strode into the kitchen. Her cast iron frying pan rested on the stove. Bacon and eggs waited on the counter.

"Not particularly," she replied.

"You always wear so many clothes. No wonder you hate snow running."

She spoke around a lump in her throat. "Why do you care? It's not as if I expect you to take them off me or anything. And I do my own laundry, although it's nice of you to offer. Oh, and thanks for cooking breakfast this morning."

He opened his mouth as if to dispute the final point, then stared at what he'd done. "Don't blame me if it's inedible."

"I promise I won't blame you for anything." Her thoughts were on memories she'd be better off forgetting. "Except for going behind my back to see Congressman Peters."

"If seeing a politician without your permission is the worst you can throw at me after a lifetime together, I'm doubly blessed."

His calm annoyed her. His assumption he would erode her determination, mate her, followed by the traditional route of lifelong companionship and children, grandchildren and service, pissed her off.

"You know," she said as she pulled two plates from the cupboard, "the only thing I've learned the past couple of days is you're not especially good at listening to me. Oh. Wait. There's something else. You don't believe a word I say if you do bother to listen."

The crunch of eggshells stopped her rant. He'd crushed an egg in his fist. Chips of shell and yellow yolk striated the silvery membrane dripping from his fingers.

So his placid act was pure pretense.

Interesting. What would she have to do to evoke a genuine, gut-deep emotion from him?

She tossed a dishtowel to the floor at his feet. "Don't stand there," she snapped. "Clean your mess."

Muscles in his face quivered. Twitched. Something flashed in his dark, unreadable eyes, and a weird satisfaction at having provoked him filled her. Life wasn't all moonlight, snow runs, and stolen kisses. Had he ever experienced grief or rage or helplessness? If she could be nothing else to him, she could be a life lesson.

"What is wrong with you?" he asked.

"You. I don't know what I'm supposed to do about you."

"You're overthinking the situation."

"You're not thinking at all," she shot back. "Except with your dick."

If she'd kicked him between the legs, he couldn't have reacted with more shock.

"What is that supposed to mean?"

"Sapien girls discuss dickheads all the time. Males think with their penises, not their brains. Everything they do is calculated to get laid."

"Well, since neither of us is sapien, your accusation makes no sense." He shook his hands over the sink before twisting the faucet. "Your sapien girlfriends are right. I see males get stupid all the time in the bars where we perform. But you know what? I'm not sapien. I'm lycan. My dick, as you so crudely put it, only twitches around you."

The water rinsed the egg guts on his hands into the drain.

"So yes, I'm obsessed with getting you naked and under me. It's my biology. Trust me, if my brain didn't have a say in the matter, you wouldn't have a say in the matter." He paused for a moment, as if repeating what he'd said back to himself to make sure he'd made sense. "If my brain wasn't working, you would be marked and knocked up by now. You do know what that sapien idiom means?"

Each of his words jabbed her. "All right!" she shouted. "I'm sorry! It's that time of the month." The phrase meant something entirely different for lycans than for homo sapien females.

"I'm aware of the time of month!" He twisted the faucet so hard the knob came off in his hand. Water gushed toward the ceiling. "Scat!" He threw the broken handle into the basin.

"Shut-off valves are usually beneath the sink."

"I know where the shut-off valve is," he snarled. "Call one of your oh-so-smart sapien girlfriends and get the name of a plumber."

Although Brittany was Selena's business partner and friend, Ethan didn't have to like her.

After she stopped sniggering about the broken faucet, she offered to call her cousin the handyman. She didn't need to show up at the house on Ash. She did, anyway. She stared at him—Ethan, not her cousin—as if she were hunting him and made him uneasy in an unfamiliar way. The honkytonk angels who loved to flaunt their stuff to the band hadn't cheapened him the way Brittany did.

The angels had been out for what they believed would be a good time. Brittany expected…more.

"Let's measure the basement for shelving units," Selena suggested. "Let your cousin and Ethan do their thing."

Ethan didn't know what his *thing* was supposed to be, but he didn't need Brittany making an already lousy morning worse.

"How'd the handle break?" the plumber asked. Scott. Brittany introduced him as Scott.

"I guess I twisted too hard," Ethan replied. "We recently bought the place. Maybe it's a faulty faucet."

"Nah. This is new. This model only came out a couple months ago."

Ethan only half listened. And not, despite what Selena accused him of, with his dick.

Didn't the female appreciate the stress she put on his self-restraint? Did she believe ignoring his screaming instincts in order to be a sensitive male was easy?

"Nope, the manufacturer introduced the Q forty-five maybe right after Christmas," Scott continued, as if Ethan cared.

What if he threw Selena onto her stomach, mounted her, and fucked her like a crazed animal? Would rough treatment make her happy?

"You know, the faucet might still be under warranty, seeing how it's not even six months old." The plumbing squealed as Scott applied a weapon or something to the pipes.

"I didn't purchase the faucet," Ethan mumbled. "No receipt."

He would be perfectly within his right to claim his mate. He hadn't chosen her. The Ancient Ones had. Older males interpreted the biology to mean the female was *given* to them. Selena *belonged* to him. He could do what he wanted.

"Yeah, it's new. The metal shouldn't have sheared off." *Squeak, squawk.*

So what if he hurt her or she ended up afraid of him? She'd recover. Other females since the beginning of lycan time functioned perfectly fine without being finessed. Selena was an alpha female. She needed an alpha approach. He'd gone wrong by being too scattin' theta with her.

"You must be a strong guy. I've never seen a new faucet snap this way."

Yeah. Overpowering Selena would be as easy as howling at a full moon. Didn't matter if she was lycan. She was female. Weaker. He could snap her like — The broken faucet.

The tone bar in his pocket.

Neither could be repaired.

"Yeah," Scott continued to ramble. "I'm going to have to run out and buy a whole new set. The Q forty-five is top of the line hardware. I assume you're going to want the same quality at least. Or an upgrade."

"The same," Ethan muttered.

He couldn't upgrade his mate. Selena was top of the line for him. Why would he want to force her? Break her? He would never have another mate. Mates were meant to be cherished. For a lifetime. He was a cur to consider anything else.

She must be pushing him for a reason, trying to get him to do exactly what he'd done: display a temper. Why?

Scott toddled off to find a hardware store or plumbing supply outlet. Selena stayed hidden in the basement with Brittany. Maybe breaking the faucet scared her. Didn't the female understand a male could be pushed only so far?

He doubted it. She'd been raised by her grandfather, a man Tokarz believed to be broken by the death of his son. Ethan needed to remember Channing's grief. Needed to remind himself the Varulv alpha was not his enemy.

"YOU TWO WERE GLOWERING," Britt said after several moments of inane conversation focused on what type of shelving they'd need for the finished product. She paced off the measurement of an outside wall.

"He made a mess in the kitchen." Selena's stomach growled. She hadn't eaten. After Ethan destroyed the faucet, there had been no time to cook anything. Breakfast had become one of her many daylight habits.

"It's his kitchen to make the mess in," Britt reminded her. "He's even hotter when he glowers."

"He's off-limits to you," Selena snapped.

"You said you don't want him. Why shouldn't I—"

"He's off limits!" Didn't this stupid sapien female recognize the words of her own language?

"Oh, you have it bad for him." Britt sounded more amused than irritated. "Why are you fighting him? He's hot, you're attracted to him."

"Have you thought any more about a name for the company? I came up with something, and a branding statement to match."

"Changing the subject isn't going to make lust go way."

"Night Shift. Handcrafted by the light of the moon."

"Catchy. Now let's discuss Ethan."

Selena clenched her teeth to keep from going for Britt's throat. "There is nothing to discuss."

"Are you in denial?" Britt's upper lip curled and her nostrils flared. "The heat arcs between you. I could come from being in the same room with you two fighting off your lust."

"You're confusing anger with lust, and you're disgusting."

"You think I'm confused only because you've never—"

"Enough!" Selena shrieked. "Just . . . enough. There are circumstances you don't understand, and I can't explain."

"Why don't you try me?"

"He . . . he wants to get married," Selena blurted. "He wants me to have his children."

"And you're upset? Why? He's a hunk. He's got money and a good future. He's being nice to you, helping you get our business off the ground. What is your problem, Selena? Are you mad?"

"I'm not good enough for him."

There. She'd admitted her fear out loud.

The confession quieted Britt's nagging.

"Commitments to my grandfather won't and don't allow me to be my own woman," Selena continued.

"You do not want to be stuck in a backwater town for the rest of your life. I don't care if it's your hometown." Britt's voice shook. "I know you want our concoctions to keep the place alive, but maybe it's time for a reality check. Maybe Ulvskog is dying for a reason. Towns lose population and industries. The world changes. From what you've told me—"

"Stop. Right now." Selena wished she could control the shaking in her own voice. Anger outvoted reason. "You don't understand—"

"What's to get? Ulvskog is devouring you. It's keeping you from having your own dreams. Do you want to be stuck in recycled plans your grandfather made for your father? You have an amazing man upstairs who wants to marry you, and you're tossing away the opportunity in order to save a dying town? Your ancestors fled their past to relocate to the new world to build new lives. Their blood flows in your veins. Their dreams are the heritage you need to tap into now, Selena. Ulvskog is dying. Face cream and bath bombs aren't going to save any town."

Selena hunched her shoulders. This venture had to work. Ulvskog needed something to survive. Her people needed their sanctuary. "Maybe you'd better leave."

"Uh-uh." Something scraped across the concrete floor. "I'm not going to let you wallow in your righteous anger toward me. We have work to do. Do you have Internet access yet?"

"I don't know."

"Why don't you go upstairs and ask your hunk? Unless you want me to."

"I'll ask him." Having been the target of Britt's manipulation skills on more than one occasion, Selena capitulated. Mating fever won. Anything to keep Britt away from Ethan.

She paused at the top of the stairs in time to hear Britt's cousin say he had to go to a hardware store to buy parts to fix the broken faucet. She waited until the front door closed and an engine coughed before she ventured off the stairs. She found Ethan in the kitchen, staring out the window.

"What?" he asked in a harsh voice.

Their gazes clashed in the reflection of the glass.

"Do we have Internet access?"

"I'll call them in a few minutes."

"Thank you." She choked out the polite words.

"You need to get used to having me around," he said. "I can't change fate. Neither can you."

She dipped her chin slightly.

"We should be civil, despite the phase of the moon."

"Stay out of my business." Her tone was low enough to pass as a growl. "My pack business," she clarified. "And my pack business includes Congressman Peters and his son."

"I can't. Congressman Peters is my pack business, too. My alpha and our former government liaison sent me to convince him to vote for keeping the treaties in place."

"Warwick isn't your pack territory. Congressman Peters is Varulv business."

"Maybe people believe your grandfather can't handle his pack."

"My grandfather is my concern, not yours. You're Loup Garou. I am Varulv. I'm serious, Ethan. Peters is mine."

His lip curled. "You fancy yourself in love with his son."

If only Ethan grasped how much she hated Liam Peters. How many times did she have to deny the idea? "Yeah. I want his babies real bad."

"Mine are the only babies you will ever have," Ethan snapped.

Selena returned to the basement without giving him the satisfaction of a single word.

"Let's go shopping," she said to Britt. "Find some food. I'm starving."

Chapter 11

Selena stared at the passing scenery as Ethan drove. When she'd suggested they go to Ulvskog for the full moon, she hadn't known they wouldn't be speaking. She had expected him to be cranky, not silent.

As obstinate a lobo as Ethan was, stupidity wasn't a factor. The full moon was best spent in the company of a pack, making a return to Selena's hometown the logical choice. Ethan driving made the trip easier.

Slightly north of the Chippewa National Forest, the closest sapien town to Ulvskog lay twenty miles west. One bus a day tied the sapien village with civilization. The bus would stop at the track leading to Ulvskog if requested.

As they neared her home, Selena sensed something wrong. If she had been in moon-mode, her hackles would have risen. Each mile disappearing in Ethan's rearview mirror only increased her trepidation. Something was wrong; dreadfully, hideously wrong.

"Do you sense anything weird?" she asked Ethan.

He glanced at her. "Weird? Weird how?"

She slipped her fingers beneath her shoulder harness to straighten a twist. "I'm going to try calling Gramps again." She'd been trying his number every ten minutes with no luck.

"I thought he hates cell phones," Ethan said after she'd disconnected for the umpteenth time.

"He does. While I was at college, a cell phone was the simplest way to keep in contact." She shouldn't have to explain cell phone convenience to Ethan. He used his to call his pack alpha and who the scat knew who else back in his precious Colorado.

"He's probably preparing for tonight, off in the woods someplace. Cell phone service might be spotty where he is. Or where we are."

Okay, he had a valid point. Reception tended to be random in this area. They were still too far from Ulvskog to ask Ethan to pull off the road to the shoulder, so she could work a quick shift and use the time-honored way of communicating by letting her howls echo across gullies and valleys as they wended their way home.

Ethan covered her hand with his huge one, making her aware she still fidgeted with her seat belt. His touch surprised her. "Why are you so antsy?"

She rolled her shoulders, trying to toss off the raised-hackles sensation. "I can't explain...something feels...weird."

"Okay." Ethan didn't mock her, didn't try to placate her, and didn't behave condescendingly toward her. "Can you call someone else? What about your mentor? The healer."

His concern and his belief in her intuition warmed her. "Old Olivia? I doubt she has a cell phone. The Varulv are a traditional pack."

"How much farther?" he asked.

"Another hour or so."

"I don't dare drive any faster. I'm not familiar with the road."

His concern was fair. She pulled her hand from his. "You might want to keep both hands on the wheel. The road gets snaky."

He barked out a laugh. "Snakier than this?"

"Oh yeah. Don't the mountain roads in Colorado have switchbacks and such?"

"Sure they do. Except I know the roads around Loup Garou. I'm a stranger here."

FROM A DISTANCE, ULVSKOG appeared peaceful. Green trees hugged the buildings as if to protect them, vastly different from the rocks and evergreens of Colorado. *Quaint*, Ethan thought.

Unlike the vicious, sinuous curves of most of the journey, the narrow dirt track shot straight into the center of Ulvskog.

"Looks nice," he lied to Selena, who sat as rigid as one of the rocks surrounding Loup Garou. Her lips twitched, as if she wanted to smile. Worry wouldn't let her.

Ethan sought her hand again, swallowing the platitudes he wanted to say. *Nothing is wrong, everything is okay.* Because he sensed the...weirdness, for lack of a better word, too.

Nothing moved. The landscape remained motionless, as if even the wind held its breath. Holding one's breath was the only way to approach the town. Something smelled...bad.

"Is the village usually this quiet?" Ethan asked. Loup Garou would have been crazy busy on the afternoon before a full moon, dealing with tasks requiring hands before the morph to four-legged form. Grannies and preadolescent children should be scurrying to the pack meeting place, parents escorting their young'uns to the care of the eagle-eyed grannies.

Selena stared at the sky. "Something is wrong. Those are buzzards."

He looked up. The landscape wasn't as still as he'd first believed. Birds, big ones, circled overhead. He hit the gas, as anxious as Selena to arrive at their destination. "Where does your grandfather live?"

"Last house on the left." The quaver in her voice pierced his heart. "Across from the full moon lodge."

His breath caught in his throat. The stench grew stronger. He slammed on the brakes. The truck skidded in the gravel in front of Channing's house. Selena opened her door before the truck completely stopped.

"Wait," Ethan growled. "Don't go in alone."

Selena ignored him. She hopped to the ground as he slammed the transmission into park. She'd climbed the porch steps by the time he'd yanked the keys from the ignition. His speed had him at her back as she crossed the threshold.

A wall of stink slammed his face. Selena's cry shattered him. He caught her arm before she could kneel beside what had been her grandfather.

The old man had been shot. At least, Ethan thought so. Murdered not with any old gun. An assault weapon of some kind. He didn't know anything about guns, but whatever had shredded Selena's grandfather had to be automatic. A strip of flesh kept his torso from being severed at the waist. Chunks of his head—hair, and something gray—clung to a wall. Blood puddled everywhere. Ethan and Selena stood in the gore. What once might have been a finger floated next to Selena's foot.

Intense, howling sobs jittered in her body. He dragged her from the room, away from the concentration of stink, to the porch where fresher air lingered.

He didn't have time to succumb to the sickening carnage. Both he and Selena were hunters by nature. Although they were familiar with blood and gore, he'd never lost a loved one, much less to something as vicious as this slaughter. She needed a moment of private outrage. So he held her. Let her pound on his chest. Shriek her fury as well as her grief.

She needed to rid herself of this poison before she could take her place in her pack. To lead them past this trauma.

Only the Ancient Ones could predict what they would find in the rest of the village.

Selena's harsh sobs should have caught someone's attention. Someone should have noticed the strange vehicle parked in front of Channing's house. Someone should have noticed that something was wrong.

No one came. Not even the wind. Only the birds of prey circling overhead in a macabre dance, performing in time with Selena's weeping, shattered the stillness.

He waited for her to calm herself. To pull her tattered pride close and use it as armor.

"Where is everyone else?" she asked in a hoarse whisper as she extricated herself from his embrace. Her brindle-colored eyes were rimmed with red, as were her nostrils. She sniffed a couple of times. Her scrutiny drifted to the large building across the road from her grandfather's dwelling. "We need to check the full moon lodge."

He waited.

"I need to check." She sounded as if she were trying to convince herself.

"I've got your back," he assured her.

She lifted her chin, as if the gesture could cosmically pull courage and strength from her depths.

Side by side, they crossed the dusty track. Ethan couldn't tell if the stench of her grandfather's house still clung to his olfactory or if new waves of death stink rolled from the lodge. His eyes watered. Selena raised her hand to cover her nose and mouth.

His blood thrummed against his eardrums. He would have sworn he could hear the air shift beneath the buzzards' wings. No. The faint hiss, the buzz came from the lodge. He quickened his step. Something inside was alive. He reached the door before Selena and yanked open the panel.

Ethan imagined he could see the horrendous smell billowing as it rolled out of the lodge. Seconds passed before he realized he did see something...undulating. Heard buzzing. He grasped what the sound meant. Flies. Flies invaded the lodge.

Selena also recognized the significance. Her whimpers hurt not only his ears, but some place deeper, in his chest, right around his heart.

The babies. The young ones—preadolescent, too young to shift. The grannies, the women too old to bear children and whose shifting days were over, but who still played a key role by tending the children on full moon nights. Now instead of vibrantly alive, laughing, crying, squabbling, or gossiping...

Dead. Forever stilled and silent.

"You don't need your last memory of your pack to be death." Ethan tried to block Selena's view.

"They were my pack." The whimper vanished, replaced by a deep, feral sound, as near to a growl as any lupin could manage while in human form. "They were my people...and I killed them."

Selena stumbled out of the lodge, off the porch, to the dirt track passing for Ulvskog's main street. How could she go on living, knowing her arrogance caused this massacre? Her lies not only killed the living, they had decimated the Varulv future. All the babies. The innocent children.

The most valuable, cherished asset of any pack.

Gone.

Due to her. She could barely control the shudders threatening her.

How many others had been slaughtered?

A better question might be, had anyone escaped?

She ran from cabin to cabin, praying to the gods of her elders someone, anyone, had been spared. She did not weep. She could mourn after the full moon rose in a few hours. Right now, she couldn't indulge in the luxury to weep, rage, or confront in her culpability. Her grandfather was dead. As his sole heir, she had to take responsibility for the state of the pack.

Distance. She needed distance.

At least Ethan, following close behind her, didn't ask questions she couldn't answer. She was glad he stayed with her. If she were alone, she might pander to her guilt, and wallowing there long enough, might drown. She deserved to drown. Deserved to die as hideous a death as the rest of her pack.

She knocked on every door. When only silence responded, she opened the door. In some homes, she found the bodies of friends or folks for whom she didn't much care, individuals who were pack mates despite personal differences. Whose souls would haunt her forever. Other houses had been abandoned, as if the residents fled.

Only the gods of her elders could know what she would find in the surrounding forest.

Ethan didn't speak. His presence, as she faced this incarnation of sapien hell, gave her the strength to continue. Without him, she couldn't have taken the census. He supported her as a mate, the privilege and honor she'd denied him. He hadn't rejected her. Even now, when she took full responsibility for the carnage, he did not abandon her. Yet.

The sun slid from the sky far too soon. Selena stood in the center of the village, closed her eyes, and inhaled deeply. She tried to find her way past the reeking threads of blood, of urine and offal. She caught a whiff of gunpowder, and the tang of hot metal.

Whoever had come to Ulvskog to assassinate the residents also left behind an imprint, an aura hiding behind the waning energy of the confused spirits of the dead trying to return to their ancestors. Confused spirits. Accusing her.

She couldn't stay in a spot the gods had deserted. She took off at a run, heading to her secret hideaway in the forest, the place where she'd spent hours questioning what was wrong with her.

Ethan trampled the bracken behind her, as if he read her mind. Her plans. Yet when she entered the grotto formed by ash and hawthorn trees, next to a brook and carpeted with moss, he didn't follow. She quickly shed her clothes and shifted. Shifting was effortless within hours of moonrise on the night of the full moon. She didn't need to sacrifice more energy.

She emerged from her hiding place to discover a black wolf awaited her. Ethan.

His clothes were wrapped in a black vinyl rain poncho. The package could easily be mistaken for a shadow. Ethan clearly had come prepared. Too bad he couldn't prepare for a mate as hideously flawed as she was.

Now he waited for her, an alpha female, to lead. He honored her position. Or placated her. She didn't deserve his patience.

She should have shifted sooner, after she'd found her grandfather. She couldn't cry in four-legged form. Her nose unclogged once she switched to full-moon mode. Only the ache in the back of her throat remained. Oh, and the agony shredding her heart.

She'd been so worried her pack and other packs wouldn't accept a female alpha, she never stopped to consider there might not be a pack for her to lead. How many times had Gramps told her to consider possible consequences to her actions? Maybe now, with his blood on her soul and the lesson too late to learn, she could appreciate what he meant. She should have known Peters would stop at nothing to protect his image. He had ordered the massacre as surely as the full moon would rise.

The moon hid her face behind a veil of clouds, mourning the loss of her chosen ones, ashamed of Selena.

I must atone.

She could never atone.

Selena picked her way up the side of the mountain, aware of Ethan snuffling along behind her. Each step on the trail reminded her tonight might be her last time to celebrate the full moon in the place her ancestors claimed as home. The leaves brushing her pelt as she passed, each rustle in the bushes betraying another creature's journey in the rapidly fading light, the rich scent of the forest floor. These were the things she needed to remember. Not the horror in the village below. Those memories were for vengeance, not solace.

She would never know peace again.

Her stride quickened as evening blanketed the landscape. Ethan easily kept pace with her. She could have closed her eyes and made her way up the familiar path to the peak of the mountain. The summit was the best vantage point for offerings to the moon, the highest spot for miles around.

The Flower Moon, sometimes called the Milk Moon, crested the horizon in the distance, dancing between the overhead branches. Tales of the moon had been a prominent part of her childhood. May's full moon, allegedly the brightest of the year, illuminated the darkest bits of the soul, bringing shame to light. Her shame, her guilt, lying in their own blood at the base of the mountain.

Behind her, the honorable lobo whom the gods of her elders chose as her soulmate, protected her back. Would Ethan still want to claim her after he learned her part in the slaughter of her own pack? The responsibility for the dead was as much a part of her as the full-moon shift.

The trail left behind the trees whose leaves changed Selena's view of the moon to lace. The moon, heavily pregnant with promise, rode low in the sky; faintly pink, as though stained by her children's blood.

Selena stopped at the apex of the clearing and lifted her muzzle. Wispy clouds still draped the sky, accented by the glitter of stars. A soft wind carried no hint of the carnage below.

Ethan nudged her shoulder with his nose. He stood next to her, his black pelt blending with the night. The moon reflected in his eyes. She could have relied on his steadfastness as she led her pack. Once he learned her part in their annihilation, he wouldn't want to shackle himself to her.

She couldn't face him, unable to bear the knowledge had she not been so...naïve, he was perfect for her. Her imperfection voided the will of her elders' gods.

He nudged her again, harder this time, as if he expected something from her. The outcropping of rock didn't have space to spare. Memories evoked a whimper. Her grandfather always claimed the spot where she now stood was the best vantage point for singing to the moon.

What better place to mourn him?

The whimper increased to a whine, a weak, subservient sound better suited to insults than a tribute to her grandfather. The whine warbled a bit, as if sapien tears were clogging her lupin throat. Her rage burst aloud in a yip. The following howl clung to the night, low, haunting, emanating from deep in her chest where her heart cowered as it splintered into shards.

Ethan joined her lament, a deeper counterpoint to her descant. She forgot everything except her sorrow. Her grief. Her need to atone. Her dirge became a plea for penance.

Mist seeped across the landscape, as if summoned by her anguish, further shrouding the moon. Raindrops pelted her. The moon wept at her confession.

Selena's voice spilled into the valley below, filling the achingly empty space with sound, echoing her culpability over and over and over so she would never forget what her impetuous words had wrought.

ETHAN STOOD NEXT TO Selena on the ledge and allowed her to take the lead in the moon song. He didn't understand her plea for forgiveness—she hadn't been the one who murdered the old and young of her pack. He wished he could find a way to comfort her.

Not everyone was dead.

The adults of the pack who could shift and hadn't been trying to save their offspring—they'd escaped. Hidden in the forest. Or so they confessed to the moon.

They were devoted to Selena, their acknowledged leader. Another time, later, he could brood about what their loyalty meant for any future he might have with her. He merely needed to be available to her, to catch her if she fell, to listen, hopefully to hold her. To lend her strength, be her mate; the other half of her soul, and the balm to help her heal. She might never be whole again. He could provide the missing pieces to help her go on.

As would her pack. They echoed her song to the moon. The lycan harmonies swelled his heart. The outpouring of sorrow, of support, of social unity was not eerie, mournful, or lonesome, as so often described by sapiens. Ethan never found the music to be so. Of course, he'd listened mostly as a wolf himself. If he were sapien, he would weep.

The pack sang for hours as the moon rode the sky. After she'd vanished below the horizon, Selena dropped her head.

Ethan nudged her side, and they turned together to return to the grotto where they'd left their clothes.

Chapter 12

One of the most satisfying experiences in the world was sleeping after the setting of the full moon. A werewolf expended a lot of energy. The deep, dreamless slumber rejuvenated.

Ethan curled around Selena in the grotto where they'd left their clothes. Her performance had to have exhausted her. She didn't object to his presence.

Ethan opened his eyes. Dawn painted the sky pearly gray with iridescent streaks, transforming the landscape into a black-and-white photo opportunity. Except he wasn't a photographer. He was a musician in the throes of mating fever, while his intended lay in his arms. Naked.

He couldn't help his reaction. A swelling penis was natural. Normal.

Her soft skin, much smoother than a she-wolf had any right to be, given only hours earlier she'd sported a lovely fawn-colored pelt, lured his fingers. He stole the opportunity to touch her, gently stroking her arm, marveling at how different they were.

Selena stirred. Moaned in her sleep. Snuggled closer to him. Her exhales ruffled the hair on his chest. One of her legs wormed between his thighs. He held his breath as her knee closed in on the danger zone.

Ancient Ones, what had he ever done to be tested in such a brutal manner?

He rested his cheek on the top of her head. He needed to focus on something else besides the want coursing through him.

Guilt. Selena made no secret she blamed herself for what happened to her grandfather and the others. Why would she believe something so absurd? She'd been with him, en route from Warwick, during the slaughter. Or did she assume the pack's fate was her responsibility as she took on her grandfather's role?

She moaned and burrowed closer to him.

He prayed to the Ancient Ones for strength. The irony of his petition didn't escape his notice. Respecting Selena was more important than claiming her. If only his cock would get the message. Selena's fingers tightened on his bicep. She whimpered. Muttered something sounding like, "No, please, don't."

She jerked awake. He could tell by the change in her respiration and the way her body tensed. He twisted until he could kiss the top of her head. Her hair smelled of the mist that had gathered as they sang.

"Ethan." Her hoarse voice rasped his nerve endings.

"You were expecting someone else?" He meant the question as a joke. Her reaction—the harsh inhale and further tightening of her limbs—betrayed her non-humorous reaction.

At least she didn't try to shove him away.

"I thought last night might have been a nightmare."

"I'm sorry." He meant the apology.

"I have to deal with...everything."

Everything a sapien would have dealt with upon the grisly discovery, but the timing combined with their physiology prevented. The corpses remained where they had fallen.

"I'm here for you." He wanted to say something else, something profound and comforting. His brain couldn't function at full capacity, mostly due to lack of blood.

"Thank you." She didn't release her grip on him.

"Selena." Such a fluid name. Graceful.

He nipped her earlobe, then drew the flesh into his mouth.

She arched her neck; he read the movement as a sign he could continue. The horror of yesterday's carnage had shown her how much she needed her mate. How key he would be to her stability and future happiness.

Selena's body became pliable beneath his roving hands. He gently rolled her onto her back. She looped her arms around his neck.

When he brushed his lips against hers, she opened her mouth, welcoming his tongue.

What blood in his body, not rushing to his penis, roared against his ears. Or maybe the air bellowing in and out of his lungs, or the bass beat of his heart battering his chest, created the sound. Or was the noise her heart, pounding against him? He couldn't differentiate because she had his heart.

He didn't think his dick could grow harder. Wrong again.

Time to stop brooding and start letting instinct rule.

Selena did not resist. She reacted as if she wanted his touch as much as he needed to caress her. They lay breast to chest, belly to belly, his penis trapped between them. Selena dropped her arms from his neck and slipped them under his.

"I need you," Ethan said, coming up for air and taking nothing for granted.

He didn't know where or how to touch her. Instinct failed him. Instinct urged him to roll her onto her stomach and mount her. Her instinct should be to let him.

He nuzzled the side of her neck, nipping the flesh around her marking spot.

She moaned, encouraging him.

"I don't want to hurt you."

Her thighs parted, allowing him to slip a hand into her secret place. Her slick inner flesh, juicy like a ripe peach ready to be devoured, tempted him.

Later. Now was for the marking. Once he marked her, everything would be okay. Sealing their union would alleviate their problems. He needed to believe mating would solve their differences.

First, though, he needed to make her happy. Judging by the sounds Selena made, extreme happiness lingered nearby. He stroked her, marveling at the different textures his finger encountered. Soft here, rough with hair there, a hard nubbin trying to elude his touch.

Selena kept her fingers busy, too. He'd have bruises on his shoulders where she gripped him. Her nails dug into his skin, a sting keeping him cognizant of what was happening between them.

His absorption in being able to touch her and taste her caused him to miss the moment her response shifted from pleasure to something else. One instant she clung to him, her soft moans encouraging his exploration of her body. Somewhere along the way, the whimpers became protests nearly drowned out by the static in his head.

He was ready. He needed her now. Flipping her to her stomach required no effort. Instinct guided him: mount her; mark her. Simple.

Except she screamed as he grasped her hips to position her for his entry. Screamed long and loud. Screamed with terror.

Ethan released her. Fell back. The shock of her reaction numbed his brain in a new way. She scrambled away from him, although he no longer touched her. Curling into a tight ball, she shielded her breasts and other vulnerable places.

His breath rasped in and out in tortured desperation as Selena huddled in a quivering mass of self-defense. Ethan dug his fingers into the detritus as much to anchor himself as to keep from reaching for her. The organisms displaced by his burrowing released the clean, seductive scent of the earth, which mingled with the stench of Selena's terror and the displaced remnants of her desire.

"I won't..." He didn't recognize the hoarse rasp of words, although they emerged from his throat.

Her sobs decreased. The shaking of her shoulders slowed to a quiver. The horrible sound emerging from her made no sense. At first. He couldn't...process the meaning of her words.

"I was fifteen..."

Too young. She'd been barely an adolescent.

"The new moon..."

She hadn't been able to shift.

"They..."

They. Not a he.

Ethan rolled barely in time to keep from puking on his clothes.

SELENA ROCKED, ARMS CLASPED around her drawn-up knees, as if she could burrow herself into the earth. Into oblivion. Gods of her elders, she'd never meant to tell anyone she'd been assaulted. Anyone. Ever.

What had happened on the night of the new moon had been her own personal assurance she would never mate, would instead be the alpha of her pack and the last of the Wolfe alphas.

She'd wickedly allowed things to progress too far with Ethan.

The attack—the endless, eternal moments—should have stayed in the past. She'd healed. After a fashion. Yet the gods decided to punish her again for being in the wrong place on the new moon.

She disgusted Ethan. She smelled the sourness of his vomit, cringed at the retching sound as his stomach emptied itself. At least now he would appreciate why she couldn't shame him by allowing him to claim her.

And now, in the aftermath of her arrogance, the destruction of her pack also weighted her soul. She wasn't alpha. She wasn't worthy of omega. Rogue. Foolish, female rogue.

Now that she'd told Ethan parts of her secret, he'd hightail his hide back to Colorado, leaving her to mourn and bury her dead.

"Selena?"

She lifted her head and stared in the direction from where her name had been called. The familiar, beloved voice was loud in the quiet of the forest since Ethan's sickness.

Old Olivia, the pack healer, entered the grotto.

"You're alive." Selena unfolded herself and swiped at her face to hide her tears, squelching the urge to run to Old Olivia. "How? How did you escape what happened?"

"I wasn't at the lodge yet," Old Olivia replied. "I ...hid in the forest. As did others."

"Others?"

"You didn't hear us lamenting with you?"

"There are others?" Once again, her self-involvement prevented her from appreciating how her actions impacted the others in the pack.

"Many adults were preparing for the shift."

Ethan pulled on his jeans. She should be focusing on the pack matters, not what her should-have-been mate did.

"And the gestating one?" The single pregnant female in the pack represented a future.

"Addy and her mate escaped."

Selena needed to gather herself. She *was* the alpha now. She needed to be calm. Needed to show compassion to the survivors. Needed to lead the pack from this moment of sorrow to a future where they could rebuild.

She fumbled for her clothes.

Ethan handed them to her.

"And who is this?" Old Olivia asked.

"I am Selena's mate," Ethan replied.

Selena tried to hide her cringe amid the motions of yanking on her sweater. How could he believe her worthy of mating after her confession?

"A Limmikin? How curious."

"Limmikin? I'm from Loup Garou. The Garnier pack in Colorado."

Old Olivia's mouth curved. "Living in Loup Garou doesn't make you any less Limmikin. You've returned to Ulvskog to claim our Selena."

"I've explained I cannot mate with him." Selena zipped the fly on her jeans.

"Mating is not a matter of can or cannot," the pack wise woman told her. "He is, or he isn't. The gods of our elders don't make mistakes."

"What is Limmikin?" Ethan asked.

"How can you be ignorant of your heritage?"

"Pa—my grandfather—never speaks of life before he joined the Loup Garou. I never persisted."

"Native. Your ancestors didn't arrive from other places, the way we originated from the Scandinavian countries, or the Loup Garou from France. Your ancestors were already here."

"You know this how?"

Selena wanted to smack him for his insolence to the revered healer.

"It's a gift." Old Olivia's sarcasm was new to Selena.

"I'm an American werewolf."

"We're all American werewolves," Selena said. "We were all born in the US."

"Most of us are dependent on the treaties for safety," Old Olivia reminded her. "The Limmikin are not."

Chapter 13

Ethan, male of the group, led their descent. Even though Selena or the crone were more familiar with the path, their protection remained his responsibility. He'd seen and smelled what waited for them in Ulvskog. The culprits might return. Selena faced a rough day. He needed to support her.

Focusing on clearing the aftermath of slaughter prevented him from reliving Selena's revelation. Brooding on what her confession meant nauseated him. Infuriated him. Someone had stolen what belonged to him, yes. Worse, though, they'd hurt her. Physically and deep in her soul.

He needed to transcend his rage and find a state of mind where he could help her heal. Help her move past the violation of her body and spirit.

Then he would hunt the men who had defiled her and dismantle them to the cellular level.

Cellular. Right.

He stopped in the middle of the trail. "Do you have a plan?"

She swallowed hard. Blinked. "No."

"We need to come up with a strategy before we..." He waved in the direction he assumed Ulvskog lay.

Selena hung her head.

Ethan smothered a flare of frustration. Reminded himself Selena had lost her only family and the generation of her pack she had expected to lead. He could be compassionate.

They couldn't trot into the village as if today were any old morning after the full moon. Bodies were everywhere. Dead, putrefying corpses who had names Selena knew. She couldn't call the local authorities, yet the dead had to be gathered and removed.

"Would you mind if I called my pack for help?" he asked. The question acknowledged her leadership heritage. He, Selena, and the old woman could not clear the bodies and bury them. Yes, there were others. Their harmonies strengthened Selena's lament. Emotions were high. Loved ones had been butchered.

Loup Garou anonymity might be a more compassionate solution.

Selena stared at him. Parted her lips as if to speak. Averted her face as if she could not bear to look at him.

"Asking for help is your choice," Ethan added in as gentle a tone as he could manage. "I won't make the call unless I have your okay. Having strangers assist might be less painful. Calling the local authorities is out. What happened is pack business. Your pack. Let my pack help."

"He's right," Olivia said. "Sheriff Wiltsey isn't capable of dealing with our species."

If the treaties weren't in question, we could have called Mitchell Jasper for federal help, like Luke had...

"The problem," Ethan pointed out, "is vampires didn't murder your pack."

"Vampires?" Olivia asked.

"They showed up in Warwick." Selena jumped in quickly, as if speaking faster could lessen the severity of the meaning.

"Two fronts." Olivia spoke slowly, as if to offset Selena.

"Yep. Selena, I'm not questioning your ability to lead. I'm not suggesting your grief would make you incapable of making good decisions. All I'm saying is you don't have to face any part of the future alone." Ethan believed he sounded diplomatic.

"You never planned for the transition of power to happen due to tragedy." Olivia smiled wearily. "What happened is nothing any of us could predict or prepare for. The situation resembles the bloodlusts our ancestors fled in the old world."

"Call your alpha," Selena said in a tight voice. "I will listen to his counsel."

Ethan pulled his phone from his jacket pocket.

Leaning against Ethan's truck, Selena wrapped her arms around her torso, as if the pose could keep her from flying apart at the molecular level. She considered pleading with the sun for another hour of moonlight, so she wouldn't have to face the results of her impetuous words. The universe wouldn't forgive her for her sins. She didn't deserve special treatment. The sight of her grandfather's body, sprawled in death, the lodge filled with the corpses of the children she should have led in their adulthood, would haunt her long after her own demise. Their slaughter belonged to her.

As did vengeance.

She listened to Ethan's side of his conversation with his alpha. The humiliation of having to ask a stranger, a male alpha from a distant pack, to bail her out of this mess mortified her. An alpha as famous as Toke Lobo only intensified her embarrassment.

What else was left for her to survive? Nothing. Nothing at all. After the remnants of her pack learned of her complicity, they would revolt. As she deserved. Maybe she should confess, lie on her back and expose her throat to let them do what they would to her.

Except her death wouldn't bring back the ones who'd died by her words.

"Who are you sending?" Ethan asked.

God of her elders, she didn't deserve the aid of an alpha.

"No, I'm not questioning you." Ethan's tone held a hint of a snap. "I want to know who I should expect."

She tried not to eavesdrop, except Ethan stood next to her.

"Being your beta doesn't make him compassionate."

Ethan listened a second. Held the phone away from his ear, exposing Selena to a deep, angry sound.

Ethan resumed the conversation. "Maybe I don't want Restin giving my mate a difficult time. He tends to be obnoxious, and she doesn't need his scat right now."

More listening. Ethan's eyes narrowed. "Selena Wolfe is my mate. I have every right to protect her, even from tail-chasing betas."

Whoa. Maybe she should remind Ethan they were not mated, they could never be mated. Clearly he hadn't recognized what brought the...process to an end.

"Selena." Old Olivia patted her arm.

Selena jerked from the woman's gentle touch. She'd already polluted too many loved ones. Yeah, once the living gathered, she would offer her throat.

Ethan disconnected the call. "Tokarz is sending his beta and a couple roadies, including our EMT."

"My pack doesn't need an EMT." *They need a leader, someone who doesn't let the need for revenge cloud her vision.*

"Someone could have survived." Ethan persisted in his misplaced optimism.

"Don't hold out hope." Her voice clogged in her throat. "We observed the same corpses. You smelled death as nauseatingly putrid as I did."

He wrapped his arms around her. No matter how she struggled, she couldn't release herself.

"Are you afraid of me or angry with me?" he asked.

"Angry." She had no reason to fear Ethan, other than for breaking her heart.

"Good. You and I are going to need our anger to get past the next few days."

"You don't need to stay."

"How can you believe I would go?" He rested his chin on the top of Selena's head. "Old Olivia, do you and the others have a safe place to stay?"

"They believed they were safe in Ulvskog," Selena reminded him, as she squirmed out of his embrace.

"Yes." Old Olivia ignored Selena. "Gambayan."

Gambayan. The old town. The place the Varulv first settled upon arriving in Minnesota. Hidden deep in the forest, Selena didn't know if she could find the place without a guide. A place so forlorn, sapiens could wander into the center and not comprehend its purpose.

She should have remembered the place. She should have come up with the solution.

"Selena and I are going back to Warwick until my pack mates arrive."

"What about the vultures?" Selena asked.

"The buildings are secure. Besides, vultures and other carrion-eaters avoid our dead."

"True," Old Olivia confirmed.

"We saw—"

"Birds of prey circle the death site, yes," Ethan said. "They sense death. If they investigate, they will flee. Your pack is safe until we can give them the farewell they deserve. Nothing will disturb them."

"Maybe we should set the village on fire. A funeral pyre. I could throw myself in the flames."

"What happened isn't your fault."

Selena forced herself to look at him. "You don't know anything."

He crossed his arms over his chest; lowered his bright, piercing gaze on her. "Why don't you tell me and let me decide for myself?"

"Doesn't matter," she said after a moment of mindlessness. "It's done. My pack, the future of my pack, is dead."

"Not all of them," Old Olivia reminded her. "The ones who remain are happy you escaped. Didn't you hear our songs?"

"I heard the gods of our elders mourning."

"Your pack mourned, too," Ethan pointed out. "They sang with you. You are not alone. And vengeance is a dish best served cold."

Selena's breath hitched. "I'm sorry. What did you say?"

"I read somewhere vengeance is a dish best served cold. It means—"

"I know what the sentiment means." A strategy. A badly needed guide.

She needed to remember the tactic.

"I HAVE TO STAY," Selena insisted. She sat on a fallen log on the outskirts of her hometown. "You have to go back to Warwick to meet your friends."

"I don't want to leave you alone." Ethan's stubbornness matched her own.

"I'm not alone. I have Old Olivia. I have the others in my pack. I can't abandon the living or the dead. Go. Now. I'll be safe in the old town." She wasn't used to having someone hover. He'd gotten on her nerves in the anti-vampire house in Warwick. Now he drove her mad in Ulvskog.

"I'm not leaving yet. Restin and the others need at least twenty-four hours to drive here."

"I have things I need to do." She barely avoided screeching. "Alone."

His eyes widened. He backed off one step.

"Your leaving is non-negotiable." He would keep at her, like a child picking at a scab, unless she drove him away. "You haven't given me a moment alone since the vampire attack."

"I can—"

"I need you to leave!" Her voice echoed in the empty streets. Her shout shocked birds from their branches, the flapping of their wings providing a backbeat to her anger. "We are not mated. We will never be mated. I get you need to stick around, but for the love of the gods of our elders, I need some space for a while."

His mouth worked, as if he were going to speak. Luckily, he reconsidered.

Smart lobo.

ETHAN WANTED TO PUNCH something. Mutilate someone. Only Selena's presence, small and solitary on her fallen log, kept him sane. Allowed him to subjugate his rage. As long as he remained with her, he wouldn't do anything to frighten or harm her. If he was alone? Ancient Ones help the universe.

His understanding of Selena increased a thousand-fold after she'd confessed—no, after she'd admitted someone had assaulted her. Some stranger abused her. Hurt her while she was defenseless. As soon as he found out the name of the violator, he vowed to leave them in a puddle of DNA.

Puking had not cleansed him of his rage.

He needed to clear his head.

Maybe Selena had a point. They needed time apart, except after seeing Ulvskog, separating might not be a good idea. Who would keep an eye on her? An old woman? A pregnant female? Okay, maybe the old town they'd discussed as a hiding spot was safer than Ulvskog. The idea didn't ease his mind.

Only blood could comfort him. Her enemy's blood.

Luke had experienced something similar with his mate. Abby had been exploited. Ethan recalled Luke's initial reaction. At the time, he'd had no sympathy. Now? He owed Luke an apology he'd never give. Too many bad times between them, late nights filled with the disgusting Internet porn Luke found so fascinating.

Ethan yawned. The morning after a full moon always exhausted him. Add shock after shock to the usual energy drain, and his wakefulness was a miracle. Selena's heartbreaking revelation, followed by Olivia's assertion he was a native American shifter... With no time to process, either idea would have depleted him.

No. He couldn't ruminate on the past, not now. Not while danger still lurked around Selena. What if the massacre had intended to eliminate her, too? He couldn't forget the vampire who had attacked her. He didn't need to further upset her with his need to destroy something or someone.

"Leave!" Selena shouted at him.

Ethan climbed into his truck and left. He called his grandparents, hoping to make the drive to Warwick less forlorn with a distraction.

"Pa, someone told me I'm Limmikin," he told his grandfather. He pictured the beloved face, etched with the deep lines of a life well-lived.

"We don't discuss the past," the old man replied. "Where are you?"

"Tokarz sent me to Minnesota to persuade a congressman to support the treaties."

"The congressman told you about the Limmikin?" The miles didn't dull Pa's sharp tone.

Ethan might as well have been standing in front of his grandfather, being disciplined for some transgression. He took the next curve in the road too close. Branches scraped the side of his truck. "No. The local pack's wise woman told me within two minutes of meeting me."

"You've met with the local pack? The Varulv?" Pa sounded more and more agitated as the conversation continued.

"You know the Varulv? Channing Wolfe?" A sharp and steeply banked curve had Ethan gripping the wheel and focusing on his driving.

Pa didn't answer.

"Channing is dead."

Still nothing.

"He was assassinated with an automatic weapon. Practically cut in half. His granddaughter found his mutilated body. Same thing with most of the pack. We still haven't located all the survivors. We hope. Tokarz is sending a contingent to help us deal with the dead."

Us. As if he were part of the Varulv pack.

Pa must have had the same reaction. "What are you doing with the Varulv?"

"Are you prejudiced? What do you have against them?" Ethan asked. Another blind curve loomed. He eased his foot off the gas pedal. "Channing Wolfe's granddaughter is my mate."

He should have told his family sooner.

Pa hesitated before offering his congratulations. No joy tinged his tone. No celebration or relief in the knowledge his line would not die out with Ethan.

"Stay alert," Pa warned. "The Varulv have their own agenda."

"And I don't?"

"Tokarz de Lobo Garnier has an agenda, and you're his tool."

His grandfather didn't mean tool in the derogatory sense. Ethan doubted Pa knew about a derogatory meaning. "I have an agenda. I've met my mate. She was attacked by a vampire. Her grandfather and the children of her pack have been murdered. I need to make sure she's safe."

"Vampires?"

Ethan could have sworn he heard his grandfather spit on the floor.

"Some things never change. You have a good agenda. Don't let Tokarz or the Varulv distract you."

"The Varulv are dead. I'm dealing with the aftermath, and yeah, I'm distracted. The smell alone—"

"You don't need to remind me," Pa grumbled.

Remind you? Ethan had no idea what the old man meant.

"The Varulv are not the peaceful, mind-their-own business pack they want you to believe." Pa's words were hesitant, as if he were reluctant to share his thoughts.

No, not his thoughts. His past.

Ethan's own heritage. He swallowed his impatience and listened, wishing he were in the presence of his grandfather instead of on the phone. Body language and facial expression could reveal as much as words. Or, if secrets were to be shared on the phone, Ethan shouldn't be driving on a treacherous road.

The missing pieces of his heritage — No, he was being ridiculous. Ethan's father never indicated he felt less of a male when Pa wouldn't speak of their lineage, and lineage meant everything in the lycan world. Ethan's mom never indicated she minded Dad's lack of pedigree.

Ethan believed he needed to prove something to Selena. Prove his worthiness. The vampire-resistant house hadn't accomplished anything. He might have succeeded after the full moon, before she'd made her horrifying revelation. Not a confession. A confession signified guilt. He knew Selena was innocent as well as he knew his own...

Did he know his own name?

Probably not.

"Are we native to the continent and not from Europe?" Ethan asked. "And don't tell me we don't discuss the past. I'm fairly certain I'm in a situation where the truth would be helpful. Ignorance isn't going to protect me."

A black pickup, covered in miles' worth of dust, passed him on the next straight away. Ethan hadn't been aware of another vehicle on the road with him. Black smoke puffed from a rusted tail pipe, and a coil of bright blue nylon rope swayed on a wooden stud.

Another long pause. "Our ancestors were here before the Europeans arrived with their treaties." Pa's voice sounded heavy, as if the topic weighed too much for him to speak. "Before they made it dangerous for us to live our way. Before the government wanted something in return for leaving us alone."

"What is our family name? Why did you leave your home?" Ethan asked only two of the many questions he had for his grandfather. "We were from Minnesota. I've figured out that much."

"Yes. Except we can't speak—"

"Channing Wolfe is dead. I saw his body myself." Somehow, Selena's grandfather and Ethan's own family's exodus were related.

"We can't speak—"

"We have to speak!" Ethan's patience vanished. "If I'm in danger, if my mate is in danger—you have to speak."

A sigh as heavy as a load of bricks tumbled across the airwaves. Ethan was surprised their connection wasn't crushed.

"I will come to you."

What? "Wait. No."

"The story is too important to trust to technology."

"Pa, vampires are after us. Murderers with automatic weapons. You should stay in Loup Garou—"

"Your father and I will join Restin and the others on their journey to you."

"No. Pa. Wait."

Too late. The old man disconnected the call.

ETHAN WISHED HE KNEW someone else to call as he drove toward Warwick. Anyone. Unless he was conversing, he brooded. Obsessed. Selena's fear, her tears, her broken words.

I was fifteen...the new moon...they...

If he wasn't careful, the steering wheel on his truck would be his next casualty.

Only one person might empathize with the emotional tornado churning in his gut, destroying his brain. Too bad the person was the one person in the world he loathed—if he didn't count Restin.

Luke. Ethan would never forget the night Luke found nude photos of Abigail on one of his favorite porn sites. Toke Lobo and the Pack were starting a new tour. Ethan and Luke were roommates in a no-tell motel. Luke flipped. Went berserk. Woke everyone in the motel with his reaction to Abby's photos. He'd attacked Restin and Tokarz, forcing a change in rooms. Tokarz guarded Luke, while Ethan roomed with Restin until Tokarz decided to head home.

Ethan hadn't learned until much later what set Luke off. Now he empathized. He'd be damned if he would call Luke for advice on how to handle his jealousy.

Except that wasn't the correct word. Ethan wasn't jealous of whoever "they" were. He wanted their blood. Their flesh caught between his teeth. Their agonized screams in his ears and embedded in his soul. He wanted a blaze of triumph instead of defeat in Selena's eyes. He wanted to tell her he didn't blame her for what happened and show her he sided with her, would always side with her. Her happiness was his priority. He had only to convince her.

No, calling Luke would accomplish nothing. Luke and Abby had nothing to do with what happened to Selena.

Rape. Selena had been raped when she was fifteen years old. On the night of the new moon, when she was most defenseless. By more than one man.

Rage narrowed Ethan's vision. He closed his mouth, so as not to over-oxygenate his brain with too much air. Blacking out while driving was not a good idea. He couldn't avenge Selena's honor if he killed himself with careless driving.

He couldn't avenge Selena's honor if she refused to tell him who had violated her. He needed those names.

SELENA BREATHED THROUGH HER mouth to prevent smelling the dank mustiness of the cabin in Gambayan. Moss carpeted the crude planks, leaving everything slightly damp and cold. She was safe, maybe secure, in the old town.

She'd been vulnerable since that night ten years ago. The night every illusion she'd ever held had been destroyed. *She'd* been destroyed, as had her grandfather and the future generations of the Varulv pack. Now Ethan had been sucked into the morass; the opposition would destroy him, too.

No future. No one left in her pack to lead. Her lie, her empty threats had backfired. She knew the individual responsible for the carnage of Ulvskog.

Me.

She also knew who had done the deed. They could sic all the vampires on her they wanted. They could murder her family and her friends. Vengeance would be hers.

She closed her eyes and rolled over, searching for a comfortable position. Futile to attempt sleep when the moon beckoned. For once she wished she didn't have to be strong. Wasn't the Varulv heir apparent. For once she wished she could wallow and mourn. The loss of her father. The newer, fresher loss of her grandfather. The loss of her innocence and the mate she'd once anticipated. The male who would treat her as she deserved to be treated.

Since meeting Ethan, her losses hurt a hundredfold. She was nothing more than scat he should scrape from the sole of his boot;

instead, he embodied every daydream she'd had until that fateful new moon.

And now he knew.

Her deepest, ugliest secret. She never should have let mating matters progress as far as they had. Of course her trauma interfered. Now he'd fetched his own pack to shield him. He couldn't stand to be alone with her. Her vileness sickened him. Hadn't he vomited after her confession?

Well, she wouldn't make excuses.

Maybe he wouldn't return. Maybe he'd pretended to want to help with…cleanup for the survivors' sakes. Claiming to fetch the members of his pack provided the perfect way to — *Vanish*.

"Relax, girl," Old Olivia said.

"I thought you were asleep."

"I don't have the full moon need. Haven't since I lost my shifting ability."

Old resentments bubbled in Selena. She *hated* being female. Female meant vulnerable. Males, once they hit adolescence, never lost their ability to shift—except on the new moon. Females, however, couldn't shift while they were gestating. Females also stopped shifting on the full moon once they were no longer able to bear offspring.

Legend claimed they could shift if in extreme danger. No one in living history had ever seen it happen; the myth explained why the older women had been killed along with the babies, toddlers, and preadolescents. Minding the young ones during the full moon took skill and the patience provided by age.

Now they were all dead.

She should have foreseen the massacre. Except she hadn't recognized true evil.

"Do you want to talk?" Old Olivia asked.

"Do you want me to confess my role in the slaughter?"

"What happened to you ten years ago isn't going away. The betrayal will always be a part of you."

Selena cringed. "Nothing happened to me ten years ago."

"You don't have to lie to me. Unless you're lying to yourself."

Old Olivia had been the one to find her after the new moon, after she'd been dropped in a ditch on the main road to Ulvskog. She'd plied Selena with foul-tasting teas and guided her into the woods to hunt for medicinal plants. She claimed Selena, the pack's alpha female, needed to learn and use the ancient healing lore.

She'd seen Selena needed healing.

"I was in the wrong place at the wrong time and trusted the wrong people." Selena's voice didn't crack.

"The past doesn't matter to your young male."

"Of course the past matters," Selena snapped. "We're lycan. Our way is one mate for life. Ethan isn't going to want a bone someone has already gnawed."

"Ethan doesn't strike me as a lobo who'd blame you for someone else's actions."

"Based on what? An hour in his company?"

"If he's any kind of a male, he not only won't blame you for what happened, he'll do everything in his power to avenge you. He's a good male. Limmikin usually are." A hint of sadness tainted Old Olivia's voice.

"What is Limmikin?" Anything to change the subject. The nightmares that still woke her were enough of a reminder. Add Ethan's courtship to the mess and maybe she would lose her mind sooner rather than later.

"Native to this continent. Not from Europe. Not from the old countries."

"I've never heard of them."

"The Limmikin used to live north of Ulvskog and Gambayan. There were as many of them as there were of us."

"Not many," Selena muttered.

"True. The Varulv have always been a lesser pack than, say, the Loup Garou. Maybe the Loup Garou success is based on their brewery."

"Ethan is Loup Garou."

"Ethan is Limmikin. What happened in Ulvskog reminds me of what drove the Limmikin from Minnesota."

Her words snatched Selena's attention. "What?"

"The Limmikin mostly kept to themselves. Oh, one or two of our pack found their mates among the natives. Mostly, though, we were separate packs. One day, a Limmikin female who'd mated with Varulv returned to visit her parents and found a slaughterhouse instead of the village."

"Gods of our elders," Selena whispered.

"No gods were involved," Old Olivia snapped. "Except the sapiens who wish they were gods."

"Someone massacred the pack?"

"Every last one. Or so we believed. At least, I did. Oh, rumors some escaped have always existed. I never believed them. Until I met your Ethan."

"He's not mine." *He can never be mine.*

"The gods have their reasons, Selena. You're smarter than you're acting. Use your head, girl."

She didn't want to think. She didn't want to remember. She didn't want to be a solution or a motive. Too bad she didn't know what she wanted. "The gods brought the descendant of the ones supposedly wiped out back to Minnesota?"

"To Minnesota. To you."

"Why?"

Old Olivia shrugged. "Who am I to try to guess the reasons of the gods?"

Chapter 14

"Interesting house." Restin Zev Garnier stood on the sidewalk in front of forty-two Ash Street. "Did you buy the place from a Syracuse University fan?"

Ethan ignored the dig as he greeted Parker and Dakota, the two roadies Tokarz sent with Restin. Parker was a werewolf EMT. Dakota drove the band tour bus. "You guys got here awfully fast."

"I found a short cut." Dakota yawned and stretched. "Nice house."

Ethan faced his father and grandfather. "Hi." He stopped himself for thanking them for coming. They weren't invited. He didn't need his family to witness his humiliation as his mate continued to reject him.

"Where is the Varulv female?" Pa asked.

"She stayed behind with her people."

"Is she alone?"

"Olivia, the pack healer, said if the survivors stayed in the old town they'd be okay."

"Olivia Hagtorn?"

"Some old granny." Ethan's grandfather's sudden willingness to talk about his life before Loup Garou threw Ethan off-balance.

"Olivia Hagtorn would be old now. She was apprenticed to the Varulv healer when—"

"When what?" Ethan asked.

Pa's dark eyes, irises as black as Ethan's own, met his straight on.

"When your grandmother and I had to leave our pack."

"Do we have to stand on the sidewalk to discuss your secret past?" Ethan's father asked. "I'd prefer more privacy."

"Sure." Ethan planted his boot heels firmly on the pavement as he led the way to the house. "The place isn't fully furnished yet."

"Not a real good neighborhood." His father studied the purple house across the street.

"It's affordable. And safe. Extremely safe." Ethan unlocked the door. The others brushed past him to enter.

"This house is amazing." Parker stood in the center of the main room and took in every detail the others missed.

"Wait until you see the backyard." At least someone appreciated what he'd done to keep Selena safe. "I have a hedge in back—"

Parker took off at a run.

As the others stared at Ethan, he explained, "This place is an anti-vampire stronghold. It's on Ash Street, between Oak and Hawthorn."

"The sacred triad of safety," his grandfather muttered.

"See this woodwork? It's all ash or oak."

"So?" Restin asked.

"The best wood for killing vampires," Pa said. "So they still use vampires to do their dirty work."

"We were attacked in Selena's old place," Ethan stressed. "I've smelled them lurking. There have been no direct attacks since I moved her here."

"Vampires." His father didn't bother to hide his disgust. "What have you gotten yourself into?"

"What has Tokarz gotten me into," Ethan corrected.

Parker rejoined the others in the front room. "The hedge is hawthorn. This place is a fortress. What's with the lot next door? Do you have plans?"

"A field to grow ingredients for Selena's botanical toiletries. She's trying to build her pack's version of Moonsinger Beer." Ethan faced Restin. "She makes creams, lotions, bombs, body wash—scented female stuff."

"Bombs?" Restin raised one eyebrow.

"Bath bombs. You toss them in the bathtub to make the water smell nicer."

"Clean water usually smells fine the way it is."

"Sapien females spend a lot of money to make water smell better to them."

"So, where's this death site we're supposed to help clean up?" Restin dismissed Selena's industry.

"North of here." Ethan wanted to hit Restin. "Don't you want to rest? Grab some food? Wait until dawn before we head out?"

"Why?" Restin asked.

"I could use some sleep." Dakota's jaw cracked as he yawned.

Pa fidgeted. Ethan figured the delay made him antsy.

"We have only two beds and a pull-out sleeper sofa." His father and Pa could share his bed, while he used Selena's room. He didn't want another lycan polluting her space.

"Two beds?" Restin infused contempt in both syllables.

Restin could sleep on the floor.

Before Ethan could outline his plan, someone knocked on the door. Other than Helga the nosy neighbor, no one ever knocked on the front door. Ethan held up his hand. Although Restin, Pa, and his father outranked him, he ruled forty-two Ash Street. Selena made Minnesota his.

He strode to the door as silently as he could while wearing his boots. Inhaled deeply to determine if some odor penetrated the thick oak panel. Nothing.

The knocking resumed.

"Who is it?" Ethan asked in a soft voice. What type of being left no scent?

"I'm trying to locate Selena Wolfe."

Ethan recognized that voice. Ethan despised the voice as much as he loathed the man to whom it belonged. He yanked open the door with such force, the wood around the hinges protested. "Why would you search for Selena Wolfe in my home?" he asked the clearly shocked Liam Peters.

"None of your business." Peters didn't quite sneer.

"She doesn't want anything to do with you." Ethan sensed his pack gathering behind him. If Selena did want Peters in her life, Ethan would have to change her mind.

"She visited me last week."

"She visited your father, not you," Ethan pointed out.

"Is she here?" Peters asked.

"She's unavailable."

"Look, I've known Selena all her life. She asked something of my father, and I have an answer for her."

"Give me the message. I'll see she gets it."

"I'm afraid leaving a message isn't possible." Peters' smarmy expression enraged Ethan's beast.

Peters should be afraid. If Ethan found out the congressman or any of his staff had done anything to upset Selena, they were going to pay. "Then you'll have to leave."

The congressman's blue-eyed son stared at Ethan with a blank expression, as if the brain behind the eyes was vacant.

"Leave." Ethan crossed his arms over his chest. "Selena isn't here, and if she was, she wouldn't see you."

"Who's with you? Your posse?"

"My family. Here for my wedding to Selena."

The blank expression twisted into a smirk. "A wedding? Right. Maybe you ought to double check with Selena."

Ethan shoved his hand into his pocket and gripped the jagged ends of the broken tone bar. Otherwise, the congressman's son might find his face rearranged. "I don't recall seeing your name on the guest list." A hand rested on Ethan's shoulders. Pa's, by the scent. Ethan's father also flanked him. "I'll tell Selena you stopped by. Maybe next time you'll bring a wedding gift."

Ethan quietly closed the door in Liam Peters' face.

"Who was that?" Pa asked.

"Congressman Peters' son." The man he'd been afraid Selena loved. If only she did love someone else.

Maybe he could cut Liam some slack.

Pa's complexion changed to the same silver blue color as the tone bar in Ethan's pocket, not a healthy shade for a werewolf. "The Peters family business," he muttered. "A dynasty, not a family."

"What do you mean?"

"The Peters family has held the congressional seat in this district since a congressional seat has existed."

"Over a hundred years?" Although not an expert, Ethan figured Minnesota had been around for a while.

"Maybe. A long time. Since at least my grandfather's time."

"He keeps getting reelected. Warwick district voters either approve of the Peters' family politics or are unaware of the truth."

"The Peters family are not honorable creatures." Pa stumbled toward the sofa. Ethan had never seen his grandfather behave with such hostility. He shouldn't get upset at his age. Whatever was going on agitated him. He needed to sit.

"What?" Restin asked.

Restin's sensitivity surprised Ethan.

Time to play host. "Do you want water? Something to eat? We have fish from local lakes."

"I'm fine." Pa stared at a spot on the bare wood floor. "The voices are the same. I could close my eyes and still hear Congressman Peters saying the unthinkable to my grandfather and father. This young one, the one who was at your door—he has his ancestor's voice."

"I would be honored to speak with your voice," Dad said.

"As would I," Ethan murmured. "Any of us would."

Dakota and Parker each nodded, while Restin continued to harangue Pa. "The era you escaped from is over. New leaders—"

"Want to break the treaties giving us the illusion of safety. What happened to the Varulv isn't new." Pa's voice creaked. "Based on Ethan's description, what happened to the Varulv is what happened to my pack."

"The Limmikin." Ethan clenched his teeth.

His father and the others stared at him.

"The Limmikin," Pa agreed.

"The what?" Dad looked confused, as he glanced from Ethan to Pa.

"We are native American shifters," Ethan explained, when Pa remained silent. "Our pack didn't negotiate a treaty with the government. We were here. We didn't need sanctuary in our ancestral home."

Dad turned to Pa. "That's why you were so upset Tokarz sent Ethan here."

"My grandson has no business fighting for something not belonging to him."

"I found my mate, so it's not all bad," Ethan reminded them.

"The Ancient Ones have their reasons," Dad added.

"Ethan's mate is Varulv. The Varulv betrayed the Limmikin not only to the congressman but also for him."

Ethan jammed his hand into his pocket and found the pieces of his broken tone bar. The jagged ends bit into his fingers. "The Varulv do treaty work for the congressman. Treaty work is why Erik Wolfe was at the Pentagon on September eleventh." Everybody knew the story. Selena's father was the only werewolf to have died in the terrorist attacks that day. He was a hero. A role model. A legend.

"Really? I've always wondered."

"Pa, are you accusing Wolfe of treason?" Dad asked.

"Or the congressman?" Ethan added.

"I've always wondered," Pa repeated. "You forget. I knew Channing Wolfe. I knew the Congressman Peters of the time. I *knew* them."

"You fled them." Restin's flat, matter-of-fact tone irked Ethan.

Pa bristled. "I approached old Bernard Garnier and asked for sanctuary."

"Service." Restin spoke with authority. "In exchange for sanctuary. The same deal we have with the government. You made your deal with the pack. This mission is as much Ethan's fight as it is mine."

"I never agreed to return to the site of my family's slaughter," Pa growled. "My mate and I were lucky to have escaped. Our deal included a ban on Peters' district."

"It's okay, Pa. Selena is my mate. The Ancient Ones have their reasons."

"She's Varulv," Pa repeated. "I don't trust them."

"They're mostly dead. If I had to guess, at least two individuals with automatic weapons emptied their ammo into the bodies."

"That's the way my people were slaughtered, only on the night of the new moon. Not one of us could shift to defend ourselves against the invaders and their machine guns. Even if we could have shifted, we couldn't defend ourselves against automatic weapons."

"The Varulv wouldn't have used guns," Ethan said.

"Why not?" Pa asked. "The new moon gave them their hands. Neither pack could shift. Rumors the congressman financed and trained his own army kept surfacing. We didn't realize fellow werewolves had been recruited. Channing's father was a greedy whelp-of-a-vampire. He didn't want to share the territory with any other pack, even though the Limmikin existed here since creation."

Ethan's head spun. He'd never heard of turf wars between packs. He believed all packs got along due to their minority status in the sapien world.

"Channing himself wounded my mate, Rand's mother, as we escaped."

"The scar on her arm?" Dad asked. "She told me she'd scratched it on a blackberry bramble."

"Our official story."

"She was pregnant with me."

"She was pregnant with you," Pa confirmed. "We could have lost you. Ethan might never have been born."

"You can't prove anything, can you, Hatch? You have no proof." Restin sounded revoltingly smug. "You had no proof when you begged my grandfather for sanctuary, and you have no proof now."

"He has me." How dare Restin question the old man's truthfulness. "I saw—"

"You observed an aftermath."

"Some of the Varulv pack survived. They witnessed what happened. Old Olivia, the pack healer, is one." Ethan offered a name.

"Olivia Hagtorn also witnessed the aftermath of the Limmikin purge," Pa added.

"Someone named Addy and her mate. She's gestating and got away. Others. They sang with Selena during the full moon."

"We haven't come to right the wrongs of the past," Restin said after several moments of tense silence. "We're to help the Varulv bury their dead. Period."

"Speak for yourself," Ethan snapped.

"I am. And for Parker and Dakota. I'm not getting involved in local politics. Tokarz sent you to convince the congressman not to break the sanctuary treaties."

"You can't prevent me." Pa straightened his shoulders and lifted his chin.

"No, Hatch. I can't stop you or Rand from doing anything. Just don't expect the Loup Garou pack to come to your rescue a second time."

ETHAN'S FATHER LEANED AGAINST the kitchen counter. "What do you have against furniture?"

"Time," Ethan snapped. Strained finances weren't anyone's business. "Selena hasn't had a chance to pick out curtains, pictures for the walls. Décor. She's had other things going on."

"He's got the most important piece of furniture," Pa added.

"Why two beds?" Dad asked. "Or haven't you claimed Selena yet?"

"I've claimed her." Marking her could come later.

"The question should be, has he made her happy?" Pa chortled at his own joke. "It's not such an easy task."

Now the elders of his family were treading in dangerous territory. Territory he didn't want to discuss. Not until he'd had a chance to discuss things with Selena. Things that still chilled him. Sickened him. Kept him awake at night. "Can we change the subject?"

Pa ignored him. "Have you tried—"

Ethan tuned out whatever advice Pa continued to give. He wasn't going to have a problem making Selena happy. Keeping her safe, making her feel secure and cherished was his challenge. Happiness could come later.

"Then there's always the hard-to-find spot," Dad said. "The one that cowers and hides."

"Finding it with your tongue is easier than using a finger," Pa advised.

"Hey you guys," Ethan interrupted. "You're talking about Mom and Gee-ma. I do *not* need the details of your happiness." He couldn't believe his father and grandfather were giving him sex tips. Sex was the furthest thing from his mind.

Dad paused. "He's got a point. I didn't need to know how you and Ma..."

Pa grinned. "Distracted you, didn't I?"

"You were making up that scat? I wanted to try—"

"Dad!" Ethan punched a cupboard door. His fist blasted through the oak. Splinters scraped his flesh. "Someone massacred Selena's pack. She's not worried about how or where I lick her."

"Might take her mind off her sorrows," Pa muttered.

"Is fucking how you coped? Stuck your dick in Gee-ma, and—"

Dad backhanded him.

Ethan spat blood into the sink and glared at his father. "Yeah. Hearing my grandparents and parents' bedroom antics isn't helping me focus on what I need to do. What's happening with Selena is deeper than sex."

Except she'd been assaulted. Only she could tell her story. If she ever told him the whole story, he would hunt the creatures who'd violated her body, her spirit, her soul.

"WHAT'S KEEPING THEM?" SELENA leaned against the mossy stone door frame. The remaining males had camouflaged the old town as best they could with fallen branches and other bracken. Her uneasiness remained.

"They had to drive from Colorado," Old Olivia reminded her for the fifth or sixth time.

Selena admitted she was being difficult. Her nerves jangled. She had no idea how long the drive from Colorado to Minnesota took.

"Your mate." Addy sounded wistful. "Mating fever is why you're anxious."

Curse Old Olivia for confirming Gramps' news, that Selena's mate had arrived.

"Selena's mate-to-be has gone for help from his pack," was what Old Olivia had shared. No one paid attention to the word *help*. Mating was the only important thing in their view.

"Your grandfather would have been pleased," Jakob, Addy's mate said.

"He met Ethan. Not especially impressed," she lied. Gramps had never shared his reaction to Ethan. He'd been happy she'd found her one-and-only. Had Gramps sensed Ethan's Limmikin blood? Would Ethan's pedigree have mattered?

"It's too bad they didn't have a chance to get to spend time together." Addy was a month from giving birth, and her naturally sweet disposition had gone into hyperglycemic mode. "Tell us about Ethan."

Selena studied the mist clinging to the treetops, veiling the worn-at-the-edges moon. A breeze ruffled the leaves. How could she tell her pack about him when he remained a stranger to her?

"Nothing personal against the males here, but he is the handsomest lobo I've seen," she admitted.

Her confession elicited giggles from the teenagers.

"What's his rank? Is he alpha?" Addy wanted to know.

"Rank doesn't matter to the gods of our elders who chose our mates." Selena was evasive. "He's a musician."

"We heard him singing with you last night," someone said.

"No, I mean he's the steel guitar player for Toke Lobo and the Pack."

A chorus of approval greeted her announcement.

"For real?" one of the teenage girls asked.

"I didn't believe him at first, either, until he showed me the CD case for *Full Moon Lady*, and yeah. He's right on the cover."

Why all the interest in Ethan? Shouldn't the pack be focused on retribution for the deaths of their friends and family?

"I love *Full Moon Lady*," the teenager gushed, stars in her voice.

Selena vaguely remembered being young. Naïve. She'd had a crush on a man. A sapien man. Her grandfather would have grounded her for life had he known.

"Could his fame be good for us?" Jakob's brother asked. Selena couldn't recall his name. "Maybe some residual money will come to Ulvskog."

Didn't he grasp Ulvskog was gone? The decaying corpses polluted everything. Torching the place was the right idea. Better to burn them than allow the bodies to rot until a mass grave could be dug.

"Not unless the Varulv are absorbed into the Loup Garou pack," she said. "Right now is too soon to make any decisions about our future."

Right now, we need to get past tonight.

"Has he sung for you? Other than at the moon?" someone else asked.

"Not yet." She remembered his deep voice crooning as he puttered around the house he'd purchased, tinkering with things to make the place more habitable and comfortable than her house on Pine Street. He'd *enjoyed* doing for her. "No. He hasn't sung for me."

"When are you going to mate? I would have thought last night—"

"I'm in mourning." Selena quickly interrupted with a valid excuse.

The wind moaned its disapproval.

"All the more reason to mate," Addy said. "He could comfort you while you grieve."

Selena didn't want comfort. She wanted revenge.

The shaking spread from her stomach until her entire body trembled like the leaves on the trees outside. Her fingers. Her toes inside her shoes. Her teeth chattered in imitation of the dead branches piled around the perimeter of the old town.

She wanted revenge. Not only for what happened to her grandfather and the rest of her pack, but for what happened to her ten years earlier. The *incident* preventing Ethan from marking her.

No. The tragedy keeping her from her destiny.

She gave her assailants power to control her. Pursuing revenge couldn't happen until she reclaimed her destiny.

"What kind of berries did he offer you?" The adolescent girls were persistent.

The males were listening, too, although they believed they were too lobo to ask how a star romanced his mate.

"Strawberries and blueberries." Maybe. She'd never opened the brown paper bag from the fast-food place. "He gave them to me within ten minutes of meeting me. He pulled into a drive-thru and ordered a fresh berry parfait."

"Wow."

She did a good job making their relationship sound normal.

"Berries were much more difficult in my day," Old Olivia said. "If they weren't in season, the males improvised to impress us. Nowadays, the drive thru."

A few chuckles salted the quiet.

"Does anyone smell something bad?" Addy asked.

Every nose immediately lifted and sampled the air.

"Your nose is overly sensitive since your pregnancy." Jakob spoke in a tender tone.

"No." Selena smelled the stench, too. Except she didn't need to ask what the reek was. She'd faced the source once. Intimately. "Quickly," she instructed, *sotto* voice. "Do we have any branches left? Here? In the cabin?"

"Why?" A male voice, belligerent and snarly asked. Philip. He'd always been argumentative.

Oh scat, this was not the time for some lobo to have his manly genes offended.

"Vampires," she replied.

"We'll be safe," Old Olivia said. "Our ancestors built the old town in a grove of ash, oak, and hawthorn."

"Nice." Selena wasn't going to risk additional lives on old world lore. If the protection worked, why didn't more packs use the spell? Why did Ethan buying a house finally make her aware the myth existed? She wanted weapons to fight back. "Except if we can smell them, they can smell us. I'm not willing to risk our safety."

Jakob didn't question her. He lifted Addy and carried her to the rear of the cabin. Others muttered since vampires smelled so bad, they could be scented at a distance, whereas lycans didn't stink. A couple of the men became shadows as they slid from the building. They returned several tense moments later with branches.

Selena had no idea from what type of tree the branches had fallen. They were wood. Wood was enough. She hoped. "Aim for their hearts," she instructed as she assisted the men breaking the limbs into usable pieces.

"Do they have hearts?" someone asked.

"They must if a wooden stake in the heart kills them," she replied. Splinters slipped into her skin. She didn't stop to remove them. Vampires struck quickly.

Once the weapons were ready, she and the males who volunteered stationed themselves at the doors and windows. She wished Ethan was with her; mating fever had nothing to do with her desire.

Her cell phone vibrated against her thigh, surprising her. *Ethan,* except they'd never exchanged numbers. She dug the phone from the snug denim of her jeans. She didn't recall cell service this deep in the forest being reliable.

Another random, anonymous caller.

"Did you enjoy your present?" She couldn't tell if the whisperer was male or female.

"Not as much as you're going to enjoy yours," she retorted before disconnecting.

It was going to be a long night.

ETHAN SAT UP, TORTURED by Selena's scent clinging to her bedding. Something was wrong. He focused all his senses, moving past the sounds of his temporary housemates snoring and farting, past the sleep scent of Selena, and the still-strange shadows of the house to what was different. Out of place. The hackles on his nape stood on end. Maybe Selena's absence disturbed him.

He swung his legs out of bed and planted his bare feet silently on the cool wood floor. He'd been moody since Peters appeared at his door.

How had Junior known where to find Selena?

Another theory intruded; if Junior found Selena in Warwick, he could find her in Ulvskog. His father had to know Ulvskog's location. He'd had past dealings with the Varulv. He'd sent Selena's father to the Pentagon to die on September eleventh.

No matter how often Olivia blathered about the safety of the old town, men with automatic weapons had penetrated whatever security measures the Varulv believed they had in place, proving the flaws in their beliefs.

He never should have left Selena alone. Restin was a big boy. Dakota's sense of direction surpassed anyone else's. They could have found their way to Varulv. As for Pa and Dad, well, hadn't Pa grown up in the area? Even though landmarks might have changed, a lobo, a territorial creature, should remember where he spent his youth.

I need to be with Selena. Now.

He pulled on his jeans. The socks he'd discarded only hours earlier. A t-shirt and Henley. He'd left his leather jacket in his truck. He carried his boots, intending to sit on the front steps and pull them on.

Parker waited on the porch. "You sense the wrongness, too."

"Maybe I sensed you." Ethan was annoyed he hadn't considered he couldn't sleep due to one of his guests.

"Nah. I didn't get out of bed until I heard you getting dressed. A disturbance in the fabric of peace woke me."

Ethan glared at Parker. "I didn't realize you're woo-woo."

"We're all woo-woo to someone," Parker said. "We need to get going."

Parker had his duffel with him. Ethan had wasted enough time. "Right. Let's go."

When they arrived at the outskirts of Warwick, the famous yellow arches beckoned Ethan. Trapped in a strange déjà vu, he hit the drive-thru and ordered a berry and yogurt cup.

Selena resisted the urge to shift. Staking a vampire would be much easier in her human form, although seeing one was easier as a wolf. Behind her, the pack was quiet. No babies remained to fuss; no more toddlers to ask awkward questions when silence was crucial.

She'd weep for them later.

She'd consulted with the upper alphabets. The gammas and deltas, the sole epsilon. They'd plotted a strategy. A weak plan. The timing was in their favor. Some males could shift and wreak havoc with their teeth and powerful jaws. Others would remain in human form wielding their makeshift stakes. The pack would not be ambushed again. They would perish fighting back.

She hadn't scented vampires in a while, but their stench could have disabled her nose. She didn't know. She couldn't risk relaxing.

THE SNAKY ROAD TO Ulvskog became a demon-possessed serpent at night. The moon shone overhead, casting her milky light where she could. Trees, hills, and valleys rejected the illumination, leaving a desert camouflage landscape.

"Spooky." Parker spoke for the first time since the drive-thru. "So you have a vampire problem?"

Why was the usually taciturn Parker so chatty? Ethan had traveled with the EMT roadie on dozens, if not hundreds of tours with the band. Of course, the roadies more or less kept to themselves, separate from the performers. More werewolf hierarchy scat.

"One. At her old house." Ethan didn't want to discuss the night he'd met Selena. Listening to her discuss making bombs, then coming home to find her in mortal battle with a vamp had been the worst night of his life. Worse even than her freak out as he tried to claim her. He could live without marking her. He couldn't live in a world without her.

"She's your mate. You're allowed to be pissy."

"What makes you believe I'm not?"

"You're awfully quiet."

"Not every werewolf is a loudmouthed alpha wannabe daring the world to take a shot at him."

Ethan regretted the words as soon as he spoke. Until Parker laughed.

"Or an arrogant beta with his head planted in his backside," Parker added. "Have you ever been on a long trip in an SUV with Restin? Way different than being on the bus. And your grandpa isn't what I'd call thrilled your mate is from the pack she's from. He muttered the entire trip."

"Varulv."

"Sounds as if he has good reason," Parker said.

"Pa isn't a fool. You wait. Mating isn't a choice. I mean, would Tokarz de Lobo Garnier, Loup Garou alpha have chosen a sapien mate?"

"No. You're right. And you're lucky your mate is as lupine as you. She's the granddaughter of an alpha?"

"Too high and mighty for a lowly theta such as me?" Ethan meant the words to be light and non-threatening.

"Are you sure you're a theta?"

Ethan tried to remember Parker's place in the pack hierarchy. The roadies weren't particularly high. There'd been a discussion of rank while they'd been undermining a cult leader in Idaho a few years back. Stoker's sapien mate kept insisting on "priests" or some such nonsense. A howling wolf was a howling wolf. Sapiens didn't give a rat's rump about a wolf's place in a pack. Most were unaware packs had pecking orders.

"I was raised theta. I don't know how to be anything else."

"Your mate is going to need your strength."

"Tell me something new," he snapped.

"You won't be strong if you're wallowing in the oh-Ancient-Ones-I'm-merely-a-theta."

"Who says I'm wallowing in anything?" He hadn't considered the differences in their status. Survival and keeping Selena safe were foremost on his mind.

"If your grandpa is a theta, I'm omega. Trust me. I ain't."

"What? You're talking scat."

"No, I'm not. My grandfather tells how the grandson of an alpha from another pack arrived in Loup Garou one day and demanded to see old Bernard Garnier. I'm going to guess the alpha grandson was Hatch Calhoun." Parker stretched his long legs, joints cracking in the process. "Remember Idaho? Joseph?"

Ethan would never forget Joseph. Rescuing the boy from the death the New Sinai leader planned was the single most heroic act Ethan had done to date. Tending to Joseph in the aftermath of his escape from the paramilitary cult was a lightbulb moment for Ethan, the moment he recognized more than anything, he wanted to be a father. He'd wanted to stay in touch with the boy. Joseph's mom and Tokarz claimed Joseph and his sister needed a clean break from their time in New Sinai. A clean break meant Ethan and Joseph couldn't maintain a friendship.

"What does Joseph have to do with anything?" Ethan growled as he peered into the darkness. Something darted off the road and into the underbrush.

"You stood up to Restin in order to keep Joseph. You won."

"You tried to argue your way out of caring for him while I played a priest in the Jericho fiasco," Ethan added with a snort.

The New Sinai operation had been a clusterfuck. Restin, who might have been the pack alpha had he been born sooner, exposed his terrible leadership skills. Operation Jericho proved the Ancient Ones knew what they were doing when Tokarz was born first.

"I lost," Parker reminded him. "My bet is the latent alpha in you is why you won."

"Is there such a thing as latent alpha?"

"Restin would say so."

Ethan couldn't decide which part was scarier: latent alpha blood in Restin—or in him.

Chapter 15

Ethan and Parker arrived in Ulvskog half an hour before dawn. The moon had set. The eastern sky mimicked the color of fog. Unlike fog, the gray light masked nothing. Nature had begun reclaiming the buildings. The stench had not abated.

"Scat," Parker cursed. "How many?"

"I didn't count. Selena might know. The worst is in that building." Ethan gestured toward the full moon lodge. "If you want to check it out."

"The babies?"

The sour taste in Ethan's mouth rendered him unable to speak for a moment. "It was hideous," he whispered. He would never be able to erase the memory of the sight from his brain. Strangers to him, whereas they were Selena's pack. He could not imagine the depth of her agony.

She'd sent him away when he needed to hold her. He had to obey, if only to show her pack even her mate obeyed the new alpha. "Selena's grandfather is across the road."

"Ancient Ones."

"They had nothing to do with what you smell."

Parker shook his head. "I'm invoking their blessing. This place needs all the help it can get."

Selena's plan to start a business to support the town, the way the Moonsinger Brewery supported Loup Garou, would have failed. Viewing the cluster of ramshackle buildings, Ethan decided nothing could redeem Ulvskog. Tokarz had been right. The Varulv should have died out with Erik Wolfe's demise on September eleventh.

PHILIP, WHO'D BEEN ON sentry duty in Ulvskog, entered the old town as silently as the sun rising in the distance. "Strangers," he whispered to Selena. "In Ulvskog."

"How did they arrive?" She'd stayed awake all night. Now she wanted to sleep, except strangers were important.

"A big red pickup truck."

Ethan. He'd come back, despite her screeching for him to leave. She was glad. She'd missed kissing him goodnight. The help his alpha had promised must have arrived. She closed her eyes and rubbed them as if she could erase the lingering exhaustion. "How many?"

"Two."

Only two? How could they deal with all the carnage with only one extra set of hands? So much for Loup Garou's generosity.

"Did they see you?" she asked. "What were they saying?"

"They didn't' see me." Philip sounded insulted she'd asked. "They were mourning our loss, as if they were Varulv."

Philip's snide comment meant nothing. Werewolves mourned the loss of any other. Their population was shrinking, not growing.

She squared her shoulders. "Bring them to me."

"Is revealing the old town to outsiders safe?"

"To my mate?"

"Right." Philip sprinted toward Ulvskog.

A GRAY WOLF LEAPT from the fringe of the forest surrounding Ulvskog. Ethan made no effort to defend himself. Wolves hadn't held the weapons used to eliminate the youngest and oldest Varulv.

Besides, he'd been expecting an emissary from Selena. The early morning sun cast sharply defined shadows across the landscape, distorting proportion and perspective.

Parker took his cue from Ethan.

The wolf stared at Ethan with eyes as yellow as the newborn sun, as if Ethan were supposed to read its mind. "Are you from Selena?" he asked.

The wolf nodded.

"Take us to her." Ethan appreciated why the wolf didn't want to shift to human form to communicate. The further away from the full moon, the more difficult shifting became.

The wolf nodded again, before facing the shadows from which he'd emerged.

Ethan exchanged a look with Parker, shrugged, then followed the wolf.

The forest grew denser. The freshly risen sun didn't penetrate the overhead canopy. Instead, the leaves filtered the light, staining the world beneath the trees a glowing green place. Like being underwater, Ethan thought. His Colorado Rocky Mountain werewolf senses found the greenness surrounding him foreign.

The wolf stopped near an enormous fallen tree. The air shimmered. Waves of familiar heat and an increase in atmospheric pressure created a micro weather system as the wolf shifted to his human form. The naked man bent to retrieve his clothing from the end of the log. Ethan examined the landscape as the stranger dressed.

"I'm ready," the man said a moment later. He wore a gray sweatshirt, jeans, and tennis shoes. His human form would be able to blend in the shadows as easily as he had as a wolf.

Good. His presence meant Selena was taking precautions. Thank the Ancient Ones.

Another twenty minutes found the trio in a clearing inside a circle of trees. Closer inspection revealed the misshapen, moss-covered humps might be buildings. Selena emerged from one into the dim light, proving his presumption correct.

Ethan wanted to run to her, hold her tightly enough to risk breaking her ribs; longed to cover her with kisses. He was afraid to touch her. Afraid to step too near to her. Afraid to speak. If he congratulated her on surviving the night, he might sound condescending, and if he didn't, he might sound as if he didn't care.

"Thanks for bringing help," was how she greeted him. Sarcasm weighted her words. She bared her teeth at Parker. "I'm Selena Wolfe, alpha of the Varulv."

"What is that smell?" Parker asked before gagging.

Ethan had been so intent on Selena, he'd failed to notice the lingering stench of vampire on the air.

"Something might have attempted to breach the security of the old town last night," Selena admitted. "At least we were prepared. Who are you?"

"I'm Parker Rowe." Parker acted as if Selena's abrupt question was normal. "I'm an EMT, specializing in lycan health."

"You can't bring back the dead."

"No, ma'am, I can't. If you have others who need healing attention—"

"We have our own healer." Selena's tone was colder than a January night on the mountain above Loup Garou.

"I brought Parker first," Ethan improvised, "in case Olivia needed help."

"First?"

"The others will arrive later today. They drove straight through from Colorado. My grandfather is old. He needs to regain his equilibrium."

"Your grandfather?" Her voice cracked.

"Yes. And my father. They hitched a ride with the Loup Garou beta and one other."

"Oh."

Something lurked behind the single syllable. Exploring it needed to wait.

"You are well?"

"Yes. Thank you." Selena addressed the lobo who'd led him to this desolate, haunted place. "Go back and wait for the others. Ethan, what are they driving?"

"A black SUV," Parker replied.

"Let someone else wait. I've done my stint," the lobo said.

Ethan wanted to tear out the man's throat for disrespecting Selena. She'd given him an order. His duty was to obey. Ethan couldn't interfere. Interfering would undermine Selena's position.

"I wasn't asking," Selena snapped. "I'm the alpha of this pack. If you prefer not answering to a female, you can leave."

Members of Selena's pack emerged from the mossy mounds. An audience gathered. Not good. Ethan found himself standing closer to her.

"Or what?" the lobo jeered. He'd caught Ethan's action. "You'll sic your mate on me?"

She blinked. Only once. The lobo would read the action as weakness.

"Do you want me to kill him?" Ethan asked Selena. "It's your choice."

"Yes," she answered in a soft voice. "I order you to kill him."

Ethan didn't bother to shift. The Ancient Ones bestowed the gift of speed on him. He caught the lobo a mere ten feet from where he'd attempted his escape. Snapping the traitor's neck required barely more than a flick of the wrist, a tightening of fingers. He tossed the body into a clump of bushes outside the clearing. The lobo had proven himself unworthy of further consideration.

"Anything else?" he asked Selena once he rejoined the cluster of people.

"No." She faced the gathered pack and pointed at a tall male. "You. Go to Ulvskog and wait for the others from Loup Garou. Signal me when they've arrived."

The lobo nodded and took off in an easy lope.

"I ORDERED YOU TO leave," Selena said to Ethan, as they patrolled the perimeter. Birdsong and chattering chipmunks enlivened the air around them. Her heart had done acrobatics when she'd spied him in his leather jacket.

"And I left. But Parker was concerned the survivors might need medical help and didn't want to wait for my grandfather to recuperate from the trip."

His deep baritone voice penetrated to the chill in her marrow and instantly warmed her. He'd returned. As disgusted as he was with her, he helped her solidify her position with her pack. He behaved like a mate.

"Thank you for your support." She hated having to say the words, but he needed to know his behavior had not gone unnoticed or unappreciated.

He kicked at the debris hiding beneath last autumn's fallen leaves. "Selena, I'm your mate-to-be. You are the alpha of your pack now—"

"Mate-to-be?" she interrupted. "Don't you get what happened on the full moon?"

"Maybe now isn't the right time or place to discuss our problems." He sounded stiff and formal, as if he had a branch jammed in his backside.

If she didn't disgust him, why didn't he demand a kiss from her? "Fine," she muttered.

"Parker and I were at Ulvskog for a bit before your lookout showed himself. The smell is worse than yesterday."

"Maybe the reek will keep the vampires away."

"Are they related?" Ethan asked. "I know you blame yourself for what happened at Ulvskog, and I'm fairly certain there's more to the vampire attack than you're saying. I have to ask. And don't tell me it's none of my business. You are my business."

His words lacked the imbued passion they'd always had before, and the absence hurt.

"Yes." If he was going to despise her, she may as well be as truthful as she could. "I believe the same person who sent the vampires is behind what happened in the village." *And the phone calls.* An overhead bird chirped in agreement.

"Vampires didn't massacre Ulvskog."

"Vampires didn't massacre Ulvskog," she echoed.

"A day army and a night army," Ethan said.

Old Olivia had suggested nearly the same thing.

"I'd be happier if you were back on Ash Street with me."

"Stop." She made her voice as low and unemotional as she could. "You don't need to pretend anymore."

"Pretend?" Ethan stopped walking. "What do you mean?"

She stopped, too. "Me. Or maybe it's become a habit with you."

"I'm not following your logic."

She swallowed. Hard. "I tried to warn you. I cannot be your mate."

Ethan pulled a brown paper bag emblazoned with the famous fast-food logo from his jacket pocket. He extended his offering.

She wanted to sob. She wanted to snatch the bag from him and devour the suspected contents. Pride prevented her. She had to be strong. Strength required sacrifice. "I hope you didn't make a special trip on my behalf."

"It's the best I could do in the middle of the night." Embarrassed and apologetic.

In the middle of the night. When he'd decided to defy her order and return to her side, he'd stopped and purchased berries for her. The traditional lycan mating offering.

Ethan's honor shamed her. No matter how much he wanted to flee from an entanglement with her, the gods of their elders had decreed their union. He had no choice.

She squared her shoulders and lifted her chin. "I release you, Ethan Calhoun. As the gods of our elders as my witness, I release you from any obligation to me."

His fists, knuckles white, were clenched at his sides, including the one still clutching the bag.

He had beautiful hands. Strong fingers. He could use them in gentle ways. How else could he play guitar for Toke Lobo? And his touch. After the full moon, when they'd come close to fulfilling the wishes of the gods, his touch had been magic, his fingers the wands delivering the enchantment. Only an hour ago, he'd killed a man for her, snapping his neck as easily as he buttoned his shirt.

She spun from him and stalked toward the old town.

ETHAN WANTED TO FOLLOW her. Grab her shoulders and pull her as close to his body as a female's body could fit. He could kiss away her objections. Except the idea of touching her terrified him. If he ever found out who had violated her, the greatest pleasure in Ethan's life would be dismantling the perpetrator's life cell by cell. Ethan now understood why Luke once told Jasper a DNA test would be required to identify what remained after his vengeance.

Ethan would survive her latest rejection. Somehow. He wouldn't leave Selena. He wouldn't give up on her. He couldn't. Being his designated mate had nothing to do with his reasons. Her strength intensified her beauty. She'd survived unspeakable horror to become a caring woman; she'd been tested and found not wanting as a leader for her pack. She longed to improve the quality of life for the Varulv. The bath bombs and stinky lotions were supposed to make Ulvskog a better place to live, were supposed to revitalize a dying town and a disintegrating pack.

She could give lessons in not giving up. He would gladly take them.

ETHAN AND SELENA FOUND Dakota and Restin in Ulvskog. The stench of decomposing bodies still stained the air. Parker stood at the forest edge, puking into the weeds. Ethan wondered if the tears in Dakota's eyes were from the stench or from mourning the loss of a generation of lycans.

Restin's clear eyes were a good indication his stomach was behaving. "Burn the place," he recommended. "To the ground."

"The whole village?" Ethan asked.

"Yes." Selena was firm. "It's been breached. The site is cursed now."

Restin's eyes gleamed, as if he approved of Selena's words.

"I'll ask the survivors if they want anything from their homes."

A polite sentiment. Werewolves didn't get attached to things. Possessions meant nothing.

"They'll want revenge." Restin's icy tone irked Ethan.

"And they'll have revenge," Selena snapped. "You're here to help, not to lead."

Ethan struggled not to grin. Selena was amazing. She wasn't going to let Restin's arrogance dictate anything.

"You—"

"I am the alpha of the Varulv. Don't you ever forget my position." Her powerful voice belied the exhaustion clouding her eyes and reshaping the contours of her face. Ethan stood proudly beside her.

The door of the SUV opened and his father and grandfather emerged.

"The village is more decrepit than I remember," Pa said. "I'd forgotten the way, although the road hasn't changed much. If Dakota didn't have his talking telephone, we might never have found the place."

Dakota drove bus for Toke Lobo and the Pack. Ethan hadn't worried he'd get lost finding his way from Warwick to Ulvskog.

"Decrepit?" Anger outweighed the hurt in Selena's tone.

Pa stared at her as if he were seeing a ghost. "You must be my new granddaughter. Channing and Selena's granddaughter. You resemble Selena."

"I *am* Selena, after my grandmother. You remember her?"

"Many years ago. Before she and Channing mated. Before I fled Minnesota fearing for my life."

Dad stood behind Pa, surveying the ramshackle structures, wincing at the smell and maybe the obvious poverty of the village. Burning the buildings would be a favor.

"Don't bother waiting for your pack to select tokens of memories," Pa advised. "The dynasty's work here is done. Your pack doesn't need memories. It needs rage. Fury. An unquenchable thirst for revenge."

"What makes you an expert, old man?" Restin sneered.

Ethan wanted to smack him. Restin had heard Pa tell his story.

"I survived a similar massacre, near here. The dynasty's secret army slaughtered the helpless. They were all helpless on the night of the new moon."

Dynasty. Pa had used the word before.

"Are you saying Congressman Bryant Peters is responsible for the slaughter?" Ethan blurted before considering the implications.

Pa winced. Selena jerked as if he'd stabbed her. Ethan extended his arm to hold her upright before remembering not to touch her, and she recoiled.

He immediately released her.

His thoughts chased their own tails as he tried to make sense of Pa's remembrances and the secrets Selena revealed.

"You're making a serious allegation," Restin said.

"I asked a question," Ethan snapped. He didn't dare look at Selena. He could sense her tension across the space between them. He needed to talk to her. Now.

Pa spoke before Ethan could figure out a way to separate Selena from the others. "A Congressman Peters has represented this part of the country since I can remember. I would imagine another one being groomed to take the current one's place after he is no longer of use."

Liam. Ethan loathed the man for a reason.

Pa had been surveying the huddle of buildings. "Restin is right. Torch the place now."

Selena made a soft sound. A whimper. No one reacted. *Delegate,* he thought. *You need to delegate, then walk away.*

Legend claimed mates developed telepathy, particularly if danger threatened one or the other. Ethan had been with Stoker the night he'd gone lame when someone smashed his mate's hand with a rifle butt. One incident was enough to convince him.

"Then do it," Selena ordered.

"We stopped for supplies. Gasoline ought to help a fire along," Dad suggested.

Nodding, Dakota opened the back of the SUV and pulled out two red gas cans. Parker took one of the cans from Dakota and headed toward the full moon lodge, where the bodies of the youngest rotted.

"Ethan, see to your mate," Pa commanded.

As if I could forget her. Ethan turned to Selena.

"Let's go. I need answers. Now."

"SELENA! WAIT UP."

Selena stopped in the entry hall of Congressman Bryant Peters' regional office. She feared delaying her departure might mean missing the last bus home. On any other night, a missed bus wouldn't present a problem. She was old enough to shift, which meant she not only could run home, she could also defend herself in the sapien world. Except tonight was the new moon; the one night a month lycan physiology prevented morphing from one form to another. As a human, Selena was vulnerable.

"The congressman wants a word," the aide—Liam Peters himself—said.

Selena hid her excitement. Liam, the congressman's oldest son, had been on the periphery of her life since she could remember—at least since her father died when a plane crashed into the Pentagon, and the congressman had publicly condemned the terrorists and vowed his unending support to the families of the victims in his constituency.

She couldn't tell the congressman no. Her grandfather would understand her lateness. Volunteering as a youth ambassador for the congressman would have been an honor without a scholarship attached. When Congressman Peters approached her with the opportunity, she couldn't refuse. Not after everything he'd done for her and her grandfather.

Besides, she wasn't eager to brave the frigid January night as a human.

Liam took her elbow and smiled at her. "If you miss your bus, I'll drive you home."

"*Thanks.*" *Her brain never wanted to work around Liam. He didn't need to be her mate for her to appreciate his smile, the dimples in his cheeks, and the sparkling lake blue of his eyes. Other girls crushed on rock or movie stars; she crushed on a sapien congressman's son.*

Liam escorted her through the now-empty outer offices before knocking on and opening his father's door. "I've brought Selena."

Congressman Bryant Peters sat behind his desk. His eyes weren't as bright a blue as his son's were, and he had taxi cab door ears, but he wasn't a bad looking man. He had charisma, or so Gramps claimed.

"Hello, Selena."

"Hello, Congressman," she replied. The room smelled of recently vacuumed carpet. Behind her, a quiet snick as Liam closed the door was followed by a quieter sound she couldn't identify.

"Is everything going well with you?" the congressman asked. "You're keeping up your grades in school, right? The scholarship depends on your grades as well as your volunteerism."

Selena nodded. Werewolves didn't go to college, especially female werewolves. Maybe she could be the one to break tradition. She would love to study the medicinal properties of plants. She was flattered to be considered for one of the congressman's scholarships.

"All is well with your grandfather?" The congressman didn't wait for her to answer his last question. In fact, he didn't seem to be paying attention to anything. Except...her chest.

He stared at her breasts instead of looking her in the eye.

She struggled to keep her arms at her sides. "Gramps is fine, thanks for asking. Is there something you wanted?" If she left now, she'd still be able to catch her bus.

The congressman lifted his gaze. Smiled as if he meant it. "Actually, there is."

He stood.

Selena took a step back. Ran into something solid. Liam. Who gripped her arms.

The congressman had exposed his — Selena's mouth went dry. Her throat closed. She tried to jerk her arms from Liam's grasp. He held her too tightly.

"I want you to bend over my desk."

She heard the words despite the thud of her blood against her eardrums. The congressman sounded as if he were discussing the weather or pork futures.

"I'm . . . I'm only fifteen," she stammered. "I'm—"

"Big enough. If you're big enough, you're old enough."

Liam forced her toward the desk. She stumbled.

This couldn't be happening. She was the granddaughter of an alpha werewolf. Good werewolf girls were never...assaulted. She couldn't shift to defend herself because there was no moon.

"Liam." She tried appealing to the younger man she'd considered a friend. His name came out as a gasp. Her knees buckled. He jerked her upright. Thrust her forward.

The edge of the desk hit her stomach. She thought she might vomit. Fingers fumbled with the button at her waist, the zipper of her pants. Inhaling deeply, Selena prepared to scream. The congressman shoved something into her mouth. Cloth. She tried to spit out the gag. Almost choked on the dry fabric.

This could not be happening. Not be happening. Not to her. Not

_ ***

Ethan hung his head and arms between his splayed thighs and struggled not to puke. No matter how much her story sickened him, he could not show weakness. He had to be strong. For Selena. For himself.

They'd returned to the grotto where they'd shifted for the full moon. Insects buzzed around them. A spider spun a web between two weeds. The sun shone bright and hot outside the mossy enclave.

His empty, open hands twitched in frustration. He couldn't wrap his fingers around Liam or the Congressman's necks yet. Ultimately blood would flow. Theirs. Spill. Gush from their mangled bodies and fill Ethan's nostrils with the sweet tang of vengeance. Fill his mouth with the taste of their horror and pain. Fill his soul with the satisfaction demanded by every molecule of his being. Still, he doubted vengeance would be enough.

Now he had to appease himself with jamming his fingers into the earth. Dirt embedded beneath his nails. Too bad no flesh was handy. Human flesh.

Selena's silence unnerved him. She huddled into herself, as if the world consisted of folded arms rejecting her. He was terrified of touching her. Scared he would spook her. Afraid to talk to her for fear of saying the wrong thing. What could he say? Sexual assault didn't matter? Her rape *did* matter. Two chunks of sapien offal had violated a young girl in the worst imaginable ways—her body and her trust. Had made her afraid in ways a living being should never have to be afraid.

Ancient Ones, he wanted to hold her. To let her soak his shirt with her tears. To encourage her to pound on his chest until she could vent her fury and pain no more, absorbing everything to allow her to get on with the greatness she was meant to achieve.

"And now you know." Her whisper barely made a sound.

His rage-fueled blood bubbled against his ears.

"I can't mate with you. I'm—"

"A survivor." Ethan spoke clearly. Loudly. "Strong. A true alpha female, one I am honored to claim as my own."

Her chin lifted. "Maybe I wasn't clear. I—"

"You were as clear as you needed to be. I'm the one not being clear. You are my mate. The Ancient Ones gave me a female I can respect. They have blessed me."

"Stop." Tremors modified her voice.

He crawled across the ground until the warmth of her body collided with the heat of his. "How? How do I stop respecting you? Admiring you? Wanting to be your mate in every way?"

"How?" An undefinable sound emerged from her. A laugh, a sob, a croak.

Chapter 16

Full dark had fallen by the time Ethan and Selena returned to the smoldering ruins of Ulvskog. Glowing embers cast brilliant orange light on the edges of the shadows. Woodsmoke replaced the stench of decomposing bodies, stinging the eyes and the lungs, and shrouding the moon with a blue haze.

Ethan's numbness spread from his heart to his brain. He needed to talk to his father or his grandfather. Privately. *Ha.* Restin, Dakota, and Parker leaned against the SUV. No privacy in the near future.

"Where are my father and grandfather?" he asked.

"Hatch is in your truck," Restin replied. "The smoke was getting to him. Parker thought he might be better off in the truck. Rand is with him."

Made sense. The smoke bothered Ethan, and he was fifty years younger.

"Selena has invited us all to stay with her pack in the old town." He didn't add the invitation had come reluctantly.

"How much of the pack is still around?" Restin asked.

"We've always been a smaller pack," Selena hedged.

"Fifteen, give or take," Ethan added.

"Is their old town inhabitable?" Restin continued to ignore Selena.

"By some standards," Ethan answered.

"I'm standing right here," Selena snapped. "Our old town is fine. It's safe. Right now, my pack needs the familiar."

"You had vampires after you last night," Ethan reminded her. "I could still smell them this morning. If you consider being stalked by the undead safe, you and I have vastly different definitions."

Of many things.

No. Forbidden territory, at least for now. He needed to pretend what she'd confessed didn't matter.

"Nobody mentioned vampires," Restin said.

"We have stakes." Selena sounded weary, hoarse from regurgitating her secrets to Ethan.

"Anything else?" he'd asked her.

"Isn't rape enough?"

She'd been right. Rape was enough. More than enough. Thank the Ancient Ones numbness had set in. If his head reeled any more, he might not have made his way back to Ulvskog.

"Do you have stakes on you right now?"

Ethan didn't care for Restin's tone of voice. "Respect my mate when you speak to her."

"You forget yourself, theta," Restin bit out.

"You forget yourself, *beta*. Mates are off limits."

"I'm going to find some stakes," Parker muttered before he melted into the dark fringe of forest.

"Great idea." Dakota followed suit.

"Have your female sit with your father," Restin suggested.

"My female is alpha. She sits where she wishes."

"Alpha of what?" Restin waved his arms at the smoking ruins of a village void of lycans.

Selena growled, low and menacing.

"Impressive. Does she want a pissing contest?"

Ethan leapt toward Restin. Someone tackled him before he connected with his target.

"Watch it," his father muttered against his ear. "Restin provokes so he can punish. Don't fall into his trap."

"He insulted my mate." Ethan struggled. Red shaded the edges of his vision. "He gets away with too much. Tokarz should have ended him years ago."

"Tokarz, not you. Besides, Selena is alpha. She can take care of herself. And if she can't? She doesn't deserve to be alpha."

Selena was vulnerable right now. And didn't need Restin, Dad, or anyone giving her more grief than she piled on herself.

"If your beta can't cut leadership in Loup Garou, he's not going to perform with the Varulv, either." Selena had regained her swagger. "He can't give solace to the grieving. He can't rejuvenate a dying pack. Let him hold Addy's hand as she brings her new babe into this crazy, messed-up world. Let him lead instead of insult."

So, she still pretended all was well. A front to the world. Not to him. Him, she let see the naked, ugly truth.

THE SEVEN WEREWOLVES TROD single file, stakes at the ready, as Selena led the way to the old town. She assigned Restin to bring up the rear. The nocturnal animals who dwelled in the woods accepted the lycan presence. Even in human form, the lycans stepped lightly. Cautiously. Owls occasionally hooted. Lightning bugs flickered in the bushes. Other creatures scrambled in the overhead branches. The scent of smoke lingered on the air.

Ethan focused on his father and grandfather who hiked ahead of him, directly behind Selena. He gripped his stake tightly, concerned the wood might snap beneath the pressure of his fingers.

When they reached Gambayan, they found the survivors huddled outside the bulkiest mound. A quick head count verified Ethan's estimate. Twelve. Thirteen until he'd killed the would-be traitor earlier. Sapiens claimed thirteen was an unlucky number. Good riddance.

"The moon makes me feel safe," a hugely pregnant female answered when Selena asked why they were not in one of the shelters.

"A glow in the sky and the smell of smoke drew us out," a man explained.

"You shouldn't have been outside breathing in the pollution," Selena told the pregnant one.

"I needed the moon."

"She's fine," the old healer affirmed.

Ethan's grandfather tensed before sliding deeper into the shadows.

"I see you, *Hache-Hi Yenal*," Olivia called. "Did you think I wouldn't recognize you after all these years?"

"Olivia Hagtorn. Are you trying to get an old man killed?" Pa snarled.

Selena caught a look between them. "You two know each other?"

"From a before time." Olivia sounded sad.

"From another time when a Congressman Peters tried to eliminate a pack of lycans."

"You were never our kind, Limmikin," Olivia retorted.

"Someone want to explain to me what's going on?" Restin clearly hated being left out of any discussion.

"No." Ethan frowned at Parker, hoping he would keep his alpha theories to himself. The last thing anyone needed was Restin challenging someone for top dog status.

"You don't believe murdering the Varulv is the same as annihilating the Limmikin?" Pa wanted to know.

"Limmikin never had a treaty with the government. Varulv do."

"The government wants to break the treaties," Selena stated.

A few members of her pack gasped.

Ethan was surprised her grandfather kept the plan from them. Tokarz had freely shared the uncertainty with the Loup Garou.

"Why?" Others echoed Olivia's question.

"Does anyone understand the new administration?" Pa asked. "My grandson's description of what happened to Ulvskog matches what happened to Oneka. Luckily, my mate and I escaped being slaughtered."

"Others survived," Olivia said. "Not many. A few."

"Where are they now?" Pa's left eyebrow rose nearly to his hairline.

"They dispersed. Without their alpha to give them direction, they didn't know what to do."

Pa snorted, then spat. "The Varulv didn't take us in."

Olivia didn't answer.

"Channing Wolfe led Peters' army to Oneka," Pa reminded Olivia.

"The Limmikin were traitors," she whispered.

"The Limmikin were minding their own business!" Pa shouted. "We are not the ones who betrayed the existence of the *homo lupus* to the government. We are not the ones who crawled on our bellies and begged for treaties to keep us safe. This was our land. We asked only to be left alone."

"Wait." The hoarseness returned to Selena's voice. "Are you saying this male, Ethan's grandfather, is a lycan alpha?"

"*Hache-Hi Yenal* is the alpha of the native Limmikin pack, yes," Olivia confirmed.

"Hatch Calhoun," Restin repeated for clarification.

Yenal. Ethan mentally tried the name on his tongue. *Yenal* fit. Tasted good.

"The Limmikin pack no longer exists. They were murdered." Pa clung to his story. "I am no alpha."

"Rand Calhoun is of alpha descent?" Restin continued. "That makes Ethan—"

"I told you so," Parker hollered from the edge of the woods.

Selena stared at Ethan. "You're alpha?"

Ethan hadn't given Parker's hypothesis much consideration. "I'm not sure," he replied. What if he didn't want to be alpha? He'd been content as a theta his entire life. He hadn't been raised to be alpha.

"Selena's mate is your grandson?" Olivia asked. "I recognized the Limmikin in him. I should have sensed he belonged to you."

"So you could knife him in the back?"

"When we couldn't find your body, we prayed to the gods of our elders for your escape."

Pa made a rude noise.

Olivia had been creeping closer to Pa. Now she got in his face. "I was your brother's mate, *Hache-Hi*. I was a good mate."

"You don't use the Yenal name. You still call yourself Hagtorn."

"Using his name could get me killed but wouldn't resurrect him. Besides, you don't use the name anymore, either."

THE SMALL MOUND ETHAN, his father, and grandfather claimed for themselves offered only shelter from the night and an illusion of privacy.

Ethan tried to wrap his brain around the idea Selena's Old Olivia was his aunt. *My great aunt.*

"Why all the secrecy?" Dad asked Pa.

"Have you ever seen bodies ripped to shreds by bullets?" Pa countered.

"I spotted Channing Wolfe's severed finger floating in a puddle of his blood," Ethan stated. "I noticed his brains spattered against the wall of his home. I saw babies, toddlers, pre-teens, blasted into pieces. I stood inside the buildings you helped burn today."

"And if you were on the list to be next, would you stick around?"

"Why did you never tell us?" Ethan wondered.

Pa snickered. "The Creator must be laughing, making the granddaughter of Channing Wolfe the mate of the grandson of a man he wanted dead."

Selena needed to hear what Pa had to say.

"The Creator has his reasons. I have to admit, I had a secret chuckle when you first told me your mate was Varulv." Pa closed his eyes. "I can call the Creator by his name again."

I can't tell you what she's been through.

"You need to go to her," Pa said. "You need to mark her. To seal the dictates of the Creator."

I'm afraid to touch her. She's fragile.

Ethan struggled not to choke. He reached into his pocket for the broken tone bar and pulled out the pieces.

Bryant and Liam Peters tried to destroy Selena. Tried to destroy the future of the Varulv, the same way Bryant and possibly his father before him had taken on the Limmikin.

Ending a pack's alpha lineage was one way to annihilate the future. If invalidating the heiress wouldn't work, eradicating them the way the Limmikin had been wiped out might.

Why was someone trying to rid Minnesota of the werewolf packs? The lycan population served the government. Yet someone had to be threatened by their existence. The Ancient Ones were undermining the enemy's effort. By joining Ethan to Selena, the grandchildren of the pack alphas, a new, stronger pack could be formed.

Whoa.

He was the grandson of an alpha. The drastic change in status would take some getting used to. He appreciated why old Bernard Garnier made Pa a theta. He didn't want the threat of an equal male.

"Why did you meekly accept such a low status in the Loup Garou pack?" Ethan asked.

"To make sure my line would survive. Pride at being an alpha doesn't do anyone any good if they're dead."

SELENA STOOD OUTSIDE THE cabin the Calhoun males had claimed as their own. She understood they needed time to talk. They had to acclimate to the secrets Ethan's grandfather had been keeping. Her matters were more pressing.

She'd attempted to voice her concerns to Restin, except he was so full of himself, she'd rather rip out his throat than continue the conversation. He wanted to seize control from her. While the pack's current mess might be entirely her doing, surrendering leadership to some lobo she'd just met wasn't an option. Some lobo who had clearly never suffered loss of the magnitude the Varulv had seen in her lifetime alone. Some lobo whose arrogance didn't win him any leeway with her pack.

Ethan was another story. An unnerving story.

You need to go to her, his grandfather said. *You need to mark her. To seal the dictates of the Creator.*

His grandfather, as much an alpha in his pack as her own had been in his, urged Ethan to fulfill his destiny.

She wanted Ethan's council. He'd earned her pack's respect by his actions. By his unquestioning allegiance to her. Although the decimated pack didn't need to lose another male, Philip's defiance had to be handled. Harshly. Ethan had obeyed.

She tried to convince herself Philip's grief over the loss of his mate and offspring created his treachery. He'd been hurting. He'd divined her role in their deaths.

Ethan should have been her mate by now. Seeking his counsel was only natural.

She didn't mean to eavesdrop.

"*. . . Being an alpha doesn't do anyone any good if they're dead.*"

The old wisdoms filled Ethan's grandfather.

Being an alpha meant nothing if no one remained to lead.

Selena had overheard the others in her pack talking. Only twelve had joined her. Other Varulv cowered in the forest. Afraid of her. Her leadership. Before knowing she'd made an arrogant error.

Rumors she met her mate had gotten around, thanks to Gramps. The pack sensed Ethan had yet to mark her. If she was unwilling to work toward a future, why should they? Or maybe Ethan, merely a lobo from Loup Garou, found her unworthy.

The realization weighed on her. The Varulv deserved a future. As did the Limmikin. The gods of her elders had to have a plan when they brought the exiled alpha heir back to his land. Back to her. Old Olivia was right.

Selena understood she had to take the next step.

She rapped on the doorpost.

The males stopped talking. Ethan said, "Come in, Selena."

How long had he been aware of her presence? She entered the cramped space. The combined body heat of the three males banished the earthborn chill.

"We need to make a plan," she started, feeling awkward and intrusive. "I need to make a plan," she corrected. "I'd like your input." She spoke directly to Ethan.

"Of course." He spoke as if he grasped how difficult this request was for her to make. He always understood. Maybe empathy was part of the mated state.

He patted the ground next to him. She sat.

"Do you mind my father and grandfather being in on the conversation?" He toyed with two cylindrical pieces of silver metal that looked as if he'd snapped them off something.

She swallowed the last of her pride. "No. I would welcome the counsel of the Limmikin alpha."

"I have never been alpha," Ethan's grandfather—*Hatch*—said. He punctuated the statement with a grunt. "The Limmikin are no more. At least, not in northern Minnesota."

"You're sitting here with your son and grandson. By my count three Limmikin still exist." She didn't have the nerve to point out she was Ethan's mate, which would technically bring her into the Limmikin fold. She couldn't read Ethan's reaction.

She braced herself for well-deserved verbal abuse.

"I am," Hatch agreed. "I never imagined I would see this day, sitting in my enemy's magic circle."

"The Varulv aren't your enemy," she blurted.

"They are. From the day the first Varulv arrived, they claimed the territory given to the Limmikin by the Creator. After they joined forces with the ruling sapiens to exterminate us, we abandoned the notion of peaceful co-existence. What happened to the Varulv three days ago is what happened to the Limmikin fifty years ago."

Selena listened with respect and an open heart.

"Except the Varulv were the ones toting the guns."

Okay, maybe not such an open mind. "I can't reconcile the grandfather who raised me with someone who would murder an entire pack. And with sapien weapons? No."

"The Varulv have a government treaty. Service for sanctuary. The Garniers blather treaty talk constantly. It's their favorite topic of conversation," Hatch continued. "If then-Congressman Peters ordered your grandfather to rid the district of the uncontrollable Limmikin, what would he have done?"

Selena swallowed her rising nausea and dug her fingers into the loamy floor. The rich scent of decaying foliage filled the mound. "He would have honored the treaty," she whispered.

"I've spent many years reminiscing, and I agree. Channing Wolfe owed the Limmikin. He paid them with betrayal." Hatch stared at the ground. "We allowed his ancestors to settle in Limmikin territory. *We* were the true givers of sanctuary. We believed the Varulv would join with us to keep the homo sapiens out. They broke their promise."

"Instead, you were given your own blood."

"We gave our lives. As far as I know, I, my mate, our son, and grandson are the only Limmikin of our pack left. Olivia Hagtorn returned to the Varulv without ever giving my brother offspring."

"Why did you go to Loup Garou instead of finding another Limmikin pack?" Ethan asked, as he rolled the steel bits between his knuckles.

The soil wedged under Selena's fingernails. She pushed aside her shame to listen.

"I hid. If the native shifters were being exterminated here, how could I trust systematic termination wasn't happening everywhere?" Hatch's face mapped a life of sadness. "No, hiding among a pack who had treaties was safer than with one who did not. Our refusal to agree to treaties made us undesirable. Why should we ask for sanctuary in our own land? We had no need for treaties."

"The treaties have proven false," Selena said. "False treaties are why we're sitting in the old town tonight, inhaling the ashes of Ulvskog."

"We should all move to Warwick tomorrow," Ethan suggested.

"What?" Selena sat straighter. She flicked nodes of moss from her fingers. "Warwick?"

"To my house."

She doubted he noticed her, since his unfocused stare bypassed her, the walls of the old town structure, and the ancient magic shielding Gambayan. "Warwick will be safer. The house has built-in vampire protection."

"We can't assume vampires are still after us," Selena protested. She *thought* she'd scented them; there had been no actual sighting since the original attack.

The anonymous caller who had traced her didn't necessarily know where she was.

"Oh, they're around," Ethan said. "They're aware survivors of the massacre are regrouping."

"They heard us moon singing. Why didn't they attack us then?"

Rand and Hatch, on the periphery of her vision, each reacted.

Ethan focused on her. "I'm too ignorant of vampire lore to answer."

"There used to be respect between blood guzzlers and shifters." Hatch sounded older than her grandfather. "Attacking a shifter on the new moon would be the same as staking a vampire at high noon."

"You make vampire killing sound like a bad thing," Selena said.

Hatch glared at her. "The problem with you younger ones is you don't appreciate courtesy."

"The need to survive trumps manners," Selena snapped. If anyone knew the truth, she was that lycan. "If I was planning an attack, you'd better believe I'd go after shifters on the new moon. We can defend ourselves better on the full moon. We can't defend ourselves at all on a new moon."

"Okay." Ethan's impatience was palpable. "They figured they would lose if they attacked on the full moon. We've barricaded ourselves in magic circles, hoping to prevent attacks when we're not in full moon mode."

"They made a mistake," Hatch said. "You lived. You both lived. You did what you needed to do."

"Stay alive," Selena muttered.

"Stay alive," Hatch echoed and lifted his chin. His dark eyes, so like Ethan's, glittered in the dim light.

"Did Peters sic vampires on you?" Selena asked him.

"I would have smelled them."

Yeah. Werewolves could scent the rotting blood of vampires far too easily. A natural, built-in defense against blood suckers.

"So, we're agreed we head to Warwick come daylight." Ethan tried for an answer again.

"The house isn't big enough."

"We're pack creatures," Ethan reminded her. "Everyone can sleep in the basement."

Her workshop space. Selena wanted to argue. Except the house belonged to him. She swallowed her hurt. Told herself to stop being ridiculous. She'd meant Night Shift to be a way to help the pack survive. The space belonged to Night Shift. The remnants of her pack needed sanctuary. Ethan was right, the survivors should use the space meant to ensure their survival.

"Good plan." She hoped no one noticed the croak in her voice.

Ethan did, judging by the way he narrowed his eyes at her.

She dug her fingers deeper into the moss and kept her eyes on him. "This is why I wanted your input." She wasn't subservient. A good leader always sought and listened to counsel. If she'd asked before she'd gone to the congressman's office, she might have averted the disaster.

If she wanted to be a brat, she could blame the whole catastrophe on Ethan. Had he arrived at Congressman Peters' office only half an hour earlier, he could have prevented her from going inside.

If her impetuous threat never crossed her lips, if she never tried to blackmail the congressman into voting to maintain the werewolf treaties, she and Ethan would not be hosting members of the Loup Garou pack and would not be mourning the massacre of her own.

Chapter 17

Selena locked herself in the basement bathroom as soon as she returned to Warwick and the house on Ash. She needed privacy to call Britt. If Britt was still speaking to her. They hadn't parted on the best of terms. "Can I see you? Meet you somewhere? Your place?"

Ethan had tried to stress how dangerous leaving the house would be. Broad daylight might prevent vampires from coming after her, although assassins with guns wouldn't care about the hour. The lycans kept their return to Warwick low-key. No one knew she was in town. Besides, rain dripped from the sky. Sapiens hated inclement weather, including, she hoped, mercenaries.

She didn't want Britt at the house for many reasons. Ethan didn't need to know her plans. Yet. The remnants of her pack were ensconced on Ash Street. Ethan and the other Loup Garou lycans were busy converting the space meant for manufacturing the Night Shift line into living quarters for what remained of the Varulv. Yes, seeing her pack sheltered and safe was her responsibility. The basement room's intent had been to support the pack. Now everything was upside down and backward. Who knew what was going to happen next?

Only the bathrooms provided privacy. She couldn't tie up one with so many others in residence. Besides, Ethan was busy. He wouldn't notice if she were gone.

"My roommate is home." Britt sounded pissy. Britt excelled at being pissy. "How important is it?"

"I need your advice on how to handle Ethan. You know, the hot country music guy I'm currently living with."

"This better be good," Britt grumbled.

"I promise, you'll be glad you did."

"You could always give him my phone number."

"What part of 'he's off-limits' don't you get?" Selena struggled to keep the flare of jealousy out of her voice. Out of her blood.

"This better be good," Britt repeated. "Spectacularly good. Why can't we meet at your house?"

"Ethan's here, and I don't want to risk him overhearing me. And we have company. A houseful." Her face heated. Thankfully no one was in the room to see her embarrassment. "Meet me at the park, at the band gazebo."

"It's raining."

"It's only sprinkling. Please. I'm begging you. I don't have anyone else I can ask."

Britt heaved a sigh. "All right, all right. You owe me."

"Lunch?"

"Details." Britt's snigger contained evil undertones.

Selena's face burned hotter. "Okay." She hoped she wouldn't regret asking for her friend's advice.

BRITT WAS LATE. SELENA worried she'd been stood up. The gazebo didn't provide protection from the weather. The cold rain didn't bother her. The gods of her elders were weeping for her.

Selena used the time to second-guess telling Ethan she'd been assaulted while hiding the rest of the story from him.

Britt arrived fifteen minutes late. She tossed her rain jacket hood off her hair. "This better be good."

"So you keep saying. I need your advice."

"So you said."

"How do I seduce Ethan?"

Britt's eyes widened. She plopped on the wet bench lining the gazebo's interior, as if shock stole her strength. Her lips formed a circle before she spoke. "Oh, this *is* good. What made you change your mind? Why do you need to seduce him? He *so* into you. All you need to do is crook your pinkie."

"He found out something I'd done and distanced himself." She missed him. She missed their moonlight talks. His kisses. Oh, she missed his kisses. She sat next to Britt. "I don't know where to begin."

"If he's a normal guy, all you need to do is show up naked with a six pack."

"Six pack?"

"Of beer."

Right. She should have remembered Britt's males from her college days. "I want to be subtler. I want to seduce *him*, not his body."

Britt squinted at her. "If it's a guy, it's sex. His body. There is no person behind his dick."

"Okay. He has a great body. I want his body. I want his body to want me."

I need him to mark me. I want to be tied to him forever. I need to make the babies the Varulv need to survive. I nearly destroyed the pack. I have to do whatever I can to help build the population. I have to let Ethan mark me.

"This is awkward," Britt complained. "I've never had to explain the basics before."

"Oh, please. Sex is your favorite topic. You're the one who wants details. How can I relay details if I don't know what I'm doing?"

"Okay." Britt brushed a strand of wet hair off her cheek. "Guys like blow jobs."

Selena couldn't process what she meant. "You blow on them?"

"You go down on them."

"Go down where?"

Britt rolled her eyes. "Didn't you ever make out with a boy in high school? I know you were the Virgin Mary in college, but come on, Selena. Have you ever kissed a guy?"

A gust of wind blew a battalion of raindrops onto Selena's back. "Not until Ethan kissed me," she admitted. "All I know about sex, I learned from rooming with you."

"Honey, a guy like Ethan, on the road with fan girls crawling into his bed, isn't going to appreciate a fumbling newbie."

Selena bit back her sharp retort. "Ethan isn't the same as the guys you pick up in bars." Maintaining a steady tone wasn't easy when she really wanted to pin Britt against the gazebo rail and scream the truth in her face. Except she couldn't alienate her.

There were no other females she could ask. Women from her own culture wouldn't have to seduce a mate. They would tell her to relax and enjoy whatever happened. Her answers had to come from Britt.

"I won't be a fumbling newbie if you tell me what to do," she snarled. "I don't have a mother. Or a grandmother or aunts or sisters or cousins. You're supposed to be my best friend."

In a softer tone, she played her sympathy card. "My grandfather died a few days ago."

"Oh, honey, I'm sorry." Britt touched her arm. "Why didn't you call me? When is the wake? Calling hours?"

"He wanted to be cremated. No fuss." If only all facts were as easily twisted.

Britt hugged her. "The rituals aren't for the dead. They're meant to comfort the living. Was your Ethan at least around to help you?"

"Yeah."

"And he didn't offer to—" Britt coughed before completing her question—"*comfort* you?"

"Do you mean have sex with me? Yeah." *Maybe.* "I declined."

"Oh, you poor thing." Britt hugged Selena again. "And now you want to let him know you're interested. Okay. Let's start with the basics."

Selena sagged in relief.

ETHAN HAD BEEN LURKING by the front door ever since he noticed Selena was missing. His nose wasn't good enough to track her in the rain.

Though he needed to process everything she'd told him, he understood why she'd sneaked out. He considered it himself. Distance should calm his hormones. She didn't need another male attacking her.

But she should have stayed in the house.

Liam Peters had traced her to Ash Street. He knew Selena was lycan. Someone could be surveilling the house. Selena could have been followed. Ethan's protective instincts were going guano crazy.

"Where have you been? And don't try to tell me you weren't out." He blocked her path.

"I won't." She was a mess. Her brindle hair, loose and wet, clung to her face and neck. She hadn't worn a raincoat. Her flannel shirt molded to her body. Her nipples were tight and prominent.

He forced himself to look elsewhere.

"Yes, I went out. I needed some alone time. Excuse me, I need to change." She brushed past him.

Ethan hurried after her.

The door snicked shut behind him. "I'm moving in with you." He addressed her hunched shoulders. "In case you were curious why my duffel is in here. Dad and Pa are in my room—Pa is conveniently claiming his alpha heritage, so Restin is stuck on the sleeper sofa. He wants us to move the sofa to the third bedroom. I said no. We need the seating."

Exiling Restin to the pullout in a public room was funny.

"We're trying to figure out what to do with the roadies and the Varulv in the basement," Ethan continued. "Everyone considers us mated anyway."

"No, the plan makes sense." She stripped off her wet shirt. The garment landed on the floor with a sodden plop.

Her white cotton turtleneck didn't reveal much. He learned she wore another shirt when the turtleneck joined the flannel on the floor. A wet, white tank top. The thicker fabric fit her much nicer than his tank top fit him. Of course, her contours were much more interesting.

His throat tightened. His mouth dried. "Where did you go?"

"To the park." She lifted the hem of her tank top. The motion exposed the smooth, pale skin on the small of her back. Unadorned skin. Every woman whose back he'd seen—honkytonk angels, every one—had a tattoo at the base of her spine. A tramp stamp. Selena's back was pure. He concentrated on counting her vertebrae, as she slipped her bra off her shoulders. Why was she stripping in front of him?

The bra plopped onto the pile of wet clothes.

She strolled toward the closet, her arm blocking his view, but not before he glimpsed the side of her breast, the flash of a dark pink nipple.

"How are we going to feed everyone?" she asked as she pulled a dry tank top from the plastic bag holding her wardrobe.

He'd seen breasts before. Breasts were for nurturing babies. His penis shouldn't be stirring in his jeans. Besides, he was still trying to figure out how to handle everything she'd told him.

"I hadn't considered food." Ethan tried to avert his eyes as she tugged the shirt over her head. The magnet of her body sabotaged his steel will. He sat on the edge of the bed, his back toward her. Her reflection in the window confronted him. She caught him staring at her and smiled.

Or did she?

Selena sure took her time getting dressed. Pink turtleneck, a pink plaid flannel shirt. She looked good in pink.

At least she was covered as she toed off her tennis shoes and socks. When the snap at the top of her jeans popped open, he struggled not to choke. He gripped the bedclothes in his fists. His fingers penetrated the fabric as Selena peeled the wet denim from her legs. Her very, very fine legs. Legs he wanted wrapped around his waist.

She bent to paw through the plastic bag holding her dry clothes. Her white underpants might as well have been transparent. He couldn't have imagined a finer ass. He could lunge across the bed, free his cock, grasp her hips, and claim her.

His alpha blood was as good as hers.

Then an image she'd planted in him wiped away his lust. A young girl, forced to bend over a desk while a person she'd trusted violated and betrayed her. Her cries for help falling on uncaring ears.

By the time the rage cleared from his head, Selena was dressed and brushing the tangles from her hair.

He had to do, say something. Something distracting. Otherwise, he wouldn't be responsible for his actions.

"How much walleye is left?" he blurted.

"Not a lot. I'd planned to restock when I was home for the full moon." Her tone was bland. Neutral. "We'll figure out something. Maybe we can raid a Hy-Vee or Cub's for meat and eggs. Or Helga will bring another hot dish. We could have a welcome to the neighborhood potluck."

"Potluck?"

"Where sapiens get together for a meal and bring a hot dish to pass." She sat on the bed next to him. "How do you not know this?"

He inched away, so her hip didn't brush his. "My interaction with sapiens consists of being a federal agent at times. And in honky-tonks. I've never mingled with them socially. Are you sure a potluck is a good idea? I don't want the neighbors to know how much company we have."

"As you pointed out, they're safer here than in the woods. Congressman Peters wouldn't dare send an army of vigilantes into a city to wipe out a house full of werewolves."

"The congressman would dare anything," Ethan reminded her. "He could twist anything. He has professional liars communicating with his constituency. And the Peters know we're living on Ash Street. The son showed up while you were still in Ulvskog. He could say we're terrorists. A religious cult stockpiling weapons. He could justify firebombing the place and killing us all."

"We've talked this to death. The woods gave the Peters false courage."

He wanted to shout at her, ask her if she trusted her judgment concerning the congressman and his son. "I'm going to kill them."

"Their deaths are my privilege," she replied. "You can help. That's what mates do. Help."

They weren't true mates yet. For some reason the limbo status didn't matter. They would be sharing the room for the foreseeable future. He planned to use a bedroll on the floor, so he wouldn't accidentally, in his sleep, give instinct the upper hand. If she wanted to believe all she needed was help from him to destroy the Peters dynasty, fine.

"I know you have your own reasons for wanting to destroy them," Selena continued in a low voice. "I respect your need. They murdered your true pack. They stole your grandfather's heritage, your father's, and yours. And if I were any other female, I would shower you with the blessings of the gods of our elders for your revenge."

Scat. He hadn't included his family's past in his need to destroy the Peters. His rage focused entirely on what they'd done to Selena.

"*I* was the direct victim. *My* words and actions triggered events."

"You are not a victim. You are a survivor." Ethan remembered Luke repeating the same words to his mate on a regular basis after he'd found the nude photos of Abigail on the Internet. "You are not responsible for someone else's actions."

The length of Selena's thigh warmed his. He must have unconsciously slid closer. Ethan squirmed away, difficult to do without being obvious.

"Pretty words," she retorted.

He had to remind himself she'd lived with the memory of her assault for ten years. It wasn't fresh to her the way it was for him. Being matter-of-fact had to be a survival mechanism for her.

"We need to lay in supplies." She spoke as if they were discussing the weather. "Do you have any money left?"

All along, she'd questioned his finances. Her practicality impressed him. If he didn't want the lycans in the basement hunting the neighborhood pets, he needed to make sure they were fed.

Then it struck him. She wasn't fighting him. About anything. Other than sneaking out in defiance of his request, she was being placid and accommodating.

"We'll manage." If he had to blackmail Restin into chipping in to feed everyone, he would.

Selena waved enthusiastically to Helga, who veiled herself behind a lace curtain at her window. "We need to talk to her," Selena said as she clambered into Ethan's truck with a smile for Helga's benefit.

He climbed into the driver's side. "Why? She's nosy, she's human, and her food is awful." He jammed his key into the ignition.

"Nosy neighbors are what keep sapien neighborhoods safe." Selena loosened the shoulder strap against her throat. "They keep an eye on things."

"How do we explain the werewolves in the basement?"

"Why does she need an explanation? She only needs to know we have a lot of company staying with us right now."

"You seem to know a lot about humans," he muttered as the truck pulled away from the curb.

"I lived among humans while I was in college. My best friend is sapien."

"I'm surprised," he admitted. "Knowing what I do now."

"Brittany was never going to assault me. I didn't always feel secure with some of the guys she brought to our room, but I couldn't let fear dictate my life."

"So you enrolled in krav maga."

"I took some self-defense courses for women first. Eventually I found krav maga. I'm more confident. Go left at the next light. If I recall, Hy-Vee is a couple of miles up."

Ethan made the turn, glancing in his rearview mirror as he did.

"Krav maga explains why you weren't afraid to confront Liam Peters and his father in the Congressman's office."

"Right."

"Are you afraid now?"

"No. I'm regretful. Mostly, though, I'm furious." All true. Baring her soul to her soulmate relieved a lot of the pressure she'd been putting on herself.

"You shouldn't be afraid. I won't let anything happen to you."

Hadn't he been listening? She wasn't afraid.

Ethan made a sudden left turn. Selena clutched the grab handle above the door to keep from sliding out of her seatbelt. He definitely wasn't listening. "What are you doing? Hy-Vee is on the other street."

"We're being followed. Black pickup."

"Better paranoid than sorry," she muttered, more to herself than to him, as he made a U-turn in the middle of an empty intersection.

"See if you can get the license plate number." Tires squealed on the pavement.

The windows were smeary with raindrops on the outside and condensation from their conversation on the interior. Besides, Ethan drove too fast.

"Sorry," she said. The truck resembled every other black pickup on the road. She didn't recognize one make or model from the other.

"He's behind us again. This is vamp-scat." Ethan veered sharply without warning, swerving into another direction.

"I don't know if there's a supermarket or a meat market this way."

"Doesn't matter. I found our favorite congressman's office."

Wait a minute.

"What gives you the idea I'm eager to see them?" She couldn't keep the spurt of panic from her voice. She'd been doing so well, too, trying not to come off as needy, craving reassurance. A she-wolf could only take so much.

"I'm letting them know we're aware they're plotting something," Ethan replied.

"I'll bet they guessed without any clues from you."

"I'm making sure."

"I have no need to prove anything to them right now." She gripped the grab handle tighter as Ethan took corners too closely, sliding on the rain-slicked pavement. "I want to get my people fed, clothed, bedded, and secure enough to defend themselves. Making us roadkill is not the way to provide for them."

"You don't trust me?"

"Pay attention to the road. I trust you with my life. I'm in this truck with you right now, aren't I?"

His low chuckle sent chills to attack her spine.

Maybe she spoke too soon. The black truck drew closer to them. Really close. Ethan could have reached out his window and grabbed the other vehicle's door handle. Selena expected to hear the scrape of metal on metal, to feel a jolt of impact.

As soon as the congressman's office building came into view, the black truck pulled ahead, sounding like the engine choked on its own exhaust. A bright blue loop of rope swayed from a wooden post in the back.

Ethan drove past the building slowly, as if counting the lighted windows. He drove around the block before parking at the curb in front of the building.

"We have a house full of hungry werewolves," Selena reminded him. "I don't want them going after the neighbors' pets."

"Punking either Liam or Bryant Peters—or both—won't take long. Keep an eye on the fourth-floor windows."

The fourth floor. Where Congressman Peters had his office.

Sure enough, not many minutes passed before the edge of one blind tilted a fraction, an example of how the congressman didn't grasp the lycan world. Maybe a sapien wouldn't have seen the twitch. To Selena, the flick was as clear as the silvery rain streaking the window.

"We've been reported and spotted," she said. "Now what?"

"We confront them."

"No!" His suggestion panicked her. She wasn't ready. She'd barely managed threatening Bryant Peters when her grandfather sent her to try to negotiate the treaty vote.

Remind him, Gramps had advised. He'd meant remind him how Selena's father had lost his life doing the congressman's bidding. Instead, she'd reminded Bryant Peters and his scat-eating son of another night, when another Wolfe lost something to the Peters family.

"They shouldn't be allowed to get away with trying to intimidate us."

"Trying?" Her voice cracked with pending hysteria. "News flash, Ethan. They arranged for the slaughter of my pack. According to your grandfather, they did the same thing to his pack. I would say their actions have far surpassed mere intimidation."

"They have to pay."

"And they will. But we need to be as cunning as our long-ago ancestors. We've lost our edge. Right now, it's Advantage Peters. They're having us followed. They know we survived and are right outside the congressman's office as I speak."

"You. They know *you* survived. They aren't aware my grandparents escaped or two more generations of Limmikin exist."

Consisting of one lycan each.

Why was she spouting strategy? Her last attempt nearly annihilated her pack.

"We need a better plan than confronting them. We need to prioritize. Right now, I have a pack to feed. We lost everything when we burned the town. Only the ones who'd hidden their clothes in the forest before their shift have things to wear. I need to tend to my pack before I satisfy my own need for revenge."

She struggled to sound virtuous and in control as she spoke the words. The alleged tasks were great shields from the truth, that she couldn't face Liam and the Congressman. Not together. Mating fever, and the guilt of knowing her words prompted the congressman to murder innocents, made her too vulnerable.

"Don't you get it?" Ethan drummed his thumbs against the steering wheel. "They're having us followed. They could stage an accident. A drive-by shooting. Any number of things could happen, and the Peters Dynasty would get away with murder."

"They already have," she pointed out. "Varulv and Limmikin. Two packs."

"No. The survivors, the witnesses in both instances are ready for justice."

"Retribution needs to be on our terms," she countered. "The moment has to be our choice."

"Then when?"

"We'll know when the time is right. We have to trust the gods of our elders."

"Trusting the gods of your elders didn't help your grandfather and the others," he reminded her.

"What happened was my doing."

"You keep saying you're to blame. Bryant and Liam Peters raping you is not something you did."

Although her insides cringed, she was proud she betrayed no outer reaction. "Maybe I'm referring to something else," she admitted, as she pulled her cell phone from her pocket.

"Who are you calling?" Ethan's tone could have shredded the truck's tires.

Selena ignored him. The Congressman's voice mail answered. "This is Selena Wolfe. Please pick up."

ETHAN WANTED TO SNATCH the phone from her hand and toss it out the truck window. He observed her closely as she waited for someone to answer. Past her shoulder, he was keenly aware of the door to the office building. The overhead security lights spilled their bluish illumination onto the rain-slicked sidewalk, a smeared reflection of shapeless blobs. He smelled wet pavement, tarry and thick in his nostrils.

He needed so much from Selena, starting with the truth. Yes, she'd trusted him with the story of her assault, and both Peters males would pay for what they'd done. However, parts of her story remained untold. Something else nourished her guilt.

"Liam," she said, shattering Ethan's focus. "I'm concerned about a black truck following me. I took photos on my phone and sent them to the police. Should I do anything else to ensure my safety?"

What a good liar.

"No, I'm not meeting with you tonight. Maybe tomorrow." She averted her head. Ethan could see only the reflection of her face, blurry in the fogged-over window glass. Her eyes were squeezed shut, the rest of her features twisted in an emotion he couldn't define. "Where?"

Ethan wanted to grip the steering wheel to keep from grabbing her phone. His track record for breaking items stopped him.

"I trusted you once, Liam," she said. "My mistake. Now we're enemies, and nothing you can do will make me hate you less." She listened briefly. "Meet you alone? What makes you think I'm suicidal? You want to talk to me face-to-face, you set up a meeting during regular business hours when there are witnesses. And yes. I am calling you a murderer."

Enough was enough. Ethan took Selena's phone from her and disconnected the call. He resisted the temptation to shatter it. "Are you out of your mind?" he whispered hoarsely, as if the phone was still active and could carry his voice to the fourth floor.

"Yeah."

He didn't know what to say.

"I'm tired," she said. "I'm tired of the prison the rapist congressman and his rapist son have erected around me. I'm tired of losing people to treaties these yakked-up hairballs don't honor anyway."

Her voice cracked. Her lips settled into a stern, harsh line. "I want the life I was promised. All this vamp-scat ends now."

"You just gave Peters more time to prepare yet another trap."

"Then let's leave. If they're smart they'll try to out think us. Except our brains don't work the same. It's our chance to make them nervous."

Ethan's smile formed gradually, as if weighing the wisdom of her words and finding them worthy.

"Besides, we have a pack of hungry werewolves in our basement."

His smile widened. "They do need to be fed."

Chapter 18

The surviving Varulv fell on the food like the pack of wolves they often were. Selena and Ethan purchased as much red meat as they could afford. The males discussed organizing a fishing trip as they tore into the raw beef. Ethan hid a couple of rump roasts to give the Loup Garou pack something to eat other than the never-ending walleye.

At least the rain stopped. Several of Selena's pack took refuge in the back yard, prowling along the hawthorn hedge as if they were prisoners seeking an escape.

"Being in the city is tough on them," Selena noted.

Ethan wasn't an urban lobo. Maybe years of bus tours with Toke Lobo and the Pack had inured him to being cooped up. Still, he understood the restlessness of Selena's pack.

Sympathizing didn't mean he had to like them cluttering his house. Werewolves posing as humans crammed the once-spacious rooms.

He wished he'd never suggested relocating to Warwick. Too much togetherness. While he was as much a pack animal as anyone else in the house, he also valued his personal space, long gone in the current circumstances. Nor were two and a half bathrooms working for twenty or so users.

Parker and Dakota had discussed finding someplace else to crash. Restin vetoed the idea. He wanted them on site. Ethan figured he needed someone to order around.

Tokarz should have sent someone other than Restin. Tokarz knew Pa's true standing; Ethan himself had told Tokarz of Selena's lineage.

Mating and fatherhood addled the alpha's brain.

"Are you ever going to claim your mate?" Restin asked after cornering Ethan on the back porch.

"Our relationship is between Selena and me." Ethan tried to sound serene.

"Yes and no. Her pack needs a reason to go on." Restin held up a hand as Ethan started to interrupt. "Yes, there's a gestating female. Hard to miss her. I'm talking about the pack alpha. Selena. You should be more desirable to her with your alpha heritage."

Ethan abandoned serenity and clenched his teeth. "I don't have any problem being desirable to my future mate." The intimacies he'd shared with Selena were none of Restin's business.

"Tell me another one."

"Why don't you go back to Loup Garou?" Ethan suggested.

"My alpha ordered me here. To help you."

"Yeah? Well, I don't need your help, so I'm ordering you back to Colorado."

"You don't have the status to order me." Restin's chin lifted. "You might be the future mate of the Varulv alpha, and your grandfather might have once inherited the Limmikin, but you haven't marked Selena, and there are no Limmikin, so no alpha is needed. You are a promise that won't be kept."

"We have nothing to do with who the Ancient Ones—the Creator—choses for our mate." Ethan bared his teeth. "Not that you have firsthand experience."

Nothing like a dig at Restin to make the day brighter.

Restin channeled serenity—or at least an arrogant version of calm. "I'll meet my mate when the time is right. In the meantime, why don't I have Luke send you—"

Ethan would have knocked Restin's jaw off his face if his father hadn't grabbed his arm. "Let go," Ethan growled, as he struggled to free himself.

"Nope," Dad said. "You called Tokarz and asked for help. He sent Restin. You're still part of Loup Garou."

If being part of Loup Garou meant enduring Restin's scat, Ethan wanted out. Now. Didn't matter if he'd marked Selena or not, if he claimed his Limmikin heritage or not.

"Luke would ignore any request from Restin anyway," Dad continued.

Random muscles in Restin's face twitched.

"Let me make one thing clear," Ethan growled, once his father released his arm. "Selena is the alpha of her pack, decimated as the Varulv may be. I am her designated mate. This is our home. You will not insult her. In any way. You will not disparage our relationship. In any way. And if I were you, I'd sleep with one eye open."

"Maybe you shouldn't have threatened Restin." Dad jiggled the back porch railing as if testing for sturdiness. "He's not one to let slights go."

Ethan lifted his chin. "Dad, I appreciate your advice, but I cannot allow him to treat Selena with the constant disrespect he's shown her. You raised me better than that."

The setting sun parted the clouds that had veiled most of the day. The orange glow glinted off the drops of rain still clinging to the grass. Behind him, the door opened. Pa joined them.

"The three of us could take Restin." Pa wadded his gnarled fingers into a fist and slammed it into the palm of his other hand.

Though Ethan approved of Pa's idea, before he could say anything, his father nixed the plan. "What's with you two? You're both acting like you just learned to shift and are going to terrorize the sapien neighborhood."

"Honor. There's been little enough honor around here." Pa punched his palm again.

A breeze ruffled the grass. Leftover rain pattered to the ground from the tree in the far corner.

The door opened again, and Old Olivia joined the trio.

No privacy, Ethan fumed. He wished the Varulv were in Ulvskog and the Loup Garou in Colorado. Then he remembered the ancient female was his great aunt by marriage.

She didn't beat around the bush. "You purchased this house for Selena?"

"Yes."

The old woman smiled. "You're smarter than I thought."

Ethan was still trying to figure out the insult when Pa spoke.

"You have no reason to speak to my grandson that way."

"Don't I?" Olivia waved her hands around the room. "This house...are you aware of its magic?"

He nodded. "It's vampire proof."

Olivia's eyes narrowed, the skin around them falling into well-worn grooves. *Old* Olivia? The female was ancient.

"The front is unprotected," Olivia pointed out.

"I'm guessing the whole block is safe." Ethan defended his choice. The bright orange house had seduced him. The structure met every one of his and Selena's needs and seemed to adjust itself as those needs changed.

Take now. Although the interior felt cramped, restless lobos could pace.

"I think you're right. This house has more." Olivia sounded thoughtful.

"The hedge—"

Olivia waved her hand, as if the tall, thorny barrier meant nothing. "You chose wisely, accidentally or not."

Selena paced. Glanced out the window where Ethan conversed with his father, grandfather, and Old Olivia. She didn't want to intrude. She wanted Ethan. Alone. She couldn't talk to him with witnesses. She needed to confess. She couldn't involve him in her revenge on Liam and Bryant Peters until she came clean about everything. Once he grasped the entire truth, he might not want to help her. As loath as she was to admit it, she needed him.

Britt's advice on how to seduce a male would only expunge a portion of her guilty secrets. Her sense of honor wouldn't let her continue until she'd purged her conscience.

Ethan stopped in the bedroom doorway, wishing he'd stayed outside talking with Dad and Pa. Selena stood bathed in the moon glow filtering through the window. She should have been asleep. He'd left his boots outside her door, hoping his steps wouldn't disturb her.

"Can't sleep?" he asked. He threw the blanket he carried to the floor.

"You were right. I do need to ditch the sapien schedule and embrace my nocturnal heritage." She spoke to his reflection in the glass.

She wasn't wearing her many shirts. Not one.

His gaze flickered lower, then shot back to meet the reflection of her eyes. Shirts weren't the only garments she lacked. His heart thudded heavily, awkwardly. "Um, should I come back when you're...ready for bed?"

She tilted her head. "I am ready for bed."

"I'd planned to make a bedroll near the closet." He gestured clumsily toward the floor.

"You don't need to sleep on the floor. We're supposed to be mates. The bed is plenty big enough for the two of us."

He closed his eyes and prayed to the Ancient Ones for strength. His jeans grew tighter. No matter how severely he scolded his body, one part refused to submit to his will. "Selena." Her name emerged as a growl.

"Yes?"

"I am not a self-disciplined lobo. My head...mating fever...I'm afraid of hurting you."

The moonlight dimmed, veiled by a cloud. Selena stopped glowing. The rise and fall of her breasts enticed him more strongly than words ever could. He tried to remember the many reasons why letting her game continue was a bad idea. His brain refused to cooperate.

She turned away from the window to face him. She wasn't wearing a stitch of human clothing.

"Planning to go for a midnight run?" he asked when his voice returned.

"No. Vampires, remember?"

"Do you usually sleep naked?" Another ungainly gesture, this time toward her.

She nodded, hesitated, shook her head. Her mouth opened, and he hoped she might speak. Instead, her tongue wet her lips.

Ethan diverted willpower to stifle a moan. He took a step back, although he continued to face her. "I'll give you some privacy until you're settled in." He sounded as if he were choking. Maybe he was. He couldn't draw a deep breath. His heart did weird things that might be scary if he wasn't a big, bad wolf.

"I'm not sure I can settle. We've had an...eventful, awful week."

Every hair on his body stiffened. He couldn't suppress his shudder.

"I thought we could, you know, try to settle each other."

She was killing him. Her words didn't mesh with the reality of their situation. "You're going to have to be more specific."

Selena hesitated. "I want you to stay here, as we planned, only in the bed, not on the floor." She took two steps toward him.

His traitorous eyes couldn't stay on hers. His gaze touched her breasts, larger than he would have guessed, her nipples tight circles of darkness. His fingers twitched before he wadded them into his palm. Her ribs cast faint shadows along her torso. And between her lovely legs, a dark triangle formed an arrowhead pointing to the forbidden. The off-limits. The source of all his sorrow.

She perched on the edge of the mattress. Patted the spot next to her.

Get out right now, his brain advised.

What male needed negative mating advice? A pathetic one.

Except he wasn't on the verge of marking his mate. Until Selena had time to heal from...

He sat, his butt on the bed, his body heat colliding with hers. Her breathing was as ragged as his. He was certain he could hear her heart battering the bony cage keeping the muscle inside her body.

"Don't play with me. I'm not a toy. Mating isn't a game."

"No game." Her fingers brushed his bicep. His skin rippled beneath his shirt. "An acceptance. An appreciation."

Her words annoyed him. Okay, maybe more than annoy. Other reactions inside him had been kickstarted. Annoyance could be pushed aside for what his body desired.

She toyed with the buttons of his flannel shirt. He covered the delicate hand with his own big one. "I do not have the patience or control of a god," he warned her.

"Good. I don't want a god. Imagine having to live up to perfection." She unfastened the top button. And the next. She placed her open palm against his chest. "Your heart is racing."

Racing could describe what was going on inside him.

"We both need what the gods intended for us." Her lips moved against his ear, her breath humid. She nipped his lobe, then sucked the flap of flesh into her mouth.

"Selena." He moaned her name.

"Shh." Her fingers made quick work of removing his shirt. "Don't argue." She ripped his undershirt from his body.

Perspective and his grasp on reality joined his clothes on the floor. Her scent drove him mad. The provocative touch of her hands and mouth on his chest as she stroked his nipples added to his delirium. He dug his fingers past the bedding into the mattress.

He forced his eyes to stay open. The moon emerged from behind the cloud and glowed brightly into the room. The pale beams washed Selena's skin with light, catching on the fine hairs of her body, changing them to glitter. She sparkled like a pristine snowscape.

He swallowed hard as she worked her way to his belt. To the snap hidden behind the buckle. To the tab on the zipper doing such a rotten job containing his erection. A moment later his dick sprang free. He raised his hips without her asking so she could pull off his jeans. His boxers. Socks.

"Come onto the bed with me," she said.

He was as naked as Selena, and most of him agreed naked was a fantastic idea. As was stretching out next to her. He reached for her.

She rolled away. "No. I have to do this."

He didn't understand.

"Stretch your arms over your head. Please."

He did as she asked.

Cold steel wrapped each wrist, closing with a snick.

"What the—?"

"Handcuffs. I have to do this."

Oh. "You don't have to do anything. Don't try to be brave or noble—"

She cut him off with a kiss.

Tasting her again. Absorbing her unique fragrance to make her a part of him, his DNA, and a promise to the future. He gripped the iron bars of the headboard, barely conscious of the metal shifting beneath his touch.

Her tongue brushed his, tentative and shy. His violent reaction wobbled the mattress.

If she halted her seduction, he would go mad. He might permanently shift to wolf form and spend the rest of his days howling at the moon.

Her breasts grazed his chest. His every muscle tensed in anticipation as she slowly introduced her body to his, nipple to nipple, flesh to flesh.

His fingers tightened on the headboard, which echoed the groans he swallowed.

She glided above him, her flesh skimming his. Her actions surprised him. After her full-moon revelation...

He needed to focus on something besides her hands and mouth on his body. If he lost control, he would belittle her courage and destroy the moment.

When the chain securing the handcuffs between the bars of the headboard snapped, he continued to clutch the iron posts. He didn't trust himself to touch her. No matter how much her mouth provoked him as she licked her way across his chest, tongue plying his nipples, lips sucking, teeth scraping; no matter how her scent curled into his nostrils, filling his head with a need so compelling, he could taste her on his breath. No matter how much he wanted to flip her onto her stomach and finish what they initiated only two nights ago, he *had* to hold on to the headboard, had to experience the iron reshaping itself under his grip.

When she threw her leg across his hips, only his hands on the metal kept him on the mattress.

"Selena," he groaned. "If you're not going to...if you're not ready, stop now. Please."

She leaned forward, her breasts dangling like fruit ready to be plucked, and kissed his mouth again.

She touched him. Below the waist. Below his hips. *Touched him.* Clasped him the way he clung to the headboard. "Someday I'll kiss you here," she promised in a husky whisper as her fingers plied his length.

Slick as a ripe peach, she lowered herself. Tight. Too tight. She was going to hurt herself.

Ethan studied her face, searching for signs of discomfort. Pain. Stress. Her expression remained neutral. Her slightly puffy lips were parted, her eyelids at half-mast. She rode slowly, driving him crazy as she sank, rose, and sank again, each time taking him a fraction deeper.

Sweat popped from his pores and beaded on his forehead. Focusing on his entire body gave him desperately needed strength. Never in his dreams of making Selena his mate had he imagined the sensations battering at his control. Letting his inner wolf take charge would be a disaster. Not all males thought with their dicks; he could prove it.

Selena's soft gasp concerned him.

"Are you okay? You don't have to do anything you don't want."

If she stopped now, he would die. His soul would flee his body and rejoin those of his ancestors, with the Ancient Ones. The Creator.

Her rough breathing matched his.

Although he wanted nothing more than to close his eyes, grasp her hips, and set the pace and rhythm, he resisted.

Selena's movements were awkward. His wouldn't be any more polished. They had to cooperate. Tonight, he needed to be as passive as he could manage.

He wasn't managing well.

He was close. Incredibly close. But she wasn't happy. He could tell. Dad and Pa and their advice be damned. He was tuned in to Selena so intimately, they could have been a single body.

He pulled the handcuff bracelets from his wrists and pushed them to the floor. Selena jerked at the clatter as they landed.

"Shh," he said, as he cupped her breasts.

Her sharp inhale whistled slightly; her nipples tightened beneath his palms.

"It's okay." He crooned the words.

He jackknifed into a sitting position, with Selena on his lap. She wrapped her legs around his waist, continuing to move on him.

Half-remembered bits of advice from his father and grandfather whispered suggestions in his head. The guidance he hadn't wanted to hear contained crucial information he could apply. He touched her. Where touching counted. One brush of a fingertip brought happiness to Selena.

And now he appreciated what the mated males in his life meant when they told him to make sure Selena was happy. The quaking, moaning, gasping mass of hot, pliant flesh straddling him, clinging to him, was what they'd meant. He hadn't hurt her, and she was happy. He'd nearly fulfilled his mating obligation.

He nuzzled her neck until he found the spot instinct led him to. Yeah, marking would be better if they used the traditional mating position; he understood why he couldn't. Her reactions intensified as he nipped her flesh, teasing her a bit with a hint of what came next.

She cried out as he bit, marking her as his. Staking a final, irreversible, irrefutable claim on her.

She collapsed. He followed her into oblivion.

When he'd regained cognizance, he found he lay on his back, with Selena sprawled against his chest. Boneless. Muscle-free. Her cheek rested against his pec. Her heart thudded as wildly as his. Their breath rasped in and out of their lungs in syncopation.

His proud, brave Selena.

All was right with the world.

"You doing okay?"

"I'm not sure." Her voice was husky. He'd done that to her.

Ethan ran his hand along the bumps and dips of her spine. "Where'd you get the handcuffs?"

"Britt. I'll have to buy her a new pair."

"Why did Britt have handcuffs? Is she in law enforcement?" A cop friend might come in handy. Except the image didn't fit the woman he'd met.

"No." Selena tensed. "She has sex toys."

Toys made more sense. Except Selena hadn't relieved his confusion. "Why would Britt—never mind. I don't want to know. Why would you borrow sex toys from her?" *From anyone?*

He didn't need help. Except maybe to dial down his sex drive.

Selena didn't say anything for a long time. He believed he understood why. When she did speak, she...shamed him.

"I asked her how to seduce you."

He couldn't decide whether to chuckle or choke. Instead, he pressed his palms against her butt cheeks, those marvelously firm globes he'd long admired. "You didn't need help."

"Yeah. I did." She rolled off him, displacing his hands. She winced as his softening penis slipped out of her. At least she didn't reject him. "You're disgusted by me—"

"Stop." He couldn't believe she'd thought her assault repulsed him. "Why you assume I'm disgusted by you is beyond my imagination. Trust me. Disgust is the last thing on my mind when I dream about you. I should get an award for my restraint."

He barely heard her answer. "You stopped wanting to kiss me."

He'd believed he was being considerate and sensitive, while she assumed he was rejecting her.

He cupped her cheek and brushed his thumb across her lips. "I was afraid to touch you. Afraid I'd hurt you. Bring back pain you don't want to remember."

Although her breathing steadied, she was still tense. "You are the last of the Limmikin alpha line. I am the last Varulv. The gods of our elders brought us together for a reason."

She pulled his hand to her abdomen. Forced his palm flat against the slight roundness. "Do you suppose we made a baby tonight? The Old Ones say our birth rates are low because a female's human cycle has to coincide with the full moon for her to conceive—"

"You seduced me because you want a baby?"

"Our packs will be gone unless we—"

"All I am is a baby-maker?" He did not like the way her motivation twisted something he'd believed sacred into something altruistic.

"The future, Ethan. We have a responsibility to our ancestors to—"

"Sex with me is your fucking duty?" Fury licked at him. He mustered all his willpower to keep from shouting at her. He'd thought in the past week she'd come to know him. To appreciate the lobo he was. He'd believed by showing her consideration, a bit of deference, and a whole scattin' lot of support, Selena would welcome his worthiness and accept the Ancient Ones hadn't bungled pairing her with him.

Instead, she considered him a sperm delivery system.

He rolled away from her and sat on the edge of the mattress. The languorous post-coital peace vanished. For a few precious moments, he'd believed everything would be okay. They'd have a happily ever after.

She was Selena Wolfe. He should have known better.

Selena lay on her back and stared at the ceiling. Moonlight created crazy patterns in the lurking shadows.

She'd succeeded. She'd seduced Ethan. He'd marked her. Their bond was now unbreakable. If he killed her once she confessed, her death would be no less than what she deserved.

Unless she was pregnant.

If I conceive tonigh, I'm safe.

Chapter 19

Helga, the neighbor from across the street, stood on the other side of the front door, fist raised as if to knock. The brilliant morning sun cast long, sharp shadows. "I guess your doorbell is broken. I noticed you've had a lot of visitors all week." Her smile put Selena's teeth on edge.

"My grandfather died unexpectedly." The truth worked. Selena didn't have to fake the hitch in her voice.

"Oh, I'm sorry." Helga's tone was sincere. The smile wattage dimmed. The brightness in her eyes did not. "Is there anything I can do? Organize the women in the neighborhood to bring meals?"

Too bad Selena's pack didn't favor hot dishes. Feeding them was a full-time job. "How nice of you. I'm sure we'll be okay for now. Thanks."

"Nonsense. I'll get it organized." Helga lifted her hand to pat Selena's cheek. Selena ducked to avoid contact. Helga's smile jerked back into place, more strained than before. Then it eased. She licked her lips. "Your grandfather must have been a handsome man to have so many good-looking descendants."

Selena turned. Ethan lurked in the background. Parker, Dakota, Restin, Ethan's family, and several males from her pack were behind her. Ethan's doing. Protecting her.

What had happened the previous evening embarrassed her. Everyone sensed she'd been marked. Finally. Their knowledge was natural. Facing Ethan was still torture.

"He was," Selena replied. Let Helga believe what she wanted. Selena wanted to get rid of her. She had too much pummeling her brain to continue human civility. "Thank you. I'd invite you in, but we aren't ready for company, what with Gramps and all."

"I understand. You don't want strangers around while you're mourning."

Selena's cheeks ached from reflecting Helga's smile. "Thank you for understanding."

"I'll work on having some food sent in. Oh, by the way," Helga said, as if her next words were an afterthought. "You do know there's an ordinance on the number of dogs you can have."

"You should have slammed the door in her face," Restin said once the door was firmly closed behind Helga.

"She was being neighborly," Selena snapped. "This is my—Ethan's house. He makes the rules, not you. And we—he decided to not make enemies of the humans around us."

"Except for the hedge," Ethan added.

"The hedge stays," Selena agreed.

"Awesome hedge," Parker said. "You should extend the hawthorn to include the front yard and the lot next door."

"How did the neighbor know we're using the back yard for...?" Restin waved his hand toward the hedge. The werewolves had been using the lawn to lift their legs, shifting to do their business. "The hedge is too thick to see through."

"Make sure no one is transforming on the lawn. All shifting has to be done inside, away from the windows." Someone was spying on the back yard, keeping track of and counting the different beasts.

Selena exchanged a look with Restin. He, too, recognized the true problem. As did Ethan. Except Selena couldn't look at Ethan without her face growing hot. "She's arranging for food. She's aware of what's happening on the street. Her nosiness is good. Someone who's aware of what's usual will be the first to spot what isn't, such as an army of vampires or thugs with big guns."

"Food is good. We'll eat sapien cuisine." Restin's agreeableness conceded the point.

"Wait until they taste a hot dish," Ethan muttered.

Selena couldn't help smiling at him. He should have returned the smile. Instead, his face lacked expression.

Something had gone wrong last night. She wasn't sure what. He'd cooperated with her clumsy seduction. Afterward, they should have cuddled and been at ease with each other. Instead, he'd withdrawn.

Don't you want babies?

I want to be a father more than anything, he'd answered.

She scrubbed her face with the palms of her hand. She was tired. Ethan had a point about following sapien hours; they had to go. Lycans were creatures of the moon. She had no business being awake and planning her day barely past sunrise.

She'd assumed appealing to Ethan's need to procreate would do the trick with him. Would make him forget she wasn't in prime condition for him to mark.

"Everyone's getting antsy." Hatch looked to Selena, as if she knew what to do with restless lycans.

She wondered if her new grandfather-in-law was testing her worthiness.

"Put them to work," Ethan suggested.

"Doing what?"

"Digging in the empty lot next door. Selena is going to be planting herbs for her business. Digging is one of our innate skills."

Her mate's matter-of-fact brilliance amazed her.

"One night in Idaho, Stoker, Luke, and I had to tunnel beneath a stockade fence to rescue Stoker's mate," Ethan continued. "Selena's business is to support the Varulv. Let the Varulv contribute. And yesterday's rain will make digging easier."

The reality bitch-slapped her. The entirety of the Varulv she led hid in a tiny house in Warwick. Why did they need a business to support them? Ulvskog didn't need infrastructure. Ulvskog needed nothing. Ulvskog no longer existed.

She wouldn't countermand Ethan's order. Oh, the words had sounded like a suggestion, except volunteering wasn't optional. Ethan owned the house. He was her alpha male mate.

Besides, Hatch had a point. Her pack wasn't used to being cooped up in a city house. They were used to trees, other creatures, and space.

Who was she kidding? She never should have let Ethan talk her into bringing the Varulv to town. They belonged in the forest of their ancestors. She belonged with them, helping them rebuild. Not that she had carpentry, masonry, or other skills. Nor did she know if the Varulv owned the property where they'd lived, or if they were squatters. All she knew was they needed to return.

Jakob, his brother, and another of the surviving males were planning a fishing expedition. She approved. The pack needed to eat. Food in Ulvskog had been plentiful. The nearby lakes and rivers provided more than enough sustenance. Feeding the pack had been as easy as shooting fish in a barrel.

She shuddered. Fish in a barrel. Babies in the full moon lodge with the grannies. Shot like fish in a barrel. The cellar of the house on Ash might be another barrel.

The Varulv needed to get out of town. She wasn't going to ignore or second-guess her instincts on this one.

ETHAN WANDERED THE BACKYARD, the sole creature for the time being. Selena lightly descended the porch steps to the grass. As much as he resented how the marking had happened, he still wanted her. Badly. Maybe if they didn't talk, and...

She crossed the lawn with an easy grace; had she been in wolf form, her stride would have been a lope.

At least she wasn't hiding from him. Of course, she couldn't get knocked up by avoiding him.

"You're upset with me," she said once she stood within arms' length. "I'm not sure why. You told me you're okay with..."

He vowed to be honest with her, always, even if honesty meant brutality. "Last night, I thought my dreams had come true. Until you mentioned babies. Wasn't I good enough to sire your offspring before you learned I have an alpha heritage?"

There. The words were out. Let her try to explain.

Except the shock on her face was real.

"Oh." Her lips twitched, as if she were planning what to say, except she didn't speak. She blinked rapidly a few times; If tears were involved, he was sunk. Her tears were poison to his willpower.

"Wow," she said a moment later. "Gee."

Maybe he'd misread the situation. "Selena—"

"No." She backed away from him. He caught a glimpse of a horrible expression before she managed to mask her face with neutrality. "No. I'm...glad you told me."

As she loped toward the house, he figured he'd stomped in scat so deep he might never be able to extract himself.

"STRANGERS ARE PARKED AT the ends of the block," Helga stated as soon as Selena opened the door to her. Her vivid blue eyes scanned the room behind Selena. She carried a hot dish. A clutch of other women stood on the porch, each one toting a pan.

Selena opened the door wider. "Come in, please. Excuse the..." she waved at the bare rooms. "We're still getting settled."

She didn't need to finish the sentence for the Hot Dish Brigade to comprehend what she meant. "The kitchen is this way." The aromas of green peppers, caraway, and cardamom enveloped the group as they followed her.

"I don't see any dogs," someone murmured.

"Doesn't smell doggy, either," someone else added.

"I do appreciate your neighborly ways." Selena ignored the stares of Restin and her in-laws as the older women trailed after her. "Did you say strangers are at the end of the block? You can set the pans here." She gestured at the bare counters. This batch of hot dishes might last them until the next day.

The females crowded the kitchen.

Helga took in the empty space. "You don't have much. I've got an extra bridge table and some folding chairs I could lend you."

"That's sweet of you," Selena said, but refused to be distracted. Helga hadn't answered her question, so she asked it again. "Did you say strangers are at the end of the block?"

Old Olivia wandered into the kitchen. Her stare fixed on Helga. "You look familiar."

Helga ignored Old Olivia, though her cheeks pinkened. "Yes. Strangers. Parked at both ends of the block. I assumed they were more people calling to pay their respects to your grandfather."

"Both ends of the block?" That didn't sound good.

"I recognize you from somewhere." Old Olivia was still staring at Helga.

Helga glared at her before setting her pan on the counter.

Selena's faith in Old Olivia as a healer remained unshaken. However, alienating Helga served no purpose. Nosy neighbors kept the streets safe. They were no different from the elders in a pack, keeping an eye on things.

"How many strangers?" she asked Helga.

Helga spread her hands, shrugging. "They're all strangers to me."

"How many is all?" Ethan stood in the kitchen door.

The visiting women stopped chattering and stared at him.

An unfamiliar irritation gripped Selena. She didn't want other females leering at her mate as they speculated how he looked without his clothes. Britt had an excuse. She was young, single, and a slut. Helga's women were primarily the equivalent of pack grannies, beyond the age of mating.

Besides, Ethan wouldn't glance at them once, much less twice. She wrangled her annoyance before it became a factor.

"Four or five strangers at each end of the block," a tiny, bird-like female chirped.

"Male or female?"

"Men. All dressed in black, too. I assumed they were mourners."

Ethan's gaze clashed with Selena's. She dipped her chin enough to signal she understood his unasked question and approved. She stretched her mouth into a smile for her visitors. "I'll bet they were confused by the orange house."

"I don't see how," Helga replied. "The orange is a beacon for miles."

Selena stilled. "A beacon? How so?"

Helga's expression shifted, as if she grasped she'd made a mistake and needed to backtrack. "It's only an expression. The color is so bright."

"I remember who you are!" Old Olivia exclaimed.

"I'm Helga. I live across the street, at forty-one Ash."

"I'm Olivia Hagtorn from Ulvskog. We met at a convocation around fifty years ago."

Helga stiffened. Her bright eyes dimmed. "Fifty years ago, I—"

"Never mind." Old Olivia inclined her head toward the other women who were busy placing the hot dishes in the refrigerator. "I understand."

Selena thought Helga looked panicked. And what the heck was a convocation? It sounded religious.

She didn't have to wait long. The women, their curiosity satisfied, left a few minutes later. Ethan sent Dakota with Helga to fetch the bridge table she'd offered.

"What's the scoop on Helga?" Selena asked Old Olivia once their company departed.

"She's a witch."

'Witch' could be defined a couple different ways. Selena wanted to be clear on Old Olivia's meaning. "Be more specific."

"Wiccan. And I'll bet the rest of those females were her coven."

"No, I don't believe so. They were ...church ladies. Hot dishes are what humans do when someone dies."

Old Olivia rolled her eyes. "How many houses are on this block?"

So Old Olivia *had* noticed the tree triad of oak, ash, and hawthorn Ethan claimed would help protect them.

"Two. Hers and ours. So?"

"Your house is on the corner of Oak and Ash. The empty lot is Ash and Hawthorne. Across the way, Witch Helga's house is on Ash. The house next to her? The address is Hawthorne, not Ash."

"I'm not following you."

"Only certain species need houses with strong magic."

"There's no such thing as magic." Selena wasn't going to let Old Olivia drag her into woo-woo. She had enough real-life problems to deal with without going all supernatural.

"Oh, I taught you better," Old Olivia chided. "There's no such thing as no magic? You don't believe it's magic when the full moon rises, and you are transformed from human to wolf?"

"Shifting isn't magic. It...just is." Selena did not want to have this conversation. She had stuff to do. Plans to make. Revenge to plot.

"When a seed falls to the ground and a plant sprouts, don't you pick the leaves so you can create a healing tisane?"

"Nature. The way life works."

"Life itself?"

"Exactly," Selena said. "Life is magic. You're only trying to attribute extra magic to the nosy neighbor and her address."

"Strong magic. The brand of magic beings like you and me should stay aware of and guard against."

"Bad juju." Selena couldn't keep the sarcasm out of her tone.

Old Olivia blasted an I-am-not-amused glare at Selena. "Go ahead and mock me, but that woman and her coven are beings you want on your side. They noticed the strangers at the ends of the block, didn't they?"

"I've told Ethan we should take advantage of Helga spying out her windows."

"Good plan."

"And Ethan is checking out the strangers. We're not foolish. We survived a vampire attack. We're aware of who was behind the attack and what happened in Ulvskog."

"You don't know anything new."

Selena chose her next words carefully. "We know...other things. Facts we hope will end the Peters' dynasty."

Old Olivia glanced around. She lowered her voice. Her eyes were bright. "Do you mean what they did to you?"

Selena cringed. Her stomach knotted.

Old Olivia grabbed her forearm before she could flee. "Did you think I didn't realize what they'd done to you? I was the one who found you after he threw you in the ditch that night. I helped you. Got you clean. I fed you pennyroyal tea so you wouldn't conceive."

"You decided I needed to learn the healing properties of plants." Selena's tone was dull. Her memories were blurred, echoing abysses she tried to avoid. She didn't remember how she'd gotten back to Ulvskog. A flash of Liam's face, green from the glow of an automobile dashboard, green like a praying mantis attacking a hummingbird, green like the monster he was. Of being tossed from the car as if she were garbage. Of cool hands. Soothing hands. Comforting crooning.

"You needed a focus."

"Focus worked. Have I ever thanked you?"

"Your plans to create beauty aids for human females using the knowledge you got from me is thanks enough."

"I'm going to kill them." Selena would have growled the words had she been in a different shape. "The Congressman. Liam. They don't deserve to share the same air as the rest of us."

"Are you prepared for the consequences?"

Okay, maybe she and Ethan hadn't planned out far enough. Motive wasn't enough. They needed to develop a strategy.

First, though, she needed to tell him the rest of the story.

ALTHOUGH SELENA MANAGED TO avoid Ethan since he'd made his ridiculous accusation, she couldn't avoid him forever. Unless he planned to spread his blanket on his elder's bedroom floor, he would be joining her in their room, hopefully their bed, at some point in the night.

She would be ready.

She considered hanging sheets at the windows, except she would be shutting out the moon. Lycans never banished the moon. Selena had a vague recollection of someone telling her the gods of the elders resided on the moon. The tale was meant to comfort a child, and many nights Selena found refuge in the myth.

Ethan wasn't going to hide under his grandfather and father's bed.

Selena stripped off her clothes before crawling between the cool sheets on the bed, careful to avoid the spots Ethan's...enthusiasm had destroyed. She had to tell him the rest of her story by confessing the extent of her idiocy.

After they'd had sex again.

She liked being with Ethan. What she'd shared with him bore no relation to what Congressman Peters and his vamp-scat eating son had done to her. Besides, Ethan hadn't made love to her yet. She'd been in control last night. Her imagination wasn't creative enough to picture how good sex between them could be if she submitted. She wanted her legacy. Tonight. Afterward, she would tell him everything. And he would cast her aside.

No, she needed the moon in the room with them. The moon would bless their union. The moon would trigger her fertility. The moon would protect her from Ethan's disgust.

THE MOON WAS LOW in the sky as Ethan crept into the room. Selena lay awake, feigning sleep until the mattress dipped as he sat on the edge.

"When I was fighting the vampire, an intense longing to have your babies kept me going."

He stilled, as if her words paralyzed him.

"Before," she added in a soft voice, "you found out you were Limmikin and not European."

He swung his legs onto the bed and reclined next to her. Their body heat merged although they did not touch.

"I believe you," he said. "I believed you this afternoon."

She rolled onto her side to face him. The broken headboard squawked.

"It's Restin," Ethan admitted. "He's unmated so he gets off on creating havoc, such as planting doubts."

"Remember the full moon?" She rested her palm on his belly. His muscles fluttered, then tensed. "My flipping out had nothing to do with your status."

"I know."

They lay still and silent for several moments.

Selena was as aware of the heavy thudding of his heart as she was of the thumps in her own chest. She struggled to keep her breathing smooth and steady. Panic battled with her calm. She didn't want him to hate her.

His stomach gurgled beneath her hand. "Rationing. Hot dishes."

"I'm sorry."

"Why did you wait up for me? Only to tell me what you were thinking during the vampire attack?"

"Partly." She massaged his belly.

"Are you hinting it's my turn to seduce you?" His voice was husky.

She plucked on one of the wiry hairs scattered across his torso. He covered her hand with his.

"I'm *supposed* to want your babies. Your status doesn't matter."

He wrapped his fingers around her hand. "You're supposed to want this." His hoarseness increased with the intimacy of her touch. He used his fingers to spread hers over his penis.

"Aren't you supposed to be seducing me?" she reminded him. She didn't want to stop touching him. Although Britt had shared a lot of sex stuff with her, she couldn't focus on anything except the way he felt in her hand. The way he'd felt inside her.

She recognized the scent of his arousal, the way the chemical changes in his body enhanced his natural aroma.

"I could be persuaded." He thrust his erection into her palm.

"Could you?"

His snicker could only be described as evil. "I owe you for doubting you."

"You don't owe me anything. We're in a bizarre situation. If we'd met in normal circumstances…"

He kissed her. It seemed forever had passed since the last time he'd kissed her. Forever, with him kissing her, was where she wanted to stay. Only the two of them, isolated from everyone, everything—and kissing.

Until he covered her breasts with his hands. Her breath caught in her throat, her lungs. When air managed to escape, it rasped as if trying to cling to her body instead of being expelled.

Ethan's touch drove every rational notion from her brain. She couldn't focus, not while her skin insisted she experience. Considering he was a novice, Ethan's instincts were faultless, his touch perfect. As he crawled between her splayed thighs, she squelched a moment of panic before welcoming him into her body.

Ethan lay on his back, his right side pressed against Selena. "Reminds me of an old sapien joke I hear in bars. Do you smoke after sex? I don't know, I never looked."

"I don't get it," Selena murmured.

"I think it has something to do with cigarettes."

"Oh."

Selena should have been relaxed, yet she was as taut as a string on his guitar. Her warm, welcoming scent had soured.

"What's wrong?"

She tensed even more. "I need to tell you something."

His stomach clenched. Not good. "Another secret?"

"The last one. I promise."

He couldn't imagine what she could reveal that would be worse than the story of what Congressman Peters and his scat-sucking son had done to her.

"I need to tell you why Peters attacked Ulvskog."

She had his attention. She inched away from him.

"Why they targeted the lodge with the grannies and..." Her voice broke.

She swallowed several times. The bed jiggled as she shivered.

One part of his brain suggested he comfort her. Another part urged caution.

He sat up and pulled the sheet across his waist.

How could anything be worse than rape?

Selena mirrored his action, pulling the sheet higher and trapping the fabric under her arms. She covered all her good bits. No distractions.

"You know how the current president wants to break the treaties. My grandfather's...liaison? Well, he approached Gramps and said we needed to petition the people who'd used our services to protect the treaties. We've been in America for a long time and have always served with honor. Sometimes serving meant our deaths."

Or the death of other lycans.

"Such as your father."

She nodded. "Such as my father."

"Our contact told us the same thing. Except he met with the whole pack." Ethan's resentment from the meeting with Jasper had faded since finding Selena.

"Nope. Only with Gramps for the Varulv."

"And your grandfather didn't lie to you?" Ethan sought an out for her; a way to negate whatever bothered her.

"You said your contact had the same agenda. Gramps ordered me to go to Congressman Peters as his ambassador."

Ethan fumbled for Selena's hand; she curled her fingers into a fist. "That's why you were at the congressman's office the day I rolled into town. I can't believe your grandfather asked you to confront Peters."

"He didn't know I'd been attacked." Selena's voice caught, as if she were choking. "He wanted me to play the my-daddy-died-for-you sympathy card."

Okay, the strategy was sick and smart at the same time. Ethan wouldn't second-guess what he would have done in similar circumstances.

"I tried to wheedle my way out of the mission. Me being at Congressman Peters' was a mission, you know. Gramps tried to convince me it was a simple meeting." Another hitch in her voice.

If not for the breaks, Ethan wouldn't have guessed she wrestled with emotion. Her flat, inflectionless tone betrayed nothing.

"I didn't know Liam would be present. Gramps called and made an appointment for me to meet with the congressman. Liam should not have been there."

Ethan couldn't stand not touching her. Telling her story cost her. Liam Peters had betrayed her in the worst way. Ethan brushed a hank of hair off her cheek and tucked the strands behind her ear.

She flinched. He dropped his hand.

The moon fled the night. Ambient light from the pinkish orange street lamps barely penetrated the uncovered window. Selena's face was a kaleidoscope of shadows, shifting with each blink of an eye, each word formed by her lips.

"Naturally, they didn't take me seriously. I was a girl they'd shared one moonless night ten years ago, maybe one of many they've violated over the years. Who was I to come to them and try to blackmail the congressman into supporting continuation of the treaties? Lots of people were killed on September eleventh. Erik Wolfe was only one."

None of what she shared surprised Ethan.

"I was angry. I was shaking." The sheet fell from Selena's breasts. She clutched at the material, twisting the fabric.

"Of course you were."

"I'm not saying this right. I stopped being scared. I was furious. Especially after Liam mentioned popping the cherries of orphan girls."

Ethan was going to kill him. Slowly. Agonizingly. Dismantle Liam Peters to his molecular level. Maybe lower.

"Long-term consequences never occurred to me," she admitted. "So I told them if they didn't support keeping the treaties in place, I would tell the world they were rapists. And they laughed." She sounded bewildered. "They laughed. They told me I had no proof. The attack was my word against theirs."

If she'd been crying, the next sound would have been a sob.

"I told them I did have proof. Nine-year-old proof. And DNA would bear me out."

Chapter 20

Selena braced herself for Ethan's reaction.

"You had a baby?" His voice cracked. He jerked back, as if he couldn't bear to be near her.

She was so stupid. "No." The denial emerged as a squeak. "I don't know why I said they'd gotten me pregnant. Maybe I thought I was being clever. Or maybe my brain froze, letting my anger take over."

"*Ancient Ones*," Ethan whispered. He pressed his fingers into his temples, his forehead. "You didn't get pregnant."

"No. I would have told you before I forced you to mark me." She wasn't entirely lacking honor.

"You didn't force me to do anything." The strength of his snap jostled the bed. "No wonder they sent their thugs to the lodge before the full moon."

She lost control. The guilt she'd been carrying around since discovering the carnage, the knowledge her careless words were responsible for the near-annihilation of the pack she'd been working to save, could no longer be compartmentalized. She drew her legs to her breasts and wrapped her arms around her shins. She pressed her forehead into her knees and wept. She hadn't suffered such despair since...the night she'd been raped.

Ethan placed his hand on her nape. Why was he touching her? He should be repelled by the careless, arrogant she-wolf she'd hidden from him. His thumb and forefinger massaged the tense spot. She knew the strength of Ethan's fingers. Maybe he planned to snap her neck, the way he'd dealt with the lobo who'd questioned her leadership. He'd been right to question her. His death, too, was on her head.

She hoped Ethan would make her death painless.

"Their actions are not on you."

The mattress dipped again. Heat surrounded her. Ethan enveloped her. His chest pressed against her back. His legs encased hers. His arms circled her, and the weight of his head rested on the crown of hers.

"Listen to me."

The vibration of his words against her shoulder comforted her more than hearing what he said.

"Maybe telling them living evidence existed was not the smartest thing to say, but those deaths are not your fault."

"They are."

"Peters wanted an excuse to get rid of the Varulv. He seized on your lie as justification."

"Stop trying to console me." At least she wasn't wailing.

"I'm not. I'm trying to get you to focus on the facts."

"I'm aware of the facts. I was there. Remember?"

"Bryant Peters ordered the murder of the Limmikin in the area. Bryant Peters hoped by raping you, your lycan sense of honor would prevent you from ever mating. If you never mated, the Varulv alpha line would die out. Without leaders, there would be no pack."

Okay. Everything Ethan said was true. True didn't make it so.

"DNA, Selena? Seriously? No homo lupus on the planet would willingly submit to DNA testing. They'd sooner shift in a room full of government scientists."

"Bryant Peters wouldn't know that."

"Yes, he would. Listen to me. You're being illogical. DNA can be lifted from dead bodies. The murder of your pack is on him. Not you."

"I killed them."

"No. What happened to the Varulv is what happened to the Limmikin. You heard my grandfather tell us the story. Your words were only an excuse Peters used to justify murder to himself. He panicked. He wasn't thinking clearly."

"But—"

"No buts, Selena. No, you shouldn't have lied to Peters. What he did afterward is on him. You really didn't have a baby?"

"No. Does it matter?" A baby probably mattered to Ethan. A lycan's female bore only his offspring.

One of his hands crept beneath the tangle of her arms and legs until his palm cupped her belly. "Your mourning of a child explains why you're anxious to have a baby now."

"I lied to Liam and the congressman. I'm anxious to have a baby now. Instinct tells me I'm supposed to have your children. Common sense tells me the best way to defeat the ones who've tried to exterminate us is by creating another generation. Limmikin and Varulv. Old Olivia was right. The gods of our elders decided to mate us for a reason."

"Then I guess I'll have to do my part to make the next generation happen." He rubbed her abdomen, flexing his fingers.

What just happened?

"Not tonight, though," he continued. "You need to sleep."

"The night is still young." She might never sleep again. "What happened to being nocturnal beings?"

"You've been awake since early morning. We didn't get much sleep last night. Tomorrow is going to be another long day. We have a lot of planning to do, strategies to form. We will have revenge... and retribution."

ETHAN, WIDE AWAKE, STARED out the window. He tried not to disturb Selena's exhausted slumber. She twitched in her sleep. He hoped she chased rabbits in her dreams instead of obsessing over Congressman Peters.

He obsessed enough for both of them. What perversion ordered the slaughter of babes and children?

Someone, he decided, who was running scared. What scared Bryant Peters? Once Ethan discovered the answer, he would know how to destroy the scat sucker.

AFTER SLEEPING ON IT, Ethan decided to research the Honorable Mr. Peters. Selena's business laptop meant he could dive deeper into the murk, without involving Luke. If he found something he couldn't manage, he figured Tokarz's order to call Luke still applied.

Helga had sent a couple of TV trays, in addition to the promised bridge table. Ethan appropriated one to use as a desk in the bedroom he shared with Selena. His mate. Their relationship might be off-kilter but claiming her had been the right thing to do. Working in the room scented by their mating kept the purpose of his task in the forefront of his brain.

Dakota and Parker were keeping an eye on both ends of the block. The strangers still lingered. The two roadies weren't happy they'd pulled guard dog day shift, but they didn't argue. Grumble? Yes, only not where either Ethan or Restin could hear them. The Varulv took the night shift. Ethan hated asking for their help while they were in a sanctuary situation. He alpha-upped and did his duty.

Congressman Bryant Peters represented the sixth generation of his family to serve the district. Pa was right. Their rule was a dynasty. Rumor declared his oldest son, Liam, would step in upon his retirement.

Oldest son. The congressman had two sons and a daughter, all with fancy Irish names. Liam, Connor, and Nola.

Ethan focused on Bryant and his number one son. The one he planned to kill, laughing the whole time he took care of business.

The congressman claimed he wanted a clean environment yet supported repealing legislation making businesses accountable for their pollution. He'd had the students who staged a peaceful sit-in outside his Washington office after a school shooting arrested for trespassing. He talked out of both sides of his mouth. Family values. Religion.

What religion endorsed raping teenagers?

Ethan's computer skills weren't good enough to dig below the official government website and the news stories. He called Luke.

Luke called back less than an hour later. "He writes a blog on the dark web. Ugly stuff. Calls himself the Sexorcist."

"The Exorcist?"

"The *Sex*orcist. He claims he can fuck the devil out of supernatural creatures. He says he's got a magic rod. He posted photos, too."

Ethan's stomach churned. "Send them to me."

"Witches," Luke continued. "He has pictures of women he claims are witches."

Selena's photo might be online, the way Luke's mate, Abigail's had been.

"Anything you want to tell me?" Luke asked. "Anything I can tell you?"

"No." What had happened to Selena was no one's business. "Can you prove it's the Congressman?"

"Not right now. Give me some time, I might be able to trace this scat back to him."

"Work on it. Oh, and Luke? This one's mine, not the government's."

SELENA PACED THE BARE rooms and muttered snide comments. Nice for Ethan to hide in their bedroom to work on the computer. In the meantime, what was she supposed to do with eighteen hungry werewolves, most of whom were confined in her basement? Dakota offered to drive some of the males to a nearby lake to fish, ridding the house of less than half the population. And her in-laws, as nice as Rand and Hatch were, made her crazy with their smarmy expressions and hints about breeding. *Fine.* They wanted the next generation of Limmikin as much as she wanted the next generation of Varulv. Did they need to bug her constantly?

Britt stopped by, wanting to discuss Night Shift and what progress Selena had made on getting their workshop in order. Selena had to tell her the project was on hold due to extended family living in the basement.

Selena gathered the pans the hot dishes arrived in, hoping Helga could help her return them to the proper people. She crossed the street to the dark purple house. The paint shimmered in the afternoon sunlight. Helga opened the door, and the overpowering scent of patchouli billowed into the neighborhood. Helga must have seen the distaste in Selena's expression.

"Can never be too safe," she muttered.

"True. Do you know a good place to buy garlic in bulk?" Selena handed the plastic bag of pans to her.

"Come on in." Helga opened the door wider.

Selena stepped into Helga's lair. "Thanks for the food."

"*You* want garlic?"

"I thought garlic ropes would look nice in the kitchen," Selena lied. "Is there a problem with that?"

"No. I'm just surprised. I thought garlic—oh, never mind. Not important."

Selena studied the interior of Helga's house. She'd imagined the rooms would be dark and sunless, filled with fussiness. Nothing could have been further from the truth. The space was as airy and open as Selena's new place. Weren't witches supposed to love the dark? Okay, the patchouli incense smoking in the fat-bellied Buddha burner was weird. Selena refused to judge. The room matched pictures of hippie houses she'd seen on the Internet.

"You need furniture first." Helga motioned for Selena to take a seat. "Can I get you a cup of tea?"

A china tea pot, steam rising from the spout, sat on the table in front of Helga's seat. Two matching cups and saucers rounded out the display. Selena stared at the pot and cups, slightly freaked out. Helga must have expected company. "Am I intruding?"

"Of course not," Helga assured her.

Selena settled into her chair. "What I can't figure out is why you asked us to get rid of the hedge. Is the hedge a test?"

For a moment, Helga looked as if she were going to keep playing her game. Then she laughed as she sat across from Selena. "Yes. But you passed."

Selena's relief was odd. Why should she care what a stranger assumed about her? "I would love a cup of tea. How long was forty-two vacant?"

"A couple of years. It's a special house." Helga continued to smile. She lifted the tea pot and poured the brown liquid into the two china cups on the tray in front of her.

The tea was hot. Fresh. Even if Helga had seen Selena leave the house, she didn't have time to brew the tea. Helga didn't offer lemon, cream, or sugar.

Helga handed a cup and saucer to Selena. "I recognized your aunt."

"I figured you did," Selena replied, assuming Helga meant Old Olivia.

"So you're shifters."

"And you're Wiccan." Selena blew on the tea. She normally didn't partake in anything caffeinated. Helga's brew had a lovely floral scent.

"Don't ask me if I'm a good witch or a bad witch," Helga cautioned.

"I wouldn't dream of asking. What's your position on vampires?" Selena sipped from her cup. "Pro or con?"

Helga's upper lip curled. "Can't stand the stink and don't trust them as far as I could throw them, and since I can't get near one without hurling, it's moot."

Since Selena had smelled one up close and personal, she agreed with the assessment. "Who do you think the thugs at the ends of the block are?"

"Minions. You have a powerful enemy."

"Let me guess." Selena sipped, scalding her tongue. "You read it in the tea leaves."

"Don't mock divination," Helga shot back.

"What else did you see? I'm serious."

Helga pulled a deck of cards from the pocket of her oversized embroidered shirt. Did she want to play a game? Cards were a human thing. Selena never learned the knack.

Helga handed the deck to Selena. "Shuffle them."

The cards were bulky and clumsy in Selena's tiny hands. The deck was a Tarot. *Fortune telling*. She'd never joined the girls in college who believed the bright pictures might foretell their futures.

More damned woo-woo.

After her conversation with Old Olivia, she tried to keep an open mind.

Helga took the deck from Selena after Selena finished shuffling. She flipped the top card. The Moon.

Selena tried another sip of tea. The moon played such an important role in her life, how could the top card have been anything else?

"The ultimate test of your soul's integrity. You can't always control what happens. Trust your instincts. They won't fail you. Don't interfere. Be a witness and let nature carry you forward."

"In other words, keep on doing what I'm doing," Selena replied in a dry tone.

"Pretty much."

So much for fortune telling.

"I had a daughter." Sadness tainted Helga's voice, polluted her eyes. "You remind me of her."

Selena didn't want to ask and suspected Helga compelled her with woo-woo. "What happened to her?"

"Congressman Bryant Peters."

ETHAN CAME TO BED earlier than he had the previous night. After supper—Restin had ordered in pizzas, of all things—Ethan had holed up with his father and grandfather. She'd thought he'd be with them all evening.

"Tomorrow night," he told Selena as he unbuttoned his shirt.

"What?" He'd lost her.

"We need to confront the congressman tomorrow night."

"Why tomorrow night?"

"It's the half moon."

Selena closed her eyes. Of course. She should have considered the lunar cycle herself. Opening her eyes, she said, "Yeah. I visited Helga. She had me draw a tarot card. The Moon. Big shocker."

"Helga?"

"Across the street. I returned all the hot dish pans to her and thanked her nicely. Old Olivia was right. Helga is a witch." Selena shared the gist of her short visit. "The congressman assaulted her daughter, too."

"He was trying to sexorcise the demons out of her," Ethan explained.

"What?"

"The Dark Net is an unregulated black hole on the Internet. People post all sorts of sordid things there."

"Like porno?"

"So Luke tells me."

Selena's lips quivered. "Am I online?"

"I don't know."

"Can we find out?" The idea of her fifteen-year-old self being exposed to the underworld nauseated her.

"I can take a photo of you and send it to Luke," Ethan offered.

"No! I don't want your friend—"

"Luke is not my friend." Ethan's cold, hard tone revealed more than his words. "He is a computer expert, who works for the FBI tracking kiddie porn on the Internet."

Selena wanted to melt into the floor. "Kiddie porn?" The words barely escaped her throat. "I might be on a kiddie porn site?"

Ethan dropped his shirt and wrapped Selena in his arms. "I'll try to get the coordinates or whatever the dark web uses and search myself."

He was her hero.

She looped her arms around his neck and prayed the night would never end.

Chapter 21

Ethan cursed the never-ending day. If being an alpha meant he had to feed a pack of hungry souls and mediate petty vamp-scat, Selena and Pa could keep their jobs. Dakota started whining something smelled funny, and Ethan snapped at him. What did Dakota expect, with twenty creatures pissing on the lawn?

He and Pa, with input from Dad and Restin, decided five in the afternoon would be the best time to confront Congressman Peters. Leaving the house would be safe in daylight. They needed to act before the half moon. Their lycan strength faded each day after a full moon until the new moon banished lycans from her realm. The half-moon marked the point in the cycle when a werewolf's strength ebbed more rapidly. The confrontation had to be today.

Old Olivia—*Aunt Olivia*—called the congressman's office and tried to make an appointment with Liam, only to be told Liam was out of town. "I hope you know what you're doing," she told Ethan.

"So do I."

Ethan asked Selena to dress in the same black pantsuit she'd worn the day he met her. "You looked professional and in control," he explained. "I need you to remember your anger while we challenge the congressman."

He, too, dressed in black—jeans, a button-down shirt, boots.

"You look mean." She made it sound sexy.

"Good."

"I hope you two know what you're doing." Restin echoed Aunt Olivia. He hadn't been informed of the details and was acting pissy at being excluded.

Dad and Pa weren't being scat-holes, and they weren't told the particulars, either.

As soon as Ethan's truck turned onto Oak Street, a familiar black pickup fell in behind him. "Remember your landlord's nephew?"

"No."

"The guy who came to put up the plywood the morning after the vampire attack," Ethan reminded her. "I'm certain he's the one who's been following us. I think he followed me out of Ulvskog the day I left to meet with Dad and Pa."

"Kirk. Yeah, I vaguely remember him. I had a lot on my mind that morning."

Kirk didn't sound right; Ethan let it pass. Nothing was going to happen late Wednesday afternoon in downtown Warwick.

Selena called Restin with the black truck's tag number. Whoever his contact, they were fast. A few minutes later, Restin gave her a name. Curtis DiNardo. Yeah. Curtis was the nephew with the plywood.

Ethan didn't care for the coincidence of the landlord's nephew following Selena; his presence meant someone had been keeping tabs on her all along.

They found a parking spot across the street from the professional building. Ethan believed it might be the same place he'd parked the morning he'd arrived in Warwick and seen Selena for the first time. He didn't leave enough space for anyone to park behind them. Curtis sped past them, his truck spewing noxious fumes, the coil of blue rope swaying.

"You'd think he'd charge the congressman enough money, so he could buy a new vehicle," Ethan said.

"Maybe he doesn't work for money. Maybe he's being blackmailed."

"Nothing would surprise me." Ethan put the truck in park and shut off the engine.

"Well?" Selena asked. "Now what?"

"We confront the Congressman."

"I know we confront him." She sounded impatient. "How?"

Ethan drummed the steering wheel with his thumbs. "I guess we haven't planned as well as we should have."

"Then we improvise." Selena opened her door. "Before we overthink what we're doing, and I lose my nerve," she added, as she slid from the cab.

Since he wouldn't let her face her rapist alone, Ethan had no choice except to follow her. He cupped her elbow and steered her across the busy street. As they reached the curb, the building door opened. Ethan recognized the congressman's snotty receptionist. She conversed with a couple other younger women.

Good. Her preoccupation meant no witnesses. Not that he planned to dismantle the congressman tonight. Putting a scare into him would make the chase and culmination all the sweeter. Ethan unreservedly approved of torture. The longer and more painful, the better.

He caught the door before it closed and pulled Selena inside. The receptionist never looked in their direction.

They waited in the corner shadows for the elevator to empty before dashing across the building lobby for their solitary ride to the fourth floor. Selena tapped her booted toe, her only outward sign of agitation.

"We got this," he assured, as the elevator doors slid open.

The office door wasn't locked. Ethan considered wiping the door knob clean of his fingerprints, except he figured security cameras captured every moment. He didn't plan to be guilty of anything, so had nothing to hide.

Today.

Selena squared her shoulders as she strode into the suite. She led the way through the empty reception area. She didn't bother to knock before opening the congressman's office door.

He was on a call and glanced up, obviously irritated by the intrusion. "I have to get back to you," he told the person on the other end. He gently replaced the receiver in its cradle. "Well, well. To what do I owe the pleasure, Selena?"

Ethan wanted to wipe the smugness from the vamp-scat-eater's face.

"Making more anonymous threatening phone calls?" Selena asked.

"I have no idea what you mean." His smirk grew wider. Although the congressman was thin, his florid complexion was that of an obese man. "Who did you bring with you? Your fiancé? Liam mentioned you were...engaged."

"He is my mate." Selena lifted her chin. "We're here for retribution. I told him what you did to me."

"Pissed me off," Ethan admitted. "You shouldn't piss off someone like me."

"Not human? Why should your opinion matter to me? You're demons. All of you. Creatures of darkness and the devil."

"I'm a voter. An American citizen. Let's start there. Then again, my Limmikin heritage ought to make you real nervous."

Peters' eyes widened; his nostrils flared. "There's no such thing as Limmikin." He sounded as if he were choking.

"Yeah," Ethan continued as if the congressman hadn't spoken. "Selena told me what you did to her, and what you did to the Limmikin is common knowledge in certain circles. I was in Ulvskog on the full moon. I witnessed the aftermath of what you did to the Varulv."

"You've stated your piece. Now, if you'll excuse me, I'm a busy man."

Selena plopped into one of the chairs facing the congressman's desk. "Searching for more devil's spawn to rape? Oh. Wait. It's not rape if the..." Selena faced Ethan. "What's the word you found on the dark net?"

"Sexorcist," Ethan supplied, his focus never leaving Peters.

"Right. Not rape if the Sexorcist uses his divine rod to drive out demons." Selena's sarcasm ranked among the best Ethan had ever heard.

The congressman's once ruddy complexion turned pale and pasty.

"You're responsible for my father's death. You murdered my grandfather. You believed you were murdering your own child or grandchild when you ordered your minions to open fire on the Ulvskog lodge hours before the full moon. Your father did the same thing to the Limmikin, on the night of the new moon." Selena ticked the crimes on her fingers. "And I've mentioned only the crimes against the shifters with whom you have treaties. If you treat your friends like scat, I wouldn't want to be your enemy. And yet, I am. Don't you find our enmity curious?"

"Nah, not curious." Ethan grabbed the back of the chair next to Selena and leaned closer to Peters. "The Sexorcist doesn't discriminate. We found photos of him raping young Wiccan females on his dark net site."

"Oh. Could Helga's daughter's picture be posted? Did I tell you the congressman and possibly Liam fucked her to death? Helga is not a happy witch."

The congressman sneered, as Ethan expected. "This great country was founded—"

"By misfits," Ethan interrupted. "By people seeking sanctuary from persecution. The Limmikin were here first."

"Limmikin doesn't exist," the congressman repeated.

"We lived here first. We didn't need your treaties. You were the invaders. This was our land." Ethan bared his teeth. "Now we're back."

"And I and many other Varulv are witness to your attempted annihilation of our pack," Selena added. She leaned back in her chair and stretched her long, gorgeous legs. "Now who's going to be fucked to death?"

The congressman had been doing something behind his desk. He now raised his hand, which held a gun. He pointed the barrel at Selena. "Your half-human bastard abomination is dead."

"What half-human bastard abomination?" Selena sounded serene. "I lied to you. And you showed your true colors. You're never going to support the treaties protecting the homo lupus. You hoped raping me would prevent me from mating and eliminate the Varulv more...gently...than your father did with the Limmikin."

"There are powers mightier than yours," Ethan murmured. "If you shoot Selena, I will have your head off your shoulders before you finish pulling the trigger."

Ethan was quick, but he wasn't faster than a speeding bullet.

"What are the coordinates of the Sexorcist's dark web page?" Selena asked.

"Don't worry," Ethan said. "The FBI has the URL."

"Whatever. How many of his good Christian constituents would approve of his method of driving out demons?"

Ethan pulled out his phone. "Here. I'll text the link to you."

The congressman's pale blue eyes darted between Ethan and Selena. "I'm calling your bluff." Maybe he'd tried to growl the threat. He failed. Miserably so.

"No bluff this time." Selena shrugged. "I learned my lesson. Boy, did you show me. Murdering innocent children and old ladies. You play tough, Mr. Congressman."

"Maybe we can't prove you were behind the massacre," Ethan said, "but we can expose The Sexorcist. You forgot one key factor about the devil spawn or whatever crap you call us these days. Our families mean everything to us. You violated our most important tenet. They say payback is a bitch. For the lupine community, payback is a way of life. Especially for the bitches."

The gun shifted targets with the jerky focus and refocus of Peters' gaze.

"Tell me, though. I'm curious. Do you fuck vampires or is sex part of your deal with them? Rumor has it fucking one is the same as sticking your dick in a snowbank."

"Why you—"

Ethan poured on the Calhoun speed and knocked the gun out of Peters' hand. "Selena, want to explain my fingers to the congressman?"

"They're scary strong. I've seen him snap someone's neck without breaking a sweat." Selena injected a whine into her voice. "You promised me I could chew off his penis."

Ancient Ones, Creator, he loved this female.

"Not today. We were seen entering the building. We only came to warn him, remember? We're going to wait. Besides, we promised the parents of the babes who were slaughtered they could help punish him. Plenty of others want a piece of him."

"But I get his penis, right?"

Another male might be jealous. "Right."

"Okay, if you're not going to let me gnaw on his penis tonight, can we stop for chicken wings on the way home?"

That's when the Honorable Bryant Peters pissed himself.

"THAT WAS FUN," SELENA quipped as they strolled into the reception area. "Let him wonder when a pack of furious werewolves are going to descend on him."

"You were magnificent." Ethan stopped and grabbed her arm, pulling her into a kiss.

Selena melted. She pressed the length of her body against his, as much for support as trying to merge with him.

A gunshot broke them apart.

Selena banged her hip against the receptionist's desk. They stared at each other for half a second before running back to the congressman's office.

"Call 9-1-1," Ethan urged, as he opened the door.

The smell hit her first. Then she spotted the congressman on the floor. "He's dead. There's no rush."

"We need an alibi," Ethan snapped.

"Right." She couldn't tear her gaze from the sight of the congressman with only half of his face—*half of his head*—in place. The rest was spattered on the window behind the desk and dripped from the ceiling.

"And try to sound hysterical."

"Can I pretend to be pissed I'll never get to mutilate his genitals?"

"Sure. Now call."

Selena lifted the receiver and punched in numbers. "Oh my god!" she cried into the handset. "He shot himself. We need an ambulance. We need the police. Congressman Peters shot himself!"

The operator instructed her to remain on the line. Staying on meant providing periodic sniffles. "I think I hear sirens," she fake-sobbed.

Ethan rolled his eyes. She stuck out her tongue. She'd wanted to be the one to kill Peters, yet if she mourned being cheated of her right to revenge, the authorities might misread her emotion for guilt. If she were merely any werewolf, she could vanish. Ethan's fame prevented him from disappearing, and she refused to live without him.

"Try to summon some tears," Ethan growled at her.

She covered the mouthpiece and lifted her chin. "I am not going to shed any more tears, real or fake, for him. I will be hysterical and put on a girly show of nerves. I will not cry."

The sirens were louder now. The crackle of radios invaded the sky and penetrated the window glass.

"The ambulance is here," she told the operator.

Ethan motioned for her to hang up the phone. He grabbed her arm and pulled her out of the reception area to the hall. "Let's wait here."

Her disappointment she hadn't been the one to kill Congressman Peters kept resurfacing. He'd stolen revenge from her, as well as her innocence and her grandfather. He was a thief. Maybe if she concentrated on her disappointment and not her rage, she'd pull off shock at his death.

"Okay, listen closely." Ethan lowered his face to hers, as if comforting her. Instead, he whispered, "They're going to separate us.

We need to get our story straight. We were here after hours at the congressman's request. He claimed the only time he could squeeze in a meeting with us to discuss Night Shift was after five."

"Night Shift?" What did her bath bombs and healing creams have to do with Congressman Peters?

"We're hoping for his assistance in getting a small business loan or grant to help launch the line. I've met with him before. And Night Shift is why you visited a few weeks ago. The congressman worked with and respected your father. You sought Peters' help for family reasons."

What a vamp-scat story. Damned if the tale didn't make sense.

Then the police were everywhere, swarming the stairwells and hogging the halls. Paramedics from the ambulance corps rattled their gurney off the elevator. Ethan tightened his grip on her arm, as if he didn't trust her to behave.

"He's in his office." Ethan gestured toward the closed door.

As Ethan predicted, they were separated immediately. Selena explained everything as Ethan had told her. Ethan, she mused, was a genius for inventing a plausible motive.

One detective acted solicitous toward her. Maybe he believed the sight of the congressman's half-blown away head bothered her. The other played bad cop and acted convinced Selena had done something to make beloved Bryant Peters kill himself.

Two hours later she and Ethan were permitted to leave. Ethan put his arm around her shoulders. They didn't speak until they were safely in his truck, across the street from the office building.

"That didn't go particularly well." Her voice shook.

"It could have been worse." Ethan twisted the key in the ignition. The truck roared to life, and he pulled away from the curb.

The sun had set while they were being interrogated. Street lamps spilled puddles of light at regular intervals, creating deep shadows in doorways and the alleys between the buildings.

The half-moon flitted between clouds.

"Should we be worried?" Selena asked.

"Maybe. I'm counting on the security camera to show we were in the reception area when he fired the gun."

"Did you spot any security cameras in the office?"

"Do you believe he'd risk recording whatever happened in his office?" Ethan's wry tone eased some of her worry.

"I guess you're right." She shuddered. A video of her being assaulted could be drifting in the ether. She wasn't certain if she wanted to know. If footage existed, it could be proof the congressman and his son had attacked her. At this point, why would she require proof?

Ethan checked the rearview mirror. "I don't see any sign of Curtis."

Selena twisted in her seat. "How can you tell? All I see are headlights."

"Too low to be a pickup," Ethan replied.

Something thudded against Ethan's truck. The truck rocked from the impact. Ethan swore.

A crack, followed by shattering glass. Cold air blasted in at the same moment a foul stench filled the cab. She swung around in her seat and came face to face with a vampire as it lurched through the broken window.

The vamp lunged for her throat at the same moment her shift kicked in. Selena fell against Ethan, who yelled something as he struggled to control the truck.

Icy fangs scraped across her human skin. Claws dug into her arm as the shift took hold and exploded from her. She leapt for the creature's heart, not caring whether her canine teeth could pierce the already dead flesh of a vampire. Krav maga taught her to use the weapons she had.

The truck cab didn't give her a lot of fighting space.

The vampire in her mouth tasted as disgusting as the bloodsucker smelled. Claws raked across her ribs. Searing pain followed. She clamped her jaw tighter and focused on not puking.

The vamp hissed as she pulled away, her mouth full of rotten flesh and surprisingly brittle bones. She spat out the carrion and lunged again. Then again. And again, tearing out chunks of the vampire's body to get to its heart.

Going for the kill wasn't a problem. The weirdness stemmed from the lack of blood. Sweet, hot fluid as she ripped out a prey's throat usually filled her mouth. The vamp was dry, its guts cold as a fish caught from a January lake. She tore a gelatinous mass from the creature's chest, praying she'd found its heart.

The vamp exploded like a vacuum cleaner bag bursting, spewing dust everywhere. The heart changed to ash in Selena's mouth.

She rested, her sides heaving with the effort of breathing. Pain welled with every inhale. The vamp's undead claws had done a number on her.

The truck had stopped moving. Her awareness of Ethan sharpened into focus. *Was he okay?* She didn't have the strength to morph to ask. She couldn't summon the energy to nudge him with her nose. Concern for him outweighed her pain.

"S'lena." He sounded weak. Distant. Her ears found his respiration, a harsh counterpoint to her own.

She whimpered to signal she was alive. Conscious. The familiar itch of healing annoyed her, but healing was good. She wouldn't want any vampire gouges to fester and putrefy.

"S'lena."

What if Ethan wasn't okay? She opened her eyes. He slumped against the steering wheel, still in his human form. She sniffed. Vampire reek continued to mask the smell of blood.

The truck wasn't moving, so he must have parked at some point during her battle. Unless he'd crashed. Beams from the headlights of passing vehicles illuminated the cramped interior in periodic flashes.

Moving hurt. She needed to check on Ethan. The view through the windshield confirmed they hadn't crashed. The engine still purred. Only the window on the passenger side was damaged.

Selena nudged Ethan with her nose. Dark shadows mottled his hands.

"S'lena?" He raised his head. More shadows marred his handsome profile.

What did it do to you? She wanted to howl. Instead, she licked his hand. The darkness wasn't blood. It wasn't anything except patterned shadow.

His gaze didn't focus for several heartbeats. She used her nose to nudge his hand.

"Okay." He shook his head, as if to clear his brain. He studied her and winced. "Let's get you home."

THE ASSAULT LEFT ETHAN more shaken than he wanted to admit. The vampire's attack had taken him totally by surprise. When he'd seen the creature go for Selena's throat, he thought his own would collapse. At least he'd managed to park the truck safely before he launched his counterattack.

He gripped the steering wheel with the same force he'd gripped the vamp's neck to keep it from getting to Selena's throat. Speed limits be damned. He needed to get her back to Ash Street as quickly as possible.

Helga's strangers formed a living barricade to prevent him from reaching his block. Their lives, their loss. He jammed the gas pedal to the floor. One of the strangers flashed fangs at Ethan. Vampires, stalking them at night. Not a living barricade, then. The creatures couldn't cross Oak or Hawthorn, which meant the sacred triad worked.

He didn't give a damn if he flattened one or all. Well, unless his truck's undercarriage got damaged in the process.

He screeched to a stop in front of forty-two and laid on the horn for several seconds before leaping from the truck. He rushed to the passenger side.

The street lights glinted off the pebbles of broken glass—fake diamonds glittering on the floor, upholstery, and Selena's pelt.

He lifted her from the seat. She whimpered. The sound pierced his soul as clearly as if she'd shrieked in his ears.

"Get Aunt Olivia and Parker," he snarled at his father, who had run out the front door.

"What happened?"

"Vampire attack."

"*Ancient Ones!*" Dad dashed toward the house.

Ethan carried Selena to their bedroom and gently lowered her to the mattress. Aunt Olivia and Parker hovered.

"A vampire attack?" Parker asked. "Did it bite her?"

"No. She gnawed her way through its chest until it exploded." Ethan didn't mention he had tried to rip off the monster's head.

"It had some vicious claws. I think it got her with those. She was bleeding."

Parker probed Selena's fur with his fingers. "She's healing now."

"She's exhausted from fighting," Aunt Olivia added.

"Why doesn't she shift to human?" Ethan asked. If she were in human form, he could better comfort her. She could communicate. Tell them where she hurt and how.

"It's the half moon," Aunt Olivia reminded him. "Be patient."

Pa spoke from the doorway. "Does the attack have anything to do with Bryant Peters' suspicious death?"

Ethan jerked his head. "Who says it's suspicious?"

"Helga stopped by because she saw the story on the news."

"He committed suicide. He waited until Selena and I were out of his office. We were still in his suite when he shot himself. He blew off half his head."

"Too bad," Pa said. "I wanted my day of reckoning with him."

"A lot of us did."

Parker straightened. "Selena needs to rest. Let her body heal itself."

"I agree." Aunt Olivia nodded.

"Where did the vampire come into it?" Dad asked Ethan.

"We were on the way home. No warning. It burst through the passenger window. Selena morphed instantly and defended herself. Us."

"How did the vampire know where you would be?" Dad continued to probe.

"Ethan, let me see your hands," Aunt Olivia ordered.

"Huh?" The request wasn't making a connection in his brain.

Aunt Olivia grabbed his hands and pulled him out of the bedroom, cursing the lack of illumination. Once she got him to the kitchen, the bright lights revealed every flaw. "What happened?"

Restin, who had followed them, leaned against the counter.

"The vamp attacked Selena. I had to stop it."

"Yes, you did." Aunt Olivia spoke in a soothing tone. "How did you get these bruises?"

"I can't remember. Not clearly. Everything happened so fast. So violently." The cramped truck cab limited the struggle. With the vampire's focus on Selena, Ethan needed to protect his mate. Not only was she his mate, but she was Selena, and he loved her strength, her courage. Her.

"I tried to choke the vampire," he finally said.

"Do they breathe?" Aunt Olivia flipped his hands so she could examine the palms.

"I . . . I don't know. I managed to keep its fangs out of Selena's throat."

"Selena was smart to shift." Aunt Olivia dropped his hands. "The bruises are broken blood vessels from your attempt to strangle something that doesn't breathe."

"I tried to rip off its head. Maybe. I don't remember. The attack was so...unexpected. Not a lot of room to maneuver."

"You have bruises on your face, too. Did it punch you?"

"It focused on Selena. I doubt it sensed me, except as an inconvenience. It was cold to the touch. Like walking barefoot on a tile floor in January. That kind of cold."

"How did the vampire know where you were?" Restin, still posed against the counter, arms crossed over his chest, echoed Dad's question.

"No idea."

"Who knew you were at the congressman's office?"

"No one. The receptionist and her co-workers were leaving as we arrived."

"What happened at the congressman's office?" Restin's tone was too sharp for Ethan's liking.

"None of your business."

"Tokarz sent me to help—"

"To help with the aftermath of the massacre at Ulvskog."

Ethan closed his eyes, replaying the moments before the attack. The vampire had to have a way to track them. And the reason kept eluding him, taunting him beyond the edge of his memory. *The black truck. Kirk. No, Curtis.* He'd seen Ethan park across from the congressman's office.

Curtis had been around the morning after the first vampire attack, too, allegedly to fix Selena's window. He was in Ethan's vicinity an awful lot and not due to any man crush on Ethan's red truck.

"You ran the report for me on a license plate," Ethan choked out, opening his eyes and fixing his gaze on Restin. "He's been following me. Maybe it's time to pay him a visit."

Chapter 22

"Don't try to shift."

Selena's eyelids fluttered at the sound of the soft, soothing voice. Someone was near her, someone whose scent filled her. Completed her.

She didn't know where she was. The only thing she grasped was a need to brush her teeth. Something had crawled into her mouth and died.

She opened her eyes. Gray light—dawn or dusk—bathed the room. She tried to sit. And realized she was still wolf.

"Don't try to shift." Ethan repeated.

Ethan. She tried to speak but lacked the body parts to form words. Was he all right? Hazy scenes teased the edges of her memory. *Was he all right?*

A pathetic sound emerged from her throat. A whimper. She shamed her alpha lineage. Alphas didn't whimper.

Ethan sat next to her on the bed. He rested his hand on her neck. The touch comforted her. "Aunt Olivia says you might have ingested some type of vampire germ when you gnawed out the vampire's heart."

His words were a garble, making no sense.

"Parker doesn't agree. He thinks you expended too much energy fighting the vampire, and with the moon in the last phase of waning, you're taking longer than usual to recuperate."

She'd fought a vampire? Yes. Days ago. The night she'd first met Ethan. Before the massacre at Ulvskog, when her grandfather still lived. No one could survive a second vampire attack.

Ethan stroked her pelt, calming her. "Don't try to shift," he repeated.

Was she supposed to wait until the new moon to pop back to human form?

A soft knock on the door interrupted her thoughts.

Restin peered into the room. She swallowed a growl. The Loup Garou beta irked the scat out of her.

Ethan padded on bare feet to the door. "What do you want?" His tone was cool and dismissive.

"How is your mate?" Restin asked.

"Resting."

Funny how Restin's name sounded like resting, when he wasn't at all restful to be around.

He peered past Ethan's shoulder to stare at Selena. She curled her upper lip, showing her fangs. Restin dipped his head in acknowledgement of her superior status. He wasn't a fool. His problem with Ethan's true status didn't help. "The authorities are here to interview you again concerning Congressman Peters' suicide."

Bryant Peters committed suicide? She wasn't going to get to chew on him as he screamed, and his life ebbed out of his repulsive body?

A vampire attack and the congressman's suicide. What else had she missed while trapped in the weary twilight of healing?

"And we still can't locate Curtis DiNardo."

Ethan buttoned his shirt. "I'll talk to the cops." He glared at her. "I'm serious, Selena. Don't try to shift."

IN THE END, SELENA didn't have to try to shift to her human form. The process simply...happened, like the first time she'd shifted to wolf shape when she hit adolescence. She slipped on her brown chenille robe and left the bedroom. Her legs behaved as if they were the consistency of dandelion stems. Vertigo clutched her. She steadied herself by putting her hand on the mattress. Several hard swallows later, she was more in control.

"My wife is extremely upset by what happened," she heard Ethan say as she forced herself from the bedroom to the living room. His words echoed.

Someone had relocated Helga's bridge table from the dining area. Other than a few folding chairs and the sofa, the room remained unfurnished.

"It's okay," Selena warbled. Her throat burned. Wife? Yeah. Right. Ethan had marked her. Longing for him welled. Needing him was natural.

Ethan leapt to her side and helped her to the sofa.

"I'm sorry to disturb you, Mrs. Calhoun," a detective, who looked vaguely familiar, said. "I have a few more questions for you."

Selena sank to the cushions. Ethan sat next to her and draped his arm over her shoulders.

"I don't know what else I can tell you." She brought her hand, still trembling from the exertion of staggering from the bedroom to the sofa, to her forehead.

The detective and Ethan didn't miss the gesture.

Memory flashes overloaded her brain. "I didn't see him shoot himself. Ethan and I left his office. We heard a loud crack."

Yeah. The confrontation was coming back to her. The taste in her mouth curdled. "We opened the door…he'd shot himself. In the head."

Gray matter oozing. Blood spattered everywhere. A milder form of what had happened to Gramps.

Selena swayed. *Gramps. Peters had murdered Gramps.*

Ethan placed a calming hand on her thigh.

"Why were you at the congressman's office after hours?"

"He couldn't see us during regular hours. I used to be an intern for him, years ago." Amazingly, she could speak the truth without gagging. "Back then, he sometimes had after-hours meetings, so we asked for one."

"And why were you meeting with the congressman?"

Ethan's story rushed back to her. "We…want to start a business. Making herbal bath and beauty products. Ethan…my husband…thought the congressman might be able to help us with startup money or something."

"And why would your husband believe the congressman would help?"

Selena lifted her chin. "My father was doing some work for Congressman Peters on September eleventh. He was in the Pentagon. The congressman always assured me if I ever needed anything…" Every word rang true.

The detective consulted his notebook.

"My wife hasn't been well," Ethan said. "Seeing the congressman upset her."

"I'm sorry. I'm only trying to figure out why someone like Congressman Peters would take his own life."

Because he was a lowlife.

"You didn't make any threats or—"

"I'm a simple woman from the north woods. With what could I possibly threaten someone as powerful as the congressman?"

"His staff claimed he was in fine spirits when they left."

"He seemed okay to me when we left," Selena retorted. Her strength increased with each of the detective's questions. Maybe anger would heal her.

"A security camera across the street from the congressman's office picked up footage of what transpired."

"I don't understand."

Ethan covered her hand with his. "I'm afraid I don't, either."

His thrumming tension transferred to her.

"The camera pans, so we can see bits of the congressman's office. We don't understand what we see. We're hoping you can help us interpret the footage."

Selena struggled to control her expression. If a camera had been in place fifteen years earlier...no. The blinds had been closed. She remembered staring at them, one of the insignificant things her brain used to protect her. *The tastefully beige vertical slats slightly swaying from the hot air blowing through the register beneath the window undulated in counterpoint to —* "We see the two of you enter the office. The next couple of frames show Mrs. Calhoun sitting. The congressman seems agitated by the time the camera pans to his office again. His body language is...odd."

He was probably jerking his gun back and forth between her and Ethan. Thank the gods of her elders that Peters' back was to the camera, so it probably didn't capture the gun in his hand.

"The next thing we see is the two of you leaving the room."

Yeah. We left him alone with his gun.

"The last sign of life we see is the congressman reentering the area of his desk. It appears he's carrying the gun." The detective's blue eyes were as sharp as lasers.

"And no sign of us," Ethan pointed out. "All I can tell you is he was alive and unharmed when we left."

"Don't you mean that's all you're willing to tell me?"

"No." Selena's insides had frosted over. "Ethan and I left the congressman's office, and the congressman was alive. I'm sure you checked the timing of the tape against our nine-one-one call. If you haven't, you should."

"What did the security cameras in the office building record?" Ethan asked. "I assume you checked them."

The detective never blinked. "We have," he admitted. "Good eye on your part."

Ethan didn't acknowledge the backhanded compliment. "He was alive when we left him."

"Maybe watching the video would jog my memory." Selena fluttered her hand. "I have to admit, seeing him...dead..." She stared at the detective.

"Selena didn't handle it well," Ethan confirmed.

I wanted to be the one to kill him.

"And you have no idea as to why the congressman would kill himself." Another statement from the detective.

"I had my own agenda. I wasn't paying attention to his mood."

"Who can tell what goes on in the mind of a politician?" Ethan added. "What did his staff say?"

"No one was aware of an after-hours meeting with you."

"After-hours meetings happen a lot in politics." Selena's stomach growled. She must have slept for a long time. "I interned in his office ten years ago, and after-hour meetings were common. Not everyone operates on a Monday through Friday, nine-to-five schedule."

The detective closed his notebook and stood. "Thanks for your time. I'll be in touch."

Ethan saw the detective out, before rejoining Selena, who remained where he'd left her.

Her stomach growled again. "Is there anything to eat?"

"Walleye." He made a face. "The Varulv males went fishing."

"Good," she said. "What day is it?"

"You were out one whole day, plus most of today. You had me worried. Why did you shift after I told you not to?"

"I didn't have a choice. It...happened. Like I was a teenager again. Was tonight the first time the detective tried to interview us?"

"Yeah."

Her memory of the attack was still mostly a blur. "How did we manage to escape again?"

"You don't remember?"

Selena stared at him.

"You chewed your way through a vampire's chest to his heart, while I stopped him from biting you. He did manage to claw you. According to Parker, healing from your wounds is why you slept so long. And according to Aunt Olivia, you accidentally ingested vampire cooties."

"This sounds vaguely familiar. Have you told me this before?"

"Yes."

"Vampire cooties would explain why my mouth tastes like I've been drinking from a septic tank."

"Septic tank?"

"You don't have septic tanks in Loup Garou? They're a sort of rural sewage system."

"We have septic tanks. When did you last eat sewage?"

She forced the idea from her head. "I'm hungry, and I need to get the vampire cooties out of my mouth."

Chapter 23

"You folks need to get a TV set," Helga groused as she pushed her way past Restin the next night. Shafts of pale moonlight followed her. "Or at least a radio."

"What's your problem?" Restin asked before Ethan could speak.

Ethan wanted to cuff Restin upside the head. This was his house. The beta had no status here.

Helga must have realized Restin's place. She addressed Ethan. "Liam Peters has been named interim congressman until a special election can take place."

"Dynasty." Ethan sighed. "Pa was right."

Selena leaned against the kitchen door jamb and crossed her arms. "I won't be cheated a second time."

Helga stared at Selena for several long moments, as if trying to read her mind.

Restin tried some alpha posturing.

Ethan stopped him. "Sometimes we have to take what we can get."

Selena had been quiet all day. The vampire slashes healed, leaving no physical scars. The emotional traumas might never disappear.

Ethan had relapsed to the place where touching her worried him. Selena acted as if nothing had happened. When he sought the privacy of their shared room, she embraced and reassured him.

Why couldn't they be like other newly mated couples? He longed to be isolated from the world. From responsibility. Bliss would be endless hours alone with Selena in his bed, memorizing every nerve ending in her body, how each cell reacted to his fingers, his lips, his tongue.

The Varulv in the basement, his father and grandfather in the guest room, Restin on the living room sofa all precluded the necessary solitude.

If constant strife was what being an alpha meant, Ethan wanted no part of leadership. He had no choice. He'd mated an alpha. His lineage was alpha. He couldn't escape.

The only place he could converse with Selena was in bed.

"My pack wants to go back to the woods. To Ulvskog." Selena drew a limp sheet across their lower bodies.

"Ulvskog is no more." As if she needed reminding.

"We should petition the interim congressman for funds to rebuild Ulvskog."

Ethan sat up. "Are you out of your mind?"

Her calm, level, steady gaze unnerved him. "Well, I don't want to build an apartment complex on the empty lot next door. And they don't want to relocate to Colorado. We're a north woods pack. We belong in the forest."

Ethan had no words.

"Liam Peters owes us."

"We owe him," Ethan reminded her.

"Only what he's earned. We can pay our debt once we get the pack settled. We appreciate your hospitality. Even though your house is painted the color of the harvest moon—"

"As seen by sapien eyes," Ethan muttered.

"Ash Street isn't home," Selena continued. "Addy wants to give birth in the forest."

"She would be safer here." He tried to be practical. "In a house painted the color of the harvest moon, surrounded by a hawthorn hedge. The basement is like a cave."

Why was he arguing with her? He wanted everyone gone, including his own father and grandfather.

"They're not any happier stuck in your basement than you are."

"I never said—"

"You don't need to say. They understand body language."

"If they hate the city so much, how are you going to entice them into working here?"

Selena's mouth thinned to a hard line. "Night Shift is going on hold. There's nothing for a business to support. Besides, I've mated. I hope to birth the next generation of Varulv alphas to lead the pack."

"Our offspring need something to lead. Rebuilding Ulvskog matters," Ethan reminded her. "Night Shift is more important than ever. You need the funds to rebuild."

"I didn't think my pack would hate being away from Ulvskog," she admitted. "I figured a few single females could live in the city during the week and work on production. Now there are no single adult females left, and the females who did survive hate Warwick."

Selena leaned on the porch rail, letting the night breeze sift through her unbound hair. The moon revealed slightly more than a sliver of light, and in a few days, would vanish before restarting the cycle of waxing toward fullness. Crickets argued with nocturnal birds. Lightning bugs flitted in the hawthorn hedge. Someone on the next block had mowed their lawn, the scent of freshly cut grass masking the smell of the unofficial privy of a diminished pack of werewolves.

She didn't want to plant anything. She'd seen holes where the digging had commenced. She normally opted for practical over woo-woo, but with everything going on, she couldn't discount the bad juju suffered by her pack being leeched into the ground by their urine. Hatred. Fear. Vengeance. She didn't want negative qualities tainting the herbs she'd planned to use for Night Shift.

Launching the business needed to wait. The pack required time to heal. Hers weren't the only deep wounds among the Varulv. Her pack might never recover.

Selena left the porch to wander across the dewy grass. The pack needed to head back to the woods if for no other reason than using Ethan's lawn as a bathroom would kill the grass. She found herself at the tree growing in the back corner of the lot.

No one hid in the branches; she'd checked. Her last encounter with a vampire had left her leery. Forty-two Ash might be safe, but the lot behind Ethan's house was unknown territory. She'd never noticed the fence behind the hawthorn. The extra barrier wouldn't stop a determined dog, yet Selena found its existence reassuring.

Being outside comforted her. She hadn't left the house since the congressman's suicide and the vampire attack.

Her cell phone buzzed against her hip. Number unknown. She answered anyway.

It's not done until the fat lady howls.

She disconnected. So much for her theory Bryant Peters had been the person calling her. Who else had the means to find her private number?

"Selena?" Ethan's rich baritone drifted across the stillness of the night.

"Out back," she replied. She'd lived among the sapiens too long. Ethan sensed she was outside, could see her and smell her. Hear her disturb the dew on the grass.

"Congressman Liam Peters is at the front door," Ethan said, as he crossed the dark lawn.

"His thugs let him through the barricade?"

"I didn't ask. He wants to speak to you."

Think. Her brain needed to be in alpha mode. "Any idea what he wants?"

"No clue. Maybe you should ask him for funds to help rebuild Ulvskog."

"Take him on a field trip to see the results of his father's actions?" Not a bad idea.

"Depends on who knows he's here. Would you trust him to tell us the truth?"

She snorted. "No."

Neither spoke for a few minutes.

"If we take him to Ulvskog, he won't be returning," Selena said.

"You make a trip to the woods sound awful."

"I vote we abduct him after he leaves."

"Vote?"

She caught the smile in Ethan's tone. "Okay, suggest. To my mate, whose counsel I value."

"I think you should listen to what he has to say and let him leave unscathed."

"Scathe him later?"

"Oh, yeah."

"Send him back."

The overhead leaves rustled, the sound too loud to be a squirrel. Besides, squirrels weren't nocturnal. Maybe a racoon. She lifted her nose to sniff.

"Selena."

She recognized his voice. It had haunted her nightmares for ten years. Liam Peters trod on her turf now. "What do you want, Liam?" she snapped. "Other than death, because your death is what's coming."

He coughed, as if her threat amused him. "I need to talk to you."

"You have nothing to say I want to hear. Your words mean nothing. Your screams as you die? Yeah. My soul listens for them."

"I'd settle for an explanation of why you're here," Ethan said.

"I want him to scream. To beg. Plead for mercy," Selena growled. "We can't kill him here. Too many neighbors."

"Good point." Ethan sounded disappointed.

"We can take him back to Ulvskog." A Varulv male spoke from the shadows. "He can die unheard."

Where did the male come from? How many others were witnessing Selena's revenge?

"Hey." Liam's voice faltered, as if he finally recognized the danger. "I come in peace. I was not involved in my father's...activities. I'm certain you had something to do with his alleged suicide, and you need to be aware I don't deal with segments of the, um, paranormal communities. I don't deal with hired guns. I want to work with your, er, people."

Selena wanted to shriek and lunge for his lying throat. Instead, she dug her fingers into her palms as if her temper resided in her flesh and she could control it with brute force. "You contradicted yourself, Liam."

"The treaties. Service for sanctuary. I plan to vote to keep them. Your species does more good than harm." Liam's voice warbled.

"We do no harm," the Varulv male added. "We mind our own business. Until mercenaries with automatic weapons kill our babies."

The rage and pain in his voice clued Selena that he was past control. Growls from the shadows betrayed the others. Her pack. They had her back, even with a different agenda.

"I had nothing to do with what happened in Ulvskog," Liam repeated. "I didn't know there was such a town."

Selena wasn't going to let him lie his way into living. "You dumped me in a ditch outside Ulvskog on the night of the new moon ten years ago."

Uh-oh. She hadn't meant to reveal so much in front of her pack.

"I saw you." Old Olivia's voice sounded distant.

"The authorities would be interested in the way you're harassing the last two people to talk to your father before he blew off half his head," Ethan pointed out.

"Wait," Restin interrupted.

Selena expected her mate to remind Restin he had no jurisdiction in Ethan's house, yet Ethan remained silent.

"Let him go," Restin advised. "Let him worry."

"Worry?" Liam asked.

"If we're going to believe you or if we're going to make you pay for your crimes," Ethan snarled.

"Your father took the coward's way out." Hatch spoke from the shadows. "Some of us have waited decades for our revenge. A few more hours, days, weeks...eh."

"This is between me and Selena," Liam protested.

"And me," Ethan added. "I'm Selena's mate, and I'm in line to be alpha of the Limmikin."

"Limmikin? They don't exist. They died out while my grandfather was in Congress."

"Liar." Hatch, again. "They didn't die out. They were killed off. Mostly."

"Werewolf wars. My grandfather told me. The Varulv against the Limmikin."

"Lying runs in your family. I was there. I remember." Ethan's grandfather wasn't going to give an inch.

Restin snorted. "Must be the political gene. Let him leave and let him wonder when it's his time."

"He needs to get rid of the thugs at the ends of the block," Selena added.

"They aren't mine." Liam raised placating hands.

"Fine. Your father's thugs. Tell them you've run out of money. The Peters family won't pay them anything more."

Liam hesitated. "All right."

Ethan wasn't finished. "And tell the vampires to back off. If I so much as sniff a bloodsucker anywhere near me, Selena, or anyone else, you will linger on the threshold of death for a long, long time. Trust me, you're not going to enjoy dying."

Selena grinned, baring her teeth. "But you'll pray for death."

SELENA AND ETHAN STOOD in the doorway as Liam strode to his car. They were clearly visible; Ethan switched on the porch light to ensure they'd be seen. Every moth in the neighborhood flew in to witness.

"Goodnight, Congressman," Selena called out as he opened his car door.

Another show of evidence the man had left forty-two Ash alive and well.

The police escort didn't hurt. Absolutely, brilliantly alpha of Pa to suggest calling the authorities. Being the last people to see the late congressman alive didn't give his son the right to harass Selena and Ethan. Showing up uninvited to their home was a bad strategy.

DAKOTA HAD DRIVEN OFF, ostensibly to buy food for the pack. If one of the thugs followed, they'd find themselves in the parking lot of the neighborhood Hy-Vee. Dakota's black SUV blended in nicely enough to use other black SUVs as cover to when they left.

"We're all set," he said after a few minutes.

Selena and Ethan, whose lycan selves had curled in the back, shifted to their human forms. Selena rested for a moment.

"I shouldn't have let you come with me." Ethan worried the constant shifting would drain her energy.

"And miss our camping trip? Not on your life. Liam Peters is mine. His father stole my revenge from me, so Liam needs to pay twice." She pulled on her underwear and jeans, then paused to rest again, panting slightly.

She tilted her head toward Dakota, as if to warn Ethan to say nothing more. Only the two of them knew the truth behind Selena's vendetta. Ethan appreciated why she wanted to keep the attack hidden. He didn't agree. But her secret was not his to share.

The back of an SUV was not the easiest place to get dressed. He helped Selena with her bra, tank top, turtleneck and flannel shirt. He'd rather be removing them.

Unlike his father, Liam did not live in a gated community. Even so, an unfamiliar vehicle might be noticed in his upscale neighborhood. Fortunately, black SUVs were ubiquitous.

"He's left his office," Dakota reported. Restin had put a tracker on the congressman's vehicle while it had been parked outside forty-two Ash. Luke, still in Colorado, fed the coordinates to Dakota.

Dakota parked at the end of Liam's block. Selena and Ethan crept from the vehicle to linger in the shadows provided by the expensive landscaping.

They didn't have to wait long.

No professional driver. No bodyguard. No reason for either. His father had committed suicide. Who could possibly want to harm the grieving heir?

Liam left his car in the driveway, next to a dark SUV.

"Liam." Selena stayed in the shadows as she called his name. Crickets kept chirping, as if they recognized and weren't threatened by her feral nature.

He paused, his shadow elongated by the angle of the motion detector light stationed at the side entrance to the house. Any security cameras were well hidden. Still, Selena refused to leave her cocoon of anonymity.

"Over here." She spoke as quietly as she could, although her insides raged.

"Selena?"

So he recognized her voice.

"Over here," she repeated.

He took a few steps in her direction. "What do you want?"

The light revealed monstrous shadows on his face.

Not shadows, Selena mused. *His true character exposed.*

"Remember how you trapped me?" she asked, as Ethan grabbed his arms from behind.

Liam didn't have the strength to fight with a pissed off lobo. He did try. No contest.

"Payback's a bitch," she continued. "And I'm the perfect bitch for the task."

In the end, nabbing Liam Peters was easier than anticipated. The man didn't have his father's self-protecting instincts. He still mistook Selena for a helpless girl instead of the strong alpha female she'd become.

Selena sat between Dakota and Ethan in the front seat of the SUV. They'd crammed Liam's unconscious body into the back.

The winding road to where Ulvskog had once existed doubled its treachery at night. The moon, a slim curved blade of silver in the sky, provided no help.

Ethan reported the success of the mission to the others in a phone call. Restin suggested everyone join the excursion to Ulvskog. They all wanted to come to the party. Addy's advanced state of pregnancy meant the females had to remain on Ash Street. The males needed to guard them. Otherwise, Ethan would have welcomed his father and grandfather and the Varulv males.

Liam would have to stand-in as the recipient of retribution for all his father's sins.

Chapter 24

D akota's knuckles whitened where he gripped the steering wheel as the SUV lumbered in and out of potholes.

"Turn here," Selena directed. Even she, who'd lived in Ulvskog all her life, had trouble finding the way.

"Stop," she said when they arrived at the spot where Ulvskog had been. The disappearance of the Varulv granted permission for the forest to reclaim stolen territory. Only two weeks had passed since Selena ordered the place torched, yet no trace of the once-flourishing homo lupus life remained.

"Are you sure we're in the right place?" Ethan asked.

"Yes. Although I barely recognize the landscape. It doesn't...it's not home."

Dakota parked the SUV. The nocturnal symphony of insects didn't cease at the disruption. The waning moon barely pierced the cloud cover.

"Now what?" Selena asked.

"You're the Varulv alpha. You get first shot at him."

"My pack should be here to help." She spoke softly, not wanting to disturb the universe with her rage. "They lost everything."

Ethan opened the door and dropped to the ground. He held out his hand to her. "The massacre wouldn't have happened if Liam hadn't betrayed you ten years ago."

She squared her shoulders and scooted across the seat to the door. "True."

By the time Selena's feet hit the dirt, Dakota had unloaded Liam Peters from the back of the SUV. He remained bound, sprawled on the ground imitating a sack of garbage.

"What shall we do?" Selena asked. Her voice rang strong in the night as she stood next to Peters. "Untie him and let him try to run for his life? Give him more of a chance than my pack's weakest had when the gunmen came?"

"Nobody said we had to be fair." Jakob's brother Isaac growled the words as he emerged from the trees. "Life isn't fair."

"What are you doing here?"

"Although you are our alpha, our families were slaughtered, too," Isaac replied. "Some of us felt strongly enough to disobey the Loup Garou and assist you in meting out the responsible one's punishment."

"Who?" Ethan's sharp tone cut through the night.

"Me and Pa." Rand sauntered into the clearing.

Two others trailed Hatch into sight.

"I ordered everyone to stay in Warwick." Ethan sounded peeved. "How did you get here?"

Selena believed they should help. That Isaac, Ed, and Harry had disobeyed Ethan's unsanctioned order was inconsequential.

"You know the black pickup truck you had Restin run the plates on?" Rand asked.

"Yeah?"

"He parked in front of the purple witch house. We borrowed it." Rand's eyes gleamed in the weak moonlight. "Made slipping past the vampires at the end of the block easy."

"Where am I?" Liam demanded weakly.

So, he was awake. Ethan had barely tapped him. He'd gone out quicker than a snowflake in hell. *Vampire scat.*

Selena summoned the alpha of her ancestors to aid her. "Ulvskog. The town your father ordered destroyed a few weeks ago. Getting nervous?"

Liam struggled against his bonds. "Half-breed bastards don't deserve to live."

Selena's insides froze. Motion and sound—including the insects serenading the night—ceased. Ethan headed toward Liam, his face twisted with fury.

Selena held up her hand. "You don't get to make those decisions."

Liam managed to spit before exposing her shame to the world. "He wouldn't have ordered the kids to be shot if you hadn't threatened him."

"You admit our congressman had our offspring murdered?" Isaac's voice carried a terrible undertone.

"What do you care? You're all animals."

Selena fought to remain calm. "We can be sporting. Tonight might be more fun if we let him try to escape. Let him hope he has a chance."

The forest resumed its night song.

"Now if you guys don't mind, I need to change."

EVERY MALE PRESENTED HIS back to Selena and Peters. Except Ethan. His focus wasn't leaving his mate.

Selena loomed over Peters, fingers fumbling with the plastic discs as she unbuttoned her flannel shirt.

Peters' eyes gleamed in the darkness. He gaped at Selena's slowly revealed form.

The shirt fell to the ground. When Selena pulled her turtleneck over her head, she exposed a strip of white skin at her waist. The turtleneck joined the puddle of flannel, followed by the tank top.

Ethan grasped her intent. He wanted to stop her. She should strip only for him. Peters, fortunately, wouldn't live to remember.

Selena toyed with the straps of her bra. "I'm bigger than I was ten years ago." Her husky voice spoke broken promises as her hands maneuvered behind her back. A moment later the front of the bra sagged, catching on her nipples.

"Selena," Ethan warned, her name coming out strangled. He didn't want Peters ogling her. She didn't have to seduce the man to death.

The bra dropped to the ground, baring Selena from the waist up. Although the moon waned toward nonexistence, she must have recognized her daughter's need. Feeble milky light washed Selena's nakedness—not enough to make her sparkle, though. Instead, her body glowed, reflecting the moonbeams back to their source.

"You're going to know why you have to die." Selena unbuttoned the waist of her jeans.

Ethan did a quick check. Everyone else's faces remained averted.

The rasp of a zipper being lowered mingled with the night sounds of the forest. Peters' chest heaved.

Selena shimmied out of her jeans, which took a long time due to her long legs. Her underwear took far less time to discard. She stood tall and naked, a goddess in her milieu. "Like what you see?" She nudged Peters' crotch with her bare toe. "Wait until you see what's next."

The shift wasn't quick or easy. The pending new moon dampened the energy. The air shimmered as the barometric pressure rocketed, along with a flare of heat as Selena's body reshaped itself.

Peters smirked at Ethan, who began removing his own clothes. "She was nice and tight, even after my father busted—"

His words were lost in his scream as Selena took her revenge. The shriek echoed, filling the gaps between the trees.

The insects paused their concert.

Pa cut the ropes binding Peters while Ethan completed his shift. "Run if you can," Pa advised.

Selena, shivering in the cool gray morning, pulled on her flannel shirt. She'd managed to return to human form, grab her clothes, and find privacy to dress.

Getting the taste of Liam Peters out of her mouth and ridding her ears of his pleas for mercy as the pack had...disassembled him wouldn't be as easy. Both should be memories to cherish. She must have been too tired to appreciate them.

Maybe later, after I recoup on my sleep.

She made her way to the SUV. Hopping into the cab used the last of her energy. Her eyes burned, and she longed to close them. She could rest on the trip back to Warwick.

These woods were no longer home. The spot was merely a patch of ground shamed by the death it had seen. Or maybe the massacre had created a holy spot. She'd have to ask Old Olivia.

No sign of anything that might have once been Liam Peters remained. Too bad they hadn't been able to savage his father as well. Maybe a trip to the cemetery on the night after the new moon might suffice. Exhume the corpse and finish the job of physical destruction the congressman had ignited when he shot himself, the cheat.

Ethan had finally ripped out Liam's throat, ending his agony far too soon. As far as Selena was concerned, Liam should have been made to suffer ten years. Still, some of her pack had been able to make him scream.

Revenge. She was glad Isaac and the others had participated.

She listened, hoping to sense the spirit of Gramps telling her how she'd done. The only sound was the breeze ruffling the tops of the trees. She studied the sky. No buzzards circled overhead, betraying the death site. Gramps was gone, residing with the gods of his elders. At rest. At peace.

If the Varulv had been a weapon used against the Limmikin, as Ethan's grandfather claimed, Gramps had believed he was fulfilling the pack's treaty with the government. He had no way of knowing Peters was a lying sack of scat. Yes, Gramps rested with his gods.

Something rustled in the underbrush. She sat straighter. Although she'd lived on this spot most of her life, the forest had reclaimed the land. Whatever plundered through the bracken was hefty enough to be a bear. Bears scared Selena. They were big and nasty-tempered.

Ethan emerged. Naked.

She stared. He was magnificent. Tall. Broad. A wedge of dark hair in the center of his chest reminded her of his sleek black lycan pelt. His package—well, she liked his more than the other two she'd encountered. The first rays of the morning burst out of the mist and spotlighted him.

He was a god. And he was hers.

Her exhaustion fled. She hopped from the SUV.

As she ran toward him, his arms opened. She leapt into them. She buried her face against his neck as he struggled not to crush her ribs.

"I love you so much," he murmured into her hair.

He loved her?

"I don't scare you?" After what he'd seen her do…talking was one thing, the follow-through quite another.

His skin was cool against her cheek.

"Scare me?" He grinned. "No, babe. You make me proud."

His penis stirred against her belly. "If the others weren't on their way, I'd show you how much you don't scare me."

"You're showing me right now."

He clasped her tighter. "I guess you're right."

"I hope I'm not interrupting something," Rand said as he emerged from the forest. Fully clothed, thank the gods of her elders. Selena didn't want to have to un-see her mate's father in the altogether.

"Not yet," Ethan grumbled. He didn't release Selena.

"I'm going to gather everyone's clothing." Rand stooped and snatched a shirt from the ground. "The Varulv want to stay here for a while longer."

"There's nothing here."

"Their home," Rand replied. "How would you feel if you were leaving Loup Garou forever?"

Selena stiffened and tried to step away from Ethan. He wouldn't let her.

"I might be," Ethan told his father. "I'm mated now. Selena is alpha of the Varulv. I'm supposed to someday become alpha of the Limmikin, who are also from these woods."

Selena released the breath she'd been holding.

"Shouldn't the Limmikin be represented?" Ethan asked.

"We are the only Limmikin," Rand reminded him.

"Maybe. Look how many Varulv escaped the Ulvskog massacre. We don't know if anyone besides Pa and G-Ma escaped the Limmikin holocaust. With news of the congressman's death spreading, maybe others will find their way back to their ancestral land. Shouldn't someone be here to welcome them home?" Ethan lifted his chin. "Why shouldn't I be the one?"

Forget breathing. Selena wanted to weep with joy.

The surrounding trees, heavy with summer, swayed in a gust of wind. As they bent in supplication, Hatch emerged from the undulating shadows into the swathe of pearly gray light.

"My grandson is right. The Creator has a reason to make Selena his mate. While I don't pretend to know the intent of the Creator, I cannot ignore the signs."

"Thanks, Pa," Ethan said.

"Pa and I are staying with the Varulv for the time being," Rand continued. "He wants to make a pilgrimage to his old home."

"Should I go with you?" Ethan asked.

Rand snorted. "You're newly mated, so you should go back to town with Selena. Males should protect the females."

"Besides, we're not in the clear yet in the congressman's suicide," Selena pointed out. "The authorities may question us again, especially now his son has vanished."

"*Scat.*"

"Let's not forget Curtis DiNardo." Rand might have been discussing the weather.

"Who?" Ethan asked at the same time Selena echoed, "Curtis DiNardo?"

"Curtis. The guy who owns the black truck following you around."

Right. Ethan's father and grandfather had highjacked the truck.

"What did you do with Curtis?" Selena asked.

"Do? Nothing."

Ethan glared.

"Okay, we tied him up and tossed him in the truck bed. Isaac checked on him not long ago. He's still out."

Selena couldn't believe her ears. Her heart throbbed, and her throat muscles spasmed as if trying to close. "You brought a witness? A sapien witness?" She choked on the words.

Ethan wrapped his arm across her shoulders to restrain her as she protested, "He has to disappear. Permanently."

"I want to question him," Ethan said. "I'm glad Dad and the others captured him."

Didn't Ethan get it? Curtis DiNardo knew what happened to Liam. "He could ruin everything."

"He won't." Ethan sounded far too positive.

Selena didn't want an audience for their argument. He would hear from her later for contradicting her in front of her pack.

"Where's the truck?" Ethan asked.

Rand jerked his thumb toward the woods. "Up the road a bit. Off the road, on the right. Follow your nose."

"Come on, Dakota. Let's go." Ethan wasn't going to wait for Selena to get over her snit.

Selena didn't speak. He knew he'd made her angry. She would be angrier before the new day ended.

The three of them piled into the SUV and headed in the direction Dad had indicated.

The black pickup was parked right where Dad said. So was Curtis, conscious, gagged, and tightly trussed in bright blue nylon rope. He glared at them, his small eyes darting like minnows in a shallow creek.

His face was puffier than Ethan remembered. He'd only seen him clearly the time he'd come to hang the plywood at Selena's place on Pine Street. Curtis hadn't looked this...bad.

"The mosquitos had quite a feast last night," Selena commented.

Ethan hopped into the truck bed and yanked the gag from Curtis's mouth. He barely avoided Curtis's teeth. "You want to get into a biting match, you should consider your opponent."

"Water," Curtis croaked.

"You don't need anything to drink," Selena scoffed. "You're not going to live long enough for water to matter."

"Sure he is." Ethan contradicted her. He wished she hadn't mentioned his death. Curtis might be more willing to cooperate if he believed he had a chance to live. Sapiens valued life, even lives as pathetic as Curtis's. "We don't have any water. Answer a few questions, and we'll find something for you to drink."

Pathetic? Curtis was dumber than vampire scat. Ethan untied him, then whipped his neck with the rope.

"Whaddya hit me for?" Curtis shrieked.

"Why have you been following us?" Selena lifted her leg, as if she were going to kick him. Instead, she settled herself more firmly on the ground. Krav maga stance at its finest. "How's Uncle Tony?" she asked.

Curtis focused on her. The sun was rising behind her, and he squinted. "What's your problem?" Belligerent. Disrespectful.

Ethan longed to teach him a lesson.

"My problem," Selena began, her low words crisp and clear in the morning air, "is your constant presence in my life. Why? Who's paying you to stalk me?"

"I think you're a hot bitch," Curtis replied.

He had no idea.

Ethan reached to grab Curtis.

Selena beat Ethan to her prey. She hauled Curtis to his feet and slammed him against the side of his pickup truck.

A she-wolf's strength didn't wane with the moon.

"Let's try again," she said cheerfully. "Why have you been following me?"

"Uncle Tony told me to." Sullen. Maybe a bit scared. "And if Uncle Tony tells me to do something, I do it. You know? You pissed him off when you moved out with no notice."

"I let him keep the security deposit," Selena pointed out, her tone still reasonable. Only the white knuckles of her fingers, still wadded in the front of Curtis's t-shirt as she held him against the side of his truck, betrayed her tension.

Ethan admired the taut muscles of her upper arm. Selena could repave the road with scrawny Curtis and not fill half a pot hole.

"You left a lot of damage."

"I told you someone broke in."

Curtis didn't respond.

Selena released him. He slid to the ground as if his skeleton had abandoned him. At least he hadn't wet himself.

"What do you want to do with him?" Ethan asked. Curtis wasn't worth killing, despite Selena's fear he was a witness.

"It's too bad he got a flat tire," Dakota said.

Ethan peered at all four of the truck's tires. They didn't look flat to him.

"A true shame," Selena added as Dakota hopped into the truck bed.

A moment later, Dakota landed on the dirt roadbed again, a chunk of metal window frame in his hand. He jammed the shank into the rubber as easily as a hot knife slid through butter. The tire deflated as Dakota withdrew his weapon.

"I guess we'll have to give you a ride back to Warwick." Selena brightened. "Maybe Uncle Tony will be so grateful to have you back in one piece, he'll tell us the real reason I'm being stalked."

Curtis surveyed his position, his panic palpable. Nothing but trees, a cloud-studded sky, and the strip of gravel passing for a road were visible. "Look." His voice cracked, though he managed to climb to his feet. "I hate to break it to you, but Uncle Tony has a bad mean streak."

"What does Uncle Tony have to do with me?" Selena asked.

"You trashed his apartment."

"I said I left the security deposit. Besides, I didn't trash the place. Someone broke in."

"But you never called the cops. You didn't file a police report for the insurance company. So Uncle Tony is pissed."

"Why didn't he contact me? Or why didn't you say something? You've been hanging around an awful lot."

"I'm only doing what Uncle Tony asked me to do."

"Have you been out this way before?" Ethan knew the answer.

"Maybe." Curtis shrugged. "Maybe not. All trees look the same to me."

"You're interfering with a federal investigation." Maybe Ethan exaggerated, but no one was going to admit publicly to the government's werewolf corps.

Except the truth flickered on Curtis's face. His expression morphed from stupid to sly.

"I'm guessing Curtis is aware of the investigation." Selena eyed him. "I'll bet he isn't as innocent as he acts. Are you, Curtis? Are you merely a minion for your evil Uncle Tony or do you add some brains to the cauldron?"

Sly shifted to a smirk.

"I thought so." Selena wet her lips. "And you know who trashed the apartment. You're working with the vampires."

A touch of swagger shaped Curtis's next action: a single step toward Selena.

"Bad move, sonny." Dakota leaned against Curtis's truck. "Ethan here is territorial. The last guy who gave Selena an answer she didn't like lost his dick. Literally. Chomp." Dakota demonstrated with bared teeth. "Lots of blood. Rumor says the story is going to be Toke Lobo and the Pack's next big hit."

Curtis's eyes bulged in his head and his prominent Adams apple shimmied in his throat. His arrogance fled, as if he remembered his captors' true nature.

Maybe he did.

Ethan leaned in closer. Got right in Curtis's face. Could smell the onions in the tuna salad Curtis had eaten for lunch a day or so ago lingering in his mouth. "Why are you stalking us?"

No answer. Curtis probably didn't know why he'd been told to follow Ethan.

"Maybe he's paparazzi," Selena said. "Hey Curtis! Are you trying to get photos of Ethan Calhoun to sell to a fan magazine or something?"

"The pregnant one." Curtis spoke in such a low voice, Ethan's allegedly superior werewolf hearing might not have registered the words correctly.

"What did you say?" Ethan's throat was so tight, his words emerged as a growl.

"She got away."

"Addy." The name escaped Selena's mouth on an exhale. "You were at the massacre."

Curtis sneered at Ethan. "Massacre?" He hawked and tried to spit. Dehydration thwarted him. "Just a bunch of dirty animals, trying to tell regular folks what to do. Yeah, I helped. Uncle Tony—a bunch of us. The pregnant one got away. Pissed off the congressman, even though we got all the kids."

"The congressman?" Ethan and Selena spoke at the same time.

"Congressman Peters. The old one. The new one." Curtis frowned. "All of them. We had our orders. The old man first. The kids and women of breeding age."

"You murdered my grandfather." Selena's voice quavered.

Curtis kept talking. "We had orders not to kill the pregnant ones, though. We were supposed to capture them."

"Why?" Ethan asked.

"As payment to the vampires."

Ethan stuck his pinky in his ear and tried to pop the strange pressure pushing at his skull. Had Curtis said—?

"Okay, he's done." Dakota raised his makeshift shank.

Selena caught his arm. "Not yet," she said. Soft. Dangerous. "What do you mean, Curtis? Payment for the vampires?"

Oblivious to how close he was to dying, Curtis snickered. "Unborn baby blood is a vampire version of champagne or something. Valuable to undead assholes. Don't worry. When the fat, pregnant lady howls, all the drama will be over."

SELENA SWALLOWED HER GORGE. "You're the one who's been calling me," she choked out.

Curtis had the audacity to grin.

"Go ahead, Dakota."

Curtis's death gurgle and the scent of blood filled her head.

"Call Restin," she told Ethan. "Addy isn't to leave the house for any reason. Keep a male guard—in addition to Jakob—with her at all times."

"What do we do with him?" Dakota nudged Curtis's body with the toe of his boot.

"Leave him with the truck."

"Give me one of your shirts," Ethan said.

She hoped he spoke to Dakota.

"Selena." Ethan sounded impatient. He stared at her, his dark eyes unfathomable. "Only your flannel."

"Why?"

"So we can wipe down the truck. The pack's fingerprints are probably hood to bed. Dad's. Pa's."

Giving him the shirt would be okay. She had on her turtleneck. Her tank top. Her bra.

"Selena? Sometime this morning?"

She fumbled with the top button. She loved this shirt. The colors reminded her of a watermelon slice. Something in her chest tightened.

"I've seen you naked," Ethan reminded her. "And Dakota could care less."

"Enthusiastically so," Dakota agreed. He faced the forest, away from Selena.

Her fingers wobbled. Ridiculous. She was more than covered beneath the flannel. And Ethan was her mate. The day was warm. She didn't need the shirt for protection against the weather. *I just prefer dressing in layers, that's all.*

Donating a shirt wouldn't put her at risk.

"Do you need help?" Ethan's impatience annoyed her.

Shedding her clothes for a shift was different. Same with removing her clothes in the privacy of her bedroom. Her safe places. The forest once sheltering Ulvskog should have felt safe. It didn't.

"No." She hated how her voice warbled. "I don't need any help."

Her fingers acted as big as Ethan's hands as she fumbled with the buttons. She couldn't suppress the shiver carousing on her spine.

"You can sit in the SUV if you're cold," Ethan suggested softly.

She pulled off the flannel shirt.

Ethan took the garment from her and tossed it to Dakota. Then he gathered the blue rope and retied Curtis. "The cops will notice rope burns."

"Rope burns on what?" she asked. "We're dragging him back to the pack and telling them what he said about Addy and the vampires. There won't be enough of him left for the cops to notice."

"Wait a minute." Isaac stood with his feet spread and his arms crossed.

Selena, Ethan, and Dakota gifted the others with Curtis's corpse, dragging the body to the center of Ulvskog on a faded blue tarp Dakota found in the back of the truck. They were preparing to return to Warwick.

"The congressman's son said some interesting scat before we killed him. I have questions."

Selena's insides clenched, then iced over. Damn Liam for spilling his guts. He'd revealed too many secrets.

"Don't speak to your alpha in that tone," Ethan snapped.

"I lost my family," Isaac snapped back. "I have questions, and I want answers."

"What?" She tried to sound as imperious as she could.

"What did Peters mean when he said you threatened his father, so his father ordered our babies slaughtered?"

Scat.

"You have to tell them," Ethan whispered against her ear.

No. The shame was too great.

"You said something to set the congressman off." Isaac wouldn't let it go.

"He was our ally," Ed continued.

"Your father died working for the congressman," Harry added. As if she could ever forget. "Why would he attack us?"

"The congressman used us." Thank the gods of the elders her voice didn't crack. "The Peters family has never been honest with Varulv. First, they had the Varulv attempt to wipe out the Limmikin. Now they tried to eliminate us."

"You threatened him," Isaac said.

"The treaty we have with the US government?" Selena continued as if Isaac hadn't spoken. She tugged on the hem of her tank top. "The current administration wants to abolish our treaties. Immigrants are animals."

"Well, we sometimes are," Harry muttered. An overhead bird squawked in agreement.

Selena bared her teeth at Harry. "We've been here for generations. We served our country with unquestioning devotion and honor. We have as much right to live here as anyone else who fled the Old World in fear of their lives. We honored our part of the treaty. The government needs to honor theirs. Slaughtering our offspring is a strange way of fulfilling an obligation."

"Peters claimed you threatened him." Isaac was as bad as a pup with a bone.

"I said I would expose him," Selena admitted, as she brushed the back of her hand against her brow. Perspiration gathered in her hairline.

"And expose us in the process?" Ed asked. "No. What aren't you telling us?"

"My children died." Isaac's haunted tone pierced her. "My mate. Why, Selena?"

Ethan placed his hand between her shoulder blades and massaged her tense muscles.

Perspiration soaked her tank top and turtleneck. How could she confess her careless words to these fathers?

"Tell them." Ethan pressed his hand deeper into her spine as his lips tickled her ear. If she didn't, would he betray her secrets to her pack?

"The congressman believed he'd fathered a child who lived with our pack." The words caught on their way out as if hawthorn spikes barbed her throat.

"Why would he think we were hiding a sapien child?" Isaac narrowed his eyes.

"I told him we were." She blinked rapidly to hold tears at bay. "I lied."

Too late she remembered rapid blinking signaled subservience. The males of her pack recognized the clue. They had been waiting for the first indication of weakness. They circled her. Ethan's father and grandfather stared at her with something she interpreted as distaste.

"Why would you say something so stupid?" Isaac demanded. "Especially when you—"

"I didn't know about the Limmikin holocaust until Ethan met Old Olivia," she snapped. Snapping was good. Not weak. She plucked the damp cotton of her turtleneck away from her skin. "I'd never heard of Limmikin when I visited the congressman to ask him to vote for maintaining our treaties. What the new administration is trying is bigger than we are."

"Tell my howling heart," Ed snarled. "My mourning mate."

"Yeah, well I wasn't your alpha at the time, either," she shot back, as if status could excuse her.

"Did your grandfather know what you did?" Harry asked.

Selena lifted her chin. "No." Didn't they sense she had her own grief to match her guilt?

"Why would you tell Peters we harbored a sapien child?" Isaac, again.

"Because he was a rapist." *There.* She'd confessed.

Except sheltered lycans couldn't grasp a concept like sexual assault.

"He forcefully had sex with women who didn't consent," Ethan explained. "Females who weren't his mate. He had a secret website where he posted movies of the ways he hurt females. Sexually. Selena threatened him with exposure. Most humans find forced sex disgusting."

"Human women conceive easier than we do," Selena added.

"Why would a human hide her offspring with us?"

Ethan's thumbs traced circles along Selena's spine. Her legs acted soggy. If he weren't standing at her back, she might have collapsed. "She wasn't sapien."

The males still didn't grasp her meaning. She was going to have to say the words aloud. Again.

"Me. He attacked me. I was fifteen." One of her knees buckled. Ethan caught her so quickly she doubted her pack noticed. "On the night of the new moon. I couldn't shift and defend myself. And after the congressman finished, Liam took his place."

There. They knew her secret. Her shame. Her unworthiness to lead them. Ethan might try to defend her, but he would be relieved to be rid of such offal as she.

She lifted her chin higher, prepared to defend herself.

Rand and Hatch strode toward her. She braced herself for their attack. She'd brought shame to the Calhoun family.

Selena was stunned when they positioned themselves on either side of her.

"We are proud to have you as part of the Limmikin." Hatch offered both of his hands. She hesitated before taking them.

"Your bravery and courage will be cherished assets," he continued. "Welcome to the pack."

"Wait a minute," Isaac interrupted. "She's Varulv born and bred."

"A direct descendant of the first Varulv to come to America." Ed's voice held as much pride as Hatch's had. "Our alpha."

Harry wasn't going to be left out of the tribute. "I don't mind trying to get Amelia pregnant again. No hardship on my part at all."

"If you can't get hard—" Isaac cuffed Ed before he could finish.

"Show some respect to our alpha. She has a long memory and doesn't mind waiting for the perfect revenge."

Chapter 25

ETHAN TWISTED IN HIS seat to watch Selena, who had been relegated to the center seating area of Dakota's SUV. She stared out the window when she should have been sleeping. Dakota had the radio tuned to a country music station. Right now, Toke Lobo and the Pack's biggest hit, "Full Moon Lady," droned out the speakers. Ethan hated Tokarz's tribute to his sapien mate. The fans adored the song, and their love kept Ethan in pocket-change-plus.

"This is you," Selena said.

Funny. In the weeks they'd been together, his career as a musician hadn't been mentioned. The focus had been on her. Tokarz might not like his steel guitarist living several states away. And Selena. How would she do without him while they were on tour or recording?

Mating created challenges in a lobo's life.

The song ended. A deep-voiced announcer teased the news headlines in sonorous tones. "Acting Congressman Liam Bryant is missing. More on that story plus weather and traffic after this message from our sponsors."

"I'm surprised he was missed so soon." Selena snorted.

"Does he have a family? Other than his dirtbag father?" Dakota asked over the commercial for a local truck dealer.

"He had at least one brother and one sister. It's not out of the question he was married."

Ethan pulled out his phone, ready to call Luke to dig around some more when an ad for a local saloon ended and the news reader returned.

Dakota upped the volume on the radio.

"Appointed Congressman Liam Peters hasn't been seen or heard from since the FBI leaked information about an investigation into his father, the late Congressman Bryant Peters. Speculation in some circles say he might have been involved in the sex scandal surrounding his father, who committed suicide last week."

"Well, well. I guess we've been out of touch," Dakota said.

Ethan tucked his phone into his pocket. No point in calling Luke, who Ethan suspected leaked the sex scandal bit.

Selena's eyes gleamed. "I've been trying to formulate an explanation in case we were asked."

Dakota shrugged. "Helga the Witch is right. We need to stay more on top of current events."

"I'm glad Luke leaked what he found. The Peters' legacy needs the tarnish." Ethan wasn't worried.

Selena didn't say anything.

"There were no cameras in his office," Ethan reminded her. "Not the night he blew off his face, not the night he attacked you."

Dakota took an intense interest in the sinuous strip of gray highway ahead of him.

"We'll never know."

"The shame is his, not yours. And you are a survivor. A triumphant survivor."

"Triumphant?" She gave Ethan a lengthy stare. "Yeah. I guess I am."

"Welcome home." Helga thrust a length of gray-white bulbs at Selena. She pushed her way into the entry. "Here's a housewarming gift for you."

"Thank you." The witch's thoughtfulness touched Selena.

"What's that?" Ethan asked.

"A garlic rope to decorate the kitchen," Selena replied.

"You're decorating the kitchen?"

Ethan's surprise embarrassed her.

"Well, yeah. It's our home. I want to make it homey." Selena spoke as if being domestic was as natural as shifting on the full moon. "You mentioned curtains and stuff."

"You haven't accepted my berry offerings," Ethan complained.

Selena's cheeks heated. He'd tried twice, and she'd been a jerk both times.

"What do you mean?" Helga asked.

"It's a lycan thing. The male offers berries to the female as part of the mating ritual."

"I know all about berries." Helga's impatience made her sharper than usual. "I mean, what do you mean she didn't accept your berries?"

Humiliation heated Selena's face. "I was being foolish. Stubborn," she admitted.

"No, you were both being ignorant."

"Well, okay." Miffed, Selena didn't bother to hide her displeasure.

"Oh, come on." Helga darted around Selena and Ethan and hurried to the back door. "Come on!"

Ethan glanced at Selena, apparently as clueless as she was.

They followed Helga down the back steps and across the lawn to the tree growing in the corner of the lot.

"So?" Selena asked.

"Look up," Helga instructed.

Berries. Still mostly white and green, a few blushing toward ripeness.

"What are they?" Ethan asked.

"Mulberries," Helga replied in a smug tone. "You bought her a house complete with a mulberry tree. She's living here. I'd say she accepted."

Ethan's grin flashed white as he scooped Selena from the ground. "You're going to have to excuse us, neighbor."

I hope you enjoyed Ethan and Selena's story.

Sign up for my newsletter, where subscribers are always the first to learn my news: titles, covers, release dates, sneak peeks of my works in progress, and occasional bonus material for subscribers only. When you sign up, you will receive a FREE short "origin" story about Toke Lobo & the Pack.

So why wait to subscribe? Click HERE for the form.

Next up: Dakota and Britt's story: BEWARE OF THE MOON.

Also By MJ Compton

COLUMBIA GEMS BASEBALL ROMANCES
PARANORMAL ROMANTIC SUSPENSE (Shifters)
THE WRITE PLACE RETREAT ROMANCES

About the Author

MJ COMPTON GREW UP near Cardiff, New York, a place best known for its giant—a hoax so successful, P.T. Barnum duplicated it. The tale of the "petrified man" convinced MJ that inventing stories could be a career.

Although her 30 years working in local television included such highlights as being bitten by a lion, preempting a US President for a college basketball game, giving a three-time world champion boxer a few black eyes, and meeting her husband, MJ never lost her dream of creating her own stories.

MJ still lives in upstate New York with her husband. Music and cooking are two of her passions, and she enjoys baseball, college basketball, and sitting on her patio on summer nights to count lightning bugs, but she's primarily focused on writing.